THE ICE-CREAM MAKERS

Ernest van der Kwast made his breakthrough with the novel *Mama Tandoori*, which became a bestseller in the Netherlands and Italy and sold more than 100,000 copies. In 2012 he published the novella *Giovanna's Navel*, which entered the *Der Spiegel* bestseller list immediately after publication in Germany in 2015. He lives in Rotterdam.

Laura Vroomen was born in the Netherlands in 1972. After an academic career teaching English Literature and Cultural Studies, she switched to translation. She has since translated a range of fiction and non-fiction, including thrillers, memoirs, and books on politics. She lives and works in London, and her favourite ice-cream flavour is hazelnut.

Ernest Van der Kwast

THE

ICE-CREAM

Makers

Translated from Dutch
by Laura Vroomen

SCRIBE
Melbourne • London

Scribe Publications
18–20 Edward St, Brunswick, Victoria 3056, Australia
2 John Street, Clerkenwell, London, WC1N 2ES, United Kingdom

First published in Dutch as *De ijsmakers* in 2015 by De Bezige Bij, Amsterdam
Published in English by Scribe 2016

Typeset in 12.3 / 16.5 pt Dante MT by the publishers
Printed and bound in the UK by CPI Group (UK) Ltd, Croydon CR0 4YY

Scribe Publications is committed to the sustainable use of natural resources
and the use of paper products made responsibly from those resources.

9781925321203 (Australian paperback)
9781925228434 (UK paperback)
9781925307290 (e-book)

The publisher gratefully acknowledges
the support of the Dutch Foundation
for Literature.

N **ederlands**
letterenfonds
dutch foundation
for literature

CiP records for this title are available from the British Library and the National
Library of Australia

scribepublications.com.au
scribepublications.co.uk

How My Father Lost His Heart to a Hammer-thrower Weighing Eighty-three Kilos

Shortly before his eightieth birthday, my father fell in love. It was love at first sight; love like a bolt from the blue, like lightning striking a tree. My mother phoned to tell me. 'Beppi has lost his mind,' she said.

It happened during a live broadcast of the London Olympics. During the women's hammer-throw final, to be precise. Since my father had a satellite dish installed on the roof, he's had access to more than a thousand channels. He spends whole days in front of the television — a beautiful flatscreen — and presses the button of the remote control at a consistently high tempo. Football games from Japan, Arctic nature documentaries, Spanish arthouse films, and reports on disasters in El Salvador, Tajikistan, and Fiji flash past. And then there are the programmes with women, of course: gorgeous, glorious women from all over the world. Buxom Brazilian presenters; near-naked Greek showgirls; news broadcasters whose bulletins, quite aside from the language (Macedonian? Slovenian?), are lost on him because of their full, glossy lips.

Usually there will only be some five or six seconds between the channels my father alights on. But sometimes he lingers, and spends a whole evening watching coverage of the Mexican elections or a documentary series about the tropical waters off Polynesia, green as a gem.

It was a Turkish sports channel that my father had stumbled across after pressing the button of the remote with his calloused thumb. The Egyptian soap that, in the space of five seconds, had homed in on just as many melodramatic women's faces, had failed to beguile him. So Beppi pressed the button, which had once been black, then grey and was now white, practically transparent. And that's when he was struck by lightning. There on the screen was his princess: creamy white skin, coral-red hair, and the biceps of a butcher. She entered the circle in the Olympic Stadium, grabbed the handle at the end of the chain, raised the ball over her left shoulder and turned — once, twice, three, four, five times — before hurling the iron ball with all the strength she could muster. Like a meteor having survived entry into the atmosphere, it buzzed and fizzed through the steel-blue skies of London. On impact, it left a brown hole in a meticulously cut lawn.

My father dropped his remote. The lid at the back came off, and one battery rolled across the wooden floor. The Turkish commentator was full of praise for the throw, but his sing-song words were lost on my father. The repeat showed his broad-shouldered ballerina a second time. Her pirouette gathered speed and ended in a brief but surprisingly elegant curtsey.

He felt like he had been spinning around, too. Faster and faster. And now he was sitting here on his sofa, in love and in awe, as if he had been hit on the head by the four-kilo ball.

Her name was Betty Heidler, it turned out, and she was the world-record holder, having broken it by 112 centimetres a year ago at an international competition in Halle, Germany. It had been a warm day in May with hardly any wind, sunglasses and short sleeves everywhere. With a spring in her step the athlete proceeded to the circle with the green nets, and almost casually threw the hammer an astronomical distance. It didn't leave a crater but bounced a couple of times, like the pebbles children throw across the water of the nearby Hufeisen Lake. In between the major competitions she worked for the police force, wearing a dark-blue uniform with four stars on both epaulettes, her red hair kept in a tight bun. *Polizeihauptmeisterin* Heidler.

In London, Betty Heidler threw a distance that was to earn her a bronze medal, but the measuring system malfunctioned, so her achievement couldn't be determined right away. It took forty minutes before a decision was reached. These forty minutes were like a romantic film to my father. He swooned over the red-headed hammer-thrower who kept appearing on screen, sometimes close to tears. Her rival, the fleshy Chinese Zhang Wenxiu, had already embarked on a lap of honour, the red flag with the yellow stars wrapped around her broad shoulders.

'No! Not the ten-ton Chinese!' my father yelled.

The Turkish commentator was a bit more nuanced about it, but he too was of the opinion that Betty Heidler, not Zhang Wenxiu, deserved the bronze. Incidentally, the Chinese athlete really only weighed 113 kilos, but that was still a full thirty kilos more than the ginger hammer nymph.

'Get rid of the flag,' my father said. 'You bloated old meatball!'

And when Betty Heidler appeared on screen, 'Don't cry, my little princess. Don't be sad, dear, fleet-footed lady.'

It was an *epitheton ornans* he was using, unwittingly dug up from the past, going back thirty-five years, to the time I went to grammar school and to everybody's shock started expressing myself in the colourful adjectives of the blind poet. According to my father, it sowed the seeds for the distance between me and the rest of my family. Or as he likes to put it, 'That's where it all went wrong.'

My epithets used to drive him mad: the long-maned girls I flirted with, the cloud-wrapped buildings my mother wasn't fond of, the wine-purple cherry ice-cream he made. And now he had used one himself for his creamy-armed hammer-thrower.

The broadcaster switched to an advert for hairspray. A bride came into view sporting a hairdo that looked like it would stay in place for at least a week.

'Betty, come back!' my father shouted at the flatscreen, on which the spray was misted across the chestnut curls of the smiling bride in high definition and slow motion. His thumb moved of its own accord

— the calloused old thumb, the thumb which for years had hooked itself around the metal handle of the *spatolone*, the large ladle with which the ice is scooped out of the cylinders of the Cattabriga.

'Oh, Betty,' my father said with a sigh, echoing the many men who had once uttered the same name with yearning. Betty Garrett, Betty Hutton, Betty Grable — enchanting actresses, now almost forgotten names.

The film starring the hammer-thrower resumed. She was sitting on a bench on the tartan inside the arena and staring into the middle distance, looking disconsolate. Meanwhile, the commentator nattered on. Every now and then, my father thought he recognised the names of athletes, but they may well have been Turkish words. He knew the satellite had plenty of other channels that broadcast the competition: in Danish, in German, in Italian, in Dutch. But the remote was on the floor and he didn't want to start zapping. He didn't want to miss a second.

Was that a tear? A silver droplet under her left eye? As if she and my father were in a film, he had to say something to her, comfort her. My mother, meanwhile, was standing in the doorway of the small room where the giant television hung on the wall like a painting. She'd heard her husband talking and called out from her kitchen: 'Beppi? What is it?'

My father's name is Giuseppe Battista Talamini, but my mother has called him Beppi her whole life.

'I love you,' my father said.

It had been twenty, thirty, maybe even forty years since my mother had heard these words from my father's lips.

'What was that you said?'

'I love you,' my father replied softly. 'I think you're beautiful.'

My mother was silent. Betty Heidler still had tears in her eyes.

'Your freckles, your powerful arms … I want to kiss your muscles.'

'What is it? Aren't you feeling well?'

Then it slowly dawned on her. The first part of his answer was aimed at the screen, the second at his wife in the doorway: 'You're the love of my life … Get lost!'

At long last the chair of the jury, a woman with a wide band around her sleeve, shook Betty Heidler's hand. Slowly, like ice-cream melting, a smile stole over the athlete's face. An embrace followed. But by the time that happened, my mother was already back in the kitchen, where a solitary pan of mince was simmering on the stove. Tomorrow was Saturday: pasticcio, glasses filled with light red wine, the afternoon spreading like a stain. It was an open secret that lasagne, like tiramisu, tastes better when you let it rest overnight.

Shouts of joy could be heard from the television room. 'Yes! She's won — Betty's got bronze!' my father exclaimed. 'Yes! Yes!' When he started jumping up and down, happy as a child, my mother phoned me. In spring and summer she always calls me when something's up. That's when my brother Luca is at work. It's an image my memory conjures up without even trying: when I hear my mother's voice down the line, I picture Luca behind the ice-cream in Rotterdam. I'm at work too, but I'm usually in a position to answer the phone.

'Where are you?' my mother asks. It's invariably the first thing she asks.

'I'm in Fermoy, in Ireland.'

There was a moment's silence on the other end of the line. My mother, aged seventy-four, is still not used to mobile phones. She has never actually held one herself. In her kitchen in Venas di Cadore, in the mountains, it never ceases to amaze her that we can communicate anywhere, anytime. Sometimes she'll phone me when I'm at the other end of the world and I'll answer with a sleepy voice: 'I'm in Brisbane, in Australia.' I use the silence to focus on the luminescent hands of my watch on the bedside table. The fact that I'm always somewhere else is something she had to get used to long before the advent of the mobile phone.

I have a home, but it doesn't feel like one. There are no plants, there's no carton of milk in the fridge. No newspaper is delivered in the morning. It has curtains and towels, but no fruit bowl. In her short poem 'Today', the Israeli poet Nurit Zarchi writes: *Tired, I want to sit on the edge of the world, to go on strike. / But I continue onward so no one will see / the short distance between me and the homeless.*' The actual distance between me and my family is short, almost insignificant, but big because of the other distance. There are days when the measuring system malfunctions.

'What's the weather like in Ireland?'

My mother is obsessed with the weather. Back in the day, when she was still working at the ice-cream parlour in Rotterdam, she'd open the newspaper to the page with the weather. And she'd eavesdrop on conversations at the supermarket checkout if they were about showers and frost. Now she's retired and many miles from the ice-cream parlour, but she still can't help asking everybody about the weather. The weather today, tomorrow, the day after tomorrow, next week. It doesn't matter where — it could always make its way to Rotterdam. She reckons the sky above the Netherlands is a vortex where everything gathers, but especially rain, wind, and frost. The beat of a butterfly wing in Brazil is bound to cause a hail storm of biblical proportions above the ice-cream parlour.

'Sunny,' I reply. 'Persistently calm and summery weather, with the odd patch of fog in the morning.' Before adding, 'No cloud-wrapped buildings.'

She doesn't say anything, but I know she's smiling. My mother has less of an issue with my choice for a different life. Just like she is obsessive about the weather, I love poetry, and my father loves tools. My brother is the only one still making ice-cream.

'Beppi's lost his mind,' she says, and repeats what she heard him say. I laugh at the muscles my father wants to kiss.

'Maybe it's Alzheimer's,' my mother says. 'Fausto Olivo pulls his underpants over his head. The doctor says he's suffering from dementia.' She's referring to the old ice-cream maker from La Venezia in Leiden. He retired only a couple of years ago. His eldest son is continuing the tradition.

'Mrs Olivo told me that Fausto thinks she's the neighbour and that he keeps pinching her bottom.'

My mother knows more about Alzheimer's than mobile phones.

She's quiet for a moment. Perhaps she's looking at the photos on the kitchen cupboards, at the portrait of her grandson, who left for Mexico a week ago.

'She's got red hair,' she resumes. 'Your father's new love has got long red hair.'

I think about the women I've seen in the street here. There are lots of red-haired women in Ireland. They're quicker to blush, because their skin is thinner and the blood shines through more easily. But often they're even quicker to look away. Yet not so the young woman who welcomed guests at the Fermoy International Poetry Festival. As she stood behind a small desk, I noticed a pink bra underneath her blouse and a milky-way of freckles on her skin. When I looked up again, I looked straight into her eyes, but she didn't bat an eyelid, neither literally nor figuratively. She'd seen what I'd been gazing at. Eventually, my eyes conceded defeat and I looked down at the form on the desk.

'What should I say to him?' my mother asks. 'He's been a bit depressed. I know he's dreading spring and finds it hard to enjoy life because he thinks it's all over. I need to lay out his clothes for him or else he'll wear the same ones, day in, day out.'

Some people become more beautiful as life wears on, as the years refine their character like a fine wine, as everything that's been ripening — the things they've learnt, experiences, major life events — turns into an elixir that may not prolong life, but does add a sheen to it. It's not that my father has forgotten anything, but that all of these things have ruined his character.

'He's still talking to the television,' my mother says. 'Would you like to hear it? Should I walk over to him with the phone?'

'That's okay,' I reply, but I can hear her walking out of the kitchen.

'I'm calling the doctor tomorrow morning,' she says to me, having made up her mind. 'He'll have to come over on a Saturday. It's an emergency.'

'It is nonsense, says reason,' I say, citing the famous poem by German poet Erich Fried. 'It is what it is, says love.'

'What's that you're saying?'

My gaze lingers briefly on the art in my hotel room, a watercolour of a grassy plain. In the distance is a boy, walking away.

'It's a poem,' I say. 'About love, what it is.'

'It's insanity, that's what it is,' my mother says. 'He's hugging the television!'

In my hotel rooms I sometimes try to establish contact with the flatscreens that greet me: *Dear Mr Giovanni Talamini, it's a pleasure to welcome you to the Ascot Hotel; Welcome G. Talamini! Enjoy your stay in Radisson Blu; Welcome to the Crowne Plaza Hotel. Dear Mr Talamini, it's a privilege to have you staying at the Crowne Plaza Hotel. To continue, please press okay.*

'Can you believe it?' I hear my mother's voice in my ear again. There's a brief glitch, and I imagine that perhaps for a split second the radio waves containing her words cross Betty Heidler's path from space into the television room in Venas di Cadore. 'I prefer to hear his usual complaints about his life and about yours.'

At long last, memory kicks in: I see my brother in the ice-cream parlour, a white cap on his head, in his right hand the *spatola*, the small flat spoon he uses to scoop ice-cream for the customers. It's late in the evening, but still mild outside. Black birds whizz through the air, and even higher up an Airbus is making its way to America, the lights in the cabin dimmed, although you can't see that from the ground. Young women are out in the street, some in skirts or denim shorts with the pockets hanging out. Luca's eyes linger on their bums. His wife is sleeping, laid out like a swimmer, one arm stretched above her head, the other beside her body. The last few customers are sitting outside on the terrace: boys and girls who've been to the cinema and now fancy a strawberry and mango cone, an old man who finds solace in a milkshake just before midnight.

The Discovery of Ice-cream by My Great-Grandfather in 1881

My father's father's father was also called Giuseppe Talamini. He had wavy hair, a big nose, and a twinkle in his dark-blue eyes. The story goes that he lost his life in an accident involving a runaway cow. The cow, a 900-kilo Tyrolean Grey, had broken through the pasture fence. After pattering down the steep slope towards the farmhouse, she somehow managed to clamber onto the roof of the small hayshed in which my grandfather took his daily nap in total seclusion and silence.

The silvery grey cow fell through the timber roof and crushed my seventy-six-year-old great-grandfather. He probably didn't die instantly, but succumbed to his injuries later. When he didn't turn up for dinner a search got underway, but he wasn't found until the sun had sunk behind the mountains. The cow was still lying on top of him, licking his clothes. My great-grandfather had a remarkably serene expression on his face. In fact, he appeared to be smiling.

The cow was put down that same evening; both her forelegs were broken, so there was little choice. Then, gradually, night fell and the foxes came out of the forest and the dogs started barking in the cold mountain air. The following morning, the people talked about the sudden death of Giuseppe Talamini and soon concluded that however strange it may have been, this was a death that befitted my great-grandfather's life. His was a life full of unexpected twists and eccentric turns, a life from which he'd always demanded the most, right up to his death. Perhaps that was the reason for the smile on his face.

What was my great-grandfather thinking of as he lay dying under the cow with nobody to come to his rescue, as he felt his life ebbing away? What do you think of when you know you're dying? As he faced the firing squad, Colonel Aureliano Buendía was to remember that distant afternoon when his father took him to discover ice. A similar image came to Giuseppe Talamini.

It was the summer when the tiny ripples underneath the dress of his neighbour, Maria Grazia, became voluptuous curves. An indecent miracle.

They had grown up together — had searched for pinecones in the forest together and had lain hand-in-hand under the clear sky of their childhood. Maria Grazia loved the sun, and the sun loved her honey-toned skin. Privately, Giuseppe called her *girasole*, sunflower. As the sun, slow as a billion-year-old, crossed the sky to the west, Maria Grazia moved her body with it, inch by inch, wanting to catch as many rays as possible and not give the shade the time of day. Giuseppe never moved, so they ended up lying in the grass like a life-sized clock.

Then came the last summer they were children. By now Giuseppe was afraid to look at his neighbour. It was as if her breasts were growing in the sun, becoming rounder and fuller by the day, like loaves rising in an oven. He fantasised about the colour of her nipples. One day they were pink, like her lips; the next, pale and transparent like the palms of her hands, or dark like hazelnuts. When a gentle breeze drifted over from the mountains one afternoon, he saw two tips poking through her blouse. While the cicadas were singing and the May beetles buzzing, Maria Grazia and Giuseppe lay quietly in the tall grass. They held hands and looked at the clear sky. Everything was the same, yet everything had changed.

And so it happened that by the end of the summer Giuseppe walked past the door he'd knocked on every single morning. He was joining his father, a lumberjack with a penchant for whistling. Sometimes Giuseppe would recognise a melody and he'd whistle along with his father. At the end of September the trees on the mountain were cut down, twenty-metre larches with dead-straight trunks. It was hard work, and not without danger. You never knew exactly how a tree would come down. Cutting, cleaving, felling — the stark sound ricocheting off the other trees, followed by the dull thud and the earth shuddering like a passing locomotive. On another slope, in another year, a tree had landed on top of a lumberjack. He was killed instantly.

Giuseppe helped strip the trees by removing all the branches with an axe. Next, he and his father cut the trunks into five-metre logs. The sweat that mingled with the sawdust, the resin that stuck to their bodies — the smell was sharp and stung his eyes. Never before had Giuseppe been as tired as after those long days in the forest.

Around Christmas, when the entire region was covered in a blanket of immaculate snow, the logs would be taken on a sledge down to the river, the Piave, which ran all the way to Venice, nearly two hundred kilometres further south. The logs were tied into large rafts, which were then pushed into the water. Hundreds of them floated downstream. Days later they arrived in Venice, where they were driven deep into the muddy, sandy soil, eight piles per square metre. Giuseppe could picture it, the fairytale city built on the water, with its countless bridges, churches, and high-ceilinged palaces. On special evenings, candles dripping in silver chandeliers would illuminate frescos of timeless tales, he imagined.

But winter was still a long way off, and snow graced only the highest peaks. One morning his father woke him earlier than usual. It was dark outside and the stars shone in the clear night sky. Giuseppe heard the voices of other men from the village. He recognised the sonorous bass of Antonio Zardus, the metalsmith. The men were talking softly, tall shapes leaning in towards one another. He felt like a witness to a conspiracy. They set off in the stagecoach. Of the seven men, Giuseppe was the youngest. As they drove out of the village, they all smiled at him. He could see the moon-white teeth of his father's friends.

They were silent, listening to the rattle of the hooves, until the sun rose above the mountains. Golden and rosy-fingered, it was a Homeric dawn. Giuseppe now recognised other faces too. Sitting beside him was the tinker, opposite him the locksmith. Strong men, each of them.

'Look,' his father said, pointing to the slope where two roe deer stood between the pines, immobile like statues, alarmed by the sound of the coach. They were only there for a split second, and then they darted off into the forest.

Antonio Zardus broke a loaf of bread; the locksmith cut slices off a chunk of dried meat. They ate open-mouthed, with great relish. The wooden floorboards of the stagecoach were covered with pickaxes and shovels, which shook and shifted to the rhythm of the horses' tread. Giuseppe had no idea what these men and he were about to do. His father had woken him, telling him only to come along. After getting out of bed, he had dressed really fast.

'They spent nearly ten years building it,' he heard someone say. 'The teams worked towards each other; more than a thousand people on either side.' It was Enrico Zangrando, who possessed more cattle than hair on his head. The other men sometimes slapped him on his bald pate for the beautiful sound it produced. He owned quite a bit of land by birth, but didn't put himself above anyone else.

'It's the longest railway tunnel in the world,' Enrico told them. 'Fifteen kilometres long, straight through the Saint-Gotthard Massif. They started off with tunnel-boring machines driven by compressed air, but when they couldn't get through the hard stone they switched to dynamite.'

The explosions had been terribly loud, like the violent noises of war. Demand was such that an explosives factory was built on the northern side, not far from Lake Lucerne. Holes a metre deep were drilled and the dynamite detonated inside. Poisonous gases filled the tunnel, causing inflammation of the workers' eyes and lungs. Forty-six men lost their lives in the explosions, until, on 28 February 1880, a breach was achieved. Hands gripped one another, hammers and pickaxes enlarged the hole, and then, finally, the first man stepped through. It was almost unreal, as though he had stepped into another world.

'We can travel through the mountains,' Enrico said. A hundred years ago men had managed to traverse the clouds in a hot-air balloon. This was just as magnificent. Not over the mountain but straight through — through the impenetrable base, the widest and densest part.

Giuseppe had to swallow his questions. Had Enrico been on that train? How long did the journey through the tunnel take? Could you see the light at the other end? The others remained expressionless; only his father winked at him. Giuseppe briefly yielded to the cadence of the coach, dreaming with eyes open of the Gotthard Tunnel, whizzing through it like a comet through the dark, infinite universe.

In Venas di Cadore, meanwhile, Maria Grazia stood in front of the window, looking out. She wanted to flee the house and lie in the grass, but the farmers had just mowed their land. Her breasts hurt. She'd seen men looking in the street, their gaze latching onto her body. At home, in her room, she sometimes held her breasts for hours. Her hips, too, had grown, and they hurt almost as much. She was becoming a woman and she needed a man, a man to hold her.

The stagecoach with the two jet-black horses climbed the mountain. It was a long, winding road. Giuseppe had no idea where they were, but judged by the mood that they must be approaching their destination. Enrico Zangrando rolled up his white sleeves. The others followed suit. They picked up the pickaxes and the shovels. All sat up straight.

They came to a halt by a railway track. On it stood a train with eight carriages, their large sliding doors open. Giuseppe jumped out of the coach. He looked around. They were in between two mountain ridges. The sun was nowhere to be seen, and wouldn't rise above the slope until late in the afternoon. But there was snow as far as the eye could see, at least half a metre high. Underneath it, water trickled and flowed down to the valley. Ice-cold water. Men waded into it up to their knees, staying in until their bones hurt because it was said to be good for one's circulation.

It was frozen snow, and they were supposed to fill the carriages with it. Giuseppe couldn't believe his eyes. They raked the snow with their pickaxes, moving it down to the track, the way farmers gather grass. The sizable chunks collected grit and mud, but that didn't matter.

Every now and then, Giuseppe leaned briefly on the handle of his pickaxe to look at the other men. The metalsmith was sweating and steaming; Giuseppe could see the vapour coming off his bare arms, his glistening and incredibly muscular arms. The other men, too, were shrouded in vapour. He was afraid to move, wary of disturbing the scene: the workers with their black hands in the blinding snow, the carriages filling up. He was scared it would all disappear the moment he stirred, like a dream upon waking.

Enrico called out his name and asked if he was fantasising about girls. The other men laughed heartily, his father included.

After two hours they took a break. Three carriages were full; their sliding doors had been shut. They rested on the trunk of a felled larch. A stone bottle was passed around, but Giuseppe wasn't thirsty. More than once he'd dug a hole in the snow and lifted a handful up to his mouth. Every time, his fingers had tingled with cold for minutes.

At first nobody had heard him, because he'd only whispered his question. But when he finally plucked up the courage to repeat it out loud — why were they shovelling snow into carriages? — everybody looked at him. Giuseppe was young and he was curious, and not just about the usual things. He suspected there might be an entire world of which he knew nothing, a brilliant light at the end of the tunnel.

'We're harvesting,' his father said. 'We're bringing in the snow.'

The word 'harvest' made him think of potatoes, beets, and apples. Not of snow in the mountains. Giuseppe looked at the carriages with the closed doors. He was none the wiser.

Enrico took over. 'It's turned into ice,' he said.

'Ice?'

'Not the ice you're familiar with, the kind you can walk and skate on.'

'There's a different ice?'

'Different flavours. Strawberry, vanilla, mocha. It's sold in the cities and tastes even better than a woman.'

It felt as if a light was beamed into his head, straight into his brain.

'I've eaten ice in Vienna made of oranges from Spain.'

'Impossible,' Antonio Zardus said resolutely, his voice dark and deep.

Enrico ignored it. 'They were selling it in the street, out of a cart with copper vats.'

Giuseppe immediately hungered for the ice described by Enrico Zangrando the way other people fall in love, in an unforgettable fever. Years later, he could still recall the exchange word for word.

'You eat it with a small spoon and it melts in your mouth.'

He tried to imagine it, a spoonful of strawberries melting on his tongue, but it was beyond his imagination. It was too big a step, from the frozen, dirty snow to the enchanting, glorious ice. As a child he'd tasted the snow that had fallen overnight, the way all children do, full of anticipation. It was like water, but impure and metallic — the universal disappointment of the taste of snow. He had been misled by the still splendour on the roads and fields. He also remembered how his younger brother, when he was still only two and had no memory of the previous year's snow, had looked outside and said, 'I want to stroke it.' As though it were a coat of fur protecting the world from the cold.

Enrico told them about the process, the various procedures. It was like alchemy. Snow was broken up with a small hammer and put inside a wooden barrel, after which salt was added to lower the melting point. The cylinder of the mechanical ice-cream machine was placed inside the barrel with the ice and salt, and then the ice-cream maker operated the hand wheel and scraped the substance around the cold wall of the cylinder. Churn, churn, churn. The first ice that formed along the surface was brittle. Air came into it; the volume increased. Churn, churn. The colour turned gradually lighter. Pink strawberry ice-cream, greyish-green pistachio ice-cream, cinnamon-coloured chocolate ice-cream. Churn.

'Until it's firm and thick and delicious.'

It was like the story you're told about love, about its consummation. It can be described in minute detail, but it will never be as good as it is in real life.

'Come,' the metalsmith said. 'Let's get on with it.'

One by one they got up again, until only Giuseppe remained seated. He felt as though he'd been churned too, the way more than a hundred years later his descendant and namesake would be spinning along with Betty Heidler's iron hammer. He sat on the tree trunk, as if he had been overcome by desire.

His father pulled him to his feet. 'Back to work, my boy,' he said encouragingly. 'I'll help you.' A moment later Giuseppe could hear him start to whistle a folk song.

Giuseppe wasn't tired. He was young and strong — if perhaps not as strong as Antonio Zardus, who was said to be able to bend coins. But he felt stunned, intoxicated by the stories and sweet flavours in the copper vats of the ice-cream cart in Vienna. His imagination flapped its wings, trying to get clear of the snow, to move beyond the mountains. Perhaps he'd have managed had he known what a woman tasted like. (In that case, he might have imagined something even better.) Now he saw what he already knew: that beyond the mountains lay yet more mountains.

What he didn't know, and nor did the other men — not even Enrico Zangrando — was that they were part of a greater whole. In countless places around the world, the harvest of the cold months was being brought in. In Boston, Frederic Tudor, the son of a well-known judge, had built up an ice-cream empire. At the tender age of twenty-three, this great adventurer had bought his first ship to transport ice to the Caribbean island of Martinique. The blocks of ice came from the pond on his father's estate. Everybody told him he was insane. The newspapers mocked his venture. Although a substantial amount melted during the three-week journey, Frederic Tudor managed to sell the remaining Massachusetts ice to the islanders. Imagine their faces, the look in their eyes. Disbelief, enchantment. Transparent blocks unloaded from the hold of a ship that had sailed 2,400 kilometres. The year was 1806.

His loss amounted to thousands of dollars.

The following year, when Frederic Tudor sailed to Havana with a frozen lake in the hull of his ship, he racked up huge debts, too — as you'd expect from an adventurer. On his return he was thrown into prison, and the next time he set sail the sheriffs escorted him to the dockyard. There in the water was his ship, which bore the bold name of *Trident*.

Tudor experimented with different insulation materials for his ships: hay, wood chips, sawdust, and the chaff of rice. But the breakthrough for his ice company came with the invention of the ice plough. Until then, the blocks had been cut from the frozen New England waters by hand. Now, with the help of horses, they moved on to mass production. The dark, graceful animals were harnessed to a plough with a metal saw. One man led the horse, another steered the plough. This resulted in a grid of perfect cubes, which were then lifted out of the water. Special tools were invented, and ice houses sprang up alongside riverbanks as well as in the ports of far-flung countries. Thousands of men found employment in the winter months, wielding saws and hatchets on lakes that had transformed into immense chessboards.

In 1833 the *Tuscany*, another of Tudor's ships, sailed from Boston to Calcutta with 180 tons of ice in its belly. The three-master travelled for four months until, in September, it reached the Bay of Bengal and proceeded up the holy Ganges River. News of the approaching ice ship spread among the local population, with many thinking it was a hoax. It had been over 30 degrees Celsius in the shade for months. But upon arrival in the port of Calcutta it turned out that 100 tons were still intact: crystal-clear ice with a bluish tinge.

It marked the beginning of a titanic transport of New England's frozen water to India. An ice house of white stone and double walls was erected in Calcutta, which was to become the most lucrative destination of the Tudor Ice Company. The daredevil who'd been laughed at and who'd spent two years of his life behind bars became fabulously rich and earned himself the nickname The Ice King of the World. He sailed to Brazil, Australia, and China.

Other companies also entered the market, including The Knickerbocker Ice Company of New York and The Philadelphia Ice Company. Railways were built to speed up transport, with steam trains criss-crossing the country. The locomotive was fed with fiery coal; the cargo inside the carriages was transparent and cold.

A flourishing trade in ice developed between Norway and England. Men in black caps and hats used tongs to fish enormous blocks of ice out of the vast lakes. These slid down long wooden tracks and into the holds of ships putting in at London and other British ports. It enabled Carlo Gatti, an Italian Swiss national, to open up a number of stalls in the capital. He had tried his luck with the sale of chestnuts and waffles before deciding to make ice-cream. He started on the street with a few carts, but soon relocated to the busy Hungerford Market. There he sold ice-cream in shells for a penny apiece. Later the shells were replaced by small glasses, which became known popularly as 'penny licks'. Until then, ice-cream had been a treat reserved for the rich. Carlo Gatti was the man who brought the frozen delicacy within reach of the masses. By doing so, he appears to have flung open the door to a dream.

Closer to home, behind the mountains that bounded Giuseppe Talamini's world, in Saalfelden, Austria, men were also wielding pickaxes. They too raked large chunks of snow into a waiting train. Those taking off in a hot-air balloon and floating through the vast, cloudless sky might have been able to see them — the men in various locations who, without knowing of one another's existence, were slaving away in the snow and longing for a hot meal.

Giuseppe's group laboured for another four hours until the carriages were full and the sun was high in the sky, suspended between the mountain ridges. The horses were given a bite of snow, and the men got back into the coach. They were silent, tired. Leaning on one another's shoulders, they slept. Only Giuseppe kept his eyes wide open. The door of the dream had been opened a crack, and he wanted nothing better than to walk through.

Why Giuseppe Talamini Fled to the New World

The girl next door had become a woman, with a body bursting at the seams. It had happened almost overnight. She had turned into a beauty, curvaceous and voluptuous, and she wasn't ashamed of her new body, either. In fact, Maria Grazia now actively met men's eyes when she was out in the street or at the bakery. She was aware of the effect when she opened her mouth a little, her lips parted slightly. It was one of the best combinations imaginable: naughty yet gracious.

Whenever Giuseppe spotted her in the street, he immediately looked away. He was afraid of her; a mere glimpse of her hair hanging in loose waves down her back was enough to set his pulse racing. They never spoke these days, but his right hand missed her left hand, the hand he'd held all summer for years on end.

My father's father's father lived in the house in which I too grew up. It's on the edge of the village, which was hardly any smaller back then than it is now. Most of the houses have thick walls that are more than a hundred years old. But they accommodate fewer people nowadays. And like the houses, the streets are less lively, too. My generation has moved elsewhere, to towns and cities. Every autumn, when the ice-cream season is over, my brother and his wife return to the mountains. He's an exception. Venas di Cadore is becoming a village of old men and women, a village slowly emptying.

When my great-grandfather was young and dreaming of ice-cream, Venas was still a village of farmers and artisans. Every now and then a fortune-seeker with a suitcase would cross the ocean, but the great wave of immigration had yet to happen. You tended to stay where you were born, and you died where you had lived. Families grew bigger rather than smaller, and they didn't fall apart. The house where Luca and I had each had our own room had accommodated my great-grandfather's family of eight. Giuseppe was the eldest son, but his grandmother was the senior resident, well into her seventies and still sharp. It was a crowded house, filled with the sounds of voices and pots and pans.

When autumn came around, the father summoned his son. 'I've found you a job,' he said. 'Bruno is looking for someone to help him.'

Giuseppe beamed. Bruno was the lumberjack who travelled to Vienna every year to sell roasted chestnuts. Their aroma filled the streets — the beautiful streets, with their imposing buildings. It was an intoxicating smell that revived memories of winters of yore. People were tempted by it, in the same way that no one can resist the seductive song of the Sirens. They stopped in their tracks and ate chestnuts from paper bags, without noticing their fingertips blackening a bit.

But Vienna was also the city where ice-cream was sold from copper vats.

That afternoon, Bruno stopped by to take a look at Giuseppe's shoulders. They had to carry a stove on which to roast the chestnuts.

'All right,' the lumberjack said, slapping him on the back as though he were buying a cow. Giuseppe saw the look on his mother's face. She was proud, but quiet, too. She wanted to put it off, keep him a little longer: the boy she'd raised, whose hair she'd stroked when he was scared. She thought he was handsome, incredibly handsome, and wanted to say so, whisper it in his ear like she used to, when she'd tell him every day how gorgeous she thought he was.

They travelled on foot, the way most people did in those days. Distances were greater then; it took you weeks to get from one place to another.

Vienna was a three-week walk away. The stove weighed a ton, but they took turns carrying it. During the first few days Bruno carried it for longer. He was a giant, a titan like Atlas. They were put up for the night by farmers with wizened faces and bad teeth. Sometimes there were cows lying right beside them. Before dawn they would wash with cold water from the mountains.

After a week Giuseppe began to find it easier; the burden appeared to have lightened. In reality, he'd become more muscular. Those first few days he thought he'd never make it all the way to Vienna with a stove on his back. But he arrived in the metropolis with a neck the size of a bull's.

They sold chestnuts on the corner of the Volksgarten, not far from the famous Café Landtmann, where artists and politicians met, and where Sigmund Freud drank his coffee. Giuseppe learned the trade in a single day. It wasn't hard. The main thing was not to burn the chestnuts, and not to scald yourself on the iron. The following day Bruno retrieved a stove he'd stored away the previous year. He set himself up down the road, and so together they filled the neighbourhood with the fumes of fire and chestnuts, and tempted residents and flaneurs alike. They came from all directions, walked up to him, and waited impatiently for their helping. For that magic moment when the blackened skin was peeled open and the sweet aroma was released. An oyster containing amber, yellow amber. The people blew into their hands as they ate.

Snow came down, large flakes falling on the knitted bonnets of little girls. Young children on sledges were pulled along by their parents. Last winter he had been on a sledge with Maria Grazia and had whooshed down a hill with her. They had fallen off, one foot deep in the snow, her red cheeks only a kiss away from his mouth. But they had been children, a boy and a girl, neighbours, and they had quickly run after the sledge, which had slid further down.

In Vienna's white world he thought of the new shape of her body. He spent hours picturing it. During some parts of the day, when the street seemed all but deserted and the snowy silence deafening, there was plenty of time to do so.

A few days later, the cold set in. The light was a chalky white in the morning, the wind biting. People warmed themselves by his stove. And then they ran out of chestnuts. He sold the last portion to an ancient man.

'*Danke*,' the man had said with a voice as delicate as paper.

During his time there Giuseppe had learned a smattering of German. He lived '*weit weg*' and had come to Vienna '*zu Fuss*': '*Jawohl, den ganzen Weg*.' On hearing that he had walked all the way, people looked at him as though he had walked on water. With a stove.

'We can head home now,' Bruno said. 'Your mother will have missed you.'

Giuseppe nodded. He was looking forward to going back, but first he wanted to visit an Italian he had spoken to over his stove a week ago. He was an ice-cream maker living in Vienna and prepared to sell Giuseppe an ice-cream machine.

'Do you know how it works?' the man asked when the two of them stood in his workshop.

Giuseppe thought of Enrico Zangrando's words. Churn, churn, churn. The glossy sheen that would come over the substance. He nodded.

'What matters most is a good recipe,' the man said.

'How do I find a good recipe?'

'The best are secret, but I don't mind giving you one. If that comes out right, you have to start experimenting.'

He lowered his voice a little, perhaps subconsciously. 'Anything is possible; you can make ice-cream out of anything.' It was like hearing a prophet.

The man was short and sinewy, in his early fifties. He had a long, rather posh name for someone from his background — Massimiliano — but in Vienna everybody called him Max. The road Giuseppe had travelled was one he had walked countless times, many a springtime, with the sharp outlines of the mountain tops silhouetted against the pale blue, cloudless sky, before heading back again in the autumn. But these days he had lodgings in the city too, above the workshop he now owned.

The ice-cream maker Antonio Tomeo Bareta had been the first to come to Vienna. He hailed from Zoldo, a small village in the Dolomites, not far from Venas di Cadore, and in 1865 he had obtained an official licence to sell 'Gefrorenes' in Austria's capital. Next, Bareta had gone to Leipzig and led a business comprising twenty-four ice-cream carts. Later he settled in Budapest, where he opened several ice-cream parlours and had sixty hawkers riding carts across town for him, men with caps and a leather pouch for the money. He had sold the Vienna licence to Massimiliano.

Giuseppe carried home the ice-cream machine, a wooden barrel with a cylinder and a small hand wheel, all by himself. He didn't need Bruno's help.

Back in the village Bruno offered him a job in his sawmill. But Giuseppe wasn't interested in cutting logs. His father shook his head. 'What are you going to do then?' he asked. 'You're a man, you've got to work.'

'I'm going to make ice-cream,' Giuseppe told him.

'In winter?'

'It's nearly spring.'

'You've lost your mind!'

The grandmother cut into the conversation. 'It runs in the family,' she said. 'My husband lost his mind during our wedding night.'

Voices filled the house. Only his mother was silent. His little brothers and sisters whispered, standing in the hallway, looking wide-eyed at the shiny cylinder in the wooden barrel. The youngest spun the hand wheel very tentatively before scuttling off.

The recipe he'd been given by Massimiliano was for cherry ice-cream, but it was February: the first cherries wouldn't be ripe until June, late May at the earliest. Every summer he would secretly climb an old tree on Enrico Zangrando's land and tumble out, drunk on sweetness.

His mother bought cherries on the market every year and made them into jam. The family ate it spread on thick slices of bread. The glass jars were kept in the cellar.

Giuseppe asked for three jars. His mother gave him five, her whole supply.

In the early morning light he headed up into the mountains, on his back the large basket he used for carrying hay down from the steepest slopes in summer. It was a warm, sunny day, but he kept going until he heard snow crunching beneath his shoes. He was now two thousand metres up the Antelao, the King of the Dolomites. Much higher up, on the north face of the pyramid-shaped peak, were two glaciers, sparkling in the sun like a jewelled necklace. Giuseppe took the basket from his back and began digging. He was the only one for miles, the sound ricocheting off the rocks. It didn't feel like harvesting, it felt like theft. He was stealing snow from the king.

Maria Grazia saw him return from the mountains, the straw basket with snow on his back. It had been months since she saw him last. His shoulders were broader, his bare forearms muscular. As he got closer, she also saw the look in his dark-blue eyes. It was a bashful, somewhat enigmatic look, which reminded her why she was in love with him and not with any of the other men who ogled her.

He had noticed her, looking young and ravishing. There's a kind of beauty that entrances, that transports you. It was her arched upper lip, her dark eyes, and the curves of her body, which her clothes failed to conceal. All together an outrageous promise. At the same time her skin retained the pallor of winter, lending it something almost sacred.

Giuseppe glanced at her very briefly. *Fall under my spell*, her dark eyes appeared to be saying. Then he rushed inside, feeling he had got away, but he knew it was out there waiting for him. The beauty that eclipses all else.

He broke eggs and separated the yolks from the whites. To the yolks he added the sugar he had bought from Tiziano De Lorenzo, a merchant who had been to Argentina and America. De Lorenzo was the son of a pioneer and had a broken nose. The world glimpsed from a hot-air balloon was small to him. The salt that must be added to the snow came from his stores, too.

Giuseppe whisked the egg yolks and the sugar until the mixture was nearly white. He wasn't entirely sure what he was doing, just followed Massimiliano's instructions to the letter. *Slowly add the milk to the egg mixture and bring to a simmer.* It was hard to do everything slowly — he wanted to do everything really fast. In his mind's eye he was already spinning the hand wheel and tasting his own ice-cream. His very first ice-cream.

He opened his mother's jars and tipped their contents into the milk mixture, spooning out the remains. He couldn't resist licking the spoon. His tastebuds were spinning the wheel of his imagination. For one brief moment he was back up Enrico Zangrando's tree.

Leave everything to cool. In the meantime he crumbled the snow into the wooden barrel and added the salt. Giuseppe and his ice-cream machine were in the cellar of the house. He had locked the door to the staircase, not wanting to be disturbed, but he knew his brothers and sisters were waiting impatiently upstairs.

The moment arrived. He poured the cooled mixture into the cylinder lined with snow, reached for the handle, and began turning the wooden wheel slowly, yet barely able to wait for the end result. The recipe had specified the proportion of water, sugar, and fruit, so he could only hope that his mother's jam met the requirements. Then again, Massimiliano had also told him to experiment.

He turned the hand wheel faster. One floor up, his little sister was lying on the wooden floor. 'Hurry,' she shouted. 'Listen.' They all lay down on the floor with their right ear to the wooden boards. Hearing their big brother churning brought the wheel of their imagination in motion, too.

'He's making ice-cream,' one of the girls said.

'It's colder than snow and sweeter than sugar.'

'When you swallow it, you start floating.'

After a while a brittle layer of ice formed along the wall of the cylinder. Giuseppe saw it happen. It was unlike anything he'd seen before, like a first enchanting glimpse of a woman's loins. The colour grew lighter, the volume bigger. His heart pounded in his chest like a fist on a door.

Churn, churn, churn.

He picked up the large wooden spoon he had borrowed from his mother's kitchen. His thumb wrapped itself around the handle quite naturally. There was no sign of any callousing just yet, but it did mark the beginning of a long-standing routine, and of the rough-skinned thumbs that would pass from father to son.

The ice was ready. It was firm, thick, and pink. Giuseppe brought the wooden spoon to his mouth, which he opened wide. He took a mouthful with his eyes closed, as though he were kissing a girl. Once again, his tastebuds tossed him this way and that. In a single mouthful he climbed up the old cherry tree, only to fall out again at once, intoxicated. He immediately took another bite. It melted on his tongue and he swallowed it in one. Then he dropped the spoon back in the cylinder and scooped out some more. It was delicious and he couldn't get enough of it. He emptied half the cylinder.

Then came the guilt, as though he had tasted of the forbidden fruit. It was prompted by the sounds above him, the fidgeting of his brothers and sisters. They were calling out his name and banging on the door, the masses calling for the king's purple blood. Giuseppe went upstairs with the cold cylinder and the spoon. They were told to line up and close their eyes. One by one, he served them and watched their faces. For a brief moment they appeared to be blushing and rising up off the floor. Then they all opened their eyes.

'More!' his youngest brother yelled.

'Me too!' his other brother shouted. 'More!'

And then they were all shouting it. His mother came out of the kitchen and wanted a taste as well. She stood in front of Giuseppe and looked at him without blinking. He raised the wooden spoon with the cherry ice-cream to her lips, and as they parted he saw just how beautiful she was. A forty-year-old woman with flushed cheeks.

His father refused to taste; he was too proud. 'Please,' Giuseppe pleaded. 'One small bite.'

'If he doesn't want any,' hollered the grandmother, who had just woken up, 'I'll have two.'

'All right,' his father said eventually. He gave in, unable to resist temptation. Giuseppe could tell he liked it by the lines around his eyes.

Then Enrico Zangrando appeared in the doorway. He happened to be passing their house when he overheard the glee. There was a little bit left in the cylinder, the very last of the batch. Giuseppe walked over to Enrico with the cherry ice-cream. The landowner instantly noticed how mature and muscular the lumberjack's son had become. As the spoon approached his mouth, his eyes automatically closed. But before he'd had a chance to say how delicious it was, Giuseppe had slapped him on his bald pate. It produced an exquisite sound.

Spring arrived and the grass awoke from its winter sleep. The land looked a little different, less drab every day. Some parts were pale green, while others had yet to be brought back to life by the sun, which was beginning to feel warmer. Logs were cut into planks by the river and the roofs of barns were repaired. But then there were days that crept up like ghosts from the night. Wet grass, wet leaves, diffuse light. A sea of mist parting slowly, wispy clouds among the trees, snow in the mountains.

When the dandelions sprung up, Giuseppe made dark red raspberry ice and pale yellow apricot ice. On the advice of Enrico he had prepared them without milk and eggs. His experiments with the fruits in his mother's jars had yielded divine sorbets. More and more people from the village stopped by. Giuseppe gave them a taste of the ice outside in the sun. It was nothing short of a miracle. With his eyes still closed, one person exclaimed, 'I can picture the colour of the ice!'

Maria Grazia plucked up the courage and knocked on Giuseppe's door. His father answered. He saw the girl who had become a woman. In her hands she held four jars of strawberry jam. The jam was lighter in colour than her lips. The father immediately summoned his son.

'I want ice-cream,' she said when he remained silent.

Giuseppe's gaze travelled from her eyes to the jam, but along the way it chanced upon her breasts. He couldn't help it. Hers was a beauty that turned heads. First he heard himself swallow, then his neighbour's voice, 'I can help you gather snow, too.'

She smiled, revealing unbelievably white teeth.

All of a sudden he felt afraid, too scared even to look at her neck, her hands, or her wrists.

Maria Grazia held out the jars as if thrusting a baby into his arms.

'Thank you,' he said as he took them, but he knew he had to say something else. There was a brief silence before he added, his eyes on the ground, 'See you tomorrow morning. I'll come and collect you.' And with that he quickly pulled the front door shut.

It was bright and early when they climbed the Antelao. The low-lying fields were dotted yellow with dandelions. As children they had snapped the stalks and watched the white juice trickling out before daubing it onto their skin. Maria Grazia had started the game.

'It's a bit sticky,' she had said, while tracing circles on her arms.

'Isn't it poisonous?'

'I like it.'

'Have you tasted it?'

She shook her head. 'It feels nice,' she said. 'Refreshing.' And she daubed some on his arms, too.

The following day Giuseppe had picked dozens of flowers. He pressed the juice from the stalks and left a trail of drops all over her body. On her feet, her tanned legs, her hands, her wrists, her slender arms.

'Don't forget my head,' she said.

He quickly picked a few more flowers and left a trail on her face as well. He even dripped some milk around her mouth.

Then she snuck a taste, a very quick one, with the tip of her tongue.

'It's bitter,' she said, and started giggling. 'Would you like to try some?'

Giuseppe shook his head.

'Are you scared?'

He didn't respond, but when she rose to her feet he yelled, 'No, don't!'

They were both equally tall and equally strong. But perhaps Maria Grazia was at an advantage; after all, she had jumped on top of him, pinning his hands to the grass. He couldn't break free from her grip. As she planted her shins on his arms, she quickly picked a dandelion from beside his ear. Giuseppe floundered like a fish, but Maria Grazia managed to hold his head in a vice with her knees. She towered over him, relishing the experience and laughing as she sprinkled the milk on his lips.

Now, years later, they walked without a word up the paths and through the fields — Giuseppe in front, Maria Grazia following. They had to climb a lot higher than he'd done the first time. Occasionally he would glance over his shoulder and wait for Maria Grazia to catch up.

'We're heading for the glacier,' Giuseppe said, pointing to the freezing cold necklace around the top.

She noticed the wet patches on his clothes beneath the leather straps of the basket. She was sweating, too; small beads were dotted around her nose. But they carried on without resting. The landscape grew quieter and more bare. First the birds disappeared, then the trees, and finally the leafhoppers that had sung the praises of morning, too. Now all that remained was the sound of their breathing in the rarefied air. Both had rolled up their sleeves.

For a while it seemed as if nothing had changed. Or only something on the outside. When Giuseppe and Maria Grazia stood in the perpetual snow and the light forced their eyes shut, their hands found each other again. There was no awkwardness, no fear, only the childlike delight in the sunshine.

Giuseppe took off the basket and dug a hole in the snow. He lifted a handful to her mouth. She sucked the water from the ice and chewed the crystals. The cold shot straight to her head. 'Ouch,' she said, her face contorted.

He knew the feeling, like a dagger through your skull.

Ignoring the pain, Maria Grazia insisted, 'More.'

She was thirsty, and she was warm. More than anything she wanted to kneel down and dig two holes in the glacier and press the ice to her skin, to her neck and to her chest, to feel the snow in her cleavage. It was the intimation of these things that left her reeling and him trembling.

As Giuseppe took in the harvest, Maria Grazia saw the steam coming off his arms. He hewed large blocks of ice out of the glacier and placed them in the straw basket she held up.

Nothing happened, just like nothing had happened when they lay under the old autumn sun.

They walked the long road back to Venas di Cadore. Like those of the *porteurs de glace* in the Pyrenees and the poor men descending the ice path on Mount Etna, Giuseppe's legs occasionally buckled under him. His limbs felt as though they were filled with lead. Blocks of ice are heavier than bags of flour and sacks of coffee beans. There's nothing quite like it. The only advantage compared to the dead weight of flour and beans was the fact that ice melts. As the meltwater dripped from the basket and fell on the thirsty earth, his yoke lightened. By the time they got home, the harvest had dwindled. Maria Grazia looked on as Giuseppe put the ice into the wooden barrel.

'Will it be enough?' she asked.

She had followed him inside, as she used to do in the old days when she came round to play. There was a game they had invented. It involved him removing his shirt and lying on his back, while she let the cascade of her hair splash down on his chest. If Giuseppe cried mercy, he had lost.

Above them, Giuseppe's little brothers and sisters were lying on the wooden floor. They heard all kinds of sounds and then the wheel spinning into action.

Giuseppe churned at a steady pace and never took his eyes off the cylinder, as though he was part of the machine.

'May I?' Maria Grazia asked after a while.

He moved aside for her. She reached for the handle and started churning. He felt the heat coming off her skin and heard her breathing quickening. Churn, churn, churn. She kept touching him ever so slightly, almost imperceptibly, and so it happened that they were both, at the same moment, witness to a miracle. Maria Grazia saw the red jam becoming lighter in colour along the edge, and the icy mass slowly acquiring an airier, creamier structure. Giuseppe discovered that her breasts were soft. Softer than summer light.

His heart was thumping so hard his chest was vibrating. He was afraid Maria Grazia could tell, could hear, perhaps. Animals can smell fear.

'I'm so incredibly curious,' she said.

'Not much longer now.'

He picked up the large spoon and clutched it, his thumb wrapped tightly around the handle. The ice-cream was a reddish pink, with small dark specks.

Maria Grazia took a bite, and as the ice melted on her tongue his fear too became fluid, less solid. Now that her eyes were closed, Giuseppe looked at her lips, her bare arms, and her breasts, which rose and fell with her breath.

'It's amazing,' Maria Grazia said. 'It's better than anything in the world.'

She had caught him at it, but didn't let on.

He held up the spoon again. Maria Grazia took a bigger mouthful of the ice-cream. This time she kept her eyes closed for longer, as if she were drifting off on the flavour, the way you drift off to a deep sleep. It was a game, an age-old game, but new to Giuseppe. It never occurred to him that he was expected to make a counter-move.

A minute passed. Maria Grazia opened her eyes. Giuseppe had been watching her nipples poking through the fabric of her clothes. He wondered if they were the same colour as the ice.

They emptied the cylinder together. When they went back upstairs, his brothers and sisters jeered. They wanted strawberry sorbet, but had to make do with the sight of the ice-cream makers' pleasure: Maria Grazia's lips were glistening like a forbidden fruit.

Summer descended. Heat and drought, the scent of hay wherever Guiseppe went. The days were long and light, the skies clear blue and drenched with the scent of lavender and lemon in the evenings.

Every morning Giuseppe walked up the glacier on the Antelao. He harvested ice and returned soaking wet. Maria Grazia picked fruits in the forest — glossy blackberries and dull, almost black blueberries. They turned them into indigo ice-cream, which he sold by the side of the road. People waited in line, ready to be surprised by a new colour, a new flavour, every day.

Giuseppe bought apricots and peaches from Bolzano. Farmers dropped off plums and pears, and later figs, too. He transformed them into frozen yellow, grey, and pink substances that had to be consumed at once — although occasionally there were children who had to take the ice-cream home, to a grandmother who had given them money. 'Run as fast as your legs will carry you,' Giuseppe would tell them.

Churn, churn, churn.

Maria Grazia's head swam. Some days they stood side by side in the kitchen or in the cellar with everything suffused with the smell of red fruit and sugar. Their fingers were sticky; even their breath smelled of raspberries.

She waited another month, but still nothing happened. That is to say, the thing that Maria Grazia was hoping for, what she was longing for, did not happen. Something else happened instead.

Looking back, people saw a connection with the increasingly outlandish colours and flavours Giuseppe produced. That's where it all started, they said. That's when we should have realised.

One afternoon he sold a pale orange-coloured sorbet along the main village road. The customers took a very cautious first bite, but loved the flavour. 'I can taste tomato,' a man exclaimed. 'I can taste actual tomato!'

Giuseppe also made ices with goat's milk, elderflower, fresh mint, and pine needles. Maria Grazia had picked the needles off the trees, and Giuseppe had put them in a pan with water and sugar. It called for the precision of a pharmacist: too much sugar made the ice too soft and sweet.

When Maria Grazia was offered a taste, she felt as if she had just taken a bite from the forest in which she had spent half her childhood, hunting for pinecones, building huts, and using branches for swords. She could taste all that, as well as the spokes of light falling among the tree trunks and the hollow sound of her feet on the root-filled earth.

This was what she had seen in his eyes, in his enigmatic gaze. She had known that he could engender this feeling in her, that he had the power to let her be in two places at once.

The following day Giuseppe made espresso ice-cream. He had added an extra ingredient, a chunk of Swiss chocolate bought from Tiziano De Lorenzo. Some ice-cream eaters detected bittersweet notes, but Giuseppe refused to reveal what it was. The best recipes are secret, the Viennese ice-cream maker had said.

'Is it camomile?' someone asked.

Giuseppe said nothing.

'How about cinnamon, then?'

That night, many had trouble falling asleep.

Maria Grazia, who had sampled plenty of spoonfuls, couldn't stop tossing and turning in bed. Her mind was on Giuseppe's strong arms, and on his hands, too. While they could not bend coins, they were all the better at stoning apricots. In the middle of the night she crept outside with a candle, stood under Giuseppe's bedroom window, and softly called out his name. When she got no response, she started throwing small pebbles at the glass.

Giuseppe stuck his sleepy head out.

'I want to show you something,' she said.

'Now?'

'Yes.'

It couldn't wait any longer. She had waited long enough.

After a short while, the door opened and Giuseppe came out in his nightshirt. He saw the wild look in Maria Grazia's eyes, but before he had a chance to say anything, she spoke. 'I love you.'

Giuseppe said nothing. He didn't know what to say. He didn't speak the language of love.

Maria Grazia stepped forward. That's when she unbuttoned her nightgown. She wore nothing underneath. He was afraid to look, but he looked anyway.

Her breasts gleamed in the candlelight. They were whiter than her belly, two dizzying copies of each other. But what struck Giuseppe most were her nipples. They had the colour of amber and the golden glow of roasted chestnuts.

This is what she had wanted to show him.

Giuseppe could barely believe that the woman standing before him was Maria Grazia. He had sawn giant trees in half and he had carried a stove across the mountains, but he was no match for this beauty.

'Give me a baby,' she said.

Instead of ripping the nightgown off her body and giving her lips a lingering kiss before taking her under the star-filled sky, he whispered only a single word, almost inaudibly: 'Mercy.'

It was August, not far into the month. Two more nights and it would be the feast day of Saint Lawrence, who, tradition has it, suffered a martyr's death on a red-hot gridiron nearly two thousand years ago. There had already been sightings of falling stars, Perseid meteors entering the Earth's atmosphere. This would reach its peak in the early morning of 13 August, with dozens of falling stars every hour — Lawrence's tears. By then Giuseppe was already walking across the hinterland. His aim was to walk to the Gotthard Tunnel and travel straight through the mountains, but he became disorientated under the hail of meteors and eventually ended up in Genoa, where he spotted the stately *Kaiser Wilhelm II* oceanliner in the port. Giuseppe had never smelled the sea and he had never seen a ship before.

The 140-metre ocean liner of the Norddeutscher Lloyd was getting ready to set sail to New York. Trunks were hauled on board, and men carried suitcases across narrow gangways. First class could accommodate one hundred and eighty passengers; second class, eighty-six; and between decks there were berths for six hundred and forty-four people. The hull was completely white.

His mother waited in his room with the window open. Maria Grazia had cried for days on end. Her dark, wavy hair hung in front of her face like a widow's veil. She clutched one hand with the other, but still felt the loss. It ran through her blood. She feared she would never see Giuseppe again.

Those first few days, people lingered by the side of the village road in the afternoon, speculating about a new, exceptional flavour that was difficult to prepare. It was said to be blue-black as the night. But when, after a week, there was still no sign of the ice-cream maker, people walked past his spot as though he had never existed, as though it had all been a dream.

Meanwhile, in the green water of the Port of Genoa, the *Kaiser Wilhelm II* had set sail. Looking majestic, with a small wave in front of its bow, the ship made its way to the sea. There had been no little jolt; all of a sudden they were sailing, they were on the move. From the quayside — with its tall cranes and the folks staying behind with handkerchiefs and hats in their hands — it looked as if the ship was barely moving, but the wake splashed and foamed. Inside, stokers toiled and boilers blazed, and large clouds of smoke billowed from the round funnels. The mood was one of parting, but also of joy, the prospect of a new life. Those standing on the afterdeck could see the coast fade from view. The ship's horn was sounded one final time.

Ten days later, at nightfall, Giuseppe Talamini was standing alone at the rail. The ship was sailing at full speed, sixteen knots, cleaving the dark waves. He hadn't travelled through the mountains, he hadn't seen the light at the end of the tunnel. But what he saw now was just as luminous as snow. There was land in sight, and above this land hung a giant sun.

'The Spirit That Creates One Object'

The hallway of our house in Venas di Cadore boasts an impressive Native American headdress. The feathers are those of an eagle, 'the biggest and strongest of all birds'.

The headdress is said to have been brought back by my great-grandfather when he returned from America. Upon his arrival in Castle Clinton, he joined a group of immigrants to work on the construction of a skyscraper. The bricks are probably still in place, but the name of the tower, with its many windows, hasn't been passed down to us. Next he is thought to have worked with other Italians on a railway up north, felling trees and putting down sleepers, the track lengthening and disappearing into the distance. After that it gets more nebulous, the picture blurry. It is said that he went to Wyoming, where he hunted buffalo, the cattle with the large heads and mighty horns, the long and stiff brown coats. I imagine it was while doing this job that he encountered the Sioux, the Blackfoot Indians who were already living on a reservation in South Dakota by then. The legendary Chief Red Cloud had led his people there after the Treaty of Fort Laramie, each feather in his war bonnet symbolising bravery in battles against other tribes — the Pawnee, the Crow, and later the colonisers, too. White feathers like bolts of lightning, representing land conquered and reconquered, and ultimately lost forever.

To the first man Giuseppe saw on his return to the Northern Italian mountains, he said, 'Greetings, paleface.' That, at any rate, is the story which has been passed down from generation to generation to generation.

My father, the other Giuseppe Talamini, walks past the Native American headdress and down the steps to the basement, which has been further excavated and reinforced with new pillars. He presses the switch. The light bounces off the cement mixer and on to the pillar drills, past the thousands of screwdrivers, monkey wrenches, files, pliers, and brackets on the walls, and against the chisels and brushes, the sanding machines and workbenches. A treasure trove of tools. This is my father's life's work — or, rather, his life's revenge. He worked as an ice-cream maker for fifty-seven years, but he'd really wanted to be an inventor.

My grandfather was an intractable man. He had no faith in his son's dreams and ambitions, and besides, he needed his son in the ice-cream parlour. At the age of fifteen, my father had to cycle through the streets of Rotterdam with an ice-cream cart. 'Some days the ice-cream would melt faster than you could sell it,' he used to tell us at the dining table when we complained about work. 'Not only would you have a sore back and arms at the end of the day, but your legs would ache, too.'

During the winter months, he would busy himself in a workshop in Calalzo fashioning nuts and bolts from large chunks of iron, his eyes screwed up a little, his black shoes planted among the filings on the floor. Every year he spent the money he earned on new tools. It began with the basic items all households have — except a bit more extensive, perhaps — but once he had taken over his father's ice-cream parlour and started earning his own money, he bought his first drilling, sanding, polishing, and cutting machines: screaming monsters with large benches, as well as lovely little adjustable wrenches and the minuscule instruments used by watchmakers and engravers. He bought everything, absolutely everything he didn't have yet, including seven-inch nails, cap nuts, lock nuts, rivet nuts, right-threaded screws, left-threaded screws, double-ended screws, endless screws, blind bolts.

One day a lorry driver pulled up outside the house in Venas, having been directed here by the ironmonger in Belluno. The man had been looking for a particular nut for years. My father listened to the driver's description the way a child listens to a fairytale and then escorted him down into the basement. When he switched on the light, the treasure chamber sparkled in all its glory. The lorry driver's pupils dilated instantly. He couldn't believe his eyes — and it probably contained only half of all the tools there are now. These days the double garage is full of shiny metal too.

Except for that one occasion, my father never showed his collection to others, 'because nobody understands'. Most people think it's an illness. But the driver congratulated my father on his wealth of tools and machines.

'I've never seen anything like it,' he said.

There probably wasn't anything like it.

My father rummaged in a couple of metal trays and a minute later retrieved a nut.

'Yes,' was all the driver said at first. 'Yes.' Then his eyes filled with tears. 'Unbelievable,' he said. 'This is it. Yes, this is it. This nut ...'

It was the best day of his life, and probably of my father's life too.

He liked to tell the story whenever my mother expressed her disapproval of a new drill or sander.

'I hope one day you'll find the screw that's loose in your head,' she would reply.

'Nobody understands, not even my own wife.'

Once she gave him an ultimatum. 'If you buy that workbench, Beppi,' she declared, 'I'm leaving you.'

My father bought the workbench, my mother stayed. My brother and I didn't get it. We were young and knew little about marriage — about the threats, the compromises, the cracks. My mother never said another word about my father's collection, but the grooves in her forehead deepened, looking as if they'd been chiselled there.

My father used the life he led as an excuse to buy tools. He had never wanted to be an ice-cream maker and had never wanted to take over his father's ice-cream parlour. But he had done so anyway.

'For seventy-five years I didn't have a summer,' he often said after he retired, before opening a box with a spirit level or a metal saw. For over half a century, no long, sun-drenched summer, no early summer, no empty summer, no sultry summer, no cool summer, no sweet, melancholic summer and no summer by the seaside. That was his lament — or the mantra with which he tried to convince himself and others.

Many are the occasions when I had fruitless discussions with him. 'Why didn't you do something else?'

'It was impossible.'

'Nothing's impossible.'

'No, not in those days.'

'You should have carved out your own path.'

'That path had already been mapped out for me,' he said. 'And when a gap opened up, when there was finally some space, you scampered off.'

My father likes to blame me for the fact that he had to make and scoop ice-cream until the age of seventy-two.

'While you were groomed by your poetry pals, I had to help Luca.'

'I wasn't groomed.'

'Brainwashed, then.'

'It's called passion.' It sounded more dramatic than intended, but I couldn't think of another word on the spur of the moment. 'The way you love a chainsaw, I love poetry.'

'You've been brainwashed.'

He was referring to the team behind the World Poetry Festival: the then director, his editors, the beautiful interns. Their offices were located across the street from the ice-cream parlour. In summer they would often come over for an ice-cream after work. But the director also came in the morning, just after we opened, when it was quiet, to drink an espresso. His name was Richard Heiman, a man with watery blue eyes and a deep voice. He was never without a volume of poetry. He would open it on the table and keep reading as he sipped.

I don't remember what volume he was reading when I first took his order for espresso, but I do remember that the dust jacket was missing and the cover was red. Dark red with golden letters, which you would have felt if you were to trace your fingers across them. Beauty is something you don't notice until you reach a certain age. It's invisible to children. It is there, but they look right through it. I like to think that the glossy letters on the burgundy book of poetry afforded me my first-ever glimpse of beauty.

I had seen plenty of customers read, at the tables both inside and out. It was usually the paper, but some women read paperbacks with sumptuous covers, while taking forever to finish their cup of vanilla, hazelnut, or chocolate.

'Your ice-cream is melting,' my father would sometimes say from behind the counter.

And then the woman would look up, blushing, as though he had read her mind, seen the images of passion conjured up by the sentences.

Richard Heiman was reading the most beautiful book I'd ever seen. Aged fifteen then, I attended the grammar school in Valle di Cadore but spent the three-month summer holidays in Rotterdam, reunited at last with my parents, so I hadn't seen Heiman before. He failed to notice me by his side. He was completely engrossed in a poem.

Even now, after all these years, I try to read the golden letters in my mind. Could it have been *To Urania* by Joseph Brodsky, or Philip Larkin's *High Windows*? Was he reading *The Last Rose* by Anna Akhmatova, or perhaps the collected poems of Paul Celan? I can no longer ask him; he has crossed the river, taking all his memories with him.

'Would you care to order something?' I asked.

He looked up, startled. 'Pardon.' One word, followed by those blue eyes trying to peer inside. 'Had you been waiting long, sir?'

No customer had ever addressed me as 'sir'. It befitted his character, but I wasn't to know that until later. Back then I saw what made him so gallant: at times he seemed to hail from a different era altogether. The era of the poets he held so dear. The Lake Poets: Wordsworth, Coleridge, Southey. And Shelley, Keats, and Lord Byron, of course.

He ordered an espresso.

The following day he opened a different book. I decided not to ask him what he wanted to drink and brought him an espresso. To my surprise he looked up from the poem he was reading and said, 'That's very kind of you, sir.' Then he fixed his gaze back on the book.

It was a month before I plucked up the courage to ask what he was reading.

'This,' Heiman replied, 'this is contemporary, impenetrable poetry with the occasional crystal-clear image. Let's start with something else.'

He asked me to join him at his table, and when I was seated opposite him he began to recite from Percy Bysshe Shelley's long autobiographical poem 'Epipsychidion'. First in English, then in the Dutch translation. '*I never was attached to that great sect, / Whose doctrine is, that each one should select / Out of the crowd a mistress or a friend, / And all the rest, though fair and wise, commend / To cold oblivion.*' His hands moved as though he was reciting before a full auditorium. The other customers were looking at us, and even my mother, who was scooping ice-cream for a little girl, turned her head. '*Narrow / The heart that loves, the brain that contemplates, / The life that wears, the spirit that creates / One object, and one form, and builds thereby / A sepulchre for its eternity.*' That was it, and he looked at me with his watery eyes, the eyes of an old man.

It was as if something had wafted up from those lines, a certain scent or perfume.

Time and again I have wondered why he chose this poem, why he recited these particular stanzas from 'Epipsychidion'. At the same time I ask myself: if I were given the opportunity to show someone the beauty of poetry, what poem would I initiate them with? Where to start? So many teachers manage to put students off with their very first poem, or worse, saddle them with a lifelong aversion to poetry. The choice seems infinite, but there's really only one option: a different poem for each student's soul. Poems should never be read in front of a class as a whole.

Heiman asked me what I thought. I didn't know what to say. I was young; my voice hadn't even broken yet. What could I have said? That I was going to change my life's course? That I was now going to open my heart to a hundred women, all of them the love of my life? Or had the poem already done so? Had the door to one of the rooms been opened a crack, without me noticing? Sometimes I think so.

He broke the silence by telling me about Shelley's premature death, at the age of thirty. 'He drowned in the Bay of Lerici after his vessel, the *Don Juan*, sank.' The poet washed up on the beach between Massa and Viareggio a couple of days later, a collection of poems by John Keats in one of the pockets of his white sailor's breeches. The poems, as well as his body, were burned on the beach. Those were the days of cholera and the plague; everything that washed ashore had to be consumed by fire. The ashes were buried in the Protestant cemetery in Rome, *a rolling green lawn beside the city wall* where *the wind whispers through the leaves* and where three years previously his young son William had been buried. 'Shelley's heart wouldn't burn,' Heiman told me, 'and was sent to his wife Mary.' After her death in 1851, it was found in one of her desk drawers. Wrapped in the poem 'Adonaïs', it had crumbled to dust.

> *Stay yet awhile! speak to me once again;*
> *Kiss me, so long but as a kiss may live;*
> *And in my heartless breast and burning brain*
> *That word, that kiss, shall all thoughts else survive.*

After the death of his last surviving son, Percy Florence, what remained of the heart was buried in Bournemouth, where Mary lay buried too. By then his mistress Claire Clairmont had already passed away. She had been buried, by her own wish, with a shawl Shelley had given her.

Before he became director of the World Poetry Festival, Richard Heiman had been a lecturer in English Language and Literature at the University of Amsterdam. Prior to that he had spent some time at Stanford, a place of low sandstone buildings and foxglove trees with squirrels clambering up their trunks. The governor had had his will drawn up by him, and the university's president had also had his deeds executed before him. But there had been an affair with a female student nearly twenty years his junior, the daughter of a prominent public notary. Despite Heiman's promise and the high regard of his colleagues, his position had become untenable. It was the only transgression of his life, but he didn't see it that way. He would always remember California fondly. The long, mellow evenings and the eternal sunshine. Her magnificent face — Natalie, her name was — and the slender chain with the bee-shaped charm around her neck. It was a present from her father or her first boyfriend; he forgot which.

But he never forgot a poet. He knew more about poetry than anyone. He couldn't imagine life without it.

'Nonsense,' my father said. 'You can live perfectly well without poetry. I've done so for over forty years.'

It was a different life, Richard Heiman meant to say. A life less beautiful. He used those words without qualms, but also without wanting to be elitist. He was like the doctors of yore who prescribed oranges; poetry enriches your life, he told others. He proclaimed it in lecture theatres, standing behind the lectern, his hands moving while he spoke.

He could recite poems in five different languages — Dutch, English, French, German, and Latin — and had an anecdote about every single poet.

'Charles Baudelaire dyed his hair green and would tell everybody at parties that the taste of children's brains reminded him of walnuts.'

'Gérard de Nerval owned a lobster that he'd walk on a blue silk ribbon in the gardens of the Palais Royal.'

'When Anna Akhmatova was under surveillance by the secret police, she wrote her poems on cigarette papers. Visitors were asked to memorise them, after which she lit a match under the paper.'

'Johnny van Doorn makes the most potent garlic soup! It contains forty cloves and is a remedy against depression, irregular bowels, sensitive skin, menstrual problems, and dizziness.'

'Edwin Arlington Robinson asked his family to carry his bed outside so he could die under the stars.'

My father had to cycle through the streets with an ice-cream cart at the age of fifteen. I listened to poetry. During the years Heiman frequented the ice-cream parlour I received daily poetry lectures, covering everything from Aesop to twentieth-century Dutch poet Cornelis Bastiaan Vaandrager. They were brief excursions, but I began to long for a more extensive sojourn in this world of autumn days and still inland lakes, of white blossom and the wide, wide ocean.

'That will do for now,' my father would say every morning. 'There's work to be done.'

In the early days he had greeted Heiman with a smile. That was back when we first had our espresso machine, a Faema E61, streamlined like a sports car. It came from Milan and drew a lot of attention from Italians living in Rotterdam. They praised its curves, and the taste of the espresso even more so.

'*Buonissimo.*'

'*Perfettamente.*'

Some claimed to detect a hint of roses in the aroma. The Dutch were less effusive. The first customer to be served an espresso by my father was flabbergasted when he saw his cup.

'What's this?'

'Espresso.'

'There's hardly anything in that cup.'

'That's the idea.'

'I can almost see the bottom.'

A week later a bucket appeared next to the espresso machine. Whenever someone complained about the small quantity of coffee relative to the price, my father's standard response would be, 'You can have a free bucket of water with it.'

Only Heiman drank his espresso like an Italian. He savoured it, as though it were a short poem, a haiku.

My father stopped greeting him warmly after I started joining him at his table a month later. It was like the song of the Sirens. Odysseus had himself tied to the ship's mast. Given the choice, my father would have chained me to the ice-cream machine.

'You can't live off poetry,' he said. 'Haven't you seen those poets swarming around him like flies?'

Every now and then Heiman would sit on the terrace with a couple of poets and treat them to an ice-cream.

'That young man over there has used sticky tape to fix the sole to his shoe,' my father whispered. 'Do you see that?'

Or, 'If it weren't for Heiman, I'd have mistaken them for tramps and chased them off.'

Heiman never looked down on others. His suits were handmade and he always wore a tie, but he hadn't forgotten his roots. His parents were simple folk, like Shakespeare's, whose father had been a glove-maker. Heiman's most vivid childhood memory was the smell of fried udder. They ate it every Saturday, and his mother always made do with the smallest portion. He didn't put himself above poets; he admired them — many of them, anyway. It didn't just take talent, in his view, but something else too, something that defied description. It had to do with seclusion and perseverance, as well as a detachment from things, from possessions. A table and a sheet of paper were all you needed. As with monks, it was a choice for a different life. There were poets who couldn't hack it. Some became addicted to alcohol or drugs. Some committed suicide. The list was long. Heiman had known two in person. They had been younger than Shelley.

I have never wanted to be a poet. I lack the talent. It's not in my blood, the sacred to which all else must be sacrificed. Of course, I tried in those early years, touched by the language of the tormented souls and the illustrious dead. I produced three poems, including a sonnet in the style of Petrach, the swan of Vaucluse. But my sonnet sought to be more lyrical than the whole of the *Canzoniere*. I was the swan of Venice, albeit not of the lagoon city, with its hazy mornings and lions overlooking the tranquil canals, but of the ice-cream parlour, with its sweet flavours in all colours of the rainbow.

Yet at least twice a year I am invited to a poetry festival somewhere in the world. They're not the most insignificant festivals, either. Sometimes I'm already on the poster. I've got several programmes featuring my name: Giovanni Talamini, renowned Dutch poet of Italian descent. My poetry is praised for its 'keen insight into the human psyche' and, on the far side of the world, for 'the light-heartedness' I combine with 'a subtle sense of mortality'.

Many festival directors are poets who are keen to appear on the most prestigious stage of all, the World Poetry Festival. They think it's a case of quid pro quo. A couple of years ago I had a spat with an Israeli poet. He phoned to tell me that he wanted to read in Rotterdam. The time was ripe.

'What do you mean that's not how it works?' he asked indignantly.

'As a matter of principle I never book poets who are also directors.'

The Israeli poet was the director of the Sha'ar International Poetry Festival. Its emphasis was on dialogue between the Hebrew- and Arab-speaking cultures. It hosted socially engaged poets from around the world. It was an important festival.

'But you get to perform at mine,' he offered.

'I don't want to.'

'On the main stage.'

'I'm not a poet.'

'You've written the odd poem, haven't you?'

'I don't want to read them, not even with a gun to my head.'

There was a moment's silence on the other end of the line. 'I've recited at festivals all over the world,' the Israeli poet resumed. 'In Medellín, in Berlin, in Struga.'

No doubt the directors or programmers of Medellín, Berlin, and Struga had also performed in Tel Aviv, but I didn't say so.

'When you're no longer a director, I may consider it.'

The Israeli poet hung up, furious, but not long ago he phoned again. 'I'm not a director anymore,' he said gleefully. 'So you can book me now.'

I told him he'd receive an invite in due course if we thought his work was good enough.

'So if I don't receive an invite, my work isn't good enough.'

That's what it boiled down to, but many poets were unable to accept this.

The Israeli poet hung up, furious again.

Since becoming the director of the World Poetry Festival I've been at the receiving end of angry emails from misunderstood poets. And I'm frequently accosted at literary festivals up and down the country. The bard's state of inebriation tends to aggravate things.

'Why would you like to appear at World Poetry?' I always ask.

'Because I'm the best poet in the world.'

'But why do you think World Poetry is so important?'

'No, I'm the one who's important!'

I try to remain professional and explain that World Poetry has become the major festival that it is because it doesn't just accept any old poet, and we're proud of our autonomy. Not a single sponsor, mayor, embassy, literary foundation, or board interferes with our programming.

Richard Heiman compared the status of the festival to the lighthouse of Alexandria. 'We're a shining example,' he used to say. If I were to say that, poets would have a go at me and call me an arrogant twat. Heiman could say anything to them. He could make them laugh, too. His imitation of Joseph Brodsky was brilliant: the same accent, the same sing-song delivery. Even Brodsky himself thought it was funny. Many national and international poets had dined in Heiman's apartment on Westzeedijk, built in the New Hague School style of the Thirties. Down in the basement were the old servants' quarters, to which he would retreat occasionally with a stack of poetry books, but in summer he would sit in the large communal garden with roses and snow-white hydrangeas.

'You must choose,' he said when I was eighteen. We were sitting at the round iron table on the lawn, a bottle of Soave in the wine cooler. 'Are you going to devote your life to poetry or are you going to become an ice-cream maker?'

My father was an ice-cream maker, his father had been one, and his grandfather had started it. They all had the same thumb, calloused and strong. At the age of four I had made my first ice. Pear sorbet. It had brought tears to my father's eyes. '*Sei un piccolo gelataio,*' he proclaimed proudly. I grew up, got an education, started shaving, and broke a heart, but in his eyes I've always remained an ice-cream maker.

'I want to break with the family tradition,' I said.

'I thought you might,' Heiman said.

He took a sip of his wine and looked at me. Despite his eyes, there was something boyish about him. Perhaps it was his clean-shaven face, the cheeks that flushed when he cycled. His hair retained traces of blond, the yellow of chicory. Every now and then he'd run his hand through it.

Then suddenly, as though he had made up his mind, Heiman said, 'Congratulations.' He smiled and raised his glass. With the sun illuminating the golden liquid, we proposed a toast.

'Fortune favours the bold.'

'And rejects the fearful.'

Those were the words of the most illustrious of Roman poets. But later that evening in the ice-cream parlour, I didn't have the guts to tell my family that after the summer I would be embarking on an English Literature degree in Amsterdam. I felt as if I was betraying them all — my father; my brother, Luca; and my mother, who held the *spatola* in her hand until midnight. She was always hunched over the ice like a farm labourer over potatoes.

In the garden, with the roses and hydrangeas, the decision had felt like freedom, like disentangling myself from a web of history and tradition. The threads appeared to have snapped. But that had been an illusion. Although so thin as to be practically invisible, the gossamer of the threads remained intact. Little did I realise it at the time, but I would never manage to free myself completely. I removed myself further and further from the ice-cream parlour — I went to university, moved to Amsterdam, and worked a part-time job at Tofani's — and yet the fine familial threads still clung to me.

'At Tofani's?!' my father yelled. 'Have you gone mad?'

'I need money.'

'They're from Bagni di Lucca. They're Tuscans!'

Most Dutch ice-cream makers came from Vodo or Venas, from the Cadore Valley. They looked down on the Tuscans, who had originally sold figurines but now made a living selling ice. The Tuscans were seen as copycats, their ice of inferior quality, at least by the ice-cream purveyors from Cadore.

'They offered you a job to get their hands on our recipes! They're thieves.'

'I'm not preparing ice, I'm scooping it.'

'Are you selling sandwiches too?' my father asked disparagingly.

Tofani's sold sandwiches as well as ice-cream. In fact, the family had a second ice-cream parlour in Amsterdam that served chips too. In my father's view there was nothing worse than an ice-cream parlour that reeked like a chip shop.

'Whatever next?' he once asked at the dinner table as he railed against the Tuscans. 'Soft serve?'

I wasn't working for the enemy. I was working for barbarians.

Luca no longer talked to me. Whenever I was in the ice-cream parlour, he pretended not to see me, or he refused to leave the kitchen, where the ice-cream was made. Since I wasn't working, he had to work. He wanted me to see it, to feel it.

Only my mother enquired after my studies and wanted to know what Tofani's ice-cream was really like.

'Their fruit flavours aren't as good as ours,' I told her, 'but they've got ice-cream made of pine kernels that is irresistible.'

My degree was everything I expected it to be. All my classes were taught in English. In lectures, the academics showed the same dedication to their subject as Heiman; in seminars, we discussed literary texts in small groups — *The Spanish Tragedy* by Kyd, Marlowe's *Doctor Faustus*, Shakespeare's sonnets. It made you feel like an aristocrat from the Elizabethan age. You ended up talking like one, too. All flowery and posh. It wasn't everybody's cup of tea. Some students dropped out after a month, switching to another degree.

I spent most of my time in the library, where I read the work of Geoffrey Chaucer, the first great English poet. *The Canterbury Tales*, *Troilus and Criseyde*. It was indeed a choice for a different life; there was the same silence that surrounds monks, except it came accompanied by young women burying their noses in heavy tomes. Sitting across from me on one occasion was a girl reading Shakespeare's tragedies. The bard had written the greatest and most powerful within the space of just a few years: *Othello*, *Hamlet*, *King Lear*, *Macbeth*. Heiman reckoned these were his best plays. They were tragedies that cut through the soul, but without the frills and the plethora of confusing names you find in history plays such as *Richard III*. Shakespeare had followed *Macbeth* with a couple of romances, but none of them achieved the depth of his best work.

The girl had blonde hair and a snub nose and came from a village in Brabant called Wouw. When she woke up the following morning, she said: 'Gosh, you move a lot in your sleep.'

'I dreamed about what we did.'

She rubbed her eyes and yawned. It made her look innocent, extremely young. Or maybe it was the snub nose that did it, the freckles on the slightly turned-up tip. She turned into a little girl when she stretched.

I hadn't been allowed to make any noise. Her housemate was already in bed and the walls were like cardboard. She had taken me home after we'd had wine in a café — glasses to begin with, and then a whole bottle. The plan had been to go for a meal, but by the end of the evening the wine had driven away the hunger. A different hunger had taken its place.

'You pedal,' she had said.

I didn't have a bike in Amsterdam at the time and used to go everywhere on foot. But now I was invited to mount an old-style granny bike that had been painted yellow, with a girl on the back, her legs dangling down the left-hand side. The headlights of the passing cars made her nylon tights shimmer.

And so I lost my virginity underneath a bookshelf that also held a diary somewhere — in between W.B. Yeats and T.S. Eliot, to be precise. She pressed her hand on my mouth. She had lost her virginity at fifteen. The person in question had been a bad boy, she told me when we were lying next to each other in the morning. Quite a bit older. He had also slept with her best friend. She had expected it to be a special experience, virginity being something you can only give away once. The second time had been much nicer. It was with another boy, her childhood sweetheart who'd stayed behind in Wouw. He had a spluttering Zündapp and a quiff.

I was afraid to tell her that I had lost my virginity to her. We spent the rest of the morning in bed. We kissed, we had sex again — and then we had it a third time. Her name was Laura. It was Saturday, it was September, it was sunny. In the ice-cream parlour I knew my mother would be leaning over the ice-cream, my father holding a tray with coffee aloft, and my brother filling the Cattabriga cylinder with a mixture of milk, sugar, egg yolks, and ground almonds.

On the train home on Sunday, I couldn't stop thinking of Laura's sex. I had kissed it, the urge stronger than myself.

'What are you doing?'

I had no idea; I couldn't help myself. My heart was pounding like a fist on a door.

'It tickles.'

I kissed the whitest part of her body until she said in a firm but velvety whisper, 'I want you inside me.'

When I got home, Luca could see it, I knew it. Just as I entered the ice-cream parlour, he came out of the kitchen with a tub of virtually white pineapple ice. Our eyes met — his dark, like Kalamata olives — and he knew it. You can tell. Sometimes you can even smell it. A certain glow, pheromones. When I'm on my way to an international poetry festival and too tired to read poems, I play a little game: I try to guess who has just had sex. The early-morning flights are the best. You see the fresh faces, the rosy glow on some cheeks, the recently washed hair of the women. And then you look into their puffy eyes, the bags under them. The alarm clock that woke them from a deep sleep, the alarm deliberately set too early so there would be some time for snoozing. You think about the men having to travel to Shanghai for work, and their wives snuggling up against them, mounting them. You think about stewardesses having to hurry and their boyfriends not wanting to let them go, hitching their skirts up and taking them with their hair still wet. Once, on the train to the airport, I saw a dark-skinned woman in a sky-blue uniform rubbing a stain from her jacket.

For a moment I worried that my brother might drop the container of pineapple ice, but he made his way stoically to the front of the shop, where my mother was serving an elderly lady. He set the tub in the chiller display, turned on his heels, and walked back to the kitchen. This time he avoided my gaze.

My mother asked if I was free to help. It was going to be a warm day. I nodded and walked to the back to fetch an apron.

'Feeling guilty?' my father asked when he saw me.

'No, I'm happy to help.'

'We started making ice-cream at six this morning.'

I knew. I could tell by his puffy eyes, the bags underneath. That was all I saw, that was all I wanted to see. I went outside and walked over to a couple sitting in the sun. The woman had to tell me her order twice. It was a late summer's day that felt like spring. 'The heart is pounding and not here,' the poet J.C. Bloem wrote in 'First Day of Spring'. I thought of Laura, of the freckles on her nose and of her sex.

Every time I entered the ice-cream parlour that day I could see my brother through the small window in the kitchen door. He held the ice ladle in his right hand like a gigantic phallus. He had never had sex. The ice-cream parlour was his future. As it had been mine once, the route mapped out for me. The two of us were going to take over Venezia like the Tofani brothers had taken over their parents' ice-cream parlour. Later they'd been joined by wives, and one of the brothers had helped the other set up his own ice-cream parlour. It had been the same story for my father and his younger brother.

Early in the evening I hung my apron over a chair. The big rush was over; it had been a good day.

'Where are you off to?' my father wanted to know.

'I'm going out for dinner.'

'We don't eat till nine.'

We always ate late; first Luca and me, then my parents. We lived above the ice-cream parlour. The dining room and my parents' bedroom were located on the first floor. Luca and I slept in the attic.

'I have to go,' I said.

'I have to work,' my father retorted. 'I have to help your brother.'

He'd never been able to do anything else, because it was out of the question in those days, or because he'd never had the guts. But I didn't have the nerve to say so.

'Go on,' he said. 'Go to your poetry pals.'

Years later I would slink out of a woman's house in much the same fashion, on my way to a mistress. The woman would be my first girlfriend, my only long-term partner. Sure, I felt guilty when I walked out that evening, under the ice-cream parlour's red-and-white striped awning and into the late summer evening. Those gossamer-thin threads kept tugging at me. Everything was connected to everything else: my stomach to the pulsating ice-cream machine; my heart to the knife in the kitchen, its blade red with strawberry juice; my head to the house in Venas; my feet to the pine forest, the earth threaded through with roots.

Heiman was already at the restaurant. He always turned up early for appointments. You'd walk in somewhere to find him reading a book of poetry. You'd always see him with a book, even on a barstool. People who didn't know him might think he was uncommunicative. On the contrary. When a conversation ran dry, it was Heiman who got it flowing again. He was a fount of stories: anecdotes about poets, rumoured nominations for a major award. Or else he scattered a few unfathomable stanzas among those present.

He sensed immediately that I was sombre. 'If you were my son I'd have hugged you right now,' he said.

And when I didn't react, 'What's the matter?'

I told him I had been helping out at the ice-cream parlour. 'I feel as though I'm betraying everyone, as if I'm leaving everybody in the lurch.'

I was hoping he would comfort me with a few lines of poetry, an ancient English quatrain I didn't know yet that captured all of my feelings. It could be saccharine for all I cared, dripping with emotions. Moonlight, dead trees, an empty heart — all of that.

'Oh, dear,' Heiman said instead. 'We all feel that way sometimes. It's how I used to feel: eighteen and all alone in the world. It's okay. It will pass.'

I couldn't imagine that Heiman had ever felt the way I felt right now. He exuded a certain unassailability. The fact that he never married didn't make him any less complete than others. He didn't need marriage as the be-all and end-all of life. There was the spacious apartment with the many paintings on the walls, some gifted by artist-friends; there were the premières and the exclusive parties. Women admired him — the prettiest interns at the festival had all fallen for him.

'Only poets stand to gain from melancholy,' he said. 'We ordinary mortals have a duty to be happy.'

He was happy, and I was keen to be guided by him in life, the way the lighthouse on the island of Pharos had guided seamen into the harbour for centuries. To this day I think of Heiman when I have a difficult decision to make. What would he do? Would he think it was worthwhile?

'Have you had a look at the menu?' he asked. 'They've got scallop carpaccio. Have you ever had that?'

I'd never had scallops.

'They're a kind of oyster,' Heiman said. 'Or have you never tried oysters either?'

'No.'

'Let's order some oysters first then, because knowing how to eat oysters is almost as important as learning to read.'

It's possible that people saw a father and son at the wooden table with the starched linen, and it's possible that my father was not only jealous of me, but also of my bond with Heiman.

We talked about my degree. He actually knew some of my lecturers.

'Paul Delissen!' he exclaimed. 'He's the son of a shipping magnate — did you know that? The father was a filthy rich man who commissioned monumental sculptures and paintings from artists, which he then donated to museums. All the nobility went to Paul. His younger brother owns a factory in Hungary that produces spreadable cheese in all kinds of flavours: paprika, tomato, herb. They're disgusting, but they sell like crazy.'

Which brother was the happier one, I wondered? What was the flipside of their lives?

Heiman took a sip of the white wine he had ordered. 'Paul's wife is called Beppie Blum. What a name! I wonder if they're still together.'

He was always curious about those things, or might point to a couple in the crowd. 'That man's wife,' he would whisper, 'is familiar with the colour of many poets' eyes.'

I told him about the writers I was reading, the poets he knew better than his neighbours, and finally also about Laura, the girl with the snub nose.

'So you're in love?' Heiman asked.

'No idea.'

'Would you like to see her again?'

'Of course!'

He laughed. 'Have you read her any poetry yet?'

'We haven't had time for that.'

The waiter served the intermediate course. A small morsel of grey mullet, a brackish fish. It was served with lamb's lettuce and a sauce made with butter, lemon, and tarragon. The waiter listed it all without stumbling. It was, like the dishes to follow, absolutely delicious. This was Richard Heiman's world. Flickering block candles, exquisite dishes, a humidor on wheels, and in the middle of the restaurant a pedestal with an extravagant bouquet of flowers.

At the end of the evening, the waiter helped us into our coats. 'Good evening, Mr Heiman,' he said.

'Bye, Marcel.'

We were standing on the footpath. I was in high spirits, but that may have been the wine. Heiman was on foot; I had my bike. I wanted to give him a hug, but I noticed the waiter standing in the doorway and looking at us.

It would be many years before we hugged, and by then it was too late really. It had started with a hoarse voice and a sore throat, but it took another eighteen months for the diagnosis to be made: amyotrophic lateral sclerosis. ALS. That's when the cramp and involuntary muscle spasms kicked in. Suddenly Heiman would clutch his calf, his face distorted with pain. He was injected with muscle relaxants, but little else could be done. He was given three years, maximum, minus the time it had taken for the diagnosis to be made.

I can still picture him in his apartment, in front of the large window overlooking the garden and the tall trees. He is sitting in a wheelchair, bemoaning the words he can no longer pronounce properly. Swallowing was becoming more and more difficult.

As soon as he received the diagnosis he stepped down from his post. I was one of the first he told the news. 'The illness is terminal and its nature progressive.' Perhaps he found the latter harder to come to terms with than the fact that it would kill him.

The winter of his life arrived like a blizzard. His muscles withered, as the signals from his brain could no longer reach them. First his legs became paralysed; then his arms. He became completely dependent. I saw him without a tie for the first time. He was nursed by a Surinamese woman, but perhaps she didn't know how to knot a tie, or she wasn't aware that he had always worn one. He could no longer tell her.

His voice was gone. That beautiful, deep voice with which he had recited the many poems he knew by heart. Memorising poems wasn't just a gift he had, it was also a matter of principle, a conviction. The time when children memorised poems in school was a thing of the past. He thought it was deplorable. All those writers, all their lines — to him they were the bedrock of his life. He could no longer recite the poems now, but his mind hadn't been affected by the illness, so they were likely still in his head. As he looked out, they must have been passing by, one by one: the words of the Lake Poets, John Keats, Emily Dickinson. The unction of their words and those of many, many others. Neruda, Miłosz, Rilke — yes, the ineffable solace of Rilke. *Lord, it is time.*

A life without poetry was a life less beautiful.

I visited Heiman nearly every day and told him about my doctoral thesis. After graduating I had specialised in the work of anonymous poets, writers whose name and image had never been passed down, but I was stuck and no longer knew what I was hoping to uncover. I had stopped going to university and hadn't done any work on my thesis for two months.

Heiman looked at me with his watery eyes, the eyes of the old man he would never be. What might he have said had he been able to speak? What might he have advised me? He would have made a brilliant suggestion, no doubt, or a remark that put everything into perspective. Perhaps he would have told me that everything was going to be all right, that the years would work their magic. I had to make do with a wink, a nod of the head, and a tear welling up — spilling over the rim and finally, slowly and haphazardly, finding its way down to his mouth.

There were other visitors, too. Mostly women. They brought flowers, which they arranged in vases. They combed his hair, knotted his tie, and pushed him in his wheelchair around the park or along the quay, where large ships kept their engines idling. They were well-dressed women, some in their forties, others noticeably younger. In many cases, I was unsure of the nature of their relationship with Heiman. I had often been tempted to ask him, in restaurants or cafés late at night, 'How many?' But he never talked about it, and I doubt he'd have wanted to disclose it.

A couple of months after his death I spotted a woman walking down the street who had combed his hair when he had become completely helpless. She approached a small group of children and opened her hand. It held chestnuts, glossy trinkets. The children chose the biggest one. She offered them to grown-ups too, women she may have thought were lonely, men with an air of mystery about them, like herself. Her tights were an intense blue, ultramarine. Had she been a lover? Had Heiman adored this woman? Her hair was wavy and grey, but her dark complexion exuded warmth and even something youthful. I tried to picture them together, in his house, in his bedroom. He sitting up straight, a pillow against the small of his back, reading to her — the most beautiful poem he had read that day.

I wanted to buy her an espresso but felt it wouldn't be right. It would have violated an unwritten law. We mustn't try to retrieve what has been carried over to the other side. The woman with the blue legs pressed a chestnut into my hands when she saw me watching her. This would have to do.

Heiman's last few days had been the worst of his life. He was emaciated and completely exhausted. He had conceded defeat and yet he was forced to stay in the ring. The hours were beating him about. Those long, quiet hours, the hours in which everything passes before one's eyes. His life had been exceptionally glorious, a charmed string of encounters, of poets and women, of art and endless evenings. All this had shaped him, like a fine wine matured to perfection. But the bottle had fallen, its contents spilled. The end was unlike anything that had gone before, like a chapter from a different book altogether.

I had held his hand, which was limp and likely no longer felt anything. Some women had stroked his head, had run their fingers through his grey hair. The nurse never showed any sign of affection. She washed him and gave him clean clothes. Perhaps, during those last few days, he thought of Edward Arlington Robinson, the American poet who had asked his family to carry his bed outside so he could die underneath the brilliance of the stars. I took him into my arms, finally gave him that hug, and held him tight. I wanted the moment to last forever, but at the same time I wanted it not to be true.

Two days later he had suffered a stroke, and then it was over. *Finis.* An end to both his splendid life and the terrible suffering. His sister, whom I had never met, inherited his house and his effects. My name was also included in his will. Heiman had left me all of his books.

I hired a minivan and one dark and dreary Monday I took his most treasured possessions to the attic of the ice-cream parlour.

My father and my brother helped me carry the heavy boxes.

'Only because it's raining,' my father said.

Luca was silent. He carried the boxes up, two at a time, showing me how strong he was. Or how insubstantial poetry.

I saw the man once more, years later, on his bike. He came towards me and passed me by at great speed, on his way to an appointment or a woman. The resemblance, which I had noticed from a distance, only increased. As we approached one another, the cyclist merged with Richard Heiman, in his late forties, with red cheeks and grey-blond hair, oblivious to the fate that would one day befall him.

How My Father Sang the National Anthem with a Bag of Onions on His Head

'He's making a hammer.' My mother phones me while I'm queuing for the check-in desk at Dublin Airport. Behind me are the two young Dutch poets who read at the Fermoy International Poetry Festival.

'A hammer? What kind of hammer?'

'He's been at it for two days now. He rarely leaves the basement.'

'Has the doctor been round?'

'Yes,' my mother says, and bursts into tears. I leave her be for a bit and shuffle up a place with my bag. A new departure time appears on the screen above the desk. The flight has been delayed by an hour. It prompts a chorus of sighs and the odd expletive in the long queue. If I were to add up all the delays in my life, I would be able to read the collected poems of Charles Bukowski, and perhaps even get to the bottom of his horse-betting strategy.

My mother informs me that the doctor came round on Saturday and that she took him aside when he arrived. She had been reluctant to tell him, but did so anyway: 'I'm worried my husband might have Alzheimer's.' She told the doctor that she had heard Beppi talk to the television, and he went on to hug it. What she didn't say was that he had seen a red-haired woman on the flatscreen whose muscles he wanted to kiss. The doctor would find out soon enough.

'I'm not sick at all,' my father said. 'I'm fit as a fiddle, actually.'

The three of them sat at the kitchen table, my father in the long blue coat he wore when he was working down in the basement. His shoulders were dotted with iron shavings. The lasagne was in the oven, filling the room with a pleasant glow.

'I'm in love with Betty.'

My mother stared at the tabletop, ashamed.

'Who's Betty?'

'The love of my life.'

'But you're married to Anita.'

'I'd swap her any day.'

It was his rotten character, the elixir that had started fermenting, the bubbles giving off stench and filth.

'Has he been forgetful lately?' the doctor asked my mother. 'Has he been asking the same question several times a day, by any chance?'

'Hello,' my father butted in. 'I'm right here.' He waved at the doctor.

'He's had some trouble thinking of certain words recently,' my mother replied. 'For instance, when he can't think of "doormat" he'll say "that thing in the hallway, next to the shoes, that *thing*. What d'you call that bloody thing?"'

'Typical.'

'I haven't got Alzheimer's!' my father shouted. 'I'm in love!'

'One of the symptoms of the disease is a change in personality.' It wasn't clear who the doctor was addressing, but perhaps he wasn't entirely sure himself.

'He's changed a lot,' my mother confirmed.

'In the early stages most patients deny there's anything wrong with them.'

'I deny that!'

'What are the other symptoms? What can family members expect?'

'Progressive symptoms include long-term memory loss.'

Something crossed my mother's mind. 'Fausto Olivo pulls his underpants over his head.'

'That's known as apraxia,' the doctor explained. 'What it means

[61]

is that the patient no longer knows how to perform certain familiar movements.'

'I wear my underpants the usual way, around my bum,' my father said. 'And when I go out, I put on a hat.'

'The rate at which Alzheimer's progresses varies from patient to patient.'

'In Fausto's case it all happened really fast.'

'Would you like me to put a bag of potatoes on my head?' my father asked. 'Would that satisfy you? Can I please you with a couple of kilos of potatoes on top of my head?'

The doctor didn't respond, but looked at Beppi with growing astonishment. My mother stared at the tabletop again.

'Fine! I'll put a five-kilo bag of waxy spuds on my head and sing the national anthem.' He got up from the table and walked over to the hallway, to the storeroom. A door was opened and closed again. Then my father re-entered the kitchen with a bag of onions on his head.

'There we have it,' the doctor said.

My mother nodded.

But after my father had sung the Italian national anthem in its entirety, he said quite calmly, 'Anita, we're out of potatoes. Will you add them to the shopping list?'

There was a moment's silence in the kitchen. I can conjure up the silence as well as the smell of the lasagne in the oven. It's not my imagination, but a memory come to life. As children, me and my brother would often sneak into the kitchen to stare at the lasagne through the oven window. It was better than watching television.

'This Betty,' the doctor said after some time. 'What kind of woman is she? Does she live around here?'

'She's a German hammer-thrower.'

'I see.'

'Her arms are incredibly muscular.'

'I'm sure they are.'

'I'd like to kiss them.'

'Beppi!' said my mother.

'She won bronze at the Olympics. For a moment it looked as if Zhang Wenxiu was going to walk away with third place, but luckily it wasn't to be.'

'Who?'

'A bloated old meatball from China.'

'My husband isn't keen on the Chinese,' my mother explained.

'There are too many Chinese.'

'Beppi!'

The doctor looked from my mother to my father. 'I think I'd better be going,' he said then.

'Aren't you going to examine him?'

A cup was shifted, the clock's minute hand moved. My mother glanced at the oven, where the lasagne was being kept warm.

'Feel free to look in my ears,' my father offered. 'Or should I stick out my tongue?' It goes without saying that my father stuck out his tongue at once. And sat like that for quite some time. Until the doctor lifted his bag onto the table and took out a case.

'All fine,' he said after the briefest of examinations.

'I don't have Alzheimer's?'

'No.'

'No other diseases, either?'

'No.'

'Do you mind if I go back to the basement then?'

'We're about to eat,' my mother said.

'What are you doing in the basement?' the doctor asked.

'I'm making a present for Betty.'

My mother shook her head. 'He's got a screw loose, that one,' she said.

'I'm making a hammer,' my father said proudly. 'A hammer in the shape of a heart.'

The woman behind the desk checks my documents. She asks if I want an aisle or a window seat. I always opt for the aisle. Every centimetre of extra space on a plane eases the pain of being a passenger. Then she hands me back my passport, accompanied by a smile. At small airports there's always a chance that the woman who checks you in will also tear your boarding pass at the gate, but more often than not you'll never see her again.

Once through security I lose track of the poets. Maybe they're buying something for the homefront, for those who stayed behind. If so, they're spoilt for choice. The area between the metal detectors and the gate is one large shopping mall. It's hard not to walk into a trap. Everything is aimed at luring you into a transaction. Giant billboards show you how beautiful life can be with a Breitling watch or a new phone; young women in tight black skirts chase you with bottles of perfume at the ready. The information boards at some airports no longer feature gate numbers, only the amount of shopping time till boarding.

Amid all of these people, all of these carrier bags, and all of these products, I sit with a book of poetry in my hands. It may look strange, but it doesn't feel awkward. Nowhere do I feel more at home than at an airport. I love the impersonal voice calling out passengers' names, the screens with myriad destinations, the flow of people coming and going — a recurring tide that swells and then suddenly ebbs again. Four hundred passengers disappearing down the silvery nose of a Boeing 747. A ribbon of tourists, businesspeople, and other travellers emerging from a jet bridge, looking around and getting their bearings before heading to the baggage carousels. You can tell right away who the infrequent fliers are and who have more than a hundred thousand kilometres under their belt, for whom arrival at an airport is like a homecoming.

Charles de Gaulle airport outside Paris was once home to an Iranian man: Mehran Karimi Nasseri. He had no documents and was unable to return to his home country. The French court ruled that he had entered the airport legally and therefore couldn't be deported, and yet he was refused permission to enter France. For eighteen years he camped out on a red bench in Terminal 1, not far from the Paris Bye

Bye bar. This is where he slept, this is where he ate, this is where he read the newspapers left for him by passengers, and this is where he became something of a celebrity, not to mention older.

Waiting for a plane back to Amsterdam, I sometimes fantasise about such a life. Lost among suitcases, in a space where neither temperature nor humidity ever change. Imagine the plane never taking off, imagine not being allowed to board … 'I'm sitting here, waiting,' Nasseri would tell people who asked him what he was doing. But he never told them what for. Maybe he no longer knew. Eventually he had gone bald at the crown, with wild tufts of hair sticking out from either side of his head. Four of his teeth were missing.

There's one problem with airports: the bookshops rarely sell poetry, with the possible exception of anthologies on certain themes, or the Four Seasons published by Everyman's Library. Anthologies — you wouldn't believe how many there are. On jazz, on the blues, on the sea, on love. On dogs, on birds, on mourning, on gardens.

It's not the kind of poetry I want to read. It's the poetry everybody knows. I want to discover poems, pilfer them if possible, from mysterious, unworldly figures — a shaman from an Indian tribe, a lonesome farmer in Siberia. In the hope they know something I don't. Their language is unrefined and independent of any movement.

Last year I was invited to attend an award ceremony in Beijing. The prize being awarded was for a national poetry competition that had received more than seventy thousand entries. They had been written by factory hands, cooks, and shop assistants. The whole country had been encouraged to take part. The jury had counted on the pyramid model, with the broad base leading to the one brilliant poem at the top. The poem that says it all. A top five had been compiled, but there was no number one, no overall winner.

The search continues. From airport to airport, from festival to prize-giving, from metropolis to village in the Gobi Desert, where eagles trace slow circles overhead.

The Fraudster Marco Polo and the Invention of the Ice-cream Cone

My father spent his whole life dreaming of things that don't exist. In summer, at the ice-cream parlour, he used to fantasise about contraptions that could change the world, or at least make many people's lives a little easier. In winter, he used to retreat into the basement to work on his ideas among the pillar drills and the sanders. He actually came up with a few inventions: a keyhole attachment that makes it easier to locate the lock's keyway in the dark; a shoehorn with a long handle so you don't have to bend down; and an extendable egg cup that doubles as a mug. But there was either no interest or else the inventions were already in the shops.

He was furious when he found out that the giant shoehorn was already available. 'They've stolen my idea.'

'Who are "they"?'

'The Chinese!'

The Chinese came in for a lot of blame, at home in Italy but also at the ice-cream parlour in Rotterdam. According to my mother, it was all down to an old Chinese man who had taken a seat outside Venezia one summer's day. We were still small at the time and would forget just about everything we heard. I certainly don't remember the argument that is said to have taken place that sunny day.

The man pointed to the text above the red-and-white striped

awning: *Venezia Ice-Cream Parlour, authentic Italian ice-cream.* 'You do know that ice-cream is a Chinese invention?' he asked my father.

'No.'

'When Marco Polo returned from China in 1296, he brought back ice-cream recipes.'

'That's the first I've heard of it.'

'It's true,' he said. 'It's in all the history books. Study them and you can reach but one conclusion: the Chinese invented ice-cream.'

My father burst out laughing. 'Ice-cream a Chinese invention?' he uttered. 'That's the funniest thing I've heard in years.'

'It's true, it really is,' the man said. 'Marco Polo spent more than twenty years in China and when he returned he introduced ice-cream to Europe.'

'Rice,' my father said. 'Not ice!'

'No, no, *ice.*'

'Rice and duck,' my father said. 'Rice and chicken, rice and turkey.'

'Peach-flavoured ice-cream, caramel ice-cream, vanilla ice-cream.'

'We've got all those.'

'Thanks to Marco Polo, thanks to the Chinese.'

'Did they invent the pizza too?' my father wanted to know.

'What do you mean?'

'Did the Chinese invent the margherita pizza too? Did Marco Polo arrive in Venice with a square box? Was he really a pizza delivery boy?'

'You're making fun of me.'

'You're making fun of my family, of our tradition. I got up at six o'clock this morning to make ice-cream according to my grandfather's recipe. He used to harvest snow up in the mountains back in the day.'

'Marco Polo got there first.'

'Would you like to order anything?'

'Do you have raspberry ice-cream?'

'We've got authentic Italian raspberry ice-cream.'

The old man shook his head. 'It's Chinese originally,' he said.

'Would you like me to put that on the sign outside?'

'It would be appropriate.'

'Do you know what would be appropriate? A ban on Chinese customers in this ice-cream parlour!'

'That's discrimination.'

My father wrung his hands. 'Would you like a cone or a cup?'

'I'd like a cone with raspberry ice-cream.'

My father went inside and passed the order to my mother, who took her *spatola* and scooped raspberry ice-cream out of the tub sitting between the chocolate ice-cream and the lemon sorbet. I can still picture the layout, and remember which flavours are next to, above, or below one another. Except my brother has since changed everything and added new flavours.

'Did you know the ice-cream cone is an American invention?' the Chinese man asked when my father turned up at his table with his order.

'And Columbus brought the cone back to Europe?' said my father.

'You're impossible to talk to!'

My mother claims that my father then plunked the cone on top of the man's head, but my father maintains that the man shoved him and ran off. He ran after him, calling out, 'Wait! Your American cone with Chinese raspberry ice-cream!' and threw it at the man. The ice-cream flew through the air, did one-and-a-half somersaults, and landed on the man's head.

My mother came out with a cloth and offered her apologies. My father wasn't allowed out of the ice-cream parlour for the rest of the day. And so he stood behind the counter, snorting like a bull and crushing four cones in his twitchy hands that day. They were a lot more brittle in those days, as my parents made the cones themselves with a waffle iron and a wooden mould. I remember the aroma vividly — perhaps the best memory from my childhood. Those calm, rainy days when the batter hissed on the small black grids of the waffle-maker. I got to press the irons together and Luca got to open them. Later we were allowed to use the mould as well, but when we were little my father would roll the cones. 'This is a gorgeous specimen,' he often said, or 'Let's hang on to this one, boys. It's too beautiful to eat.'

My mother scraped any remaining bits of dough from the iron with a spatula and we would fight over them, like young birds opening their beaks to be fed.

And yes, the ice-cream cone was indeed invented in America, although the inventor wasn't an American. At the World's Fair in St Louis, Missouri, in the year 1904, Syrian pastry chef Ernest A. Hamwi sold sweet, thin Persian wafers from a stall. Standing next to him was an ice-cream maker who ran out of plates in the afternoon, so he could no longer sell his ice-cream. The inventive Syrian came up with the idea of rolling his wafers into horns that could hold ice-cream. The customers loved it, and before long Hamwi was also baking cones for other ice-cream makers at the World's Fair.

Fifteen years later, at the convention of the Association of Ice-Cream Manufacturers of Pennsylvania, the American ice-cream maker L.J. Schumaker was recorded as saying, 'The ice-cream cone is the biggest little thing in the ice-cream business.' Its advent had transformed the industry, opened it up enormously. Up until that point, ice-cream had been sold exclusively in pharmacies and sweet shops, served in small glasses or on plates. The cone brought ice-cream to the street, to stalls at junctions and schools, to fairgrounds and squares, to zoos.

There's a story about two brothers who ran an ice-cream stall at Coney Island. Whenever business was slack, they hired pretty girls to walk along the promenade with an ice-cream cone in their hands. They ended up selling more than on the hottest day in summer.

Two years ago, at the Oslo Poetry Festival, the golden-blonde Norwegian programmer blushed when I told her I came from an ice-cream-making family and that making cones was one of my fondest childhood memories.

'Let me tell you something I've never told anyone before,' she whispered. We were sitting at a table in the Green Room, drinking red wine. All around us poets were talking in bigger or smaller groups. The official programme had ended hours ago and the auditoriums were empty, but things were pretty lively in this room with private bar. Here's where the translators, poets, volunteers, and organisers got together. They are beautiful times, those endless evenings at festivals when the audience has gone home.

'As a girl,' the Norwegian programmer said, 'I always thought of sex when I ate ice-cream.' She fixed her grey-blue eyes on me, perhaps hoping to shock me. 'When I was only fourteen and I'd never even done anything like it, I'd roll the tip of my tongue around the top of the ice-cream, twirling it around the scoop, before sinking my lips into it and slowly licking them. I thought that's how it was done, that it would be like that.'

I told the programmer that in the Thirties respectable girls didn't eat their ice in the street. They were supposed to take it home, tip it onto a plate, and eat the scoop with a spoon.

Actually, it's questionable whether Ernest A. Hamwi really was the inventor of the famous cone. Like the bikini, which was invented by French car mechanic Louis Réard in 1946 but had already been worn by Etruscan women, the ice-cream cone had popped up before. *Mrs. A. B. Marshall's Cookery Book* from 1888 features a recipe for 'Margaret Cornets', cones filled with ice-cream. But I wasn't going to bother my father with that. He was convinced that an Italian from the Dolomites had helped the Syrian pastry chef in St Louis, and he wasn't the only one. According to local journalist and amateur historian Serafino Dall'Asta, an ice-cream maker from Vodo di Cadore is said to have been involved in the invention of the cone.

'So the ice-cream cone is more of an Italian than an American invention,' was my father's firm conviction.

And it goes without saying that ice-cream didn't originate in Asia. After chasing the old Chinese guy away, my father asked the neighbours' son to borrow a stack of books on Marco Polo from the library. That evening he discovered that the original of *The Book of the Marvels of the World* had been lost and that the oldest extant manuscript dated back to 1400, some seventy-five years after the death of the Venetian trader and explorer. It contained no mention of the Great Wall, and not a word on eating with chopsticks or drinking tea, let alone ice-cream. Some historians question the authenticity of the travel document and there are suspicions that Marco Polo simply recounted the stories of others. This was years before the London-based sinologist Frances Wood published her controversial study *Did Marco Polo Go to China?* But by then my father was already one hundred per cent sure that the world-famous explorer had never set foot in the country he wrote about.

'Marco Polo is a fraudster!' my father called out in the middle of the night.

'Go to sleep,' my mother reacted.

My father waited for the old man who had pointed to the text above the awning for days on end, but he never returned. And so my father approached another Chinese customer sitting in the sun.

'You guys didn't invent ice-cream at all,' he said. 'It's historically inaccurate.'

'I don't know what you're talking about,' the man replied.

'The Chinese didn't invent ice-cream, nor did they come up with the giant shoehorn!'

In the Sixties, Dutch ice-cream parlours had been plagued by southern Italians who had come to the Netherlands as migrant workers. On their days off they would go to a parlour in a small group, each sit at a separate table, and be really boisterous. Or they would make a nuisance of themselves by sitting next to a girl who had ordered an ice-cream. Some ice-cream parlours put up notices in their windows, stating (in Italian) 'No Italians allowed.'

My father wanted to put up a notice saying 'No Chinese allowed.' But my mother wouldn't have it.

'Everybody is welcome,' she said. 'Young and old, rich and poor, men and women. Ice-cream is for everybody.' Thereby echoing what Carlo Gatti had envisioned with his penny-licks in London more than a century ago.

My father accepted the defeat, but the seeds for his lifelong grudge against the Chinese had been well and truly sown.

When, years later, I came across an anthology of classic Chinese poetry, I discovered a poem by Yang Wanli, born a hundred years before Marco Polo's death. To my great surprise, the poet wrote about a milky substance that 'appears congealed and yet it seems to float' and 'as with snow, it melts in the light of the sun'.

I read the poem to my father — to tease him, I guess. But all he said was, 'I don't like the Chinese and I don't like poetry.'

The Snow of Yesteryear

I was six when my parents packed me off to the boarding school in
Vellai di Feltre. Such was the fate of the children of ice-cream makers.
As a baby, toddler, and pre-schooler you get to join your parents at
the ice-cream parlour every season, but after that you have to go to
school. In Italy. The advantage was that you got to spend the winter at
home and the long summer holidays — three months, in Italy — in the
Netherlands. The disadvantage was that you spent the rest of the time
in a boarding school run by nuns.

The nuns at my school were conservative and authoritarian, but
they taught me reading, writing, and arithmetic. I was one of those
children who liked learning, who liked sitting bent over my exercise
book, pen in my right hand. And my tongue sticking out of my mouth,
if Luca, who often mimicked me, is to be believed. He came to Vellai di
Feltre two years after me, but he never took to the nuns' regime. They
were extremely strict and sometimes hit us with the flat of their hands.

'Don't you miss Mamma and Papa?' Luca asked me almost every
day.

'A little,' was my standard reply. I was trying to be strong.

'I miss them a lot.'

'They have to work,' I said. 'The ice-cream machines have to keep
churning.'

'Churn, churn, churn,' Luca said. As my father had put it to us: we had to learn, the ice-cream machines had to churn.

Luca had great trouble reading and writing. Unlike me, he didn't enjoy it. He hated books, and preferred to run up and down the long corridors of the boarding school whenever the nuns weren't looking. Every so often he was caught in the act and given a good hiding by the eldest nun, who had a wart on her chin that had sprouted three thick hairs. But that wasn't the worst of it. She stank, according to Luca.

'Can't you smell it?' he asked me.

I shook my head.

'When she lifts her hand, her robes go up and you catch the weirdest smells.'

It may have been because I always had my nose stuck in a book, but that's the boarding school smell that has stayed with me. That wonderful smell of old, damp books. I would put my finger on the paper and plough my way through the lines. It may have been because of the books that some days I missed my parents less than my brother did.

At night Luca often crawled into bed with me. We would each clutch the other's hand, forging a link of an unbreakable chain. As I whispered a story in his ear, something I had read during the day, I would wait for his breathing to grow calm and regular.

When we switched to *scuola media*, or secondary school, Grandma Tremonti started looking after us. She had dark-grey hair and crooked hands due to arthritis, but she was proud and strong. Her father had run an ice-cream parlour in Ulm, in Germany. When the British bombed it during the war, the family had sheltered in the cellar. 'Don't be scared,' the father told his daughters. 'It's like thunder; it will pass.' His wife shook her head, but the girls never cried. They lost everything — the ice-cream machine, the refrigerators, the gondola-shaped glass plates — but they survived. They walked away from the rubble and the dust.

On her bedside table, Amalia Tremonti kept a framed photograph of her husband, who had lost his life in an accident on the road from

Dobbiaco to Cortina d'Ampezzo. One winter he had tried to overtake a tourist just before a bend. Friends had knocked together a wooden cross and planted it by the roadside, but Amalia had never visited the scene of the accident. As the father had passed on to his daughters: step out of the rubble, brush yourself off, and carry on.

With her bony, bent fingers, Amalia Tremonti sliced onions and tomatoes and made us pasta every day. She was caring, but hardhearted at times. She rarely allowed us to phone the ice-cream parlour in Rotterdam. I felt responsible for Luca. When he struggled with his homework, I helped him. And sometimes I even did his sums for him, so that we had more time to play outside. In the street he always held my hand. In fact, we walked to school like that. Grandma didn't like it one bit: two boys holding hands was not appropriate.

Come the summer holidays we took the train to Rotterdam, escorted by my mother's sister. At that point we hadn't seen our parents for four months. For the whole of spring, the days when the grass turned a pale green, the dandelions sprang up and lent the meadows a yellow complexion, and the sun began to feel warmer. All this happened at a dizzying pace, as if life was being fast-forwarded, and yet to us time passed like frozen December days. We had been looking forward to the reunion for months.

I remember my mother's tears, and her arms that enclosed us, not wanting to let go.

'Can I have a go?' my father would ask every year. 'I want to have a go, too.'

And then he'd squeeze us tight. He placed his bristly cheeks against our smooth boyish ones, but we didn't mind. At least not until my stubble began to scratch, too.

We helped out in the ice-cream parlour and relished the days, which were longer than those in the mountains. My parents were usually out front, while Luca and I were in the kitchen, making ice-cream. We were trying to improve the recipes.

'Have you tried the mango ice?' Luca asked. 'It doesn't contain enough sugar, it's far too hard.'

'Let's look at the vanilla ice-cream first,' I replied. 'The texture could be a lot smoother, and the vanilla isn't evenly distributed.'

This was before the discovery of poetry. As in Shelley's poem, our spirits created just one object: ice-cream.

'What do you think will happen if we add white chocolate?'

'Watermelon ice with white chocolate?'

'Yes,' my brother replied. 'Stracciatella, but different. Totally different.'

'Don't let Beppi hear it.'

On more than one occasion we had suggested introducing new flavours: banana with caramel, orange-gingerbread, sweet and salty peanut.

'Our customers aren't interested,' my father always said. 'They want to eat the same ice-cream day in, day out.'

'Surely we can try?'

'Later,' was his answer. 'Later, once you've taken over the ice-cream parlour.'

We swore we would make the weirdest flavours once we were in charge at Venezia.

In the evening, in the attic, in our separate beds, we would anticipate this fantastic future, this science-fiction world of flavours.

'Honey ice-cream,' my brother said.

'Ricotta with pine nuts.'

'Coconut-cinnamon.'

'Carrots and walnuts.'

'Asparagus ice in April!'

'Cucumber sorbet.'

'Ice made with blood.'

'As in blood pudding?'

'Yes, but frozen.'

Later, when he had taken over the ice-cream parlour and I was flying around the globe like a sardine in a can, my brother, as promised, made all the flavours we had listed that night. And many more besides. My father's conservatism was no match. Like a curious child, he would take a huge bite whenever he was offered a spoonful. 'This is amazing,' he would say with his eyes closed, like the people who had tasted his grandfather's ice. 'But what is it?'

'Blue cheese with apple and pear,' my brother replied.

'Unbelievable.'

On one occasion, after I had eaten ice-cream with a couple of young poets outside Venezia and I settled the bill with my father, he said, 'Are you expected to pay for those scroungers?'

'They're poets.'

He gave them a disdainful look. 'Tell them to look at Luca if they want to see a true artist.'

My brother was always the better ice-cream maker of the two of us. He could separate three hundred and sixty eggs in fifteen minutes, whereas I needed nearly forty minutes to do the same job. But Luca never mentioned it. There was no tension or rivalry. We made ice-cream together, had the same dreams, and would be overcome with longing for our parents at the same time. Before our final day in Rotterdam had even dawned.

The beginning of September marked our return to Venas. The ice-cream parlour would stay open until late October. And so we would spend two months at Grandma's, breathing her smells, feeling her hands ruffling our hair and trying to emulate her strength, but when winter finally arrived, our strong family roots would prevail. The four of us would once again be sitting in the kitchen in front of the hot stove, each in our usual chair, twisting a fork in a deep plate.

The return of the ice-cream makers galvanised the village, the way spring breathes new life into nature. But unlike the arrival of spring, everything happened within the space of a few days. The slumber in which Venas had rested for eight months was broken quite suddenly. Cars drove around with their engines roaring and horns honking, shutters were opened, heads were stuck out of windows. It was like the arrival of the Allied forces.

The pizzeria was full again, there was a queue at the bakery, and people were gossiping about turnover and who had come back in a new Mercedes. In the morning the butcher couldn't keep up with demand. The streets were no longer just the reserve of elderly people and little children. In the evening, men would head down to the pub to play cards, staggering home hours later underneath a clear, starry sky. They were blind drunk and blissfully happy — freed from the long working days in Utrecht, Arnhem, or Maastricht. On Sunday the same narrow footpaths would see a procession of families in their finery; all the pews in church would be occupied. Afterwards everybody meandered home, to roast meat served up alongside small glasses of red wine, accompanied by views of the mountains, chit-chat about other families, and finally the gurgling moka pot spreading its familiar aroma.

A wind swept through the entire valley, from San Vito to Lorenzago di Cadore. It was like Christmas — the same joy and exhilaration, except two months earlier. Everybody was free. This is what they had been working for, this is what they had sacrificed the summer for. The body came to rest, minor ailments vanished, and here and there a baby was conceived. Most children of ice-cream makers come into the world in summer. Luca and I were born on dog days.

Of course there was the never-ending competition. Which ice-cream maker created the most delicious flavours? Who could churn the perfect frozen yogurt? The rivalry tended to be confined to the Netherlands, but some would carry it back to the mountains and insist that their ice-cream was smoother, creamier, or tastier. Sometimes things got out of hand, as the infamous street brawl between the owners of two ice-cream parlours in Zwolle testifies.

'Your strawberry ice-cream tastes of raspberries,' one ice-cream producer yelled at his rival across the street.

'Your banana ice-cream tastes like pear,' the retort came.

'Your vanilla ice-cream is indistinguishable from snot!'

'Your chocolate ice-cream is cow shit.'

And then came the ultimate insult, which nobody could have anticipated and which was not universally understood, either.

'My apricot ice-cream tastes of your wife!'

The ice-cream makers squared up in the middle of the road and clenched their fists. They fought like teenagers in the schoolyard until they were separated by Guido Zardus, who was as strong as his coin-bending grandfather.

The following day, several ice-cream makers joked about the incident in Bar Posta.

'My blackcurrant ice-cream is as black as Gregori's right eye.'

'My cherry ice-cream is as dark as Belfi's blood!'

Then there was another controversy. Not as bloody, but almost as fierce. Most of the villages in Cadore — Venas, Vodo, Pieve, Valle, Calalzo, Cibiana — boasted an ice-cream maker who claimed that his grandfather or great-grandfather was the one who had invented ice-cream. Some ice-cream makers joined the debate because it was simply a way to pass the time, but others were dead serious. In our attempt to unravel the mystery together, Luca and I went to visit wrinkly men whose children now ran ice-cream parlours in Austria, Hungary, Germany, or the Netherlands.

Sometimes we were done in less than a minute because the ice-cream maker in question was deaf. Then there were the elderly men we could barely understand. The word 'gelato' we could just about make out, but the rest was gobbledygook to us.

Signor Zampieri tried to bribe us.

'We heard your grandfather invented ice-cream,' we said the first time we appeared on his doorstep. 'Do you have proof?'

'Come in, boys,' Signor Zampieri said. 'I've got delicious chocolate biscuits.'

In the living room he presented us with a plate of biscuits. We were allowed to take as many as we wanted.

'My grandfather started out on the market in Dresden,' Signor Zampieri told us. 'He churned ice-cream by hand, but nobody was buying it. The people had never had it, had never even heard of it. When it started melting, he began to hand it out to passers-by. "Free ice-cream!" he yelled. My grandmother thought he'd lost his mind, just giving it all away. But once the people had tried it, their ice-cream started selling quite well.'

'When was this?' Luca asked.

'Let me think,' said Signor Zampieri. 'Have another biscuit, boys.'

A couple of minutes later he told us another story. 'Oh, times were hard. My father cycled back to Italy in winter to save money. All the way from the Netherlands. When he arrived in Venas, my mother was furious. He'd worn out three pairs of trousers! They came to about as much as a train ticket.'

'Mr Zampieri,' I cut in, 'my brother asked if you happen to remember when your grandfather sold ice-cream in Dresden.'

'A long time ago,' he answered. 'Before you were born, before I was born.' He pointed to the view outside, to the Dolomites. 'Nobody knows exactly when the mountains came into existence.'

I looked at my brother. He snatched another biscuit off the plate.

'Did you know we're living on top of gold? We just can't reach it. It's too deep down.'

'Would you mind sticking to the subject?'

'Oh yes, ice-cream. We used to work with Italian hawkers,' Signor Zampieri told us. 'I'd give them bed and board and pay for their return journey. On top of that, they were paid six hundred lira per month plus ten Turmac cigarettes a day.' He pondered this for a while, perhaps adding things up in his mind. Then he said, 'If you two were smart, you'd dig a hole. Maybe you'd manage to retrieve that gold.'

Luca's interest seemed piqued, but then he asked, 'Why do you think your grandfather invented ice-cream?'

'He was trying to sell it at the market in Dresden,' he said again. 'But nobody was buying it, because they didn't know what it was. Nobody knew what it was! He'd only just invented ice-cream, you see.'

My brother shook his head.

'Mr Marinello from Pieve claims his grandfather invented ice-cream,' I said.

'Marinello is in his nineties. His memory's like Swiss cheese, full of holes.'

The day before, we had gone to visit the ancient ice-cream maker from Pieve. He had fallen asleep after sitting down in the armchair opposite us. We had been afraid to wake him.

'If you asked him whether his family invented the hamburger, he'd say yes, too.' Signor Zampieri got up and pulled a photo album out of the cabinet. 'This is me,' he said. 'Back when I was young and handsome.' The photo showed a man with a hat in his hand. 'Do you see that station? It's in Zuel, close to Cortina. The station doesn't exist anymore, but it used to be right opposite the place where the ski jump is now.'

'Do you have a photo of your grandfather, by any chance?' I asked, but my question was ignored.

'If you asked Marinello whether he went down the ski jump at the 1956 Olympic Games, he'd say yes, too.'

Then something sprang to mind. 'The invention of ice-cream came before the invention of photography.'

'So you can't prove that your grandfather invented ice-cream,' Luca noted.

'Nobody can prove that,' Signor Zampieri exclaimed, a tad exasperated. 'Just like nobody can prove that his grandmother invented spaghetti carbonara.'

He showed us his calloused thumb, the same calloused thumb my father had, the thumb my brother would one day have but that would never be mine. No hard skin forms on my thumb, however many poems I read, however many pages of poetry I turn over. It remains sleek and smooth in the light of my reading lamp.

'Here's the proof,' Mr Zampieri said. 'This rough, rusty thumb and the stories, my father's three pairs of trousers and the free ice-cream at Dresden market. My grandmother thinking my granddad had gone mad.'

The biscuits were finished, but there was no end to Signor Zampieri's stories.

'Will you stop by again soon?' he asked.

We said goodbye and promised to be back soon. A little later we walked hand-in-hand through the valley of the ice-cream makers. It was something we continued to do, even when our parents were in Venas. Sometimes people would stare at us, thinking we looked funny.

It was a dazzling winter's day, the air clear and cold, the outlines of the mountains razor-sharp. We hadn't had any snow yet. It would be another nine days before the first flakes fell, delicate ones, as though made up of only a single ice crystal. They blew through the valley like goose down and struggled to land on the ground. They didn't melt as they touched the earth — they sublimated, seemingly swallowed up by the roads and the fields. This was in the morning; by noon the snow was as thick as a swarm of locusts. The mountains were invisible.

There was always something magical about the first snow of the season, while at the same time it was quite earthy for the people in the mountains. They had known it, sensed it; some had even smelled the snow. It had been in the air. Three days before the first flakes, they talked about nothing else. It will come soon, the people said. It will come tomorrow or the day after. They all agreed.

And then it came.

We retrieved the sledge from the attic and whizzed down the white sloping meadow. Right through the fresh snow. Me in the front, Luca at the back, our legs stretched out before us, my back on his stomach. We pretended to be on a bobsleigh and tried not to brake. In the Sixties, the brothers Enrico and Italo De Lorenzo from Pieve had become bobsleigh world champions. Now they owned an ice-cream parlour in Utrecht. In our dreams, a similar fate awaited us.

We asked Beppi to make us a sledge with shorter blades, which would enable us to dart across the snow even faster. He retreated into the basement and emerged a couple of days later with a sledge you could actually sit in. It was a kind of cocoon you had to push and then jump into one after the other.

'Now,' Luca yelled, and I dove into the cocoon, feeling his body behind mine a split second later. At first we often got it wrong and ended up lying on top of each other and overturning. There was snow everywhere, even in our underpants, and Luca's red cheeks were barely a centimetre from my laughing mouth. After a while we began to master the technique, and we'd be whizzing down the slopes like proper bobsledders. We shot across bumps, careered around impossible bends, and hurtled ever faster towards the future. But the dream would never come true.

At the dinner table we were quizzed on our search for the inventor of ice-cream. 'You must go and talk to Serafino Dall'Asta,' my father said. 'He knows who invented the ice-cream cone. Maybe he also knows who invented the ice-cream itself.'

We no longer believed that we might one day discover the origins of ice-cream. Signor Marinello had been awake throughout our second visit, but his story failed to bring us any closer to the truth.

'Isn't it beautiful?' he had said while gazing out of the window.

'What is?'

'The snow.'

Luca and I said nothing. It had been snowing for days on end. As far as we were concerned, it was about time it stopped.

'It's the same snow my grandfather trudged through,' Signor Marinello said. 'In winter he'd practised the art of confectionary in the Po Valley, and in Venice he'd learned how to cool a mixture. The necessary salt was brought in from Sicily.'

He didn't sound like someone who was forgetful and might suddenly claim that his great-aunt had created the hamburger.

'Round about what time was this?' Luca asked. 'When was your grandfather in Venice?'

'It may have been my grandfather's father,' Signor Marinello replied. 'Or even my great-grandfather's father.'

Luca's left eyebrow shot up, but I was prepared to hear the story out.

'I was born nearly a hundred years ago,' Signor Marinello elaborated. 'My great-great-grandfather would have been born another hundred years earlier.'

The distance of time was too great to get our heads round. Hardly anything had been passed down: no photos, no objects; only a story, which had been twisted and turned by each new generation.

'It's the snow,' Signor Marinello explained. 'Everything gets buried, the tracks erased.'

And yet many could picture their grandfather up in the mountains with his sleeves rolled up and a pick-axe in his hands. Maybe they could picture it because their fathers had followed in his footsteps, and they themselves in their fathers', and some of them could see even further back, through the snow that was identical to the snow in their own lives. Once upon a time, the very first ice-cream maker must have stood there, shrouded in mist, in that blinding, frozen landscape.

Snow. Snow is unbelievably common in poetry, even more so than falling autumn leaves. The cheerful snow of Ralph Waldo Emerson; the snow of Ted Hughes, which is sometimes masculine, sometimes feminine; Henry Wadsworth Longfellow's flakes, descending 'silent, and soft, and slow'; the hurried flecks of Alexander Pushkin; and of course *les neiges d'antan*, as envisaged by François Villon. But it was only after reading the English poet Maura Dooley that I began to view snow differently. This was more than thirty years after Luca and I had interviewed Signor Marinello. When I read the poem 'The World Turned Upside Down', about 'a skein of snow', I was instantly cast back into the past.

> *Everything drained, thinned*
> *to a blankness, pattern that lost*
> *all pattern, a bleakness that took*
> *Wilson Bentley a lifetime to define.*
> *Snowflake, no two ice flowers alike.*

Until then, the name Wilson Bentley had slipped my mind but it had not been lost forever. As my eyes skimmed over the letters, it was as if the sulphurous head of a match was lit, instantly igniting the story.

'I'd like to show something,' Signor Marinello said on that day Luca and I interviewed him. He rose from his armchair and walked over to the bookcase. For a moment I thought he was going to take out a photo album, like Mr Zampieri. Not so. The book he removed did contain photos, but not of himself as a handsome young man at a station that had long ceased to exist.

'This book contains two thousand five hundred photos of snowflakes,' he said. 'They were taken by Wilson Alwyn Bentley.' He told us that Bentley hailed from Jericho, a tiny place in Vermont. As a teenager he became fascinated by snowflakes and tried to draw them with the help of a microscope, but the ice crystals were too complex to copy before they evaporated. A folding camera with bellows offered a solution. Bentley hooked the camera up to the microscope and caught the snowflakes on a velvet cloth. It was exceedingly complicated. Even below freezing, snowflakes evaporate without melting first. But on 15 January 1885, Wilson Alwyn Bentley photographed his very first specimen. Many more were to follow. During his lifetime he photographed more than five thousand snowflakes.

'He held his breath for each photo,' Signor Marinello said.

Despite the technical limitations, his photos were so good that for nearly a hundred years hardly anyone else would photograph snowflakes. Later, Bentley would also turn his attentions to measuring the size of raindrops.

'He died of pneumonia after trudging six miles through a snowstorm,' said Signor Marinello.

We looked at the photo book, at all the pictures of snowflakes, the dazzling ice crystals. To Bentley each specimen was a masterpiece in itself, whereas we leafed through the book the way we walked through the white streets — young and indifferent.

'He looked right through the snow,' Signor Marinello told us. 'And when he did, he saw miracles of beauty. That's what he called his snowflakes: miracles of beauty.'

We had gradually begun to give up hope. It may well have had something to do with the new girl who had moved into our village.

There was no direct correlation, but it wasn't a complete coincidence either that the end of our search for the original ice-cream maker of Cadore coincided with our first infatuation.

We had spotted her in the snow. She had her head tilted back and her mouth wide open. She must have noticed us staring, because at some point she said, 'It's funny to see you're holding hands.' Then she walked off and disappeared among the riot of flakes.

Luca had immediately wrenched his hand from mine.

We wouldn't see the girl again until several days later, when we also saw just what a long tongue she had. She could easily touch the tip of her nose with it.

'You mean you can't do that?' she asked, baffled. Her eyes were grey-green, I noticed.

Luca was the first to try, then me. But neither of us managed to pull it off.

'Again,' the girl said, and pulled Luca's nose without warning. 'You're nearly there now,' she said. 'You're just a hair's breadth away.'

I was up next. I felt her cold fingers around the wings of my nose. I stuck out my tongue as far as possible and she pulled as hard as she could. It hurt. Luca must have felt it too, but he never let on.

She shook her head. 'You can't do it either.'

'I'm Sophia,' she said then.

We introduced ourselves and told her where we lived. She came from the south, from Modena. Her parents weren't ice-cream makers. Her father was the new boss of one of the glasses factories in the region.

'I can catch two snowflakes at once.'

We gazed at her long, narrow tongue, which appeared to hover in the cold air, and at the masterpieces landing on it. We held our breath.

That evening in bed, Luca asked, 'What's on your mind?'

I was thinking of Sophia's tongue, but replied instead, 'A new jump for our sledge.'

'Same here.'

She was thirteen, a year younger than me, a year older than Luca.

We had the tacit agreement that boys his age were his friends and boys my age my friends. But with Sophia being in between the two of us, the question was who she belonged to.

The following morning we rang her doorbell. Her mother answered. Like her daughter, she had blonde hair and a wide mouth. But she also had long and smooth tanned legs sticking out from under a yellow dressing-gown. We were too young for them, just as we were for the buttocks she clothed in tight skirts when she was out and about. The men in the village were all exactly the right age, but they couldn't believe their eyes the first time they saw her. A mirage, a summery woman in the middle of winter. Everybody wondered what she was doing here, this big-city beauty.

The same was true for her daughter. She turned our world upside-down.

Luca, who was usually so chatty, had been rendered speechless. I had to do all the talking. 'We've got a sledge,' I said. 'Do you fancy coming with us?'

'I'd like to stay in for a bit,' Sophia replied.

'All right.'

And so we stayed in, but we had no idea what to play with.

'You can take your coats off if you like,' Sophia said after a while.

Her mother brought us all a cup of tea and then must have left to get changed, because shortly afterwards she re-entered the living room in a purple dress with flowers on it. There was July in that dress, the sun high in the sky. Sophia smiled when she saw her mother.

Meanwhile Luca and I hadn't said a word, just taken turns sipping the hot tea.

Eventually Sophia said, 'Who'd like to brush my hair?'

Suddenly it was Luca who was the quickest off the mark.

He was handed a brush and set to work on Sophia's blonde hair. It gleamed like the halos of the statues in church. My mother had strong black hair with a blue tinge to it. We had often brushed it when we were little, so we knew how to move the brush through and how to get the tangles out without hurting. Still, every now and then I could see Sophia grimacing with pain, but that may well have been feigned. Perhaps she didn't want to let on that she was enjoying it. I used to brush one half of my mother's hair and Luca the other, but this time he didn't hand the brush over to me.

'Have you been practising?' Sophia asked me.

I didn't know what she meant until she stuck out her tongue and brought the tip to her nose.

I shook my head. 'Does practising make a difference?'

'It did for my father,' she replied. 'He can do it now.'

We hadn't seen her father yet. He was the boss of one of the bigger glasses factories, or so we had heard at the kitchen table. 'They hired him to outwit the Chinese,' my father had said. 'To crush them.'

'Ouch,' Sophia said with a smile as Luca finished brushing.

She looked prettier when Luca put the hairbrush down on the table. 'What next?'

I glanced at the bristles, at the spool of golden hair caught in them. I had to stop myself from pulling it out and slipping it into my pocket.

Since Luca wouldn't say it, I did. 'Let's go outside.'

The sledge's cocoon wouldn't hold all three of us, so we took turns going downhill with Sophia. I had no idea whether Luca talked when he was alone with her, whether he held her, and what the exact distance between his mouth and her cheeks was when they lay in the snow after a tumble. I only knew what happened when I slid down the white meadow with her and hurtled across the bumps. I ended up with her hair in my mouth when we veered off the track. She pulled it out with her index finger and thumb. Her eyes darted from my lips to my eyes and back again. I had no idea a moment could last that long.

That evening Luca and I lay awake again.

'What's on your mind?' Luca asked.

Every single thought seemed to evaporate instantly, assuming the shape of a girl's face instead. 'Signor Zampieri,' I lied. 'His biscuits.'

'I'm thinking about Sophia.'

All was quiet for a moment.

'I'm thinking about her hair. I want to brush it again.'

My brother had decided to be honest with me, seeing as we had always shared everything. He opened up his heart, while mine remained closed.

'You're in love,' I said.

'Aren't you?' He sounded as though he couldn't quite believe it.

'No,' I said, but I couldn't quite believe it myself. And that's why I took it one step further, so there was no way back. 'You can have her.'

Luca was silent, and it took a while before he said, 'You've got to help me. I don't know what to do.'

'I'll help you,' I said. I made him a promise. I was his older brother; I would always help him.

The promise meant that every single time Luca went to her house I had to come along. I told him it would be better if I stayed at home and he went on his own, but he didn't have the guts.

'That way you'll have to talk to her,' I said.

'What am I supposed to say?'

'How would I know?' I replied. 'Why don't you tell her you dreamed about her?'

But he didn't speak the language of love. At least he wasn't as bad as our great-grandfather, who had actively fled from love. When Luca saw Sophia he just said, 'Hello.' And when he left, 'Bye.' Or 'See you.' But in between he remained eerily quiet, and I had to make sure we didn't come across as two socially challenged idiots.

Sophia didn't make things any easier for us. One morning, when she was catching snowflakes again, she asked, 'Do the two of you taste the same as well?'

She simply held her head tilted back and waited for a response while the occasional flake whirled down onto her tongue.

'Well?' she demanded after neither of us answered. Now she actually looked at us: first at Luca, then at me. She took a step towards us, and then another one. I knew I had to say something.

'I taste of broccoli,' I said, 'and Luca of strawberry mousse.'

'Broccoli's my favourite vegetable,' Sophia said at once, 'but I quite like strawberry desserts as well.'

Either Luca hadn't heard the latter half of the response, or it felt like second-best to him, because when we were in bed that evening he was livid. 'You should have said you tasted of horse piss.'

'Who tastes of horse piss?'

'Who tastes of broccoli?'

It goes without saying that I was just as ignorant about love as Luca, but I wasn't shy or scared. That's how it started. Maybe Sophia was perfectly aware of Luca's debilitating love, but equally aware of something else — of me, trying to swallow my love, hiding it deep inside.

We both played 'hard to get' to an absurd degree. It was a question of waiting until another would walk away with our bone. But it never came to that; there would never be another.

In bed I assumed the role of Cyrano de Bergerac, whispering useful lines into Luca's ear. 'Tell her you want to know what she tastes of'; 'Tell her you want to touch the tip of her nose with your tongue'; 'Tell her you'd like to be a snowflake on her tongue.'

But he didn't say any of this.

'Tell her you want to brush her hair for ever and ever. Tell her you can't hold your breath much longer, that you're suffocating and dying without her love.'

He never said a word.

Of course, there's no knowing what might have happened had he actually said all of this. They say love is a chemical reaction in the brain, but I reckon it's a mechanism that lacks any logic. Try too hard and you put the other off. Do nothing and the other will want you — although there's also a chance they may never even notice you. What do we know about the workings of a heart? How to make it beat faster, how to conquer it and make it yours forever?

On the day it stopped snowing, Sophia suddenly said, 'My mother claims the two of you are in love with me.'

We were at her house, sipping our tea. Tiny sips, but Luca still managed to swallow the wrong way.

'She says I have to choose.' She looked at both of us in turn. Even though I didn't feel entirely at ease, I did meet her gaze. Luca couldn't stop coughing; he had tears in his eyes.

I decided to slap him on the back, and after a couple of slaps he was doing better and we returned to our tea as if nothing had happened.

I waited a bit, during which time all three of us took two sips of tea, and then I said, 'I'm not in love with you.'

And what did my brother say? The twit, the oaf, the tongue-tied idiot said, 'Neither am I.'

Of course Sophia had to follow suit. 'I'm not in love with you two, either.'

I should have drained my glass, put on my coat, and left them to it — the two of them, in the spacious front room. But I was afraid that Sophia would come after me, and if not, that Luca would finish his tea and run off to catch up with me.

So the three of us just sat there and drank the herbal tea Sophia's mother had made for us. I was the one who finally said, 'Shall we go outside?'

There were some clouds in the sky, a veil the sun was trying to pierce. No more snowflakes were coming out.

Sophia bent down and used both hands to scoop snow off the ground and fling it in the air. It was like a haze descending on us. We followed suit, shovelling up snow and throwing it high up in the sky.

Needless to say, Sophia opened her mouth and tried to catch the powdery snow with her tongue. But the flakes also ended up in her hair and inside her collar. Before long, we were caught up in a snow fight. We did fashion balls of a kind, but we didn't take enough time with them. While still in flight they turned into an ever-growing flurry. At first Luca only threw at me, me at him, and Sophia at us, but at some point we began to throw back. Together. She got completely inundated by snow. It landed in her collar and in her neck, and she felt it between her shoulders and on her arms and her yet-to-develop breasts and her stomach — just about everywhere. I threw and scooped and tipped snow all over Sophia.

She begged for mercy. 'Stop!' she yelled. 'No more!'

But I carried on. I felt like shouting: *You have to choose. You have to choose one of us. Go on, choose!*

Then she fell over and took a direct hit on the head. It was one of my balls. She refused to give in and scooped up as much snow as possible with her small hands and hurled it at me with all the strength she could muster.

It was cheerful snow and hurried snow, it was masculine and feminine snow, and it was also the snow of yesteryear, the same snow Signor Marinello's grandfather had trudged through, in which my grandfather had stood, and my great-grandfather, too. It was a flurry that stretched from the distant past into the future. Into now. And it is now that I see that no two flakes are alike, as Maura Dooley writes in her poem, and it is now that I too look through the snow and finally see the miracle.

Luca threw a snowball at me, a ball he had taken pains to shape: rock-hard, unexpected, it was like a slap in the face. I felt the cold burst on my forehead before it trickled down into my neck. And when the snow slid further down to my chest, I felt the betrayal. Luca was standing up for Sophia; he was protecting her. He threw again, a ball that turned into a mist that briefly obstructed my view. It was the miracle I wasn't aware of at the time — I didn't realise the incomparable mechanism that had been set in motion. Luca had done not too much, not too little. He had done exactly the right thing.

I stumbled and fell and got showered with snow. Four hands at once. Snow in my eyes, snow in my mouth, snow in my nose. I didn't get it, and I wouldn't get it for a long time to come. But now I get it, now I know that he couldn't have done it any other way. This had been the only way for my brother: without words, without tenderness, issuing a blow so hard it knocked me down.

Years later, when I had already turned my back on the ice-cream parlour, my brother and Sophia got together and she became his wife. But it was decided back then. Back then, in the snow, while I lay on the ground and the final few flakes fell down on me, silent, soft, and slow.

In Amsterdam

After finishing my first degree I embarked on a PhD, but what I really liked to do was hang out in cafés with writers, journalists, and editors. And it was in a café, amid a haze of cigarette smoke and conversations sustained by booze, that I was offered a job at a publishing company. It was more of a suggestion than an actual offer, really, but such distinctions fade as the evening draws to a close. It came from a short man with a bulbous glass in his hand. His eyes were barely visible, since he tended to squeeze them shut, like someone sensitive to light. In reality, the squinting came with the generous smile of Robert Berendsen, a man who not only loved literature but also had a great appetite for life, especially after a few glasses of De Koninck, his favourite beer.

'Why don't you drop by tomorrow,' he had said. 'I'm looking for a poetry editor.'

As it did all other evenings, the conversation had revolved around books and authors. Someone had mentioned K. Michel's debut, *Yes! Bare as the Stones*, which had been published a few days previously. Some poets thought it was loudmouth poetry. Noise. 'Too many exclamation marks,' one man shouted over everybody else. 'I've lost count.'

Others thought it was a spectacular collection introducing a wholly new voice. 'I've never read anything like it,' said a man who wrote for a paper. 'It's frivolous, fresh, and profound at the same time.'

'I don't think it's poetry,' another person said.

It was an observation made at least once a week. It seldom elicited a response. Some people expected poetry to deliver the same as tap water — clarity above all else. And yet the conversations in the pub were almost always interesting, if only because everybody had different ideas about a particular poet or collection. And because they involved alcohol.

The discussions could get pretty intense. Every so often an exchange would become so heated it degenerated into a fight, at which point the barman would step in. 'Out,' he would say. 'Get out! Go and fight outside.'

At university my fellow students and I had studied writers who were six feet under and buried under layer upon layer of literary criticism. We were expected to form our own opinions, but we didn't feel free to do so. Now we were in the thick of it, in the smoke and the buzz, because only a few doors down poetry was being written, and we could say what others hadn't said before.

A young woman joined the conversation. 'I love K. Michel's sense of wonder,' she said. 'It's a totally different way of looking at ordinary things.'

I felt compelled to make some qualifying remarks. While I thought it was an incredibly strong collection, neither the language nor the form were new. 'That outsider perspective,' I said, 'isn't that something it shares with Martian poetry? And that goes back ten years.' It was a movement which had arisen in Britain in the late Seventies, with Craig Raine and Christopher Reid its trailblazers. In their poetry they viewed the world the way someone from Mars would look at the things around us. *In homes, a haunted apparatus sleeps, / that snores when you pick it up.*

'If anything, I thought it was liberating to read poems that weren't written by a melancholic for a change,' I said.

Robert Berendsen nodded. 'Away with wistfulness.'

Another round of beers was bought. 'To the Martian poets,' someone toasted.

The following year K. Michel would be nominated for the C. Buddingh' Prize, given for the best Dutch-language debut poetry collection published in the previous year, but failed to win the award. It didn't detract from the poet's dream start, though. He had shaken up the literary establishment, or at least a section of it — its crowning glory, poetry. For many, his book opened a door to another world. Young poets tried to bring an even greater sense of wonder to the things around them. Cue experimentation, agitation, hallucination. During that scintillating time of innovation I started a job as an editor at a company that boasted over a hundred years of publishing history.

'Why don't you drop by tomorrow.' It had sounded like a promise that evaporates the minute you exit the bar, but when I climbed the steps to an impressive canal-side house the following day I received a warm welcome from the publisher. Robert Berendsen's eyes looked even smaller. I was to start the following week.

I shared the news with my parents at the ice-cream parlour. We were sitting in the dining room on the first floor. My brother was downstairs, making coffee for the first few customers. 'I've got a job,' I said. 'On Monday I start work as a poetry editor for a publishing company.'

'What about your thesis?' my mother asked.

It was a question I had anticipated, but had no real answer to. The truth is, I was stuck with my thesis on anonymous poets. 'I want to work,' I said. 'I don't want to waste this opportunity.'

'He says he wants to work,' my father exclaimed. 'He can't wait to get started. Well, you know what? It's August: grab a *spatola* and get started. I'll have a nap for an hour.'

He got up from the table and walked to the door that opened out onto the roof of the ice-cream parlour's kitchen. There was a lounger there, on which my father now lay his weary body. As he did so we could hear the tubing creak under the tightly stretched fabric. It was only later, after he had retired, that my father started complaining about the many aches and pains in his body: in his back, in his legs, in his hands. Everything ached, even his crotch and his teeth. All his life he had fought the pain, not given in to it, and had simply carried on bending, stoning, pounding, pureeing, pressing, and walking up and down the terrace. There was no time for suffering.

'He's having a hard time accepting it,' my mother said after a while. 'He's still having a hard time accepting it.'

I walked down the stairs to the ice-cream parlour. My brother was out front, serving a boy with short, spiky hair. A small queue had formed, mainly children with their parents. It was a warm morning.

I put on an apron and joined Luca. 'Hello,' I said, and when no reaction was forthcoming, 'I've come to help.'

Luca nodded, just as he had only nodded when I walked into the ice-cream parlour half an hour earlier.

'I've got a job,' I said as I filled a cup with vanilla and strawberry ice-cream.

No congratulations, no nothing. He looked at me as though I were a Martian.

In the years to come Luca would do his utmost to say as little as possible to me. Just as he had said hardly anything to Sophia when a boy, he limited his contact with me to a few words. Only when I insisted would he say, 'I heard you.' It was supposed to be an answer to a question, except that it wasn't. At times I felt like charging at him with the *spatola*.

My father did speak to me, but everything he said resonated with the hope that one day I would convert back to ice-cream. I had strayed, and it was his job to make me realise I had made the wrong decision. I had chosen a life without the ice-cream parlour, without family. Sooner or later I would come to regret it.

'Do you hear this music?' he said. 'It's Rino Gaetano.'

It was after midnight; the chairs outside had been stacked up, the doors closed. My father had switched on the stereo, something he only did after a good day. A good day for an ice-cream maker is when it's scorching hot and he has to work like a dog.

I knew the song: 'Ma il cielo è sempre più blu', or 'But the Sky is Always Bluer'. It was a classic, a song with a heart of gold. You couldn't help but sing along when it came on. As little children we had often hollered it without knowing what the lyrics meant.

My father kicked things off. *'Who lives in a shack, who sweats for his salary / who loves to love and dreams of glory.'* Luca joined in: *'Who robs pensions, who has a short memory / who eats once a day, who plays at target practice.'*

For a fleeting moment I felt like an outsider. It was a protest song. Rino Gaetano had written the song for all those who suffered, day in, day out. Not for me, not for someone whose job had fallen into his lap, who did have a summer, who had sex with angelic girls and slept till noon. But as Gaetano's voice got louder and the chorus built, I couldn't help but sing along: *'But the sky is always bluer, uh uh, uh uh, / But the sky is always bluer, uh uh, uh uh, uh uh ...'*

My mother's eyes filled with tears as she heard us sing and scream. We sang with the same passion as Rino Gaetano, who had been born in Crotone, a small town on the Ionian Sea, had moved to Rome — to the big city — and achieved immense success, becoming a national hero before losing his life in a car accident at the age of thirty. Life was unfair, but the sky is always blue, always bluer.

Perhaps it was this section that my father loved the most. He certainly sang it at the top of his lungs, an exclamation mark after each line:

> *Who hasn't got a house, who lives alone*
> *Who earns very little, who plays with fire*
> *Who lives in Calabria, who lives on love*
> *Who fought in the war, who just scrapes by*
> *Who makes it to eighty, who dies with his boots on*

My father didn't earn very little, didn't live in Calabria, and hadn't fought in the war, but he did die with his boots on. Not literally, but very gradually. To him that was the crux of the song. And of his life.

After the song had finished, all three of us were panting, our chests rising and falling in sync, and my father said, 'That's what I call poetry.'

He had to have a dig at me.

And kick me when I was down. 'Rino Gaetano is the greatest poet in the world.'

This was supposed to be followed by the line, 'Not Shelley, not Szymborska, not Kaváfis, not Atwood', except he didn't know the names of any of these poets, 'with their difficult words and their incomprehensible language'.

According to my father, there was only one poet, and that was Rino Gaetano, who had managed to break through to my father's heart and touch his invisible soul. The young man from Crotone thought of himself as a writer first and a singer second. After he'd written his first album, he was rumoured to have told the producers to go in search of someone who could actually sing his songs. He didn't think his own voice was good enough. Too rough, too gravelly. They had to force him into the studio.

I believe you can be both poet and singer. A bard. It's the way Achilles' rage was sung, and the way 'Mr Tambourine Man' reached us. I have invited Bob Dylan to the World Poetry Festival several times, but have yet to receive a letter back. Perhaps he is waiting for the Nobel Prize for Literature. In the olden days the world was divided into prisoners and guards; these days it's made up of people who think Dylan deserves the Nobel Prize and those who think the very idea is preposterous.

That night I stayed over in Rotterdam, in the attic, with my brother. He pretended to be asleep, but I could tell from his breathing that he was still awake. I waited for the question he had asked so often when we were children; I was hoping he would ask me what was on my mind.

I was thinking of him, or of us really. Of the silence between us.

'Are you thinking of Sophia?' I asked after a while.

No reply.

'I asked if you were thinking of Sophia.'

Last winter I hadn't been to Venas, because I had intended to work on my thesis. It was the first time I hadn't come along to Italy.

The winter before last I had chopped down a fir tree in the forest with my brother, we had celebrated Christmas together, and we had drunk beer and wine with Sophia in Bar Posta until late. She sat between the two of us on the corner bench and we played Uno. The good thing about playing cards is that you don't have to talk. The way Luca played, you'd have thought there was an astronomical sum of money involved, ten million lira or something. He was completely focused on his cards and silent, like a professional poker player.

I noticed that his right leg was resting against Sophia's left leg. A little later, her right leg touched my left leg.

He let her win, but it was blatant only to someone who was his brother. When we played Uno at home in the warm kitchen, my father and Luca were the most fanatical players. Both were bad losers and were known to occasionally whack the table in anger or shout, 'The two of you are cheating! The two of you are in cahoots together!' The 'two of you' in question would always be my mother and me. There were two distinct camps in our family.

There came a point when I could no longer stand Luca's silence, the hypocrisy.

'You're letting her win,' I said, and put my cards on the table. 'It's no fun this way.'

My brother didn't say anything. Of course he didn't say anything.

Sophia turned over the cards I had put on the table. 'You'd never have won with these,' she said without batting an eyelid. 'You're just a bad loser.'

At times it felt as if there were two distinct camps in Bar Posta too. As if I was the common enemy. But then there were times when Sophia enjoyed seeing Luca in a tight spot, or encouraged me to goad my brother by laying down a particular card. The snowball had been thrown, and I was down but not out.

'Shall we carry on?'

'Yes,' replied Luca, the sneaky bastard.

The cards were shuffled and dealt again. This time I won. I felt vindicated.

We carried on playing until last orders. The place stayed open for another half hour after that.

'Tell me more about Amsterdam,' Sophia said. It was a regular question towards the end of the evening. I had already told her about the cafés full of writers and cigarette smoke and the parties after premières and book launches, but every evening she demanded to hear more.

'You're not telling me everything,' she said. 'You're holding back information.'

'What kind of information?'

'About girls, about women.'

Luca said nothing. Sophia had no way of knowing that he wasn't talking to me. He had always been like this when the three of us were together.

'Shall I tell you about Rosa?'

Sophia nodded. 'Let me guess,' she said. 'She's tall and blonde.'

'No.'

'She's short and she's got troll's teeth.'

'No.'

'She's fifteen.'

'No.'

'She's fifty.'

'Almost.'

I was glad the sip of beer Luca had just swallowed didn't go down the wrong way.

'She's forty-two.'

'My mother is forty-four.'

'You've got a young mother,' I said.

We had seen her walking down the street. None of the lustre had gone with the years — her skin was as luminous as ever. The women in the village gossiped about her at the baker's. She was said to be cheating on her husband with the roofer: last summer she had been seen emerging from a field with hay in her hair, followed a few minutes later by the stocky, slightly boorish Salvatore Grigio.

Or that was the story that did the rounds and left the village buzzing with excitement, eager for more.

Luca and I had reached the right age for her tight skirts. We looked over our shoulders and stared at her on the street. Last time we saw her, I wanted to tell him that Sophia was his, her mother mine, but Luca had already walked on.

'I want to know everything,' Sophia said. Again, she didn't bat an eyelid.

Everything. That included the collection of poetry I had spoken to Rosa about and the question that always rears its head in discussions, the 'to be or not to be' of poetry. In the words of Martinus Nijhoff: 'Should a poet express what we feel, or should we feel what the poet expresses?' But Sophia wasn't interested in any of that. I could skip the poetry.

'What does she look like? What was she wearing?'

'She was wearing a short dress and had the sort of breasts any woman would like to have for a day.'

There was nothing wrong with Sophia's breasts. They were not too big, not too small. Pears, I know now. Beautiful little pears.

Rosa's breasts were of an entirely different order, a double-sized portion. Not those immense breasts that turn to jelly without a bra. They remained firm and round, like a juicy fruit that takes two hands to harvest.

'How did you know?'

'I didn't know at the time, but it was plain to see.'

Her nipples were erect, as if an almond had been inserted into each breast. It may have been the wind that blew in every time the door was opened. The occasion was a book launch, the location the sumptuous, marble-floored lobby of the publisher's headquarters; a wooden staircase led to the offices on the upper floors. At the start of the night there were no more than twenty people; by late evening their number had tripled.

Sometimes you find yourself talking to someone and you think nothing is happening. There are no clues, no signs, but then suddenly a single remark changes everything.

We were talking about polka dots. There was a girl there with long braids who wore a dress with cheerful dots on it. She walked right past us.

'I like dots,' I said. 'On men too, on their shirt or socks.'

'Does that mean you like moles as well?' Rosa asked.

I couldn't help it. My gaze immediately darted to her neck, to her arms, to her breasts. There's the speed of light, and there's the speed of pupils. I saw moles everywhere.

From poetry to polka dots, from moles to the sheets on the bed that awaited us in a virtually empty attic.

I wasn't allowed to undress myself. 'Hang on,' she said. 'Let me do that.' She undid the buttons of my shirt. Her fingers were still cold, but that's the sort of thing only spouses mind. I moved my hands across her transparent black tights and squeezed her buttocks.

'Take it easy,' she whispered.

It was the age difference. Twenty years. You'd never guess, looking at her body, at her skin, which was soft and firm in equal measure. I wanted to touch every centimetre of her.

'You've got beautiful fingers,' she said. It was the first time anyone had told me that.

'You've got delicious breasts.' I couldn't possibly be the first to have told her that.

I slid the straps of her dress off her shoulders, but the bra had to stay on a while. 'What's the hurry?' she said.

'I want you.'

She laughed as she looked at my erection jabbing at the fabric of my trousers.

'I take it you know the difference between a woman and a girl?'

For a moment I didn't know what to do, what the next step was. Standing before me was a woman whose breasts I wanted to uncover, but who deemed it too early for the ceremony.

'Kiss me,' she whispered.

I kissed her skin — I kissed every single mole I saw. The trail led to her armpit, and from there to her cleavage. She moaned softly.

'I want to see them,' I said.

She took my hand and led me to the bed. She took her time. I fell back on the mattress, and it was only then that I heard the music in the room. She must have put it on when we came in. It was a deep male voice, accompanied by a languid bass. Old soul music. I took a fleeting look around. I had no idea where I was, which canal her house was beside.

Rosa kicked off her high heels and climbed on top of me. Her fingers reached for the buttons on my trousers. She did it with one hand, one button at a time. My prick shot forward. I tried to sit up but was pushed back. She shaped her mouth into an O and wrapped her lips around the fabric of my boxer shorts.

'Jesus.'

I pulled her up by her wrists, bringing her face close to mine. Her cheeks were red, I noticed, and she had crow's feet.

'What's up?' she asked.

'Nothing.'

'Something is, I can see it.'

'I think you're amazing.'

Her bra came off; she did it herself. Such beauty.

At first I only touched them with my fingertips; it felt almost sacrilegious.

She said something vulgar, but very softly. I could barely make it out. Or had I misheard? I grabbed hold of her breasts and brought my mouth to her nipple.

She no longer put up any resistance, but gave my hands free rein. I rolled her tights down her legs. Her knickers were soaking wet and smelled of her. She kissed me feverishly. Her fingers enveloped my prick.

'Would you like to go in my mouth?'

She started off tentatively, only the tip at first, but when I was almost completely inside her she let me put my hands on her head and determine the rhythm.

I made her move faster.

It was too much. I closed my eyes.

She must have realised, because suddenly she stopped. 'You mustn't come,' she said. 'Not yet.'

And then, 'Fuck me.'

I slid in seamlessly, a canoe cutting through water. She had moved onto her stomach, but raised herself up at one point. Leaning on the palms of her hands, she looked back at me. I saw the fine lines around her eyes, which deepened the more she exerted herself. She moved her buttocks, her entire divine backside.

'Keep going,' she urged me.

I didn't share this last bit, nor do I remember where exactly I broke off the story. Would Sophia figure out what had happened next? Luca had drained his glass by now. He looked over to the barman, who was eager to go home too.

'I wish I could quit,' Sophia sighed as we walked under the dazzling December sky.

She worked in admin at her father's glasses factory. The days were monotonous, the same people and the same work every day. They were at odds with her joy, the joy of the girl who continued to catch snowflakes, who could touch the tip of her nose with her tongue. Although she had grown older, she was still extremely young, and more beautiful than her mother had ever been. Gracious and innocent. With eyes that showed no fear.

'Why don't you tell me what's on your mind?' I said to my brother, who was still pretending to be asleep. He gave me no answer. It wasn't hard to guess, of course.

He was to become more and more like his father. It had started with a thumb, and this would be followed by the physical ailments, the twinges in his back, the pain in his knees. He would develop a more pronounced stoop and take an increasingly bitter view of the world around him — the world that had betrayed him, that had denied him his chance of immortality. And finally, he would start hating the woman he had once loved so much.

I wondered if Sophia had enquired after me at all, whether she had missed me, perhaps.

'Have you kissed her?'

Still no response.

'Well?'

My brother turned over in bed.

'Sleep well.' I counted to twenty. 'I said, "Sleep well."'

'I heard you.'

In Amsterdam I worked with poets on their manuscripts. I discussed their work with them in my office at the publishing company. All I had to do with the most talented writers was point out a lesser poem, one dodgy oyster in a big heap. We spoke about words, their meaning, the stress on particular syllables, their sound. These were conversations nobody else was having. It was like looking at language through a microscope. Then there were poems I had pored over for hours and still couldn't figure out. When I took it up with the poet, they usually offered a faltering clarification that shed some light on the mystery. But sometimes it only deepened.

'I don't really understand it myself,' a female poet told me once.

'What do you mean?'

'I mean, I don't understand the poem myself. Or perhaps I ought to say I only partially understand it.'

I looked at her. She was dead serious.

'It's like a dream,' she said after some time.

I remembered a conversation with Heiman about T.S. Eliot, who once said, 'I write my poetry under a kind of divine inspiration so that often I myself don't understand what it means.' According to Heiman, this amazing statement touched on the very essence of poetry. Unlike prose, poetry required patience. It didn't take the reader's comprehension into account. In fact, sometimes it seemed as if a poem couldn't care less about a reader. 'A novel speaks to you,' Heiman said. 'The writer tells a story. A poet talks to himself.' Obviously, some poetry strikes an immediate chord, like an arrow into your heart, but equally it can take a while before you get it. There were no rules, there was no recipe. Poetry could overwhelm, touch, comfort, weigh on you or be absolutely weightless. And much more besides. Incomprehensible poetry could be brilliant poetry.

In summer, with the sash window open, fresh air would blow into the office along with the sounds of the canal. You could hear women laughing. If you went over to the window, you would see them sitting on the stern of a small boat. They invariably had long, blonde hair and bare shoulders. Their beauty was reflected in the water. The world was a mirror; everybody told them how beautiful they were. They sailed past, brimming with confidence. This was their time. These weren't the women in the smoky cafés — these were unapproachable women, women who were already taken or destined to marry a rich lawyer or the heir of a family with a double-barrelled name.

It would be many years before you got to know them. By now they were well into their forties, still blonde, but no longer naturally so, and with long, horizontal creases in their foreheads. Their husbands were older, their children had moved out. Some had bought themselves a dog, a fox terrier or a dachshund, and would walk it in the woods on the outskirts of Amsterdam every day. Others wanted more. They reckoned it was their turn now. They had raised the children while their husband had pursued a career. You would see them at readings. They wore expensive shoes, their legs still shapely, as though they had been embalmed rather than clad in shimmering nylon. Some wore corsets. Maybe they had been keen readers when younger, or they had once been in love with a book, a novel they had devoured in their girlhood bedroom. At any rate, literature was a favourite hobby now. Many of them had never been to university, or else they hadn't finished their degree, but people who read books radiate the same erudition as a graduate. Or at least that's what they thought, what they believed.

One of these women was Joan Foks. She wasn't married, nor did she wear a corset, but she did belong to the circle of affluent reading women. Her husband, a renowned orthopaedist, had died unexpectedly. She had been divine when I was still only a toddler, but she appeared before me with a broken capillary in her face. It hadn't happened right there and then, but a couple of months earlier. Age had come like a thief in the night.

Robert Berendsen had invited her to dinner at his house, along with five other guests. His wife had cooked, four courses; she had started in the morning. In daily life she was a partner at a prominent maritime law firm, but she knew all the major authors on the list personally. She cared deeply about the publishing company and would read the occasional manuscript when her husband asked her to. Unlike many women in her social milieu, she was independent, and people envied her for her intelligence and dress sense.

I was the only guest who hadn't been round before. Robert introduced me as a professor of poetry. 'He knows almost as much as I do,' he added.

He had met Joan Foks at a performance of *A Midsummer Night's Dream*. His wife had been ill and she was on her own, since she enjoyed going to the theatre but never phoned anyone. They got talking during the interval. Despite being behind him in the queue for the bar, she had been served first.

'*C'est la vie*,' had been her response when he commented on it.

'You might have bought me a drink too.'

'I never buy men drinks.'

It was a joke, albeit one with a grain of truth. 'Beautifully staged,' Joan said in an effort to steer the conversation in another direction.

A proud Robert Berendsen had told her that both the translation and the adaptation had been done by a poet from his list. And so it happened that the following day she climbed the steps to his office. Her heels had echoed through the building.

During their lunch, Robert listened to stories about her life. Her husband had become unwell in a restaurant. He thought it was the bisque when in fact it was his heart. He collapsed, surrounded by white tablecloths and people in evening wear. She would never forget the woman who carried on eating. 'She kept bringing her fork to her mouth,' she said. 'Fair play to her, the food was amazing.'

He smiled. She was wearing an all-but-transparent silk shirt. Her nose was dead straight, like that of the Venus in Villa Borghese, the marble statue Canova had made of Pauline Bonaparte, Napoleon's sister.

She had been to Rome several times and was familiar with the statue.

'Am I the first to note the resemblance?'

She didn't answer; that is to say, she didn't address it directly. 'The question is whether she posed nude.'

'What do you think?'

'She told everyone it was warm enough in the artist's studio.'

'That doesn't sound innocent.'

'She was a promiscuous woman. Canova wanted to immortalise her as the goddess Diana, but Pauline insisted on being portrayed as Venus Victrix, with the golden apple in her hand.'

The wooden base contained a rotating mechanism so visitors could view the statue from every possible direction by candlelight in the evening. Canova had treated the marble's surface with wax so it acquired a certain sheen.

'The story goes that Pauline came to regret it,' Joan said, 'and that she asked her husband to remove the statue. He granted the request and had the statue stored in a wooden chest.'

'Shame,' was all Robert said, his thoughts on the statue's skin illuminated by candlelight.

Joan herself had never cheated on her husband. She knew of at least four cases of adultery in her social circle — that's to say, of at least four women with lovers. She didn't approve. If you married, you made a promise. If you were unable to keep that promise, or didn't really believe in it, you shouldn't have got married in the first place. But perhaps that was easy for her to say. She had married late, and prior to that there had been many men. Which is not to say that she was uncomplicated. She did have certain standards, criteria.

Her husband's suits were still in the wardrobe in the bedroom. All of his shirts, neatly ironed and arranged by colour, were there.

His most romantic gesture was to give her a piano Erik Satie had once played.

'Do you play an instrument?'

Robert shook his head. As a boy he had played field hockey, and the love of literature had come after this.

She told him that she had started playing the piano at an early age. The teacher made home visits and told her mother that she had never come across such a talented child, and Joan had overheard. It was a golden childhood memory.

'I was supposed to go to the conservatoire, but something came up. I went abroad instead.'

She fell silent, perhaps thinking it was too early to tell the whole story, her whole life. Suddenly another memory surfaced: her younger self on the quay of a French seaside resort, bent over. An unimaginable girl wringing her hair. A silver ribbon of droplets splashing onto the hot cobbles, all but hissing.

'Anyway,' she said, 'that piano was the most beautiful thing I ever received in my life.'

It was the kind of glorious weather that makes you forget your coat in a restaurant. Nothing happened between them, except that they went for lunch again the following day. In fact, it happened so often that people began to notice, and Robert Berendsen had no choice but to invite her home. The three of them had dinner together, which was awkward to begin with, and in fact later that evening in bed his wife remarked, 'She really is rather beautiful.'

But now she sat at the large table in the living room as a good friend. She looked magnificent, like a woman ten years her junior. The conversation revolved around the work of poets. Not the sacred, the vocation, but the jobs needed to make a living.

'Joost van den Vondel was a hosiery salesman,' said one of the guests, an editor at another publisher. 'He had a shop on Warmoesstraat.'

'Gottfried Benn worked in a mortuary,' said a man who had written several biographies.

'What kind of poetry does that inspire?'

'Beautiful, degenerate poetry.'

'Rimbaud was an arms dealer,' said the young woman who had come along with the editor.

'But that was after he'd stopped writing poetry.'

'I didn't know he ever stopped.'

'At the age of twenty,' Robert told us. 'He spent the rest of his life travelling. Europe, Indonesia, Africa.'

'Is it possible to stop writing poetry?' the biographer asked.

'Borges tried,' I said. 'But after a thirty-year break he picked up the pen again. He published another ten books.'

'He was blind by then.'

'Beethoven was deaf when he wrote the Ninth Symphony.'

'Not completely though, right?'

'Oh, yes,' Joan replied. 'At the end of the première they had to turn him round to face the auditorium so he could see the audience applauding him.'

Nobody knew whether or not Borges could still see towards the end.

'He began to live in his memories,' Robert said. 'His poems consist of enumerations. You could read them over and over again.'

Something occurred to his wife. 'François Villon was a thief,' she said.

'And didn't he kill someone too?'

'Yes, but he received a pardon,' I clarified. 'It was a love rival. He was jailed for theft.'

'If you want to be rich, you shouldn't become a poet,' Robert noted.

'Byron sold ten thousand copies of *The Corsair* on the day it was published,' the biographer said.

'That was two centuries ago.'

'You could win the Nobel Prize,' the editor contributed, 'and become a millionaire in one fell swoop.'

'How many poets have won it?'

'The first Nobel Prize laureate was a poet: Sully Prudhomme.'

'There have been quite a few: Pablo Neruda, Czesław Miłosz, Joseph Brodsky.'

'Yeats,' the young woman said.

'T.S. Eliot.'

'Salvatore Quasimodo,' I offered.

'Who?' someone asked.

'A truly major poet.'

'Says an Italian,' Robert said with a laugh.

'He thought his work was better than Shakespeare's.'

'Has he been translated?' the biographer asked.

Robert thought for a moment. 'No idea.'

'His wife said the Nobel Prize was the beginning of the end,' I explained.

'Why?' Joan asked.

'Twenty-two million lira at once,' I said. 'At long last there was money, but Quasimodo spent it like a sailor. On other women, of course. The year of the Nobel Prize was also the year of their divorce: 1959.'

'I once had a relationship with a billionaire,' Joan said. 'Well, relationship is a big word. I was one of many. It was a long time ago and I was extremely young. I can't even remember the currency unit. Drachma, was it? Or dinar?'

Joan's laugh was infectious. Her stories were good, too. How many women can say they have shared a bed with a billionaire, but can't remember the currency?

'He had a Swiss watch which was more expensive than ten Lamborghinis combined. He kept saying it, ad nauseam, but as a young girl I was impressed.'

We all looked at her, and then she said, *'C'est la vie.'*

The evening was coming to an end. The dessert plates were on the table, the cutlery placed together on top of them. Coffee was served, and Robert came round with a bottle of Armagnac. The conversation no longer involved the whole table; instead, people talked among themselves. The young woman talked with Robert's wife, while Joan Foks talked with me. She told me she had spent a lot of time in Italy, but none in the north. 'Or maybe I have, in Cortina d'Ampezzo.'

'It's great for skiing,' I said.

'Oh, I never saw any mountains. We stayed at the hotel that's featured in that James Bond film.'

'*For Your Eyes Only*.'

'That's right,' she said. 'Except that it was filmed much later. I was in my early twenties.'

'I actually saw Roger Moore,' I told her. The truth of the matter was that I spotted a man in a blue ski jacket who was said to be the English actor. Luca claims it was a stunt double. We had taken the bus to Cortina in the hope of meeting the film's stars, but had to make do with the autograph of a champion skier.

'The Miramonti,' Joan said. 'That's what the hotel was called.'

There were three lives: before her marriage, during her marriage, and after her husband's death. It was into that latter life that she was now gradually admitting new people. She could come across as shy, but wasn't really. If she seemed shy, she didn't like you and didn't fancy talking to you.

There was a time when men had vied for her attention, but most of them never stood a chance. She always asked if they were married. More often than not, the answer was yes.

It was impossible not to picture the young woman she had been, unmarried, available. A Venus. To imagine the pleasure of looking at her, of talking to her, of touching her.

'I'm renting an apartment on Herengracht,' she said. It might have been interpreted as an invitation, a remark giving the conversation a different turn, had she not gone on to say, 'I'd have bought it if the piano had fitted through the window.' The piano remained in the detached house in Haarlem, which she didn't want to sell. It's where her husband's shirts were still in the wardrobe and she always left a small light on for him. She could see it gleaming in the distance when she entered the gravel driveway.

I asked her if she had children.

She shook her head. 'I wanted them, though,' she said.

The conversation ground to a halt. Maybe she thought the question was impertinent, or she found it a difficult subject. To be honest, I had expected her to have children — sons studying abroad or travelling through Southern Europe without a care about the rest of their lives.

'Do you want children?' she asked suddenly.

'I'm twenty-four,' I replied.

'That's a wonderful age.'

'For children?'

'For anything.'

'I don't think I'm suited to family life.'

'That's what I always thought,' she said and looked me straight in the eye. 'Until it was too late.'

I looked away, at the broken capillary. It was a small crack in an otherwise perfect face.

'But men don't have that problem.'

Simon Vestdijk came to my mind. He had written twenty-four books of poetry and had fathered a son and daughter at a ripe old age. His wife was forty years his junior.

Joan pushed her chair back a little, getting ready to go home. I was going the other way, but offered to escort her to Herengracht.

'There's no need,' she said. 'Really.'

A brief, awkward silence ensued, as though I had made a different kind of offer.

'*Au revoir*,' she said eventually.

We sold some five hundred copies of most of the poetry collections we published, sometimes fewer, and on a rare occasion we had an upward blip. From a commercial point of view, books of poetry were totally uninteresting, but they represented a different sort of value for the publishing company. Its reputation hinged on it. Poetry had a certain grandeur. It was my job to see to it that as many of our poets as possible were nominated for various awards. To this effect I had to maintain contact with critics who served on juries. It always helped to slip a brief note into a collection, or to take them out to lunch and brazenly recommend a poet.

'Are you trying to bribe me?' a female jury member once asked me.

'I wouldn't dare.'

'I think you are.'

'It's not unusual for me to have lunch with colleagues in restaurants; it's part of my job.'

'Am I a colleague?'

'We're in the same boat,' I said. 'Of course there are differing interests, but at the end of the day we've got the same objective.'

'Which is?'

'To serve literature.'

'And that's why you're picking up the tab?'

'The publisher is paying,' I replied. 'Robert Berendsen.'

I signed the credit-card receipt and put the pen down on the white tablecloth.

'Are you taking the other members of the jury out for a meal too?'

She was teasing me, I could tell by her upper lip.

'The chairman of the jury is on the agenda,' I said. 'But I intend to take him to a more expensive restaurant. Do you have any suggestions?'

'The Excelsior. It's got a Michelin star.'

'Sounds like a good choice.'

'I need a new dress,' she then said.

'For the ceremony?'

'Yes,' she said. 'And high heels.'

She could no longer suppress her laughter.

Lobbying was like flirting, albeit less egotistically. It didn't revolve around you, but around the poet and his collection. But there were no guarantees. In the end, the prize went to another poet, an established name. A safe choice, which wasn't uncommon when it came to the bigger awards.

The jury member I had lunched with came over to me after the ceremony. She wore a red silk backless dress. 'What do you think?' she asked.

'I think the dress is better than the winner.'

*

In an attempt to attract fresh talent, I joined forces with some of the poets on the list and founded a poetry journal. It was to come out monthly and also feature translated poetry. To this end I contacted the World Poetry Festival. I hadn't been back to the office since Richard Heiman's death, although I had attended the festival every year.

The new director was older but no less passionate. His name was Victor Larssen and he wore beautiful shoes, two-tone brogues in brown and dark green. Next to his desk stood a basket from which a pug stared at me with beady eyes that wouldn't have looked out of place on a human child.

Victor Larssen sat at the same wooden desk at which Heiman had written his letters. The portraits of poets still graced the walls, too. Clara Janés, Seamus Heaney, Herman de Coninck, Margaret Atwood, Hans Magnus Enzensberger, Sarah Kirsch, Tomas Tranströmer — they had all appeared at the festival, along with hundreds of other poets from all over the world. The bookcase was full of jacketless hardbacks, each annual volume in a different colour. These were publications for internal reference, printed in a very limited edition, no more than ten copies. Every now and then you might find one in an antiquarian bookshop. They contained all the poems that had been read at the World Poetry Festival in both their original language and translation. The paper was thicker than that of a prayer book, and larger too, but ultimately the reading experience was just as powerful.

There were sound recordings as well, countless tapes. The readings had been recorded right from the inaugural festival, in 1969. On many an occasion Heiman had pushed a pair of headphones into my ears, saying, 'Listen. This is 1973.' I would hear the tape whirring, white noise, crackling, followed by a poet's voice. Often they were reading in languages I didn't understand — Chinese, Spanish, Norwegian — but the tapes were always a pleasure to listen to. The rhythm, the sounds, the silences.

The portraits, the books, the sound recordings — it was a glorious, borderless world. History in poems. It was all there: wars, assassinations, and tsunamis, as well as the sound of summer, the birth of babies, and the scrapping of a Chevrolet Impala.

It felt good to be back. The publishing world was more frantic. Books were meant to follow one another in quick succession, new writers meant to be discovered all the time. If you took your eye off the ball you ran the risk of seeing a promising debutant lured away. It was less of an issue for poetry, but you were surrounded by editors who wolfed down their lunch while quickly making another phone call. Robert Berendsen was not immune, either. He had actually bought a foreign title without having read it first. Fortunately it became a bestseller, the way you can strike it lucky on the roulette table.

'Have you read Patrick Lane?' Larssen asked after we had talked about the festival's most recent edition. 'I think he may be right for your journal.'

I knew the name, had perhaps even read a poem of his, but no lines sprang to mind.

'A Canadian poet.'

His dog sat up and barked. 'Hardy,' Larssen said. 'Quiet!'

The animal lay down again and stared straight ahead with those cute little eyes in that sad, wrinkled face of his.

'I read a terrific poem by Patrick Lane,' Larssen told me. 'About a logger who saws off his hand.' He patted his dog on the head absentmindedly. 'You don't happen to know it?'

I shook my head.

'It was an accident, and a colleague took him to hospital — a five-hour drive over mountain roads, the severed hand in a bucket of ice water between them. The nurse wanted to know the man's name and date of birth and asked for a piece of paper with his address. That's when his colleague lifted the logger's sleeve. The nurse averted her head from the veins and tendons. The doctors examined the wound, but it was too late for the hand: it was dead and couldn't be sewn back on. The colleague drove back to the north. After several hours he stopped by a bridge and took the hand from the bucket. He couldn't keep it and he couldn't really give it to the logger's wife, either.

He considered burying it, but it was cold and dark and he was working the morning shift. And so he threw the hand "high off the bridge and for one moment it held the moon still in its fingers".'

Victor Larssen slid a stack of sheets towards me. 'I hope they're of use to you,' he said. And then, 'That image of a hand tumbling in the night sky, appearing to hold the moon. I think it's phenomenal.'

He laughed. Larssen didn't have Heiman's boyish charm, but he did have the same cast-iron faith in poetry. Without it, life was less beautiful for him, too.

We talked about the poets I mentored, and about Robert Berendsen. The two men used to write for the same university paper. Then Larssen shook my hand and escorted me to the door of his office. He didn't invite me for a drink or a bite to eat in a nearby restaurant, the way Heiman had often done. When we got to know each other better, perhaps. We scheduled another appointment and I was to send him the journal proofs.

Standing on the footpath outside the World Poetry offices, I looked over to the ice-cream parlour. It was November. The awning had been folded away and it was darker inside than out. A note had been stuck to the window of the door: 'Back in March!' It was in my mother's handwriting and included a drawing of a small sun. In the old days Luca and I got to do that. Luca drew a sun and I drew a sun. So we wouldn't fight.

I stood there for quite a while, not trying to suppress my thoughts. *Let them come*, a rebellious voice inside me said. *Come on then! I can handle you!* And so they came; they besieged me. All the thoughts and the questions, the memories, the images. Had it snowed in Venas yet? What did the kitchen smell of? I saw my parents sitting at the table with Luca. I saw my chair. What was Sophia doing? Was she walking around the village, was she looking at the warm lights behind the windows? March was still a very long way off. But not for an ice-cream maker. March came closer every day.

That evening I translated Patrick Lane's poem in bed. The ice that had melted in the bucket and the water that was thrown away.

The severed hand on the river bed like a 'dark blue spider sleeping'. And then the question: 'What do you do with the pieces of yourself you lose?'

Like Sophia Loren's Buttocks

The following spring, Sophia stood in the ice-cream parlour. She wore her long, blonde hair in a thick braid down her back and held a *spatola* in her hand. She served the customers, together with my mother. Beppi made coffee and waited on the tables outside. Luca was in the kitchen, boiling milk and churning scandalously thick ice-cream. There were four again.

It had happened the previous winter, or the one before. Luca never told me. He was still not talking to me. The fact that he had won Sophia and she had taken my place in the ice-cream parlour made no difference to him. Yet he failed to suppress a smile when, in late February, I walked into the parlour and our eyes met. I had already spotted Sophia. I had seen her right away, even before my hand had reached the doorknob, through the glass my mother was cleaning, past her blue apron, behind my father who was polishing the espresso machine with a cloth. There she was. It was unbelievable, yet perfectly natural at the same time. She was holding a mop and greeted me with a kiss on the cheek.

'Hello, brother-in-law,' she said with a smile.

I spied Luca through the small window in the kitchen door and he too was smiling, but it was a sardonic smile, like that of a boxer who sees his opponent sprawled on the canvas.

They were cleaning, making final preparations before re-opening, perhaps as early as the next day.

'It will stay dry,' my mother said, sounding pleased. 'Sunny spells this afternoon, with temperatures rising later in the week. The wind is moderate, southwest.'

I knew it. Spring was in the air.

My father made me an espresso. 'Have a taste,' he said. 'I connected the machine this morning. The beans are freshly ground.'

I took a sip. It was only warmish because the machine hadn't heated up properly yet, which made the coffee a touch sour.

'Nice,' I said, 'but there's so little of it. I can see the bottom of the cup.'

There was no bucket of water for me, but I did get a hug. I could feel his stubble scratching my cheek, and mine his. On the first day of the season, there was no resentment. It would come after a few weeks, when the ice-cream machines were churning non-stop, the espresso machine was wheezing, and my father's joints were creaking. He would start cursing me as he walked back and forth between terrace and parlour for the umpteenth time, suddenly visualising me in a chair with a book of poetry in my hands — a vision in the blazing sun.

He attached a double portafilter to the espresso machine and pressed the button. Two caramel-coloured jets gushed into the pre-heated cups. It would take exactly twenty-six seconds, not a second shorter and not a breath longer.

For most ice-cream makers, coffee was just a sideline. They sold it in the morning or used it to attract customers on rainy days, and of course it was nice that they could drink proper espresso themselves. But ice-cream was their livelihood. For many it was a passion, or even more than that: some ice-cream makers couldn't stop talking about their trade. It continued in Italy in winter. Endless conversations in Bar Posta about vertical and horizontal ice-cream makers, about the ideal temperature, about proportions; discussions that often carried over to the kitchen table. It drove some wives to distraction.

My father simply withdrew into his basement in winter, to his treasure trove of screwdrivers and sanders. He rarely talked about ice-cream, but when the subject was coffee he liked to get involved. Other ice-cream makers often talked about smells. They praised the extraordinary aroma of their coffee: chocolate, cinnamon, nutmeg, cedar. One ice-cream maker even claimed that his espresso smelled of the colouring pencils of his childhood.

My father swore by a percolation time of twenty-six seconds. Aromas were unimportant to him, hogwash. 'A good espresso smells of espresso,' was his opinion, 'the way yoghurt ice tastes of yoghurt.'

He tried to convince other ice-cream makers of the ideal percolation time he had established after years of experimentation.

'Why not twenty-eight seconds?' an ice-cream maker from Vodo had once asked him teasingly. 'Or twenty-four?'

'Twenty-eight seconds is far too long,' my father replied, deadly serious. 'It makes the espresso bitter, because the roasting notes are dominant. After twenty-four seconds the espresso is sour and watery. The coffee hasn't had enough extraction time.'

'What about twenty-three seconds, Beppi?'

'At twenty-three seconds there's a risk of the cup exploding.'

'Twenty-six seconds per cup, you say?' another ice-cream maker remarked, sounding as if he had just made a difficult calculation. 'I haven't got that much time.'

'What's the rush?' Beppi replied. 'Ice doesn't melt at minus fifteen.'

'But the customers walk away when they have to wait too long.'

'Let them walk away.'

The other ice-cream makers frowned at my father.

Perhaps it was an escape, a way of withdrawing every so often. My father could hide behind the Faema E61, behind its gleaming hood, behind the steam taps and manometers. Twenty-six seconds per cup. Atomic time.

As a bitter old man, stranded in Venas di Cadore, my father would admit, 'At first I only hated the ice-cream, but then I started hating the people buying the ice-cream, too.'

When exactly the loathing had started and when it assumed an extremely rare form of misanthropy is hard to say. My father had never wanted to be an ice-cream maker in the first place; he never had a vocation for it. The fact is that as Luca and I grew older and began to make the ice-cream, Beppi spent less and less time in the kitchen. After I went to university and Luca took over the ice-cream parlour, my father often had to help out, but my brother was the one who was in charge of the ice-cream.

The machine ground to a halt. The espressos were ready.

'For you and your brother,' my father said.

I picked up the two cups and took them through to the kitchen.

'Right,' was the first thing I said to my brother. 'So you're engaged.'

He said nothing. He didn't even look at me. He looked at the tiled floor and listened to the Cattabriga, to the scraper blade moving back and forth, going *slll, slll, slll.* A good ice-cream maker doesn't have to peek inside the cylinder; he can tell by the sound of the machine when his ice is ready. 'It's like a marriage,' an old ice-cream maker from Tai di Cadore had said in Bar Posta once. He was tipsy, but not quite drunk. 'I know the ice and the ice knows me,' he said. 'It talks to me.' The other ice-cream makers, their eyes equally bloodshot, all nodded.

We were silent and downed our espressos at the same time.

Maybe there was nothing to talk about. What had happened couldn't have happened any other way. I was the eldest, I was the one who would have inherited the ice-cream parlour had I not renounced it. Luca, on the other hand, had accepted it and had received Sophia as a bonus. It made sense. He needed her. I didn't. What more was there to say?

There were no other subjects for discussion, and my brother must have realised it. Our lives had become too different. I read, I wrote, I edited. I had meetings, ate baguettes and brie with poets, and attended book launches. He worked sixteen hours a day, churning ice-cream, selling it, cleaning the machines, and then sleeping like a log at night. The ice-cream parlour was his whole world; mine began where it ended.

Slll, slll, slll.

Luca switched off the machine and picked up the *spatolone*. His thumb closed around the metal handle. He leaned over the open cylinder and straightened up again. The left corner of his mouth was a little higher than the right one — you couldn't quite call it a smile. It was what he had expected. It was good.

He had made vanilla ice-cream. It dripped off the large spoon and into the metal container like cement.

Luca saw me looking, like my great-grandfather's brothers and sisters had looked at his ice-cream, like everybody looks at ice-cream. What could be better? Do you know anyone who doesn't like ice-cream? Who doesn't feel happy at the sight of an ice-cream parlour? The cone that takes us back to childhood, the cardboard cup we've all stirred with a flat plastic spoon until we ended up with a new colour and flavour. Are you ever too old for ice-cream? Outside Venezia stands a giant cone with three scoops: strawberry, vanilla, and chocolate. The thing is made of polyester and filled with polystyrene, but I've seen plenty of toddlers waddle over to try and lick it. They won't remember it when they're older, but the longing will never go away.

Luca approached me with the metal container. The ice-cream didn't move in sync with his steps. It was soft yet firm.

'Like Sophia Loren's buttocks in *Yesterday, Today, and Tomorrow*,' my father was to say after tasting it.

My brother held up a spoon. I looked into his Kalamata eyes. He returned my gaze. Then I opened my mouth and he fed me his ice-cream. The texture was unbelievably fine and smooth, velvety and soft. The millions of tiny ice crystals in the thick cream formed the backbone of the ice-cream, even though they constituted only a fraction of the overall volume. The air bubbles that had been locked in during the churning had produced a lighter consistency, but not a brittle one — you could almost chew the creamy ice. And then it melted and my eyes involuntarily closed. It felt like floating, the way you're briefly suspended from everything when you kiss a girl.

Luca had improved the recipe, perfected it. The structure was creamier, the flavour richer, and the vanilla evenly distributed across the ice-cream. I swallowed and opened my eyes. His gaze had never once left my face. The sardonic smile had gone. Both corners of his mouth were equally high now. He knew what I knew. I had helped him by doing nothing, by being absent, by not coming back. That's how he had won the most beautiful girl in the village. He couldn't say it. His ice-cream was tasked with the job.

That afternoon the five of us sat around the dining table on the first floor. My mother had made pasta — spaghetti with tomatoes, garlic, capers, and anchovies. There was a bottle of red wine on the table. It was like a Saturday in the mountains.

Sophia came down from the attic after changing her clothes. We all looked at her and saw a field full of daffodils. She had started wearing her mother's dresses, the way Luca had stepped into my father's work gear. I glanced at her tanned legs and wondered whether my brother had touched them this morning. She twirled her fork in the spaghetti and took a bite without splattering her dress.

My mother couldn't help herself and talked about the weather. On the radio she had heard that it was going to be seventeen degrees tomorrow. 'It's never been that warm on the first day,' she said with a twinkle in her eye.

Beppi told us that one year the temperature had been ten below zero when they arrived back in Rotterdam. 'The icicles were hanging from the lampposts. You could skate on the Westersingel.'

'Had Giovanni and Luca already been born?' Sophia asked.

'Giovanni, yes,' my mother replied. 'But not Luca. He was still in the womb.'

'We were both born in summer,' I said. 'Ice-cream makers only do it in winter.' It was meant as a joke, but it didn't elicit a laugh. Everyone fell silent. The only sound was the twirling of my brother's fork.

Luca didn't talk — never said a single word during the meal. I wondered if he talked to Sophia at all, whether he had the guts for it now. I hadn't heard him say anything to her so far.

When the plates were empty and we had all finished our glass of wine, my father started telling us about a hammer drill he had seen in the window of Spijkermand, a hardware shop down the road.

'It's a beauty,' he said.

'Don't even think about it,' my mother warned him.

'I've already bought it.'

Sophia and I laughed.

My brother looked up, his mind already on the ice-cream. I recognised my father's old nervousness. Back in the day, he could never enjoy a meal, either. Not in Rotterdam, anyway. There was always something to do: separating eggs, mashing pineapple, squeezing oranges. We had two ice-cream machines, but twenty-two flavours. The ice-cream maker was the linchpin; one miscalculation and everything ground to a halt. The worst thing was running out of a flavour — an empty metal container in the display and a child bursting into tears and starting to screech. It meant you never had a moment to yourself. It was all work, work, work. Churn, churn, churn.

'May I have another glass of wine?' Sophia asked.

'Of course,' Beppi said and emptied the rest of the bottle into her glass. He was delighted with his future daughter-in-law. 'My wife never drinks more than one small glass.'

'One of us has to stay level-headed.'

'I've never been drunk in my life,' Beppi said.

'When you're drunk, you think you're sober.'

Suddenly my father remembered something. 'Stefano Coletti tried to make ice from his urine once.'

'Beppi!' my mother exclaimed. 'We're eating.'

'Everyone's done.'

'Those stories aren't suitable for a young lady.'

In due course she would get to hear all the stories, and the names of all the ice-cream makers, too. We had heard them as well. Stefano Coletti came from Pieve di Cadore, and one night he had emptied his bladder in the cylinder of his ice-cream machine. Drunk as a skunk, he had then switched in on. The resulting sorbet, which he put in the freezer, was hard and grainy. The following morning he had to work as usual, and with a stabbing headache he carried the metal containers to the display counter. He didn't look properly and put the new flavour where the lemon sorbet was supposed to go, but when his wife tried to stick the *spatola* into the container ninety minutes later, she couldn't get through. Without any added sugar, the ice had become as hard as stone at minus eighteen Celsius.

'Stefano!' she had yelled. 'Come here.'

He looked at the sorbet, but failed to make the connection with the night before.

'What's this?' his wife asked.

'Lemon sorbet.'

'It's rock hard.'

'Strange,' was all he said.

Only when he tasted some in the kitchen did snippets of the night resurface.

'He didn't think it was too bad,' my father told us. 'In fact, he took a second bite!'

There were countless stories about ice-cream makers and their machines. The most tragic one of all was the story of Ettore Pravisani, from Valle di Cadore. Pravisani was a true gentleman who was never seen without a tie. He had a shop in The Hague, and one morning in July he was churning strawberry ice-cream, his most popular flavour, as it is in so many other parlours. The machine was going *slll, slll, slll,* but Signor Pravisani couldn't tell from the sound when his ice-cream was done. So he leaned over the Cattabriga for a look inside the cylinder. His tie got caught by the driveshaft and he was strangled above the red ice-cream.

Sophia was spared this story for now.

'I tasted my wee once as a little girl,' she said, 'but I didn't like it at all.'

'Perhaps it's better cold than warm,' my father remarked.

He laughed at his own joke, and we joined in. Only my brother rose to his feet and said, 'I'm going back to work.'

It was Saturday, the afternoon like a spreading stain, except that we weren't in the mountains.

It turned out to be a good season — a warm spring, a sizzling summer. On days when the mercury rose above thirty, my thoughts were often with the ice-cream parlour. The window of my office was open and on my desk lay a stack of papers, a pencil beside it. With my sleeves rolled up, I read the latest work from poets on our list. It felt magical to read poems that nobody else had had the privilege to see, like walking through virgin snow. It had something to do with the silence, the complete solitude, and the words, which had been extracted from deep down like gold. But now and again I got lost between two lines and my thoughts would suddenly drift to the ice-cream parlour. I wondered what dress Sophia was wearing and how many men were trying to catch a glimpse of her cleavage as she scooped ice-cream for them.

At the end of the summer, Victor Larssen invited me to Rotterdam. There was something he wanted to discuss with me, but not over the phone. We agreed to meet outside Venezia. It was late afternoon and all the chairs were bathed in sunlight. My brother was helping my father, but it was Beppi who took our order.

'For me, a cup with vanilla and raspberry,' I said.

Larssen wanted a cone with hazelnut, mocha, and cinnamon.

'With whipped cream?' my father asked, but he didn't wait for an answer. He had served Larssen so many times that he knew he wanted whipped cream on his ice. Likewise, I still remembered what flavours some people wanted. One man had been coming to Venezia for more than ten years and always ordered the same: a five-scoop cup filled completely with pistachio ice-cream. His dog, half-hidden under his chair, was always given a cone, which it devoured in a couple of bites.

I could tell by the way he walked that my father's joints were aching. How many times had he walked back and forth between the terrace and the parlour today? How many times this season? These had been peak months. He would have to keep walking back and forth, like Sisyphus in the underworld. I knew a snide remark was imminent. He had cursed me on the hottest days this summer, and now I was sitting here on a stiflingly hot afternoon, wearing a goddamn t-shirt no less, and I had the audacity to order an ice-cream from him, a man in his late fifties, a man who had risen at five-thirty to help his younger son peel apples, a man who had started working at the age of fifteen, who hadn't had a summer for over forty years, who had started hating ice-cream. I made him walk while I sat in the sun.

Sophia was scooping ice-cream. To her left my mother was also serving a customer. A queue snaked around the giant ice-cream cone and the lamppost. I tried to catch Sophia's eye, but every time I looked she was bent over the ice-cream. Larssen told me that he had liked the most recent editions of our journal, and that he was really impressed with the translations.

We were interrupted by my father, who was holding a tray in his hands. He put down my cup and handed Larssen his cone. And then he stayed put for a while. Not that it would have been immediately apparent to an outsider, a customer, who probably just saw a middle-aged man dragging his feet. Larssen didn't notice anything out of the ordinary, either, but I knew what was coming. The hard feelings, the accumulated resentment.

'Would you believe this weather?' my father said. 'It's a good thing we've got some outside space so you can sit and enjoy the sun.'

I nodded, hoping he would leave it at this. But he remained beside our table.

'You'd better eat your ice-cream quickly or it'll melt.' He was only addressing me now.

Larssen had already taken a bite. Cinnamon with whipped cream. I was afraid to touch mine.

'Or would you like me to spoon-feed you, Giovanni?'

Perhaps he had already started hating the people who bought ice-cream; perhaps he hated me at that moment.

I decided to risk it and dug my flat plastic spoon into the vanilla.

'Good?' my father asked.

I had been looking forward to my brother's ice-cream, the way you long for a flavour or an aroma from childhood. In Amsterdam I had ordered a cup at Tofani's, and later I had also joined the queue at Gamba and Verona Gelati, but their vanilla ice-cream was no match for my brother's.

I felt my eyes involuntarily closing, but I immediately opened them again. It was just as soft and firm as it had been on that early spring day when my brother had held up a spoon for me in the kitchen. Unbelievably creamy. It was as if time stood still during the transition from solid to fluid.

'It's like Sophia Loren's buttocks in *Yesterday, Today, and Tomorrow*,' my father said. This time he was addressing Larssen too. 'Luca is a genius.'

'My brother,' I clarified.

'My other son,' my father added. 'He makes vanilla ice-cream that is just as firm and irresistible as Sophia Loren's buttocks in *Yesterday, Today, and Tomorrow*.'

Larssen looked at him. At first he seemed shocked, but then he said, 'Now I know where your son gets his love for poetry.'

We both laughed, my father and I. Except that he turned red in the face and nearly choked. The idea! It brought back memories of the old man who'd claimed ice-cream was a Chinese invention. He'd had an ice-cream cone flung at his head and had been forced to run for his life.

Victor Larssen was allowed to remain seated and finish his cone. After turning round, my father walked back to the ice-cream parlour, slowly and laboriously, pushing the invisible rock before him.

'Where's Hardy?' I had looked at Larssen's handmade shoes and then under his chair, but the pug with the sad face wasn't sleeping by his feet.

'He's at the office,' Larssen replied. 'He's doing the honours.'

'What happens when you travel?'

'My wife looks after Hardy.'

She wasn't his wife — they weren't married — but he wouldn't reveal this to me until later. Victor Larssen didn't wear a wedding band. He used to have one, which he had put next to his toothbrush every evening for twenty-two years. He had children, too; a grandchild, even. After his divorce — they had separated when their youngest daughter moved out, the documents signed before her boxes were unpacked — he had met a French woman who worked at the embassy. Her name was Valérie and they now lived together, and despite a great deal of respect for each other they also lived very separate lives. Not so much when it came to tastes — in composers, wine, literature — but definitely when it came to their jobs. She worked long hours, he travelled a lot, but it never caused any friction. They were inseparable only in summer, when they spent a month sailing the Mediterranean, sleeping side by side in the fore-cabin.

His youngest daughter was my age. She was a civil servant in Utrecht, where she worked for the Executive Councillor for Finance. 'She has no truck with poetry,' Larssen told me.

'Nor does my father,' I said. 'And my brother even less so, if that's possible. It's a miracle we share the same genes.'

'I used to wonder whether she was my daughter at all.' He laughed. 'Unfortunately she's got my nose.'

His wasn't a big nose, but a distinctive one. It had a strong curve, a proper hook.

'I used to fantasise that I'd been adopted and that one day my real parents would turn up on the doorstep. A Brazilian man with a white hat, a father like Carlos Drummond de Andrade.'

'What about your mother?'

'Antjie Krog.'

'Why?'

'Imagine her sitting at the foot of your bed, reading you a bedtime story,' I replied. 'In that beautiful language, in that gentle, charming voice: *I dearly want to make you happy / I would write verse for you / sober and supple as you are / I would sing for you / each night while you sleep.*'

Larssen commented, 'Didn't she write that for her husband?'

'Doesn't matter,' I said.

That's when I finally caught Sophia's eye, as the *spatola* in her hand went from the ice-cream to the cup in her other hand. Somewhere halfway, for a split second, our eyes met.

'I wanted to see you,' Larssen said, 'because I want to ask you something. Or make you a proposal, rather.' He shifted in his seat and straightened his back. He carried on talking, but I missed a bit, the essential bit.

She had smiled, and I must have done the same, because Larssen asked me, 'Does that smile mean you'll accept the job?'

When I didn't respond straightaway, he added, 'It's a great job. As an editor you get to travel the globe. Zagreb, Havana, Quebec City.'

I was familiar with the magical list of cities. Struga, Istanbul, Michoacán. I had hung on Richard Heiman's every word whenever he returned, tanned, from a festival on the other side of the world.

'I work for a publisher,' I stammered. 'I already have a job.'

'Robert Berendsen would understand your choice. He'd be happy for you.'

I looked over to Sophia again. She continued to return my gaze, her mouth a little open, the lips parted slightly.

'Would you like the job?'

'Of course,' I replied. 'Of course I want to be an editor of the finest poetry festival in the world.'

I thought of Heiman, of the lighthouse of Alexandria to which he used to compare the World Poetry Festival. He had piloted me to this harbour; now it was time to go ashore.

'In that case, we've got something to celebrate,' Larssen said. 'Do they have champagne here?'

I shook my head. The most festive dish on the menu was the Coupe Gondola with fruit, ice-cream, and whipped cream. But if I were to order that, my brother was sure to kill me. What was I thinking? Sit outside in twenty-eight degrees and order a large coupe to boot! As if he didn't have enough work to do!

I tried to establish eye contact with Luca, but he avoided my gaze. He looked tired, an ice-cream maker in summer. Six more weeks, the tail end of September and October, and they would head back to Venas. And then he would finally get to sit in an easy chair, watch television, nap after lunch, and in the evening, after popping into Bar Posta, make a baby. *Un piccolo gelataio* who would one day have a calloused thumb, like his father, his grandfather, his great-grandfather, and his great-great-grandfather before him. That was the order of things. And this new offshoot of the Talamini family tree would one day take over the ice-cream parlour and beget yet another child who would churn ice-cream.

This winter I was due to travel to Italy, too. In December Luca and Sophia would be getting married in the new San Marco church. He hadn't yet asked me to be his witness, but he was going to, according to my mother.

'Let's go to the Veerhaven and have a drink over there,' Larssen suggested. He settled the bill with my father. A note was handed over, coins were given back. No words were spoken. The silence was as bad as a snide remark.

While Larssen retrieved his dog from the office, I waited outside on the footpath and observed the ice-cream parlour. Our seats had already been taken by other people. My brother took their order with a friendly smile. Children were running around in high spirits. A breeze had got up and the edge of the awning was flapping. Thunder was imminent. My father retreated behind the espresso machine.

The door to the office opened. Larssen came out first, the pug traipsing after him. 'Hardy fancies a drink too,' he said.

I saw my mother waving at me with her free hand, the one without a *spatola*. Sophia waved too, over the heads of the children, the fathers, the mothers, the tourists, the senior citizens, the lovers, the lonely, the well-to-do, the skint — all those wanting an ice-cream on this muggy day.

I would see them again the following day. It had rained in the night, a summer thunderstorm. The footpaths were dotted with large puddles, but the asphalt was already drying. I was with a woman I had met the night before. Kitty. She worked for a communications agency downtown and had woken me at seven in the morning because that's when she got up during the week.

'Oh look, it's one of our regulars,' my father said as he approached our table.

I was asking for trouble, of course, but Kitty had insisted on going for a cappuccino at Venezia. I had bumped into her in the café in the harbour where Larssen and I had gone to drink a glass of champagne. At some point both of us got talking to other people: he to an architect friend, me to an unknown woman whose bare back was sunburnt. If you pressed it, your hand briefly left a white mark.

I had interrogated her, and she me, in the unashamedly curious way of people who have just met. Heiman told me once that Isaak Babel wanted to know everything about beautiful women. He even asked to look in their handbags. 'Did Babel write poetry?' I asked, surprised.

'No,' Heiman answered. 'But he loved a lot of women.'

I found out that Kitty had been the mistress of a plastic surgeon for almost a year, she that I came from a family of ice-cream makers.

'Is that your brother?' she asked after a sip of her cappuccino. I looked up from my espresso and spotted Luca in the ice-cream parlour with tubs of ice in both hands. My mother took them from him. Sophia was probably upstairs. It was early and not all that warm yet. The first ice-cream of the day had yet to be sold.

'He looks a lot like you,' Kitty noted. 'He's got the same build and the same posture.'

'I'm more than an inch taller.'

'He's got the same nose, too.'

'Other than that we're completely different.'

'Your skin's a bit darker, I grant you that,' Kitty said. 'You've spent more time in the sun.'

'My brother works the whole summer.'

'He's more muscular, too.'

Luca came out, not looking at me but at Kitty's legs. She was wearing a short skirt and pale blue lace knickers underneath, but I was hoping those weren't visible.

'You've got the same ears,' Kitty said.

'Now you're teasing me.'

'Such cute little ears.'

She took another sip of her cappuccino.

'And I bet he's got the same buttocks too, but to be sure of that he'd have to turn round and show us his other side.'

'Shall I ask him to?'

She turned towards me and kissed me on the mouth. I could taste the milky cappuccino on her lips. 'But I suspect he doesn't have your beautiful long lashes,' she whispered.

Sophia had come down. From behind the ice-cream she looked at Kitty's legs, just as my brother had done. Judging by the look on her face I was all but sure that she could tell what colour the lace was. Then our eyes met, but this time I got no smile, no nod, no wave.

'Who's she?' Kitty asked.

'My brother's fiancé. They're getting married in winter.'

'What a beautiful girl.'

Sophia turned her back on us.

'Is she Italian?'

'Yes, she's from Modena. She was thirteen when she moved to our village.'

'Tell me more.'

'What do you want to know?'

'Didn't you fall in love with her?'

'She's my brother's future wife.'

'Not in those days.'

Luca had gone back in. And as he made his way to the kitchen I suddenly felt a stab of longing, nostalgia for the ice-cream machines. I couldn't help it. It was there, the wish to be beside him in the kitchen right now. To prepare fruit, grind nuts, fill the cylinder of the Cattabriga. To listen to the scraper blade together.

'Yes, even in those days,' I replied.

Kitty looked at Sophia, at the blonde braid between her shoulders. 'Do you know how the plastic surgeon's wife found out?' she asked then.

'Did she catch you in the act?'

'No, that would have been painful.' She briefly touched her back, which was still sunburnt. 'His wife could tell just by looking at him. That's what she said to him, one morning, over breakfast. Nothing had triggered it. She could tell simply by looking at him.'

'Would you like to order anything else?' It was my father, standing behind us. He wasn't feeling the new day in his legs yet. The resentment was there, but it wasn't that acute yet. 'Maybe you'd like another cup of coffee?'

'I kind of fancy an ice-cream, actually,' Kitty said. 'Shall we share a cup?'

'One cup for the two of you?' my father said. 'How many flavours?'

'You decide.' Kitty smiled at me. She had a small mouth with thin but supple lips.

'What would you like?' Beppi said. He smiled at me as well. He took pleasure in his role. He had all the time in the world and didn't require me to play along. I *was* a customer. I was sitting outside their parlour, after all.

'Three flavours,' I replied.

'And which will they be?'

There was no way back now. 'Vanilla, mango, and blueberry,' I said, ordering the first ice-cream of the day.

My Brother's Wedding and My Father's Songbird

The wedding in Venas took place on a blue day. The sun had risen above the mountains in the morning, setting fire to the sky. The fields were blanketed in a thick layer of snow, covering even the needles of the larch trees, but the roads were clear. My father had come to pick me up from the station in Dobbiaco. I had travelled from New Delhi, where I had visited a poetry festival with Victor Larssen. We had spent most of the time in a minivan. Although poetry was read in locations across the city, there wasn't much of an audience. Larssen had explained to me that the festival aimed to bring poets together so they could translate one another's work. 'The audience comes second,' he had said. In my hotel room, with its view of Connaught Place, a rat had spent all night trying to find a way out through the air-conditioning unit. I hadn't slept a wink.

My father looked well: relaxed and in high spirits, an ice-cream maker in winter.

'How was your trip?' he asked as we drove out of Dobbiaco. He had come in the white Land Rover. When you accelerated, the engine growled, a sound my father loved. He had bought the four-by-four for the mountains. For the longer distances, such as the annual drive to Rotterdam and back, he had a green, virtually silent Mercedes.

'Long,' I replied. I had flown from Delhi to Rome, where I had boarded the night train to Verona before continuing my journey via

Bolzano and Fortezza. I felt as if part of me had yet to arrive.

'Here you go,' my father said. 'Your mother made you a *piadina*.'

I unwrapped the aluminium foil and took a bite, tasting the prosciutto and stracchino. It was better warm, but it would do for now. I couldn't get it down my throat fast enough.

'Luca is dead nervous,' my father said. 'I can't remember finding my wedding day that daunting. Your mother had to help him with his cufflinks.' He laughed while he stepped on the gas. 'Maybe he's scared she'll say no!'

The engine growled like a bear as we zipped through the white winter landscape. I clung to the grab handle whenever we tilted in a hairpin turn. Every now and then my eyes fell shut, but I would jolt awake when my head hit the car door.

As we drove down the main street of Cortina d'Ampezzo, my father started talking again. 'I'm curious to see if the church will be full,' he said. 'When Valentino and Anna got married, some people had to stand.' He was referring to the wedding of his brother's son. 'Practically the entire village turned out.' Deep down my father was nervous, too.

'I wouldn't mind a drink,' he said as we approached Venas, 'but I promised to head straight home. Your mother is worried we'll be late. No surprises there.' Still, he slowed down when we spied a bar by the side of the road.

'No, Pappa,' I admonished him. 'We have to get there on time.'

'We've got plenty of time.'

'No.'

'One beer,' he pleaded. '*Una bella bionda*.'

'Beppi!'

'His mother's son,' my father muttered and stepped on the gas. 'There goes my *bionda*, there she goes.'

In winter he liked to drink a beer in the morning, something nearly all ice-cream makers did. But most of them didn't know when to stop. After retirement, their noses tended to get redder and redder. The empty days, the deserted streets — that's what did for them.

We drove past Sophia's parents' big house. Lights were on in every single room. Her father was sitting in the living room, I could see, but I couldn't see his wife and daughter. Maybe they were in the bathroom at the back of the house. I thought of Sophia's long, blonde hair, the hair I had never got to brush.

Smoke billowed out of the chimney of our house, the grey dissolving in the cold blue sky. My father parked the Land Rover next to the Mercedes. A cement mixer blocked the entrance to the garage. 'It's new,' he said proudly.

'I thought you already owned a cement mixer?'

'A different kind. This one's got a greater volume and it's orange.'

My father would never, ever make cement or mortar. Not in this life, anyway.

My mother hugged me and told me how pleased she was with the beautiful weather. She was beaming.

'Come,' she said, 'freshen up and get changed. We'll talk when we're in church.'

Just then Luca emerged from the bathroom, wearing a brand-new suit. His hair was slicked back, and it shone like ebony. In order to squeeze past each other in the narrow corridor, we both had to do a quarter turn, and so it happened that for a brief moment we were standing with our backs against the wall, a tiny space between our bellies and noses. I noticed the bags under his eyes, and presumably he saw mine.

'The big day,' I said.

'Yes.'

'You're looking good.'

'See you later.'

Then he walked on, leaving me, his older brother, his witness, in the corridor. Four words he had spoken to me, four in one year, and they were absolutely meaningless. They were sounds more than words.

The bathroom smelled of him, of his body, the odour I knew from his bedroom, but even more so from the attic in Rotterdam, the sheets he pushed back in the morning, the warm air that spread and reached my nostrils, sometimes in a dream.

I washed my face and put on the suit I had carried with me across more than ten thousand kilometres. The jacket was badly crumpled, but the trousers had retained their sharp crease.

The four of us walked to church, the heels of our shoes tapping on the cobbles. My mother kept glancing at my brother with a smile, and then at me. She looked unbelievably happy, and the wedding ceremony had yet to take place.

There were already quite a few people on the oval square in front of the San Marco Nuovo. They all looked splendid, the men sporting ties and some even hats, their wives smelling of soap and wearing dresses that showed more leg than usual. They looked younger, and their daughters a couple of years older, than their age. Ice-cream makers shook hands and exchanged a few quick words. Little puffs of steam came out of people's mouths. And then the church bells started ringing and everybody went inside.

I sat in the front row, next to my parents and Sophia's mother, who was also a witness. The fur stole she wore did little to conceal the fact that she was the only one in church with bare arms and shoulders. Her dark-blue skirt stopped above the knee.

When the organist started playing, all heads turned, practically as one. Sophia walked down the aisle on her father's arm. She wore white, a long dress with a bodice that gleamed like the inside of an oyster. Her blonde hair was braided in a single plait and wrapped around her head, a golden crown. She all but glided across the church's smooth flagstones, gorgeous and self-assured, looking straight ahead the whole way. Luca beamed as she came towards him.

Although the church was packed — the pews were all full, with people standing at the back — it was dead quiet when they got to the vows. The priest, in his long robes with gold stitching and purple patches on his shoulders, gave the bride and groom a long, hard look before asking them to rise and hold hands. He started saying the age-old words that Luca and Sophia had to repeat.

I watched, I listened, and I would remember this for the rest of my life, but part of me didn't want to be here, in these wooden pews in this church, but in India instead, at the Indira Gandhi International Airport, terribly delayed, waiting for a sky-blue plane while an English voice reads out names and a new load of passengers is disgorged.

Everybody appeared to have been holding their breath, and now that the vows were complete, they relaxed and let go. Applause rose from the pews, my mother cried, and Sophia's mother dabbed at her eyes with a handkerchief. The bride and groom turned around and looked into the church. My brother's eyes found those of my parents', mine found Sophia's. The winter light illuminated her face and her fairytale dress. Only now did I see the change in Sophia, from a girl who caught snowflakes with her tongue to a woman in her prime. She smiled and I smiled back. It felt as if we touched.

Outside, children threw handfuls of rice at the couple. Sophia bowed her head and closed her eyes. Luca turned towards her and they kissed in the white rain. And as I joined in and threw rice at them too, my memory built a bridge back to that day we threw snowballs at one another and I went down.

They got into the old Alfa Romeo, hired from Belluno, which had driven countless newlyweds to married life. The chauffeur wore a cap and smelled of tobacco, and while his nails were yellow, the old-timer car didn't have a scratch on it. Standing in front of the church, I watched the car drive off as a castaway on a desert island watches a ship in the distance.

To touch it isn't necessary for someone to sit close / Even from very far it is possible to touch. It was the voice of the Hindi poet Manglesh Dabral, whom I had heard in Delhi, which now made its way across the sea to me. *Rather, touch the way the tall grass appears to caress the moon and stars.*

My parents walked towards the car. Others followed. A small procession formed, as it did on Sundays, made up of families dressed in their finest, moving along the narrow footpath.

'The next wedding will be yours,' someone said, and I felt a big, strong hand with a calloused thumb on my shoulder.

*

We met again in spring. I had expected her to be showing, but Sophia was as slender as ever. She looked a little bored behind the ice-cream.

'Hello, brother-in-law,' she greeted me with a smile. 'I'd like to give you a kiss, but I'm not tall enough to lean over the counter.'

'You can make me just as happy with an espresso.'

I sat down at a table inside and listened to the noises produced by the espresso machine. As the coffee trickled into the cup, I counted the seconds. Twenty-six, not a breath longer. The machine stalled like an engine.

'It's been raining all morning,' Sophia said as she walked towards me with a tray in her hands. 'It's going to be a bit warmer this afternoon, but still wet.'

'Welcome to the Netherlands.'

'It will remain overcast all week while the wind is set to pick up.'

I thought I heard my mother talking.

They had been open for a week, Sophia told me. But they were off to a bad start. They were selling more coffee than ice-cream.

My parents were out grocery shopping. Luca was in the kitchen; I had glimpsed him through the window, and he me, I would have thought.

I took another good look at Sophia's apron, but nothing showed. Her face didn't look any different, either.

We used to pass rainy days in the ice-cream parlour making cones, but once we got those delivered in boxes we had enough time on our hands to count the rain drops. I read poetry, collections lent to me by Richard Heiman or ones I had bought myself in the bookshop two doors down. The bookshop had a tall window display and a red tomcat traipsing jauntily past the crammed bookcases; the owner was a blonde lady who had written a few books herself, all since long out of print. The reverse of our shop was true for hers: on cold and dark days it was busy, on muggy days people stayed away. But she had come up with a solution. In summer she wore flimsy tops with a plunging neckline. Some men couldn't take their eyes off as she gift-wrapped a book, prompting her to once ask a customer, 'Shall I wrap these two as well?'

At the stroke of five, sometimes earlier, she would open a bottle of wine, while the tomcat in the window basked in the sun breaking through the clouds.

Looking back, it was inevitable really, with the World Poetry offices across the street and a bookshop less than ten metres away. The street was a magnetic force field. It was a miracle my parents and my brother didn't feel it and just stared into space on rainy days. If I ever left a book of poetry on the freezer, nobody picked it up.

Sophia didn't seem to feel it that week, either. Sometimes she enquired after my work, but more often than not she just wanted to hear about the city I had visited: the footpath cafés, the restaurants, the popular night spots. On the rare occasion when I read out a poem, she quickly turned to something else, as though I was doing something illicit. She was my brother's wife and she knew that ice-cream and poetry were incompatible. It was one or the other. Those who listened to the song of the Sirens were lost.

The kitchen door swung open. Luca walked over to us with two spoons in his hands. He wanted us to have a taste.

'Tomato,' said Sophia.

'And basil,' I added.

'Amazing.'

'Extraordinary. I wonder what Beppi will say.'

But Luca had already turned round and gone back into the kitchen.

That dreary spring, three things happened that were seemingly unrelated. My father bought two birds, my brother threw himself into making new ice-cream flavours, and I moved to Rotterdam.

Until then I had lived in Amsterdam, where I continued to work at the publisher's one day a week. Robert Berendsen had made me promise him two things: I would keep a hand in the poetry journal, and I would get as many of his poets as possible onto the World Poetry programme. They were promises made in the pub. I had told him the news after he had taken a sip of his first De Koninck. Many more beers were to follow that evening. As Victor Larssen had predicted, Robert understood my decision. He was happy for me to have the job. 'I think it's a great opportunity,' he said, 'and I'm really curious about the poets you'll discover.'

We talked about the festivals he had visited. 'Liège is very intimate. It's the oldest festival on the calendar. The poets are practically on your lap,' he told me. 'But Medellín beats all the others, hands down. More than a hundred poets are invited and performances take place at lots of different locations: in cafés, in little backrooms, in the street, at the university. It's as if poetry has taken over the city. You have to see it to believe it. During the opening night, over ten thousand people spend seven hours listening to poets out in the open air. And even if it starts raining they stay seated. It goes on until the early hours.'

His eyes got smaller and smaller. We were among the last to leave the café. 'I'm really pleased for you,' he said again as we put our coats on, before adding with a broad smile, 'And of course for our poets, who will all be invited to Rotterdam now.'

With Victor Larssen's blessing, I had established a partnership between World Poetry and the poetry journal. Every year we would publish a special festival edition with poems by the performing poets, supplemented with interviews and essays. My first festival as editor had yet to take place, but I was already spending my days reading, translating, phoning, and writing letters. I was assisted by an intern who was studying Russian. She had spent her childhood in St Petersburg and reckoned there was no greater poet than Marina Tsvetaeva.

She would brook no contradiction.

'*Thinking of something, carelessly, something invisible, buried treasure, step by step, poppy by poppy, I beheaded the flowers, at leisure. So someday, in the dry breath of summer, at the edge of the sown, absentmindedly, death will gather a flower — my own!*' she would recite at me.

Xenia, her name was. Platinum blonde hair, pale skin, and bright red lips. Her boyfriend usually picked her up at the end of the day. He had black hands and occasionally even smudges on his face. He worked in a garage, which is where she met him, when she dropped off her Volkswagen. The V-belt was squeaky and needed replacing; she had fallen for him like a brick.

'Does he read poetry?' I asked after hearing how they had met.

'No, of course not. He's a car mechanic; he likes long-legged blondes.'

'And you like him?'

'Yes,' she replied. 'Are you surprised?'

I didn't know what to say. I thought it was a curious combination, but I didn't want to come across as conservative.

Xenia told me about her lecturer who, when she was studying Russian herself, had an affair with her professor for many years. But now she was married to a window cleaner. They had two children and a beautifully furnished house together. She set off for the university every day while he drove to the suburbs, where he leaned his ladder up against the walls of other people's houses.

'And do you think they're happy?'

'Yes, I think they are,' she said, before immediately correcting herself: 'I know they are.'

My father had married a woman who also hailed from an ice-cream-making family. When she was young, my mother vowed never to work in an ice-cream parlour. She wanted to be a nurse or a kindergarten teacher, but things didn't work out that way; it had been inescapable. Luca had lost his heart to a girl from Modena, the daughter of a factory boss, but she had picked up the *spatola* like a natural.

Meanwhile I had bought a top-floor studio apartment in Rotterdam. The ceiling had been knocked through to the attic, making the room more than six metres tall. But the place was not very big: the kitchen was part of the living room, and my bedroom just a screened-off area. There was no scope for growth.

The apartment was a five-minute walk from the World Poetry offices, and therefore also from the ice-cream parlour. When I went to work, the doors of Venezia were still closed, but I usually glimpsed someone in the semi-darkness. Occasionally my father would gesture for me to come in and have an espresso. On one of those mornings he showed me a cage with two small birds. He had bought them from a Surinamese customer who came in regularly to eat ice-cream with some buddies.

'They're songbirds,' my father told me. 'That's to say, the male is a songbird.'

'What about the female?'

He shrugged his shoulders. 'He's supposed to sing to her.'

I looked at the birds in the cage. They did nothing, and struck me as rather fearful.

'The man I bought them off is the chairman of the Surinamese songbird association,' my father said. 'They have competitions in the park.'

'What kind of competitions?'

'Singing competitions. What else?'

'Do the birds sing well?'

'That's irrelevant. What's the point of a songbird whistling a Puccini aria? The thing is for them to chirp as much and as often as possible. No matter how shrill or out of tune.' My father grabbed another cage and put the female in it. 'The trick is to place them further and further apart,' he explained, 'to encourage the male.' But the male didn't start singing. Instead he just flapped about in his cage and pecked frantically at the small feeding dish. The seeds ended up on the floor.

I was curious to hear what my mother made of this new hobby. 'Will you be entering those competitions as well?' I asked him.

'I can't,' my father said curtly. 'I have to work. I have to help your brother.'

It was time to cross the road; I could tell from my father's face, from the look in his eyes. He had all the tools in the world for a major invention, but he didn't have the time to create it because he had to work in an ice-cream parlour. He owned a songbird, but he couldn't enter competitions because he had to work in an ice-cream parlour.

'Come on,' he urged the male. 'Sing for your female. Go on, then.'

Those were the exact same words I heard him say a couple of days later, except louder and harsher. My mother was standing behind him.

'They don't want to,' she said.

'Sing for your female, damn it. Sing! Go on.'

'If you scream at them, they get scared.'

He moved the female. The distance between the birds was around three metres now, but still the male wouldn't sing. It fluttered around its cage.

'Stop fluttering,' my father yelled. 'You're meant to sing, not flutter. You want me to show you how? Well? *Tweet! Tweet!* It's not that hard, is it? *Tweet! Tweet!*'

'Beppi, please leave those birds alone.'

'Leave *me* alone!' he said. 'You're driving me mad. Don't do this, don't do that. You're watching me all day long. Why don't you leave me alone? I want to be alone with my birds. Go away!'

I had never heard him have a go at my mother like this. There had been plenty of disagreements and discussions over the years, but my father had never yelled at my mother. He had always managed to crack a joke. Some of them were funnier than others, but still.

It turned out to be the opening gambit, the first of many arguments. The beginning of what would become years of vitriol that, strange as it may sound, culminated in an infatuation with a hammer-thrower weighing eighty-three kilos.

'I want peace and quiet!' Beppi roared through the ice-cream parlour.

My brother didn't appear behind the little window in the kitchen door. He was busy weighing sugar, separating eggs, and experimenting with new ingredients. He churned, he listened, he tasted, he improved. He worked even harder than my father had ever done: eighteen-, nineteen-hour days. All for a new flavour. Ice-cream made with gorgonzola, with rosemary and chocolate, with yoghurt and Amarena cherries — a swirling dance of red and white.

Sophia was still in bed. She was getting up later and later. The ice-cream parlour opened its doors at ten in the morning, but some days she wouldn't come down before eleven, my mother told me.

'Maybe it's the weather,' she said. 'She's bound to feel better again when the sun comes out.'

Her hair had grown darker; it had taken on the dull shade of a gold picture frame. It was the summer spent in the ice-cream parlour, the winter in Italy, and the spring without traipsing through fields of dandelions. The sun's rays had struggled to get through to her.

And then the female died. My father found the bird early one morning, lying on the bottom of her cage, her beak in the male's shit, or her own, perhaps. At first he was inconsolable and refused to talk to anyone. 'Dead,' he muttered. 'Dead.'

I made him an espresso, but he didn't touch it. He just kept staring at the lifeless female in his hands.

'Dead, dead, dead.'

As if he foresaw his own fate.

'Beppi, we can buy a new bird.'

He didn't react to my mother's suggestion, exceptional though it was — at long last, he was allowed to buy something.

We left him to his grief, but when I shut the World Poetry office to go out for lunch, I saw my father beckoning to me in high spirits. Had the female risen from the dead? Had it just been a fainting fit?

'The male is singing!' said my father, happy as a child. 'He's singing, whistling, chirping. Listen!'

I had already heard. And so had everybody else in the ice-cream parlour. The male was making the noise of an aviary full of birds. He was singing like nobody's business, as if all this time there had been a stopper in his throat that had now been removed.

'He's elated,' my father said. 'His female is dead.'

The bird kept cheeping and chirping, but my mother and Sophia were quiet. They were standing behind the counter, even though there were no customers to serve. They had all the time in the world to stare at the rain.

'Look how cheerful he is. It's as if he's celebrating. Fantastic!'

I observed the male, which looked like a far cry from the bird that had been silent all this time.

'What did you do with the female?'

'The female?' my father replied. 'Forget about the female, she's history. Listen to him singing. Like a champion.'

'Did you bury her?'

'All this time he was unable to sing because he was unhappy, because he felt oppressed — who knows, perhaps he even suffered from depression.'

The way he said it, you would have thought that he had just made a discovery, the invention of a lifetime. And he had once more linked his fate to a bird, albeit to a living specimen this time.

'Yes, go on. There's no need to be sad now,' my father encouraged the bird.

Suddenly, my mother started sobbing. She didn't make a sound and I couldn't see her tears — she had her back to me — but I could tell by the hand Sophia put on her shoulder.

My father was oblivious to her silence. All he heard was his tweeting bird. It was an infernal noise — very rapid, with brief, intermittent pauses. You stopped hearing it at some point, like a ticking clock, but that was really the only point in its favour. It drove the customers who came in for a cup of coffee absolutely insane.

'He's cheery,' my father explained to everyone. 'His female just died.'

Some customers laughed, others shook their head.

One person said, 'You ought to cover the cage with a sheet.'

My father replied, 'He's been through so much already.'

In the end it was my brother who banished the bird to the first-floor kitchen. The customers would no longer be bothered by him, but it meant my mother was forced to look after and listen to him day after day — my parents' bedroom was next to the kitchen-diner.

Every time we chatted when I stopped by the ice-cream parlour, she complained about it. 'He starts singing at five in the morning, and then Beppi jumps out of bed to encourage him. He goes downstairs to fetch a spoonful of sweets. As a reward.' The sweets my mother referred to were those children liked on their scoops of ice-cream: sprinkles.

Mamma, can I have sprinkles? It was a question asked upwards of three hundred times a day.

'The minute there's nothing to do he rushes upstairs to listen to the twittering.'

Did she mind the attention given to the little bird more than the dreary weather? The forecast for the next couple of days wasn't very promising, either. It may well have been the worst start in years. Of course, some people always fancied ice-cream, regardless of the weather. 'It tastes just as good under an umbrella,' they would say, or 'We won't let a bit of rain get to us.'

The folk of Rotterdam were pragmatic, and yet they all craved the sun and long, lazy days.

One day when I visited, Sophia was wearing a pink dress. The colour had come back: she was wearing lipstick and had put a ribbon in her braid. Just as her mother was an unlikely apparition in the mountains, Sophia stood out in the grey city. She gave me the briefest of smiles, but it wasn't like touching.

Luca was experimenting with ice-cream in the kitchen, my father was with his bird, and I would shortly go to my apartment and sit down on my second-hand Chesterfield with a book of poetry. All three of us in our own worlds.

A couple of years later, in a hotel room in Paris, where I was attending the Marché de la Poésie festival, I was lying naked on the bed, looking at the pink wallpaper. I'd just had a shower and was staring idly at the repeating pattern of poppies and curlicues when I discovered that everything in the room was pink: the carpet, the curtains, the sheets, the bedside tables, the desk, the phone, the ceiling. And to my horror, I noticed that the head of my dick was the same colour. That lonely day in Paris, Sophia's summer dress came to mind and I disentangled the threads that had got all jumbled up during that miserable spring.

I realised why my brother was trying to make ice-cream out of olive oil, why he mixed melon and mint, why he tinkered with a recipe until the early hours, and why Sophia sometimes stayed in bed until ten-thirty and spent the rest of the day staring at the deep puddles and the little children in rubber boots jumping into them.

Finally summer arrived, in all its glory, and everything that comes with it: pale blue skies, clammy sheets, short skirts, the lingering light followed by seductively twinkling stars, freckles, wasps, hailstones, and sunburnt noses. It was as if the summer was aware of its brief reign and now erupted in all its intensity and eagerness.

A common mantra among ice-cream makers is this: 'It's better to have a bad spring than a bad summer.' But in Bar Posta, late in the evening, you would often hear this profundity: 'It's better to be thirsty in winter than in summer.'

With the heat came the new flavours. For the first time in the ice-cream parlour's history, the display was rearranged. Some regulars were put out. One week, there would be no container of raspberry sorbet next to the chocolate ice-cream, but fig-and-almond ice-cream. The week after, the raspberry sorbet might reappear, while the chocolate was replaced with coffee-cardamom.

'You're chasing all of your customers away,' my father warned Luca.

'One spoon and they're sold.'

'But they're not brave enough. I've been selling ice-cream for over forty years and I know my customers. They don't want surprises; they want strawberry, vanilla, mango, and chocolate. There's the odd eccentric who likes cinnamon or After Eight, but nothing too fancy — no weird combinations, and certainly no ingredients they have to look up in a dictionary.'

'I'll let them have a taste.'

'Don't,' my father reacted. 'Don't give your ice-cream away.'

'I'm not giving it away. I'm giving people the chance to try flavours they're not familiar with.'

'You don't know what you're letting yourself in for. You know what the Dutch are like. They'll want to try everything. A spoonful here, a spoonful there, and how about a bite of this and a bite of that. Like in the supermarket. They're happy to try, but they never buy. I've seen it with my own eyes. They'll all wheel their trolleys straight to the stand where a woman is preparing an Asian stir-fry. Would they like a taste? So? What's it like? Delicious? Yes? But all they take to the checkout is a loaf of bread, a carton of milk, and a pound of green beans.'

'Have you had a taste yourself?' my brother asked. He held up a spoon. Fig-and-almond ice-cream.

'You'll go bankrupt if you let everybody taste your ice-cream; you don't have the margins for that sort of thing. I haven't worked hard all these years to build up a viable business to pass it on and see it go bankrupt within a matter of months.'

'Open your mouth.'

My brother inserted the spoon, as one does with little children who refuse to eat.

All was quiet for a moment. Then my father smiled. 'This is terrific,' he said. 'This is delicious, this is unbelievably good.'

The news about the wonderful flavours spread across the city like wildfire. People came to have a look and a taste and were instantly sold. The newspapers wrote about them, and new customers joined the queue. People came from all over, even from across the border. It was busier than ever.

I, too, had to join the queue. Every single seat outside was taken. The school holidays had started and it was a glorious day. Mothers held their hyperactive children by the hand. 'I want strawberry with sprinkles,' I heard ahead of me, and behind me two little brothers shouted almost but not quite at the same time, 'Mamma, can we have chocolate with sprinkles?'

My mother and Sophia leaned over the ice-cream and scooped it into cups and cones. I was able to watch them without being seen myself. I was peeping, really, but couldn't help myself. My mother was faster than Sophia, and moved effortlessly. It was all down to experience, although even her *spatola* occasionally faltered above the tubs with the new flavours.

'I want sprinkles,' I heard a little girl say to Sophia.

'And what flavour would you like?'

'Sprinkles.'

'No, the flavour,' her mother prompted her. 'You need to tell her the flavour.'

The little girl thought long and hard before answering, 'I can't remember.'

All I could see was her back, the butterfly bows in the blonde, almost shoulder-length plaits. I couldn't see her small greedy mouth, her golden eyebrows, her deep-blue or grey-green eyes.

'Vanilla?' the mother said to her daughter.

'Oh, yes, vanilla with sprinkles,' she exclaimed in delight.

But Sophia's left hand didn't stir to pick up a cone. Her right hand didn't reach for the ice-cream with the *spatola*. Nobody in the queue noticed — they were all discussing the ice-cream, the flavours they were going for — but I saw my mother putting her hand on Sophia's shoulder.

'And for me, a cup with pineapple-grapefruit and fromage frais with prunes,' the mother said. 'I'm really curious to see what it's like.'

The news even made it as far as Venas di Cadore. Serafino Dall'Asta had written a piece in *L'Amico del Popolo*, the local paper. The journalist had phoned Luca and asked him whether he had come up with all the flavours himself. My brother told him that he spent hours on end experimenting with combinations, but that he liked to take inspiration from customers as well. Just as once upon a time people brought fruits to my great-grandfather, they now came up with suggestions for new flavours. Cherry and chocolate, banana and coconut, blackberry and vanilla.

And just like my great-grandfather, Luca kept creating new ice-cream varieties. He introduced a flavour of the week and a board advertising special combinations. A second display was built into the counter for yet more tubs. And so the summer went by, with long queues and bare legs on the terrace, with gleeful noises and beaming faces around midnight.

*

Together with Victor Larssen I travelled to poetry festivals across Europe and, at the end of July, as fat raindrops hissed on the runway, to Medellín for the first time. The festival's opening night took place in a theatre hewn from rocks halfway up Mount Nutibara. We drove there in large buses, travelling across one of South America's biggest cities. Cars, scooters, and minivans were everywhere. Larssen told me that not so long ago Medellín was the most criminal city in the world. People were afraid to leave their homes. The newspapers were full of political assassinations; the streets were the scene of massacres. There were fatalities every single day, most of the victims young and anonymous, but the puddles of blood also spread around gang leaders, FARC members, and senior military figures. 'The festival is a response to the evil,' Larssen said. 'It was set up by the poets and editors of the Latin American poetry magazine *Prometeo*. They wanted to offer an alternative to the corruption, the violence, the brutal murders in broad daylight, and they've pulled it off. What was once South America's capital of crime has now become the city with the world's biggest poetry festival.'

I looked at the mountain range in front of us. Medellín was situated in a bowl, at the bottom of a basin. The city was surrounded by mountains, and one of those was Mount Nutibara. As the road became steeper, the engine of the bus struggled with the gears at times. We drove through a jungle, flanked by trees with dark green leaves. The scratching sound of insects and the occasional loud screech of a bird came in through the open windows.

On the bus were poets from Italy, Somalia, Mexico, Canada, Norway. A total of seventy poets would be reading on opening night. I had heard stories about the thousands of visitors, the seats hewn from rock, the applause that rose up to heaven. 'You won't believe your eyes,' Robert Berendsen had said.

The bus came to a halt on a widened verge, the kind of spot where a couple of years back corpses might have been thrown out of a car. I heard some poets wonder whether we were in the right place. Surely this couldn't be it? The Parnassus: a ghastly place in the forest.

One after the other, we got out and started going down a steep stone staircase. The oldest poets crept down slowly, like beetles, their younger colleagues hot on their heels. Every now and then the procession halted and a poet would stare down, but the theatre was nowhere to be seen. At the bottom of the staircase was a small hut you had to walk around. And that's when you saw it: a gigantic amphitheatre with ascending stone rows, an arena in the jungle. Here and there people were already seated, as the audience poured in via gates on either side.

'It's possible to approach the theatre from below,' I heard Larssen say above me. 'There's a car park at the foot of the mountain from where you take a very steep staircase up. But this is the best way, with the theatre suddenly looming up ahead.' Like a square in Rome, after navigating numerous narrow alleyways — unexpected and grandiose.

I walked further down until I reached the stage. It was around forty metres wide and covered by a roof. Enormous rows of speakers were suspended from grids on either side. Although not on yet, the spotlights were trained on some seventy white plastic bucket seats on stage. We had the same chairs on Venezia's terrace. My father put them out every morning and stacked them up again at night. There were two lecterns with a microphone each: one for the poet, one for the translator.

Seats had been reserved for us in the front row, but Larssen wanted to sit higher up, among the general audience. At other festivals, too, he rarely sat in the seats with the white 'reserved' slips. At the World Poetry Festival he always stood to the side of the stands because he was too nervous to sit down.

The stone rows of the theatre filled up. The festival was to open at seven o'clock, but a full thirty minutes prior to the official start all the seats were occupied. You could see men and women climbing trees and sitting on branches, and in a field higher up, a clearing in the forest, there were people too.

The scale of it, the crowds: it all felt like a concert. They were ordinary city folk — labourers, bus drivers, market traders, as well as families with children. They had brought food (deep-fried *empanadas* with chorizo and grilled corn on the cob) and beverages (Coca-Cola, Águila beer, cheap whisky). The sky was clear. We would have no rain tonight, unlike that time when Robert Berendsen was here and everybody simply stayed put under a poncho or an umbrella, listening to poetry.

Meanwhile all the poets had taken their seats on stage. I spotted Lars Gustafsson and Breyten Breytenbach, as well as poets I didn't recognise.

As they do at concerts, the audience sensed that the programme was about to begin. People wolf-whistled and clapped their hands. Children stood up and joined in. 'Not long now,' Larssen said. It was like Cadore before it snowed — when the snow was in the air and the people could smell it. Everybody knew it could be any moment now.

No lights came on. In fact, they wouldn't be switched on until several hours later, when the sky had turned a deep blue. The festival director walked on and welcomed the audience and the poets. He clenched his fist and whipped up the crowd. It sounded as if he was chanting battle cries. 'This is nothing,' Larssen said. 'Wait till he starts speechifying.'

Every poet read ten poems, with each poem followed by the Spanish translation. Again and again, a man or a woman got up from one of the white chairs and walked to the front, to the microphone. Seven hundred poems in a single night. It was a marathon session, but the poets did everything in their power to retain the audience's attention. They would start with a declaration of love to Medellín, for example, or bow deeply to the audience. 'This is the most beautiful day of my life,' a poet from the Congo said. The applause was a tsunami crashing from the top row down.

At one o'clock in the morning we were still listening to poems, with frequent revolutionary speeches from the festival director thrown in. He roared into the microphone that poetry could save humankind from capitalism and imperialism. The people whooped and clapped under the stars. And then another poet would rise to his feet and read his work to more than ten thousand listeners. I forgot all about the poetry readings in badly lit library rooms. I forgot the presentations drowned out by noise in pubs and cafés. I forgot the dismal literary afternoons where people felt obliged to clap after each poem, sometimes even when the poet merely paused between stanzas. I tilted my head and tried to make out a falling star, while poetry poured into my ears. This is what it must have been like to stand atop the Parnassus and be enchanted by poetry. This is what it must be all about.

After the opening night, Medellín itself was taken over. For eight days, the poets were driven around the city of millions in minivans. Huge audiences turned up wherever they were: in theatres, in the open air, at the university. Larssen and I immersed ourselves in this city of poetry only to resurface a week later in Parque Lleras, where we came up for air and drank a glass of ice-cold Águila.

Meanwhile, in Rotterdam, my brother created ever more unusual flavours: herring ice-cream; rose ice-cream; ice-cream made of fennel, with pear and basil notes. Very rarely was there a flavour that didn't work out, or a result that wasn't quite what he had in mind. An Italian man had asked Luca if he could make ice-cream from *prosciutto crudo*, dry-cured ham. Luca set to work, juggling ingredients and listening to the sound of the scraper blade. A quick glance told him that the ice-cream had come out right, but when he took a bite the flavour disgusted him. It was revolting. Ham ice-cream simply didn't work. Even the most committed carnivore wouldn't like it.

Ice-cream made of alcoholic beverages was difficult to prepare, too. Luca had made ice with Moscato d'Asti, a dessert wine, and he was experimenting with the combination of prosecco and red currant. He wasn't happy with the result, and the tubs never made it into the display. But Luca refused to give up. He kept tinkering with the recipe; he kept retreating into the kitchen.

This experimentation went on for two more years — two short winters and two long ice-cream maker's summers; two years during which Sophia's hair became duller and duller and my father's songbird chirped louder and louder; two years during which I flew around the globe from festival to festival and I felt like a stranger in my own apartment. Two years chock-full of poetry and ice-cream, and then my brother started talking to me again. He took me aside in the kitchen. I noticed that he had a new system for the dry ingredients, and that the freezer had been replaced, too. He had bought a third ice-cream machine, a smaller, horizontal model. The white tiles on the wall were pristine; the worktop gleamed like never before. Or was it new, too? As we hadn't spoken in years, the silence had become familiar, however uncomfortable and painful it was.

Two years on top of ten years. That's how long he had been silent.

'You've got to help me,' he said then, and looked at me with the same dark eyes I had. 'You've got to get Sophia pregnant.'

Jacuzzis and Ironing Boards

Hotel receptions are almost always staffed by women, while the night porter is usually a man in his late forties. Hotel corridors are like streets, with identical doors on either side. The light is diffuse, the walls matte, and the carpet muffles all sound: heels, rattling wheelie suitcases, voices late at night. Sometimes, somewhere halfway down, there is a random shoe-polishing machine.

The bigger hotel chains all have keycards for their rooms, but in smaller establishments the receptionist will hand the guest a key on a ring with the room number. In Ljubljana, in Hotel Center, the keyring came in the shape of a fluorescent gnome; at the Hotel Royal in Tetovo, the key was attached to a heavy bullet. ('Do not lose key,' were the receptionist's only words when I checked in at Tetovo.) There's a greater risk of the room door not opening with keycards than with keys. They can be inserted in four different ways, and even when you get it right the unlocking mechanism may refuse to comply and you have no choice but to return to reception.

Whether two, three, four, or five stars, the room will contain a chair, a desk, a lamp, and a television. There's usually a window with curtains on a rail and a bed flanked by two cabinets. The drawer of the one on the left often has a bible. In Oslo, in Hotel Rica, I also found an opened packet of condoms. In Medellín, they were actually lying on top of the bedside table, along with a packet of Lucky Strike and a strip of paracetamol. In Brisbane, a shiny green apple awaited me; in Edmonton, a box of mints.

On the desk there'll be a folder with information about the hotel, the restaurant menu, a tourist leaflet, or a map of the city, as well as two sheets of writing paper and two envelopes. There will be a tray with a kettle. The welcome note on top of the television will be in two languages, sometimes even three. The Metropole Hotel in Brussels has the message in nine languages.

There's a safe in the wardrobe; the ironing board either folds out or leans against the wall. The larger wardrobe will have clotheshangers — a single plastic one at the Van der Valk Hotel in Maastricht, twenty-four wooden hangers at Grand Hotel Karel V in Utrecht. An extra blanket lies on the bottom shelf.

In the bathroom you will find two small glasses beside the wash basin, a shoe-polish sponge and a shower cap in separate bags, a small guest soap and a shampoo and a shower gel, or a shampoo and shower gel in one. The hairdryer is in a drawer. And there will usually be a sewing kit, matches, and a ballpoint pen with the hotel logo somewhere.

The colours are different wherever I go, but yellow, pink, and pale blue are popular. Modern hotel rooms are as white as the walls of a dental practice. The paintings are never crooked. Nine times out of ten they are reproductions — sometimes an old master, more often something by Picasso, or Michelangelo's angels. Jim Morrison is popular, too. I may have woken up with him on no fewer than twenty occasions, sometimes in Pop Art colours or as a gelatine silver print, always half-naked. Room 9 of The Albany in Scotland's St Andrews has three identical reproductions on the wall. It's a plate from a botanical book, a black-and-white drawing of a milk thistle. It took me four days to realise there were three completely identical drawings in completely identical frames.

The breakfast room at the Monasterium Hotel in Ghent, a former monastery, boasts drawings of bodies with copious pubic hair.

Some chains decorate their rooms the same the world over. Hotel beds may be two thousand kilometres apart and yet surrounded by identical lamps, tables, and wardrobes. Walls, ceilings, and carpets are no different, either. The hotel guest wakes up not knowing whether he is in Berlin, Toronto, or São Paulo. What differs is the view. The Museuminsel from the tall windows in Berlin; the CN Tower in Toronto; and in São Paulo, a whitegoods store selling second-hand sofas.

Hotel Panorama in Bologna doesn't have a view. At the Sea View Hotel in Durban, where each corridor has a security guard, the windows overlook the Indian Ocean. At Hôtel du Lac in Cotonou, the view comes courtesy of the Atlantic Ocean. Stand on the balcony and you can see whale fins come to the surface with the naked eye. Reservations for the corner room have to be made three months in advance.

Room 16 of the Roxford Lodge Hotel in Dublin has a sauna. You actually hit your knees against the timber wall when you get out of bed. The bathroom door opens only partially. All the rooms at the Bristol Hotel in Odessa boast a jacuzzi. The folder with information and the restaurant menu also contains a leaflet for a marriage agency, would you believe. There is a mirror above the bed of Room 402 of the First Hotel in Paris; the curtains are made of shiny black satin. The porter of The Courtyard by Marriott in Tbilisi wears a handsome blue uniform, helps carry suitcases and, in a whisper, offers to supply young ladies for the night. The Cinema Hotel in Tel Aviv has two free porn channels.

It's rare for a room to have fishbone parquet flooring.

The air conditioning in Hotel Tryp by Wyndham in Leipzig can't be switched off. In Room 126 of the Novotel in Beaune, the iron blows the fuse. The items that can be faulty in a room: the light, the television, the kettle, the phone, the alarm clock, the hairdryer. You wouldn't believe how many rooms have defective showerheads. In Room 13 of Hotel Balkan in Belgrade, the toilet seat looked as if someone had taken a bite out of it. Normally, a problem gets fixed after a phone call to reception, but the strategy at this hotel was to blame it on the guest.

I was told the seat had been intact in the morning and had broken after my arrival. This could only mean one thing: I was the one who had taken a bite out of the toilet seat.

The roof of the Oovotel in Ulaanbaatar is leaky.

In Room 404 of the Bayclub Hotel in Haifa, I found fingernails in the windowsill.

The chambermaids at Hotel Catalunya in Barcelona will enter the room regardless of a *Do not disturb* sign on the door. The housekeeping staff at the Novo Hotel Impero in Trieste is made up of stunning Slovenian women — I saw red lace peeking out over the trousers of the chambermaid on my corridor — but more often than not they are hefty ladies in drab aprons. They rarely wear the white caps Gabriel Dan dreams of in *Hotel Savoy*.

Fresh flowers or a poem on your pillow are rarities, too. Hanging on the wall of Room 612 of the Royal Marine Hotel in Dún Laoghaire is the head of a wild boar.

Bellboys are threatened with extinction.

Some hotels are so big they can accommodate all the delegates of a conference. Before it's even seven in the morning, the place will sound as if a market is being set up in the corridor. The walls of the Travelodge in London are made of cardboard. If someone in the neighbouring room farts under the sheets, it sounds as if you let one off yourself.

In Hotel Spreebogen in Berlin, I heard a knock on my door in the middle of the night.

The bed in Room 109 of Het Paleis in Groningen is inside a closet. Five minutes after checking in, well-trained staff phone the room and enquire whether everything is satisfactory, and whether the guest would like to order something to eat or drink, perhaps.

The hotel in Bombay was still under construction when I stayed; the upper storeys had yet to be completed. I could hear drilling and hammering high above me, and the occasional loud bang. My room overlooked the construction workers' rubbish tip. Mangy mongrels ran in front of a bulldozer, and rubbish was being burnt on several pyres. The extractor fan in the kitchen hadn't been connected yet; the entire hotel reeked of onion. Rats crept up and down the long bare corridors. Out of a pipe in the corner of the room, rusty brown drops splashed onto the untreated concrete. The bottom of the bathtub was covered in dust and sand.

Every thirty minutes, reception would call the phone beside the bed: 'Are you comfortable in your room, sir?'

My Brother's Seed

They may have been at it for three or four years. 'It's not happening,' my brother said when I still hadn't answered his question. We stood face-to-face in the kitchen. One of the ice-cream machines was churning.

I didn't know what to say. All sorts of questions ran riot in my mind, but I couldn't actually formulate one. We hadn't spoken for so long.

'It's not working,' Luca said. 'It's my fault.'

For years I had been trying to talk to him, to tear down the wall he had erected. He had ignored me, had looked at me like a total stranger, had turned his back on me, had attended to the Cattabriga, had pretended to be asleep. And now that I had given up, now that we both had completely different lives and we were strangers more than brothers, he began to talk.

'My sperm isn't viable, it's not moving.' He didn't point down at his crotch, as I might have; his eyes remained fixed on mine. 'We've been to the hospital — we've been to the hospital dozens of times. To begin with they said we ought to be patient, that we had to keep trying. We were young, we had all the time in the world. But that's the thing that alarmed me most: the fact that we were young and it wasn't happening.'

On a couple of occasions I'd been terrified that I might have gotten a woman pregnant. I hadn't always used a condom — either I didn't have them with me or they had run out. One time a woman had taken the morning-after pill. At least four girls brought me out in a cold sweat when they didn't get their period on time, and twice I watched as the line slowly appeared on a pregnancy test. Thankfully the second line failed to materialise.

A girl at university had told me about her abortion. A boy in Portugal had gotten her pregnant. All she knew was his first name: Eduardo. Another girl's pregnancy had ended in a miscarriage. She had been incredibly relieved. Both girls had sworn never to have unsafe sex again. They had pulled a condom out of their purses.

That's as close to having children as I ever got. All around me I saw contemporaries — friends from Rotterdam, poets, former classmates — pushing prams, and on a warm day Venezia's terrace was full of young mothers and photogenic babies. But so far I had felt no longing for a child. I couldn't imagine having my own family.

Luca listened to the ice-cream machine for a moment, but didn't move. The scraper blade told him he had enough time to continue his story. 'We were always acutely aware of people's eyes on us,' he said. 'The winters were dreadful. Sophia's mother kept asking, "So? When am I going to hear the patter of tiny feet?" Or, "Am I going to be a grandma soon?" When you get married, you're expected to have children straight away. Nine months, that's how long it can take, at most. Beppi kept asking too, quite openly at the kitchen table, whether we were cuddling enough. What do you say to that? What can you do, except stare at your plate? We were so ashamed. Sometimes we'd stay in all day. Beppi would be in the basement, Mamma in the kitchen, and we'd sit on the sofa in the lounge. A childless winter is as dead as the summer in Venas. But meanwhile we had to keep trying. Sophia kept track of when we were supposed to do it and then we'd both undress in the dark, as if at the clap of a hand. Sometimes she would only pull down her pyjama bottoms. I could hear the bed frame creaking, the mattress squeaking, the floor crunching. I could hear everything. I could even hear the church bells ring twice. Except I didn't hear Sophia. She would be dead quiet and pull her bottoms back up when it was over.'

He kept nothing back. He poured out his heart, like he had done when we were little. Back when he had fallen in love with Sophia and had turned to me for advice, when I had whispered lines into his ear and used to come along to her house. Back then he had told me everything and I had listened to him.

'And when I simply wanted to make love, because I happened to feel like it, she'd tell me it wasn't the right time. She didn't turn her back on me, but jabbed her knees, her sharp bones up against my stomach.'

The long years of silence meant nothing. Silence was nothing but air. It could be compressed quite easily, until there was nothing left. Twelve years — every year a little snowflake that sublimated before it hit the ground.

'Finally we got a referral and we ended up going in for a battery of tests. It was awful. All those waiting rooms, they drove me mad. All those women with big bellies waiting there, as well. And the two of us among them.' Luca paused a moment, as though checking whether I was still listening. I nodded for him to continue. 'Everything was fine with Sophia,' he said. 'Her ovaries, her ovulation — everything was in working order. It was me. The problem lay with me. With my sperm.'

I had never been frank about women with my brother. I had always kept everything to myself, except for that time in Bar Posta when we were playing cards. But that was only because Sophia had been present. She was the one I had told the story to. He had just been sitting there with an empty beer glass in front of him.

'It wasn't viable; it had no motility. It was doing absolutely nothing. According to the gynaecologist, the chances of pregnancy were nil. We could only hope for a miracle.'

I glanced at his crotch, very briefly. I couldn't help it. Luca noticed.

'It felt like I'd been emasculated,' he said. 'My seed was worthless. I'd lost my function.'

It reminded me of a story I had heard in Amsterdam when I was working at Tofani's. It was an anecdote about an ice-cream maker, one of many, but this one had never made it to our dining table. I never had the guts to pass it on. Besides, I didn't even know whether it was true.

One time it was set in an ice-cream parlour in Zwolle, the next in Breda. The story revolved around a young ice-cream maker, not the owner's son but an assistant from Cadore. He was really ugly, with a face covered in acne. The girls looked right through him. All those beautiful young girls in their summer dresses, sitting outside the store eating ice-cream — some days it looked as if a swarm of brightly coloured butterflies had descended on the terrace.

The ugly young man had his revenge in the kitchen. Thinking about their bare legs and shiny lips, he jerked off above a metal container filled with a fresh mix of ice-cream. And while out there in the glorious sunshine they continued to ignore the ice-cream maker, wouldn't deign to look at him, the most beautiful girls in town licked ices with his sperm in it.

My brother had conquered the most beautiful one of all, had managed to secure her for himself, but his seed did nothing inside her body.

'I remember walking out of the gynaecologist's consulting room and getting into the lift. Inside were a couple of men in white coats, pagers in their breast pockets, and two or three other people. I saw the tears rolling down Sophia's cheeks and wanted to put my arm around her, but I couldn't. I was afraid she'd push me away, that she'd be angry because it was my fault.

'We were blinded by the daylight as we walked through the sliding doors. We didn't say a word on our way back to the ice-cream parlour. It's a five-minute walk, if that, but it felt like five days. I remember crossing at a red light while Sophia stopped, waiting for the light to turn green. It's the kind of image you keep seeing long after, even with your eyes closed, one that stays with you forever. We were on either side of the road. Cars whizzed past; a motorbike revved and roared. I looked at Sophia and saw an unhappy woman.

'In the ice-cream parlour she tied on her apron and picked up the *spatola*. I went to the back, to the kitchen, and got stuck in. It was one of those sweltering days, warm and incredibly muggy, with big, ponderous clouds in the sky. But the thunder and lightning never came.

By the afternoon the queue stretched out into the street. Sophia's back was drenched, as were Mamma's and Beppi's. I'd haul in new tubs of ice-cream before quickly fleeing back into the kitchen. The machines were scraping non-stop and would keep on churning deep into the night. The following day was set to be even warmer. They were dog days, the days it dawned on us that we would never have children.

'When I finally went upstairs, Sophia may have been in bed for hours, but I could tell by her breathing that she wasn't asleep. I thought she might want to talk and reached for her hands under the covers. "Leave me alone," she said. It was the only thing she'd say that week.'

Luca stopped, and there was a brief silence between us. Lasting three or four seconds, it was long enough for a thought to surface and unfurl while we kept looking at each other: we were no strangers, and we never would be. I was older; he was stronger. I was darker; he was shorter. But we were brothers.

'IVF wasn't an option for us. And there were no other treatments, either. All we could do was hope for a miracle, as the gynaecologist had said. We'd been given a leaflet on adoption, but Sophia had thrown it away. She wanted a child of her own. Every time she looked at me her eyes told me that. And that I'd failed, that it was my fault. At some point I actually became afraid to look at her. We only talked in the pitch dark, in bed, when I was worn out from ice-cream making and she was shedding all the tears she had held back during the day. She refused to accept it, couldn't accept it. "It's different for you," she said. "No," I replied, "it's not." "Yes, it is." But she didn't explain what was different. She was probably right, anyway. Something inside me was resigned to it. Maybe because it was my fault. It was me who was infertile, not her. That's what allowed me to accept it. It was a coping mechanism of sorts. I don't know how else to put it. But don't get me wrong, I also dreamed of a child. Of a boy I'd carry on my shoulders and kick a ball with. Of a daughter like Sophia, enchanting and blonde.'

I could smell pistachio and a very faint whiff of citrus. As the air bubbles were incorporated, taking their place among the ice crystals and the cream, the ice began to release its aromas. It became lighter, the volume gradually bigger. It was orange, I was almost certain of it. Orange and pistachio ice-cream.

'Sophia could be rattled by a line she read somewhere, a song on the radio, a random remark, or a kid ordering an ice-cream. You know what they're like, standing in front of the counter — they can just about see the ice-cream, and the sight of all those flavours practically makes their heads spin. More often than not they only get to choose two flavours, two out of twenty-two. That's a mind-boggling task for a child of four. The brain tries to get to grips with all the possibilities and gets everything mixed up. Sophia is bringing the *spatola* to the ice and asks what flavour the boy or girl wants, but there's no answer, and time stands still as they look at each other.

'The guilt began to weigh on me. It was as if something broke between the two of us, the way something broke between you and me when you went to Amsterdam. When you chose poetry and left the ice-cream parlour behind. When you left me behind. Did you think I had no dreams? Did you think the ice-cream parlour was the only thing on my mind? Did you have any idea of the consequences when you packed it all in? Well, did you? There aren't that many options, there's only one answer: I had to stay here, I had to keep the ice-cream parlour afloat.'

This moment would come back to haunt me. These sentences, this accusation. It would surface when sleep eluded me in another time zone, in a small room with a chair, a desk, a lamp, and a television. Outside it was night, but I was wide awake and my mind kept churning. *Well?* This was the question I kept hearing. In New Brunswick, in Sydney, in Chicago. Why hadn't I answered my brother? Was it because I never had any doubt that Luca wanted to take over the ice-cream parlour? It never occurred to me that he might have wanted to do something different, that he too had wanted to stray from the path mapped out for us. I was eighteen when I made the decision; I was completely self-absorbed.

Well?

Not that there had been room for an answer. Luca carried on talking after his question. I could have interrupted him, but maybe I realised, like my brother, that there was no time, that the ice-cream was nearly done. The scraping blade was making an ever-longer sound. I couldn't hear exactly when the ice-cream was done, only when it was nearly there. It was nearly there.

'When you left,' Luca said, 'I no longer had a choice. It was out of my hands. And yes, I really went for it, I shouldered my responsibility. But I decided to stop talking to you, to say nothing, not a word. However much you talked to me, however hard you kept trying, I kept my mouth shut. You could get lost, with your poetry and your trips to South America and Asia while I was working like a horse over here. But now I have to talk to you because we can't carry on like this. Because everybody is quiet. Sophia is sad all day and becoming more and more withdrawn. I can barely look Beppi and Mamma in the eye. They've stopped asking, but that's not to say they're not thinking about it. Mamma is mumbling prayers the livelong day. When she scoops ice-cream, when she counts change, when she gazes at the rain.'

I had noticed that my mother seemed to be praying more than usual, but I thought she was praying for Beppi, for his mental health.

'Sometimes I wonder how it's possible. How can you be sad about something you don't have? But then I look at Sophia and I see her dull hair and her red eyes and there's no trace of happiness left. I'm sad because she is, and I'm not functioning properly because she's not functioning properly. All we're good for is making and selling ice-cream.'

There were countless images I could see with my eyes closed. Sophia sticking out her tongue and catching snowflakes. Sophia pulling at my nose with her cold fingers and shaking her head in mock disapproval. Sophia in her mother's summer dresses. The spool of golden hair in the brush. Her smile at the altar as the winter light fell on her shimmering dress.

'You must help me,' Luca said.

That word *must*. As if I still owed him.

I had helped him by coming along to Sophia's house and by talking when he was silent. I had helped him by being elsewhere and not coming back. And now I was expected to help him again.

My younger, stronger brother. He needed my help.

'Have you spoken to Sophia about it?'

'Yes.'

'Was it her idea?'

'No.'

It was as if he had started talking in sounds rather than words again.

'What does she think about it?'

Luca didn't reply. It had to be awful for him. But there was no time for silence. The revolving blade was scraping in his ear. The ice-cream could start talking to him any moment now, the way it does to ice-cream makers. It would whisper that it was firm and soft, sigh that it was thick and creamy and could wait no longer.

'She wants a baby. She wants a child to hold in her arms and nurse.' I saw a glint in his left eye. He wiped away a tear, keeping his emotions in check. At boarding school he had cried a lot, but I couldn't remember ever seeing him in tears afterwards. Ice-cream makers don't cry, they sweat. They suffer, they have no summer, they have no life.

He looked at me with tears in his dark eyes. I still owed him. He had taken my place in the ice-cream parlour, and now I had to take his place with Sophia.

Perhaps I had moved my head, or perhaps he had seen something in my gaze. Luca's chest heaved almost imperceptibly and then he said, 'You can't tell Mamma and Beppi. You can't tell anyone.'

This time I nodded more vigorously, not realising, at least not at that point, that I would also have to keep it a secret from the child I would father. The child that would be mine and Sophia's.

'And now you'll have to let me get on with work, because the ice-cream is ready.'

What's a Couple of Seconds?

The trees are closing in. It's something I have started to notice in Venas di Cadore in recent years. My father reckons it's nonsense. 'Trees can't walk,' he says, behind the wheel of his white Land Rover. 'Trees have roots.' I must have read too much Shakespeare.

And yet. In places where no trees used to grow, I now see slender, supple larks. 'Over there,' I say. 'And there!' Beppi looks at the places I indicate, but shakes his head. He refuses to see new things.

My father had come to pick me up. As I got off the train, I spotted him on the platform: an old man with a walking stick.

'You've put on weight,' he said to me.

'You've become a cripple,' I told him.

We hugged and for a split second our stubble rubbed up against each other's cheeks.

Once my father had finally retrieved the key from the right pocket and had fastened his seatbelt, he started the Land Rover and stepped on the gas with a smile. The engine growled like a bear. It was a different car, a newer model, but it produced the same noise as the previous SUVs.

'You see that house?' he asked as we drove through Dobbiaco. 'The guy who used to live there won the lottery. Over a million! A week later he was found dead in bed. A heart attack.'

Shortly afterwards we drove past the Grand Hotel Dobbiaco, a fantastic hotel in Austro-Hungarian style that I had never seen from the inside. It boasted fifty-seven rooms and a private chapel in one of its wings. My father slowed down a moment and said, 'The owner took his own life last winter.'

'Did you know him?'

'Everybody knew him.'

'I mean in person.'

'That's irrelevant.'

He seemed irritated for a moment, but maybe it was a permanent frown, wrinkles that were there to stay. The legacy of a lifetime of looking annoyed.

'Do you know why he did it?'

'He had no debts, no problems,' my father replied. 'He was ten years younger than me. And there was a white sports car in his garage.'

I thought he was going to say more, but my father made the bear beneath the bonnet growl again and we sped up the deserted road to Cortina d'Ampezzo.

It was the end of September, and cool. Several mountain tops were covered in snow, but it was too early for skiers and too late for hikers. The oncoming cars were few and far between: a Mercedes, a Toyota, a Volkswagen. In hairpin bends I clutched the grab handle.

At a particular point, after roughly half an hour on the road, you can glimpse the Tre Cime di Lavaredo, three colossal rock formations — the middle one is 2,999 metres high. These spectacular peaks attract thousands of mountaineers every year. You won't find more photogenic mountains in the Dolomites; stand before them and you can't keep your eyes off them. But the ice-cream makers from Cadore only know the Tre Cime from a distance, from the gap between two mountains on the road between Cortina and Dobbiaco, from the second and a half the peaks are visible from their car. A little longer than a flash. Yet they know exactly when to look to the left (coming from Dobbiaco) or to the right (coming from Venas, Vodo, Pieve, Valle, Calalzo, or Cibiana). I remember the first time my father alerted me to the Tre Cime. 'Quick, Giovanni,' he said. 'Look to the right!' But I was too late and had no idea what my father wanted to show me. Luca was asleep in the car.

The best time to walk up to the gigantic rock formation is in the middle of ice-cream season. My father, like Luca, had never stood before them, his head thrown back, his eyes darting back and forth between the peaks before lingering on the Grande Cime, with its vertical north face of some five hundred metres high.

In Vodo my father stopped the car by the side of the road. I thought he was going to buy bread at the bakery, but he remained seated behind the wheel.

'Are you not feeling well?' I asked.

He gave no answer and stared at the footpath.

'This is where Osvaldo Belfi collapsed,' he said eventually. 'Just like that, on the street. Seventy-eight years old.'

I looked at my father, at the sagging skin under his chin, at his watery eyes. He had turned eighty not that long ago, but hadn't bothered to celebrate his birthday. I had phoned him from Sibiu. The phone call lasted two minutes. He was watching television, one of the thousand satellite channels. Maybe he was watching an Arctic nature documentary or a volcanic eruption in Ecuador; maybe he was looking for Betty Heidler, in action during a Diamond League competition, her hammer whizzing through the skies of Berlin or Paris.

'And that's where Ernesto Zangrando used to live.' His finger pointed to a house some way up the slope.

I waited for him to continue, but no elaboration followed. Belfi, Zangrando: these were the names of ice-cream makers. They conjured up a long history — carts with copper vats, broken cones, love affairs, and grandmothers who thought their husbands had gone insane. But my father accelerated and manoeuvred the Land Rover out of the village.

The closer we got to Venas, the more ghosts he saw. They emerged from the deserted houses along the road, out of the draughty, crooked wooden doors. Shutters were hanging by their hinges, window frames were rotting. Birds had built their nests in the gutters.

'That's where the Tamburini family used to live.'

Again, no explanation, no biography, as if he was talking to himself, just testing his memory.

'And that's where the Gregoris used to live. Or was it the Battistuzzis?'

I didn't know. I didn't remember the names, only the colours of the window shutters and the flowers in the balcony boxes. Red geraniums.

They had left, these families, and never returned. The ice-cream makers who had parlours in the Netherlands or Germany now often stayed there all year round. Some remained open in winter, selling coffee, sandwiches, and soup.

'That's where Elio Toscani used to live,' my father said after we had pulled into Venas. 'And Pietro Soravia, over there.' I looked at the houses. The shutters were open, the curtains pulled back. There was life, albeit slow and shuffling. Women growing older, widows falling asleep on the couch. Their children in Deventer, Groningen, Hamburg, Mannheim — in the middle of the day the phone might suddenly ring, waking them from their afternoon sleep.

'Tito Dall'Asta has passed away as well.'

Tall, jolly Tito. He had taught me to ski and I had been in the same year as his daughter in school.

'He had a good ice-cream parlour,' my father remarked, 'but a difficult wife.'

We drove past their house, with laundry hanging on the balcony. There were large white underpants, stockings, tea towels. The women lived longer in Venas — in the whole of Cadore, actually. The men had worked their bodies to the bone. By the time they retired, they were spent.

'Fausto Olivo didn't live to see winter, either. He died last week. You'll still find flowers on his grave.'

'Did you go?'

'Yes, I go to every funeral. You're expected to. People my age have no excuse to stay away. We've got nothing better to do.'

The Land Rover turned into the steep road our house was on. We sped to the top.

Beppi gave a brief chuckle. 'It's becoming a time-consuming hobby,' he said. 'The ice-cream makers are dying out.'

The trees were advancing since they were no longer chopped down for use in the kitchen or to heat the houses. The cold, empty houses, with their walls full of cracks.

My mother is in the kitchen. When she hugs me, I feel her bones jutting out. She has lost weight. 'The sun's out,' she says when we let go of each other, 'but it's not all that warm.' And while she discusses the weather forecast for the Belluno province and for greater Rotterdam, I notice my father slipping into the hallway, on his way to the basement, to his treasure trove of tools.

'Is he still working on the heart hammer?' I ask my mother.

'He's already made three.'

'Is he planning to send them?'

'I've no idea what he has in mind. I just hope he's not going to throw them around.'

She picks up the wooden spoon and stirs the sauce on the stove. I smell tomato, bacon, onion, and courgette. It's for the pasta we're about to eat — the table has already been set.

I look at the photos on the cupboards. There is a black-and-white portrait of Luca and me, taken in Alfredo Vissa's photo studio in Pieve di Cadore, not far from the house where Titian was born. The painter spent twelve years in Pieve, before being apprenticed to Giovanni Bellini in Venice and painting saints and doges. Aged fourteen and twelve, we were captured as fat-cheeked boys with neat partings in our hair. We had been to the hairdresser's especially for the photo. I remember the flashlights and the sweet we were given by the photographer, but not whether Luca and I held hands on our way to the studio. It is the only photo with a wavy white border. The other photos are more recent, most of them in colour. One shows our family in front of the ice-cream parlour in Rotterdam. The photo is blurred and the colours have lost their brilliance. You need to look twice to make out the faces, to tell Luca and me apart.

There are photos of Luca's family, too. I look at one of Sophia with her newborn son in her arms, a baby with deep furrows in his forehead. Giuseppe, named after his grandfather and great-great-grandfather. He has their dark eyes too, but his mother's blond hair. People felt compelled to run their hands through it, through those first, soft wisps. Before long it became clear that he also had his mother's long tongue. There's a photo of that too, of Sophia and her son both touching the tips of their noses with their tongues. But that one's not here. His hair has grown noticeably darker over the years. In his most recent portrait he is seventeen and sporting shoulder-length, almost black hair. 'A terrible hairstyle,' according to Luca. 'Impractical for an ice-cream maker. Dangerous, and unhygienic to boot.'

My mother tastes the sauce and adds a pinch of salt. Her back is hunched. She may not have touched a *spatola* for years, but her posture suggests she's still leaning over the ice-cream counter.

'Can you get Beppi?' she asks. 'The food's ready in ten minutes.'

'Do I need that long to get him upstairs?'

'Probably a lot longer. If it's up to him he'll stay down there all day long.'

I walk past the feather headdress and down the stairs to my father's bunker.

He doesn't hear me because he's busy grinding. Golden-white sparks fly off the iron, and the floor is littered with filings and gleaming curls. Not wanting to startle him, I sit down on the bottom step. And so I watch him for a while, the ice-cream maker who wanted to be an inventor. He retired eight years ago. That's when he called it a day in Rotterdam. 'Or else there'll be casualties,' he told my mother. Enough was enough. Fifty-seven summers.

There was no stopping my mother, but then she was seven years younger than my father. She couldn't abandon Luca. He badly needed her help. Those first few years she joined him when he and Sophia went to Rotterdam in February, leaving Beppi on his own in Venas for eight months, the entire ice-cream season. Every evening my mother phoned him at the stroke of seven and asked how he was doing. 'Better every day,' was his response.

The truth was that the kitchen counter was stacked full of dirty plates and food-encrusted pans. And instead of washing his clothes, he just bought a new pack of socks and underpants every week. The sheets smelled sour; his pillow was yellow. He hauled machines to the garage and drove over to other black-fingered guys once a week to talk crown drills, saw blades, and sanding discs. The rest of the time he spent either in the basement or watching his one thousand television channels.

I visited him in summer and was shocked by the filth.

'What are you doing?' my father exclaimed as I opened all the windows.

'Doesn't the stench get to you?'

'It doesn't bother me.'

'Don't you think you should do the dishes?'

'I haven't got the time.'

He was too busy grinding, drilling, sawing, and sanding in the basement.

I stripped the bed, throwing the sheets and clothes into the washing machine. Then I rinsed all the plates, pans, knives, forks, and glasses; swept and mopped the floors; scrubbed and scoured the walls; and hung up the washing to dry in the warm sunshine.

'*Now* I could do with the windows open,' my father said. 'What's that smell?'

'Detergent. Lavender.'

'It stinks.'

I'm sure he would have been happy if Luca had cleaned the house. I was the son who couldn't do anything right. And always would be. No matter that I had succeeded Victor Larssen as director of the World Poetry Festival and that in the past year I had been chairman of the jury awarding the most important poetry prize in the Dutch language.

I took him to Ristorante Il Portico in Valle, where he always ate the same pizza: a margherita with *bresaola* and rocket. Accompanied by *una bella bionda*, of course. He drained his glass in no time and asked the waitress for another. While clearing up at his place, I had come across countless empty beer cans, all dented, as though they had been attacked by a bored schoolboy. On one occasion I had caught him whacking a can with a flat, vertical hand. 'Hi-yah!' he had said while doing it.

'Don't you miss Mamma?' I asked.

'I just talked to her on the phone.'

He cut a slice of pizza. I wondered how much I took after him. Was it his doing that I had never missed a woman, that I had never woken up feeling lovesick?

'Do you still love her?'

'Jesus, Giovanni. I'm eating my pizza.'

'Did you miss her back in the day? When you fell in love, Mamma had to go to Ulm to help her parents in their ice-cream parlour while you were working in Rotterdam. How was that summer?'

'How do you know that?'

'Mamma told me.'

He took a bite of his pizza, stuffing the strip of *bresaola*, which was left dangling from his mouth, back in with his fingers.

'Did you write letters to her? How did you feel back then?'

My father nearly choked on the sliver of dried beef.

'Did you ever miss her?'

'Why won't you let me enjoy my pizza? What's gotten into you?'

I don't know why I was so blunt. Perhaps because we had never sat opposite each other in a restaurant with the opportunity for a conversation, just the two of us.

'Marriage is really complicated,' he said then, 'but that's something you'll never understand.' It was a sneer, a stab in the back, and for a moment it seemed as though he envied me for this aspect of my life, too. The lonely part. As though he had not only been forced to become an ice-cream maker, but to marry, too. After all, you need a woman in an ice-cream parlour.

We spent the rest of our dinner gazing at the atrocious frescoes the owner had applied to the walls of his restaurant. Beppi didn't want an espresso. He ordered another beer.

'I'm leaving tomorrow afternoon,' I said.

There was no reaction, just a brief smile after a few seconds. That was all.

Back at the car, we nearly had an argument because he insisted on driving.

'You've had too much to drink.'

'They rarely stop anyone,' my father countered. 'Besides, it's only a short distance.'

'I'd like to go over to Pieve.'

'Pieve? Why do you want to go there?'

'I'd like an ice-cream.'

'You're bonkers.'

'I fancy it.'

'I fancy another beer.'

'Then we'll go to the ice-cream parlour first and to Bar Posta afterwards.'

Like a miffed child, he sat down in the passenger seat. I didn't hear another word from him. Until we entered Pieve. 'I'll wait outside,' he said then.

I thought he was kidding, but once we had parked the car and walked over to the ice-cream parlour, he waited at the corner, some twenty metres from the display counter.

Gelateria al Centro had been in Pieve for almost fifteen years. The owners used to run a parlour in Tilburg, but they no longer wanted to spend eight months away from home every year. It took some getting used to, an ice-cream parlour in Cadore. 'It's like having a restaurant in a stable,' someone had remarked in Bar Posta. And although it had been harder in recent years because the villages were getting quieter, the owners managed to earn a crust. They had outstanding sorbets, made of fruits from the mountains. Strawberries growing at an altitude of 1,736 metres made for delicious strawberry sorbet.

With a cup containing two scoops of raspberry sorbet in my hands, I walked over to my father.

'Go away!' he yelled, when I was still a few metres away.

'Surely I can come and stand next to you?'

'Stay away from me.'

'I'm your son.'

'I don't want you to stand next to me with that ice.'

'It won't explode.'

That didn't get a laugh.

Thinking he was being childish, I walked over to him. But Beppi quickly took a couple of steps back.

'Wouldn't you like a taste?'

'Over my dead body!'

'Fine,' I said. 'I'll eat it here.' I sat down on a low wall and brought the plastic spoon to my mouth. It was a balmy evening. The windows of some houses were open, and children ran through the narrow streets. The ice-cream was refreshing and sweet. The raspberries and strawberries were said to have been picked by women in their underwear. I had never seen them in the fields, crouched down, in the burning midday sun. More likely than not it was an ice-cream makers' tall tale, like so many others. But those who believed it enjoyed their ice-cream even more.

I let the last bite melt on my tongue and tried to savour the moment. My father stood with his back to me and to the ice-cream parlour, staring at the asphalt. He looked as if he was staring into an abyss.

Back in the car I wanted to put an arm around him. No big deal. Just a hug of sorts. But my father shot up in his chair, practically hitting the roof of the Land Rover.

'What are you doing?' he exclaimed. 'Get your sticky fingers off me!'

Finally, the grinder is switched off. My father runs his calloused thumb along the edge of the iron heart.

'The food's almost ready,' I say, as softly as possible.

'That gives us a couple of minutes,' my father replies. 'Look at this beauty.'

I walk over to him and look at the heart materialising from the dark iron.

'It has to be exactly four kilos,' my father says. 'That's the tricky thing. There's a fifteen-gram margin, but that's nothing.'

He shows me the other hearts. They're all different. 'This one here's the biggest,' my father says, sounding like a sculptor. 'But the bigger, the slimmer.'

I pick up another heart, smaller and thicker.

'Great, don't you think?' my father says. 'I want to make a whole series, maybe as many as ten.'

The melancholy is gone. The ghosts have dispersed. Down here, in his basement, he's the young man who used to make nuts and bolts in a workshop in Calalzo.

'I'm also planning to make one with a jaunty tail. Imagine Betty Heidler becoming world champion with that.'

I can't imagine.

'Maybe she'll improve her own world record.'

'Shall we head upstairs?'

'The magic frontier of eighty metres! An unbelievable distance.'

I look at the pillar drills. Back in the day they had seemed gigantic, but now they tower only a couple of centimetres above me. Luca and I were never allowed to touch them. Unlike the Cattabriga, which we were allowed to fill and switch on.

'Have you seen a picture of her?' Beppi asks.

I nod. I had checked out a photo of her on the internet. She was a woman with red hair and enormous upper arms. I didn't get it. But when my father picks up the smallest heart and holds it in his hands, in his open palms, and starts whispering sweet nothings to it, my memory harks back to almost twenty years earlier, and two images slowly elide.

The songbird has mutated into a hammer-thrower.

We are sitting at the kitchen table, my father, my mother, and me. All three of us are twisting our forks. When the plates are empty and the napkins covered in tomato stains, we shall have to talk so as not to hear the silence. We're not there yet. We chew, we swallow, we drink the red wine. Every so often I look into my mother's eyes, her irises grey under her long lashes, surrounded by the craquelure of her skin. Only once do I catch my parents looking at each other.

It's the empty chair. Giuseppe's chair. He has been travelling for nearly two months now, around Mexico, Guatemala, Belize.

He had phoned once, to say that he had arrived in one piece. Luca spoke to him. It was a Saturday afternoon, warm and therefore busy. The terrace was heaving, and customers were jostling in front of the display. The telephone must have rung about ten times before my brother finally answered. 'Ice-cream Parlour Venezia,' he said. 'Luca speaking.' His voice must have betrayed his grumpiness. It always did when you phoned him in summer.

There was noise on the line and a faint beep quite far off. It took forever before he heard Giuseppe's voice, 'It's me.'

It was morning in Mexico City, bright and cool, but the air was already thick with smog. I was familiar with the airport, Aeropuerto Internacional Benito Juárez. I had been there twice — the first time for the festival in Michoacán; the second time for a new festival in Colima. There were pay phones beside the taxi rank. I remembered a young woman in a tight skirt. While on the phone, she had leaned against the pillar with one arm above her head, her eyes hidden behind jet-black sunglasses. But perhaps there were phones inside too, in the immense arrival hall, and Giuseppe was calling Rotterdam from one of those. My brother doesn't know. He cannot remember whether he heard the sound of cars and buses, or the buzz of the departure lounge: hundreds of voices, children's screams, and trolleys and suitcases being wheeled in a hurry.

'I had a tub of ice-cream in one hand and the phone in the other,' Luca had told me. 'It was a Saturday and it was sunny. Half the city was queuing.'

'What kind of ice-cream was it?'

'Does it matter?'

'Yes.' I wanted to know every single detail.

'Lemon sage.'

This was a new one to me. For a moment I tried to imagine the combination: the tart flavour of the lemon and the sharp, robust sage. It must have been divine on a summer's day.

'I could barely make out a word he said,' my brother told me. 'It was a poor connection.'

'What did you say to him?'

'Not much.'

'What did he say?'

'I've told you a dozen times. That he had arrived in one piece and that he was off to find a hostel in the city.'

'And you didn't say anything in return?'

'Not much,' my brother replied. 'I didn't have the time to be on the phone, and he should have known that. He knew what time it was in Rotterdam, how busy we are then.'

'What's a couple of seconds?'

'You have no idea! Or you've forgotten. But Giuseppe knew. He knew perfectly well. Ice-cream is churned. It's churned all the time. Churn, churn, churn. But when it's churned too long, it becomes grainy and doesn't come out right. It's ruined.'

Luca resented him for going travelling in summer, for insisting on seeing the world while his father was working seventeen-hour days.

'Who hung up?'

'I don't remember.'

'Yes, you do.'

'All right, I was the one who hung up.'

The plates are empty. My father presses his napkin to his mouth and drinks the last of his wine. I'm curious to hear if my mother will bring up the weather or if Beppi will get to the basement before she can.

'He's bought a new shower,' my mother says to me, gesturing at my father. 'One with a seat.'

'The old one was completely knackered.'

'That's what you thought.'

'Would you like to see it?' my father asks. 'It has eight adjustable massage jets.'

'What?'

'Plus a hand-held showerhead and a ceiling-mounted one.'

'It's a gigantic plastic contraption,' my mother says.

'It's a shower cabin and it's made of acrylic and safety glass.'

'There are no taps to turn on.'

'It's all electronic,' my father says proudly.

'Push the wrong button and it's like someone empties a bucket of water over your head.'

I can't believe my ears.

'Your mother is afraid to sit down.'

'I don't *have* to sit down. I don't have mobility problems.'

'Why don't you try it tonight, Giovanni? Just sit down and activate the massage jets.'

'It feels like being attacked from all sides by kids with water pistols,' my mother says. 'And do you know what the thing cost?'

'It was cheaper than a pile driver.'

My mother slaps her forehead. 'Don't talk to me about that pile driver!'

'It's a thing of beauty, Giovanni. The most beautiful machine you've ever seen. And just a tiny bit bigger than the shower cabin. Ninety centimetres wide by two metres high.'

It doesn't take them long to break the ensuing silence.

'He's eighty and he wants to buy a pile driver,' my mother despairs. 'If that isn't Alzheimer's, I don't know what is.'

'It causes hardly any vibrations. And that's because you can drive in steel piles.'

'I won't have any pile driving here!'

'I'm not going to use the pile driver for driving in piles, am I?' my father says. 'I just want to look at it.'

'We're going from bad to worse.'

'I wouldn't mind an espresso,' I say.

'Me too,' says Beppi.

My mother gets up and walks over to the kitchen cabinet. She picks up the moka pot and fills the base with water. Once the cups are on the table and she is back on her chair, she glances outside. Then she turns her gaze to me and says, 'There's a mirror in the shower cabin, but it keeps misting up.'

We're back to square one.

'You're supposed to switch on the built-in ventilator.'

'I want my old shower back.'

It's as if both of them are suffering from dementia. Their grandson is in Central America and hasn't been in touch for two months and they talk about a shower cabin and a pile driver.

With the empty cups in front of us on the table, we wait for the coffee to be ready. The silence is palpable by the time the moka pot starts gurgling. The aroma of espresso fills the kitchen and finds its way to our nostrils. Sticking out of my father's are black hairs that he used to trim with a nail clipper, something my hairdresser now does for me, unsolicited, with mini trimmers.

Just as you can tell from the sound of the scraper blade when to take the ice-cream out of the machine, and you can tell from the poetry whether a poet has reached the summit of Mount Parnassus, you can tell when the coffee is done. The lid of the pot sounds as if it's trying to take flight.

Sometimes, when I'm miles away, the memory of that wonderful, warm aroma from this particular shiny coffeepot with the black handle that gets incredibly hot will suddenly creep into my nose. Oddly enough, this tends to happen to me at large, modern airports, all air-conditioned and sterile. As I walk across the smooth, square tiles of a terminal, the kitchen in Venas springs to mind: floor and ceiling, kitchen cabinets and table, chairs and pendant lamp, spice rack and calendar.

My mother lifts the moka pot and pours our coffee. Nothing is as familiar as this espresso, and yet everything is different.

'Right,' my father says once he has emptied his cup. 'I guess I'll be going back down.'

A couple of days later Beppi takes me back to Dobbiaco, where I'll catch the train to Verona before going on to Bergamo. My plane to

Rotterdam The Hague Airport leaves in the evening. I should be home just before midnight.

We drive past the dilapidated houses and the advancing trees. I wait for my father's melancholy, for the ghosts to emerge. But what follows are not the names of families, of ice-cream makers who are only alive and kicking in his mind. Instead he yells at a driver who shoots out onto the road: 'Salami!' A second or two later, he mutters, 'Women are trouble.'

For a moment I fear this is going to be a very long drive, filled with resentment and rancour, but after Beppi has made the bear under the bonnet growl, he appears to become calmer with every kilometre we cover. As we leave the valley of the ice-cream makers, he says, 'We're living on top of gold, but we just can't reach it.'

'Yes,' I reply. 'That's what they say.'

I look out of the window, at the steep slopes, where the first skiers will be in action in a month's time. Snow or no snow. Hypermodern snow machines will create white pistes.

'It's true,' my father says. 'Venas comes from *vena*, or vein.'

'I reckon it's just a myth.'

'The gold is buried very deep down. Bringing it to the surface would be too expensive.'

In school we were taught the geology of the Dolomites, including that of the rocks underneath Venas, the many different rock strata with million-year-old fossils of shells and sea urchins, but nobody ever mentioned a seam of gold deep beneath our village.

'Has anyone ever tried to bring it to the surface?'

At first my father doesn't react, but after a while he says, 'I've been living on top of gold my whole life.' He starts chuckling. 'Would you believe it,' he exclaims. 'What a joke!'

His father, too, had spent his life living on top of gold, Beppi resumes once he has stopped laughing. And so had his grandfather. They had slogged and slaved away, had worn out their backbone and joints, and all that time they had been walking across a stretch of earth that hid, deep down below, like a great secret, a vein of the purest gold.

If so, we had all walked across it. Luca and me, too. In our youth, in winter, in the snow with Sophia.

As we drive through Dobbiaco, the house of the man who won the lottery looms up. The curtains are drawn, and there is a rusty drying rack in the garden. My father slows down. 'It really is unbelievable,' he says. 'To win a million and then die. Perhaps he never even lived to see the money in his account.'

Friedrich Hölderlin, the German lyrical poet, comes to mind. Not when I'm standing on the deserted platform with my father and we gaze in silence at the rails in the distance; nor when I'm waiting for the Milan train among countless other travellers in Verona; nor at the airport, where the names of passengers are announced non-stop. But hours later, high in the dark sky, far above the patch of earth with gold.

Some poets descend into the darkest regions of their soul and never return, and some poets reach for the light, for true happiness.

The plane bores through the night, but then encounters turbulence. We are tossed about in our seats. The woman next to me clutches her handbag, squeezing the handles like the bridles of a horse. Lightning is visible in the distance and briefly illuminates the clouds below us.

In a letter to a doleful friend, Friedrich Hölderlin wrote that there are few who are compelled to catch lightning in their bare hands.

The Night My Brother Made Grappa Ice and I Fathered My Nephew

Right after Luca asked me to get Sophia pregnant, I had to leave for Struga Poetry Evenings, an international festival in Macedonia. Larssen wasn't coming with me. He and his wife were sailing the Mediterranean, not far from where Shelley had drowned with Keats's poems in his pockets. Xenia accompanied me instead. It was the first time she came along to a festival abroad.

The director of Struga Poetry Evenings came to pick us up from the airport in Skopje. A fat man in a tight suit, the buttons of his jacket undone, he stood at the bottom of the escalator bringing down the passengers and gave me a firm handshake. 'How many poets have died at your festival?' It was the first thing he asked me.

A poet from Nigeria got lost in the city once and didn't resurface until three days later. A Polish poet had been too drunk to read. A female poet from Chile never arrived. But no poet had ever died in Rotterdam.

In his chauffeur-driven car, the director told us that he'd had to accompany two coffins back to Russia. Poets who had disembarked too early from the boat cruising Lake Ohrid. 'Russian poets love drinking,' he said, 'but they're not good at swimming.' Xenia wasn't amused.

The festival's programming was peculiar, to put it mildly. Every year the director invited twenty Russian poets. Usually these were the same group of boozers, with the occasional new poet in their midst.

The Russians were invited because the director received funding for it from his friends. The independence that the World Poetry Festival prided itself on was conspicuous by its absence in Struga, but there was compensation in the form of ten leading international poets invited by a programmer. His name was Clive Farrow. He taught English at the university and had been working for the festival for many, many years, a dinosaur surrounded by books. He was said to live like a hermit, but on opening night he walked up the Cultural Centre's illuminated stairs with a gorgeous woman on his arm. He had brought them all to Struga: W.H. Auden, Ginsberg, Enzensberger, Neruda, Hughes.

The twenty Russians didn't mingle with the other poets. They moved differently around the festival, like something of an autonomous element. A stray caravan of poets, battered and dirty, always thirsty.

That very first evening, Xenia got harassed. After a shower, she had come down in a long gown. It revealed little more than her ankles and a hint of her calves, but still, her legs were bare. The Russians were smitten. They closed in on her and fought for her attention.

Most of the poets had arrived in Struga in the course of the afternoon and met in the bar of Hotel Drim. One or two were due to arrive the following morning, the day of the opening ceremony. Having shaken everybody's hand, the director was now surrounded by a group of men who looked like they might be the festival sponsors: heavy-set guys who were chain-smoking cigarettes. Parked outside was a line of cars, some with tinted windows.

I got talking to the Israeli poet Yehuda Amichai, who was the festival's guest of honour and the recipient of the Golden Wreath, a prize first handed out in 1966. The guests of honour at Struga Poetry Evenings were also honoured with a memorial stone in the Park of Poetry and given the opportunity to plant a tree there. Yehuda Amichai had travelled here with his wife, yet another privilege not extended to the other poets: only the guest of honour's partner had their plane ticket paid for.

Amichai's wife was a head taller than, and very attentive to, her husband. She fetched his drinks and sometimes even answered a question I asked him. It's something I was familiar with from my festival. The wives of internationally renowned male poets were extremely dedicated. They did everything for their husbands, allowing them to concentrate exclusively on their poetry, on the sacred. The women paved the way, they walked in front. To the hotel reception, to the buffet, to the presenter in the room where the reading was to be held.

So it was too in Struga. At one point the guest of honour's wife started making her way to the elevator. Tomorrow would be a busy day, she said. The poet left without a word, to be swallowed up by the telescopic door a little later.

'I told them you're my fiancé,' Xenia said to me. She had put her hand on my shoulder. I felt her upper body against mine, but more than that I felt the hot breath of twenty drunken Russian poets. They stared at me with glassy eyes. They had raised their voices, I noticed.

'They'd give their life for you, if you ask me.'

'You have to protect me.'

'There's twenty of them.'

'My boyfriend wouldn't be scared.'

The guy with the black hands, the car mechanic. Xenia had told me that when they were in the pub he had to keep the other men at bay. On one occasion he had pulled a wrench out of his overalls and threatened a man with it. All I had in my bag was a book of poetry.

'Can't you say you'll spend the night with the strongest?'

'I told them I'm spending the night with you.'

'They'll lynch me.'

'No, they won't.'

'They're Russians,' I said. 'And they've been drinking.'

'I don't think Russian poets are violent. The only one that springs to mind right now is Sukhovo-Kobylin, but he was a playwright.'

'What did he do?'

'Murdered his mistress.'

That failed to reassure me. The Russians at the bar kept staring. Hungry like wolves. They had a view of Xenia's back, of the dress that fit snugly around her hips.

'It's a lot more common the other way around,' Xenia said. 'The list of murdered writers is long. The same is true for poets who committed suicide.' She raised her wine glass to her lips. 'Only the list of Russians who step into a lake and go home in a coffin is short,' she said. 'To date, anyway.'

By now most of the poets had gone upstairs, to their hotel room. Likewise, the director's entourage had halved.

'Shall we go?' I suggested.

'Oh, yes. We're spending the night together.'

We were alone in the lift, but didn't say a word. There was the silence that fills most lifts, alongside the usual phone and a mirrored back wall. The lift at Hotel Rinno in Vilnius has a vase with plastic lilies, and at the Hotel Jianguo in Beijing, saccharine music pours from invisible speakers. The lift at the Ramada Hotel in Berlin smells of apples.

Just before the doors opened with a ping, Xenia threw me a sideways glance. We walked down the corridor, which looked like any other hotel corridor. The thick carpet absorbed all sound, making Xenia's high heels inaudible. She was an elegant and fast-moving hind. The rooms in this wing overlooked Lake Ohrid. In the morning the sun would bathe the balconies in bright light and there would be ripples on the water's surface.

'Shall we have a quick listen?' I said.

'A listen to what?'

'To the poets in the night.'

It was something Richard Heiman had done for years, he confessed to me once. When everybody was in bed, he would stroll up and down the long corridors of the Rotterdam Hilton and eavesdrop. With his ear to the doors, he had heard them coughing and snoring, tossing and muttering, in their sleep. Then there were the poets who lay awake half the night; the sound of the television filled their room, or else they'd be on the phone to the home front, a wife in Romania complaining about bills that needed paying and children who wouldn't get out of bed.

I pressed my ear against a door.

'Well?' Xenia asked.

'Nothing.'

She walked to the next room and listened. 'An ox,' she giggled. 'Or is it a bear?'

I stood behind her, but there was no need to press my ear against the door. 'Jesus, listen to that.'

'Who could it be?'

'Perhaps it's Yehuda Amichai.'

'Or his wife.'

Richard Heiman probably knew who slept in which room and which sounds belonged to which poets. Who received nocturnal visits.

'Sleep well,' I said when we were both in front of our respective doors.

'Sleep well, fiancé.'

She gave me a mischievous smile, the smile of a woman who knows she's in control. Not wanting to be rejected, I didn't respond with a countermove. But less than a minute later there was a knock on the door — not the door opening out onto the corridor, but another one, in the room's internal wall. I had to unlock it. Behind it was Xenia.

'A secret passage,' she said, and walked straight into my room.

This wasn't the first time I had slept in connecting hotel rooms, but I had never bothered knocking on the door. I always considered the chance of a young, blonde woman who knew everything about poetry walking into my room to be nil.

'There's a bottle of vodka in the minibar,' Xenia said.

I opened the small, square fridge and spotted a few mixers and half a litre of vodka. The glasses were on the desk beside the kettle.

Xenia slid open the balcony doors and sat down on one of the plastic chairs. She kicked off her heels and rested her feet on the balcony railing. Her long dress ended up around her knees.

We sipped from our glasses and looked at the dark lake. Over by the quay the shoreline was visible, but further down it was all one big black smudge. It was a warm August night, with music playing somewhere.

'Nice,' Xenia said.

'Yes.'

She wasn't really trying to get a conversation going. Perhaps she thought it was my job, or perhaps she was happy to just sit here after the long day, outside, with her bare feet on the railing and a cold glass of vodka in her hands.

'What did the Russian poets ask you?' I said after a while.

'Oh, the usual,' she replied. 'The thing men always want to know when they've been drinking.'

'Were they that brazen?'

'First they asked me where I was from. Then, one by one, they tried to impress me with Russian poets. The big names — Pushkin, Lermontov, Tjutcev — as well as twentieth-century poets. They thought I was just a silly little girl. They cited poems and wanted me to say who'd written them. Classic lines by Blok and Bunin. You'll find them in any anthology. I hit back with a poem by Sergei Yesenin, a poet who was sober for barely an hour a day towards the end of his life, but still managed to write brilliant poetry in that one hour. He wrote his final poem with his own blood, because he'd run out of ink.'

'Did you recite that one?'

'I was sure they didn't know it. They carried on drinking, but I'd clearly showed them up.' She rubbed one leg against the other, calf against shin. 'Then one of them asked how many men I'd slept with. His friends all laughed at that.'

'What did you tell them?'

'At first they all came up with a figure themselves. Of course several poets claimed I was still a virgin. I told them the number equalled the number of volumes Boris Pasternak published during his lifetime.'

I didn't have the faintest idea how many volumes of poetry Pasternak had written. Not many, I would have thought. Poets didn't publish a lot in those days.

'Eight,' Xenia said. 'But I didn't tell them that. I let them rack their brains over it first.'

We were silent. I looked at her white ankles, at the toenails which she had painted purple, the colour of her dress. She finished her drink before me and poured herself another. 'And what do women want to know when they've been drinking?' she asked casually.

'Everything.'

And after a large mouthful, 'Well, how many?'

'I don't know,' I answered.

'Have you lost count?'

'No, I never kept count. It's not important to me.'

'Pushkin married his one-hundred-and-thirteenth lover. That's what he claimed, anyway.'

'There haven't been that many, nowhere near. I'm only thirty.'

'So was Pushkin when he got married.'

She looked at my glass and gave me a top-up.

'I reckon you're the kind of man who'll never marry and have kids,' she said then.

'That sounds like a disqualification.'

'I don't mean it like that,' she clarified. 'But it strikes me as a bit ... dull.' It sounded as if she'd had to pick from a number of words — *lonely* and *superficial* among them — and had opted for the least awkward one.

It was something I often sensed. If there was no partner, people thought you had no story to your name. No life.

'I can't really imagine you doing any of that, anyway,' Xenia said. 'You're always travelling, and whenever you get the chance you hide behind a collection of poetry.'

I couldn't imagine it either, and yet it was about to happen. Not marriage, but a child. If I wasn't also infertile like Luca, that is.

'Where does it come from?'

'Where does what come from?'

'All the travelling, the love of poetry.'

'Not from my family. Although my great-grandfather once got on a boat to America. He was involved in the construction of a skyscraper and hunted buffalo. But whether he read poems too? I doubt it.'

'Pushkin's great-grandfather was Czar Peter the Great's adopted son. He'd been presented to him as a gift, a little Ethiopian boy. He wasn't even ten years old.'

'I didn't know that.'

'Pushkin's passionate nature has been ascribed to this swarthy ancestor.'

It sounded made up, like a fairytale, set in a distant period, in a time of palaces and silk-brocade suits, of carriages and pristine white horses, a tale distorted, embellished, and inflated by each new generation. A tale about a Moor, a czar, and the greatest poet of all.

The story behind a name.

Two days after the closing ceremony had taken place and more than two thousand people had listened to the poets reading on the wooden bridge across the Drim, I was supposed to get Sophia pregnant. By then, Yehuda Amichai had planted a tree, 'the way Russian astronauts do before they go into space', as Xenia put it. His wife had helped. A stone had been placed during a formal ceremony in the Park of Poetry and we had taken a small boat to the island just off Struga. The island was home to an ancient monastery, and a well that produced an eternal murmur. One by one, the festival poets leaned over the edge and listened to it, as though it were the well of Castalia from which the poets of Parnassus derived their inspiration. Although the Russians had been drinking, nobody disembarked too early. Everybody flew back home, alive and well.

At Schiphol Airport, Xenia was met by her boyfriend. She offered me a lift, but I decided to take the train. The guy with the oil-stained hands looked at me with misgivings, the way men look at someone who has just spent a couple of days with their woman. (On the balcony, during another night, drinking from a new bottle, Xenia had confessed to cheating once. 'Does that mean Pasternak has nine volumes to his name?' I asked. 'Some claim there are ten,' she replied with a naughty smile.)

On the train to Rotterdam I read Charles Simic's prose poems, which Clive Farrow had given to me in Struga. Despite winning the Pulitzer Prize, the Serbo-American poet was reviled by literary critics. Not everybody was enamoured of poetry in prose form, even though the genre had been practised by some of the greats: Baudelaire, Lautréamont, Rimbaud.

As we approached Delft, I turned a page and read, *'I was stolen by the gypsies. My parents stole me right back. Then the gypsies stole me again. This went on for some time.'* One day the child drank from the dark breast of his new mother; the next he was sitting at a long table, eating breakfast from a silver spoon. *'It was the first day of spring. One of my fathers was singing in the bathtub; the other was painting a live sparrow the colors of a tropical bird.'*

It was a short poem, two paragraphs, but I didn't resurface from the lines until the train had long since come to a halt at Rotterdam Central Station and the compartment was empty.

I joined the mass of people walking into the city, past the hundreds of parked bikes and the jingling trams. Back then there was an old pontoon bridge opposite the station where a boys' choir used to rehearse. Walking past, you would sometimes hear the high voices of the young boys in sailor's outfits. *O Lamm Gottes, unschuldig. Am Stamm des Kreuzes geschlachtet.*

I knew every street and every stone, but the city was under constant development. You might come back from South Africa and find an entire building gone, a building you always used to look at while cycling past. New towers sprang up, squares were transformed, railway lines disappeared underground. This had been my second visit to Struga, but despite the six years separating the two occasions I hadn't seen any major changes. No shiny new flats had been thrown up. The city felt familiar. The only thing familiar in Rotterdam was the pounding of pile drivers.

On the kitchen table I found a couple of envelopes. The cleaner had been round: the sink was spotless and the counter empty. In hotels I always lay down on the bed for a while, with my shoes on the covers, looking at the wallpaper pattern, the fly droppings on the ceiling light. I had to fight the urge to do the same in my own apartment.

That evening I sauntered over towards the ice-cream parlour, but turned on my heels when I got to the street corner. There was a long queue. Maybe it would be better to pop round the following day. On the plane I had heard it was going to get colder, it was going to rain. Tourists flying home are just as obsessed with the weather as ice-cream makers.

It turned out to be the last fine day of summer. When I walked over to the ice-cream parlour the following evening, the street was full of large puddles. It was nearly ten and quiet. My mother was alone behind the ice-cream, while my father lingered beside the espresso machine. Three Somali men sat at a table. They were regulars, drinking coffee and talking in their mother tongue about subjects we could only guess at. Luca was in the kitchen. He was making ice-cream, of course.

I greeted my parents and walked past the displays and round the back of the till, through the door leading to the stairs I hadn't climbed in months. Nobody asked me anything, neither Beppi, nor my mother. It was as though they were expecting me, as though they knew what I was about to do. When I questioned Luca about it years later and accused him of telling them everything, he reacted furiously. 'Yes, I told them you were coming!' he exclaimed. 'And no, of course I didn't tell them you came to go to bed with Sophia. How could you think such a thing?! I'm not stupid, you know!' He told them I was going to read her poetry, in the hope it would make her feel better, cheer her up a bit. My mother hadn't said a word, but my father had shaken his head. 'I won't be surprised if she never got out of bed again.'

I had expected it to be dark and musty in the attic, with Sophia under the covers with her eyes closed, not saying a word. I thought she wouldn't have washed and would be looking tired, exhausted. I was expecting a sad face, bone-dry lips, and bags under her eyes, the strands of her long hair spread across the pillow like the tentacles of an octopus. But Sophia had opened the door before I had even taken the final step and welcomed me with braided hair and rosy cheeks. She looked enchanting, in a dress with a peony pattern in pink, purple, and white.

For a moment we faced each other without a word. Then, 'Hello, brother-in-law,' she said with a smile. Just like she did when I first saw her in the ice-cream parlour, with a mop in her hands. It had been unbelievable, yet perfectly natural at the same time. That's what we were aiming for now — unbelievable and natural in equal measure.

As I planted a kiss on her cheek, I felt her take my hand. She didn't lead me to the beds in which Luca and I had once slept — which had been since pushed together to make a double bed — but to the middle of the attic, to a rug under the small, square skylight. Had the sky been clear, we might have kissed under the stars. Instead, our lips drew near under colossal blue clouds. Her eyes closed and she gently squeezed my hand, pressing her body against mine. I looked at her straw-like eyebrows and the blemishes on her skin, the pigmentation, the small dents in her forehead.

Her lips disengaged from mine. 'Giovanni,' she whispered. 'Close your eyes.'

I closed my eyes and felt her hand on my face — her soft hand, the round pillows of her fingers. She slid them across my cheeks, across my lips. She kissed my ear without a sound.

My right hand was guided to her lower back. 'Touch me,' she said softly and kissed me on the mouth again. Her lips parted. I thought of snow, of innumerable flakes, millions of ice crystals. I also thought of my brother — of Luca as a boy, and how enchanted we had been by the girl who stuck her long, narrow pink tongue into the cold air.

She smelled lovely. She had showered, but not especially for me. Her hair wasn't wet and I could smell her body, the body I had never been allowed to touch or see. The sheen, the dappled light on her skin. Her cleavage.

I had dreamed of her breasts, had fantasised about them hundreds of times. They were perfect and fit neatly into my hands. Her nipples were girlish, light and small, practically transparent. But none of this I had ever actually seen. The light never reached that far; the fantasy always stopped, however much she leaned over and smiled.

I heard the floorboards creak as we made our way to the beds.

I thought everybody could hear — Beppi and my mother two floors down, Luca in the kitchen, the Somali men at their table. Everybody knew.

Now we had reached the bed. Now it was about to happen.

Sophia turned round and lifted her braid. Dimples appeared in her shoulders. And so she stood for a while, like an artist's model. I didn't know what she wanted, what she wanted me to do.

'My zip,' she said, and giggled.

It was like the first time: the same insecurity, the same clumsiness.

I took the cold fastener and pulled it all the way down. Her hips were white as milk. She dropped her dress on the floor and stepped out of the peonies around her feet. She lay down on the bed, on her side, resting her head on her hand.

'Come here,' she said.

'Don't you think it's weird?'

'A little.'

'Just a little?'

Her chest rose and fell. 'Yes, a little.'

She sat up and unbuttoned my shirt. My clothes fell to the floor beside her dress. I felt her hands on the fabric of my boxer shorts and then her fingers behind the elastic. She planted a kiss on my prick.

'You don't taste of broccoli at all,' she said. 'And Luca doesn't taste of strawberry mousse.' She laughed out loud.

How could she be so light-hearted about it? This beautiful young woman who had grown sad and sombre, who could be silent for days — the woman who got tears in her eyes when a little boy ordered ice-cream from her. Had she somehow found a passage to the past within this darkness, back to the enchanting young girl she had been, the one who could touch the tip of her nose with her tongue?

She began caressing me again, and I let my hands wander across her skin, too. Her silky soft calves, her wonderfully warm thighs. Why all the tenderness? Shouldn't we just do it? Fast and hard. Sophia on her stomach, me behind her, thrusting like a stallion.

Instead we kissed as if time hadn't made a giant leap and we were still young and innocent. I unhooked her bra. Her breasts, which would get

[199]

bigger, nipples which would get darker, right now were small and pink.

The light-heartedness was gone. We were making love; bodies not yet used to each other, but keen to know everything there is to know. Every nook and cranny, every millimetre of skin.

She took off her knickers herself. Her skin was paler underneath, her pubic hair curly. My fingers went down there instinctively. *Neither white petals nor snails have skin so fine*, the poet Federico García Lorca wrote, *nor moonlit crystals shine with her brilliance.*

'Use your thumb,' she whispered. 'I want to feel your thumb.'

I didn't know what she meant, not immediately, not when she first whispered it. But when she repeated it, effectively ordered me to, I did as I was told. I touched her with my smooth, perfect thumb. Not the calloused ice-cream maker's thumb, but the thumb that had turned countless pages of poetry. The thumb Luca didn't have.

She moaned and writhed, as though a shock passed through her body. Only then did I notice just how sallow her skin was and how dull and dark her hair. I saw my brother's wife. Unhappy, deprived of sunlight. The colour on her cheeks was blusher.

'Go on,' she said.

'We mustn't.'

'He's fine with it.'

'But it's not okay.'

She put her finger on my mouth. 'He won't come up here, he's making ice-cream.'

For a split second I could picture him, in the white-tiled kitchen. The ice-cream machines churning, murmuring in his ear. The next day, I would hear what flavour he had made while I slept with his wife. Everybody would be talking about it. It was the first time Luca had ice made from an alcoholic beverage in the display. Grappa, barrel-aged, forty-three per cent. The trickiest ice to make.

Despite the rain, people queued. The regulars of the pub across the street. They had gotten wind of the new flavour and ordered grappa sorbet after grappa sorbet. The structure was amazing, which was a miracle in itself. Alcohol lowers the freezing point; the higher the percentage, the faster the ice crystallises. It becomes granular, slushy. But Luca had pulled it off; it was perfect. Perhaps he had spent all night on it — who knows, perhaps he had gone through ten bottles. When I peered through my office window in the morning, I saw him leaning on the counter, looking for all the world as if he had a terrible hangover.

But Sophia smiled and beamed and fluttered around the ice-cream parlour like a butterfly. They say some women are so familiar with their body they can actually feel the fertilisation of an egg-cell. Sophia had felt it and was blissfully happy.

In the attic, she kissed me. The fresh taste of her mouth yanked me out of my thoughts. Her hands slid across my legs, my groin, my balls. She was giving me a hand job.

'Shall I use some oil?'

Before I had a chance to reply, Sophia reached for the bedside cabinet and pulled out a small bottle. She dripped some oil into the palm of her hand and started massaging me. Her right hand moved slowly up and down and enclosed the tip of my prick in her fist.

'Nice?'

Yes, bloody nice. This really wasn't right.

'Any other requests?'

She laughed and continued the massage. She was using two hands, her fingers entwined. It was a particular technique, an undulating movement. I felt a continuous pressure on my prick. It was divine.

'Don't come just yet,' she said and squeezed my penis hard.

My eyes opened. You wouldn't believe what your eye can alight on. I saw the flaking paint of the frame. Luca's bed. We were in his bed. As a boy, Luca had scratched the paint off when he was angry because we weren't allowed to go out and play. I remember it well.

Why had I not booked a hotel? The executive rooms at the Bilderberg Park Hotel were spacious and light. It's where, in recent years, we'd accommodated the poets invited to the World Poetry Festival. The views across the centre of town were gorgeous.

Her hands were everywhere. Her whole body, in fact; her legs, her mouth, her hair. Everything was spinning around me — the sheets, the pillow, her bare feet. Or was it the thought of my brother, who was making ice-cream? Churn, churn, churn.

I felt her nails in my back. Now she was sitting on top of me. As she looked down at me she began to move slowly. She found her rhythm, controlled, infinitely patient.

'Giovanni,' I heard her say at some point. 'Where's your mind?'

'Nowhere.'

'That's not true.'

I was in Venas di Cadore the day of their wedding.

She stopped moving.

'Don't stop,' I said.

'You men tend to bottle it all up.'

'What do you mean?'

'You and your brother. Your whole family.' She stopped those wonderful movements of her cunt around my prick.

I had slept with her mother. I had seduced her after the wedding party. Her husband had already gone home. She'd had too much to drink and we left without saying goodbye. We did it in the street, standing up, in the small square behind the bakery. Her fur stole around her shoulders, her dark-blue skirt hiked up to her waist. Her hands against the plaster wall.

In one fell swoop I rolled Sophia over, onto her stomach. She looked over her shoulder, obviously startled, but she soon relaxed when I ran my fingers across her back. Her white buttocks, her curvy hips — she was immaculate. I entered her and began thrusting, in and out, harder and harder. I supported myself with my hands. She bit my fingers.

I had to stop thinking about my brother, stop thinking about the ice-cream churning in the machines. I had to stop thinking about the flaky paint of the bed we were lying in. I had to stop thinking about her mother. Lines of poetry spun around in my head; they plunged into my mind like water from a great height, and purged everything.

And so it felt as if that night, like in Lorca's poem, I rode the pick of the roads, on a mother-of-pearl mare without bridle or stirrups.

'A Soft, Feathery Breath'

My son was born one cold morning in May. It had been raining when Sophia and Luca drove to hospital, fast and anxious, a small suitcase with baby clothes on the backseat. It was night and the streets were quiet, the traffic lights flashing.

The labour took hours. Luca stood behind Sophia, holding her hands. Never before had he felt so close to his wife — not in front of the altar, nor in bed. He caressed her forehead and encouraged her. By the time the contractions had become more frequent, the clouds had drifted off towards the north. The sun rose above the river, the sky turned pale and blue, container ships set sail for the sea. Giuseppe Talamini, all crumpled and wet, washed ashore into the arms of the midwife. He weighed a paltry five pounds. Squinty eyes, glistening lips, barely a hair on his head. The birds sang in the flowering trees.

I was in Barcelona. It had been a clear night, the morning warm and lively. Men in suits drank their coffee standing in small cafés, cars drove bumper to bumper along the wide avenues. It was hot and close in the metro. The news from Rotterdam didn't reach me until the evening. I had spent the whole day listening to poets and sound artists. They had gathered at the Festival Internacional de Poesia de Barcelona to experiment with words and sounds. A French poet was accompanied by singing sand dunes; another poet was impossible to understand, which seemed to be part of the piece.

Along with my key, the receptionist at Hotel Catalunya handed me a folded note with the ice-cream parlour's phone number. That instant I knew Sophia had had a child. A boy, as she had confided in me the day the parlour opened.

'Come here,' she had said. 'I've got something to tell you.'

I was standing in front of the display, she behind it, a *spatola* in her hand.

We leaned towards each other, over the first ice-cream of the season. 'It's a boy,' she whispered.

I didn't know how to react, what to say.

'We're having a son,' she said.

All I could do was stare. Her cheeks had filled out and her eyebrows appeared to be coarser. The blue apron no longer concealed her belly, her bigger breasts.

'Don't tell anyone,' she said. 'Beppi and your mother don't know yet.' Then she straightened up again.

'Are you pleased?'

'Yes, really pleased.'

She beamed as if she had only just heard the news herself and I was the first she shared it with. She had a little boy growing inside her, a little curled-up creature with hands and feet, nails and hair. The son of my brother and me.

'I think he's asleep now,' Sophia said, still in a whisper. 'But when he's awake you can feel him move.'

A couple of days later, she let me feel it. I was standing outside the World Poetry offices, key in hand, when she came running out into the street. It was morning — the ice-cream parlour hadn't opened yet. Sophia wasn't wearing her apron; in fact, it looked as if she wasn't wearing anything at all. Her body practically burst out of her clothes. I could see everything: hips, buttocks, breasts. And her belly. She took my hand and placed it on the tightly stretched fabric of her shirt.

'Can you feel him?'

Not right away. It took a couple of seconds before I felt a tiny but distinct movement under the palm of my hand.

Sophia put her hand next to mine. I could feel her fingers. So this is what it was like to become a mother and father. We stood still while everything around us was in motion: the clouds, the leaves on the trees, the trams on Westersingel, the cars, the schoolkids on their bikes, the twirling knife of the butcher slicing ham.

Luca had come out. I had pulled my hand away. A reflex. I didn't even think about it.

'Good morning, uncle,' he said.

Yes, that was my role, my function.

'He felt him,' Sophia said.

'His little hand,' Luca said with a smile. 'He's dreaming of churning ice-cream.'

We hadn't spoken much since. I had travelled a lot in autumn and then winter had come. The whole family had been in Venas while I was in Rotterdam.

Sophia walked back to the ice-cream parlour. Time to start work.

'A boy,' I said to my brother.

'Yes, terrific.'

'All fingers and toes accounted for? Is he healthy?'

'The gynaecologist says he's developing well.'

'Good.'

'How are you?'

I didn't respond at once. He had never asked me how I was.

'Busy,' I replied eventually.

Luca didn't react.

'Lots of reading,' I explained.

'Are you staying in Rotterdam for a while?'

'I'm off to Scotland in two weeks' time.'

Let's face it, perhaps we had been avoiding each other. I had slept with his wife.

'What name would you give him?' he asked.

'I haven't given it any thought, to be honest.'

'What names do you like?'

'You're putting me on the spot.'

'Surely you can think of something?'

I thought for a moment.

'Otello.'

'Otello? What sort of a name is that? Must be a poet.'

'No. Shakespeare wrote a play with that title, a tragedy, but I'm thinking of Otello without an "h".' I didn't want to saddle Sophia and Luca's son with the name of a man who murders his wife and then takes his own life. 'It's the first name of the inventor of the mechanical ice-cream machine,' I said. 'Otello Cattabriga.'

Luca nodded. He spent more hours with those machines than with people. My father had bought them second-hand. They outlasted an ice-cream maker.

The name had a ring to it, I thought. The rhythm, the combination of long and short vowels — there was something grand about it. With a name like that you were bound to make a major invention sooner or later. When Otello Cattabriga patented his mechanical system in 1927, his machine went global. Otello Talamini. If my father had borne that name he might have invented something huge.

'We're thinking of Giuseppe,' my brother said. 'His granddad's name.'

'And that of his great-great-grandfather.'

'Yes.'

A traditional name. The name of an ice-cream maker.

My mother said the name after I keyed in the ice-cream parlour's number on the cordless phone in my hotel room. It was the first thing she said. 'It's a boy,' she exclaimed, not knowing I already knew. She knew nothing.

I lay down on the bed, the phone pressed to my ear.

'He's so cute,' she said. 'Such a beautiful baby. He's got hardly any hair on his head.' The joy of a brand-new grandmother.

My father came on the line, too. 'Giovanni,' he said. 'Where are you? Get yourself over here at once. You've never seen such a gorgeous little fellow.'

'I'm flying back the day after tomorrow. I'll pop round straight away.'

'He smiles in his sleep. He's amazing. He's a marvel!'

There was interference on the line. Or perhaps it was noise from the ice-cream parlour. I looked at the kettle on the desk, at the folder with information. The Museum of Contemporary Art was only a stone's throw from the hotel.

'Are you still there?' my father asked.

'Yes. How's Sophia doing?'

'She's doing well. She did a great job. We're expecting her home tomorrow.'

'Where's Luca?'

'He's in the kitchen, making ice-cream.'

He had gone straight back to work, right after the delivery, I would have imagined.

We had no cordless phone in the ice-cream parlour, not back then anyway. 'I'll call him later,' I said. 'He must have lots of ice-cream to make.'

'Yes, the ice-cream machines have never been idle for this long in spring.'

The next day I didn't bother about work. I told the organisers of the Festival Internacional de Poesia that I wasn't coming and hung the *Do not disturb* sign on my room door. Sunlight fell through a gap between the curtains. Motes of dust swirled around in that bright strip. I thought of Sophia's hands. I didn't want to think about them. I wanted to think about the little boy lying next to his mother in the hospital bed, peaceful, dreaming of the velvet womb. They were going home today. But the thought of her hands won out. It was a film that kept playing in my head. The oil, her intertwined fingers, the undulating movement. Was this the pleasure my brother enjoyed? Each time I tried to stop the film, to see how much oil there was in the bottle she took out of the bedside cabinet. It had been divine, so delicious, that even now, nine months later, I still thought about it, still wanted her hands. Just her hands. It was lust, pure and simple.

Late morning a key was inserted into the lock and then the door to my room flung open. It was a chambermaid, dark hair in a bun, white apron.

'Mi disculpa,' I heard her say. 'Disculpa!' The door slammed shut.

The sense of loss came later. After I had seen little Giuseppe. From the station I went straight to the ice-cream parlour. It was a clear day in May, the sun high in the sky. I arrived at Venezia bathed in sweat. My mother stood behind the counter; Luca was working in the kitchen, my father hiding behind the espresso machine.

'She's resting,' my mother said. 'She'll be down shortly.'

I shook my head. I wanted to go upstairs, eager to see the baby.

'Let her sleep, will you,' my father said. But I walked right past them and up the stairs. When I had gone up to impregnate Sophia they hadn't said a word, but now they looked at me like I was a criminal.

In the row ahead of me on the plane there had been a young mother with a baby, a three-month-old girl with dark eyes and hardly any hair on her head. The mother had walked up and down the aisle with her, trying to rock her to sleep, but she had looked at all the passengers. Me included.

I saw babies everywhere on my journey home — in Barcelona, in the queue for the check-in desk, at Schiphol — and I very briefly entertained the hope that Sophia would be in the arrival hall with Giuseppe in her arms, among the people with roses and balloons. I had never been met by anyone in the Netherlands.

Giuseppe was absolutely tiny, his onesie far too big. He was sleeping on his side, arms stretched out, little fists clenched. There he was. I wanted to pick him up and hold him tight.

Sophia opened her eyes. 'I didn't know you were coming today,' she whispered, not yet fully awake. She was lying on the bed in her knickers, the sheets pushed back. It was boiling hot in the attic. She didn't cover up. She didn't mind.

'I wanted to see him.'

She looked at Giuseppe with a smile on her face. We both looked at him, at his flat little ears, his soft head.

'Isn't he gorgeous?'

I felt tears in my eyes and was unable to stop them. They rolled down my cheeks.

'I think he's going to wake up soon,' Sophia said. 'He's been asleep for two hours.'

He was a miracle to behold. The little boy who had brought the ice-cream machines to a standstill in the middle of spring, with his small hands and rosy arms.

Leaning over him, I studied his face. His eyebrows looked as if they had been applied with a delicate paintbrush. Briefly, very briefly, his hand moved, and then his fist opened, but he remained fast asleep. *A soft, feathery breath*, as Ida Gerhardt wrote in her poem. In and out. Very gently, almost imperceptibly.

Sophia rolled over on her side too, turning her body to her child. 'I'm going to try and get some more rest,' she said.

'Would you like me to leave?'

She shook her head.

'In that case, I'll stay.'

She murmured her assent.

It was only then that I picked up the scent Ida Gerhardt describes in her short poem. *Scent of honey / and fresh milk, / of a nestling / fast asleep.*

Sophia's nipples had grown bigger and darker. Her breasts were huge. She looked strong, stunning. And not just her. They looked beautiful together, a union of mother and child. Her nakedness was natural; it protected them.

Luca was at work downstairs and wouldn't come up until late in the evening. I didn't really belong here, either.

Sophia's eyes were closed. She appeared to be asleep, one leg crossed over the other. I planted a careful kiss on Giuseppe's head and inhaled his scent. *The scent of what has happened: / birth, / secret.* He seemed unaware of the kiss. My first touch had passed him by. I had seen him. He hadn't seen me, but I was fine with that.

Not long after Giuseppe's birth, I travelled to the Sha'ar International Poetry Festival in Tel Aviv for the first time. I had been in Rotterdam for a week, if that, but I had held Giuseppe and he had stared at my face with a furrow in his forehead, as though he couldn't quite comprehend it — the gleaming teeth conjured up by my smile, the profuse stubble of my three-day beard. I had pressed my nose against his nose.

Every morning and evening Luca would work in the kitchen, preparing thirty different ice-cream flavours. In the afternoon, he helped my mother behind the counter. He was curt, to the point of not even greeting the regulars. That week I never once saw him with Giuseppe in his arms. Sophia, meanwhile, spent every waking hour with her child. If I happened to spot her sitting outside from my office, I would rush downstairs. Most of the time he was asleep, one hand on his mother's breast.

Sophia told me that babies tend to get a bit lighter straight after birth, but then gain a little weight every day. The health nurse reckoned Giuseppe was doing really well. But in the seven days I spent in Rotterdam, I didn't detect any changes. Giuseppe was still tiny and his onesies were far too big. Maybe his hair grew a bit lighter, but such minimal differences slip through the filter of memory.

The changes were more obvious in Luca. His eyes were small, and the circles underneath them seemed to be getting darker by the day.

'Your son is keeping me awake,' he said one afternoon. It was a joke, but he failed to crack a smile.

Maybe that's what Giuseppe saw when I held him and the furrows appeared in his forehead. Two faces that looked alike, but one with smooth cheeks and the other with a smile. One with a frown, the other with a suntan.

*

In Tel Aviv they had flown in an interpreter from Brussels for me. The poets read in their native tongue, but were also translated into Modern Hebrew. I had requested English translations, and so it happened that I was followed around the festival by a small man with a cravat. He worked for the European Parliament and had no affinity with poetry whatsoever. Wherever I sat down, he would sit down behind me and bring his mouth to my ear. He translated the poetry literally and simultaneously, while also providing a running commentary. 'Not a fucking rose again. No, not again! Fuck the rose, fuck the rose.' He wasn't too keen on imagery.

One of the programme strands featured Israeli and Palestinian poets translating one another's work. All the poetry dealt with the conflict, so in order to translate the work the poets had to understand their colleagues' view of the hostilities, get inside one another's heads. It created the necessary debate; the interpreter in my right ear sounded like a match reporter. The poets seldom agreed, but at least they heard the other side of the story.

Back in Rotterdam, I was swallowed up by preparations for the World Poetry Festival, which would take place mid-June. I had preliminary talks with interviewers, corrected English translations, and conferred with the other editors about the schedule. On some days I was in the office until ten o'clock at night. The hours were long, but never as long as in the ice-cream parlour. Luca lugged metal containers and carried cones and milkshakes to boys and girls sitting outside. His back ached — you could tell by the way he walked across the cobbles. He had acquired our father's gait.

Sophia was blossoming. She took the pram for long walks along the Nieuwe Maas. Sometimes she would sit on a bench by the river, watching the ships heading for the hinterland while breastfeeding Giuseppe. He giggled whenever she caressed his upper lip with her index finger.

It wasn't long before she had regained her slender figure and was back in her summer dresses.

She was a sight for sore eyes. Her svelte shape, her amazing bosom.

I bumped into her by accident on Parklaan, where I'd had a meeting with a festival sponsor. It was the time of year when the poplars were losing their catkins. There were places around town where it seemed to be snowing softly, with innumerable little seeds floating through the air.

'Giovanni!'

I turned round and saw her walking through the June snow. She came towards me with the pram, white catkins in her hair.

Giuseppe was wide awake. He was lying on his back, watching our faces with a twinkle in his eyes. Everything was wondrous. He was flapping his little arms about and producing happy sounds.

Something got caught in the filter of memory. I noticed that his cheeks had become fuller, a little chubbier. This was the first time I noticed a difference, saw that he had grown a little.

'Are you in love yet?' Sophia asked.

'Yes.'

I *was* in love, like I had been in love with her.

Giuseppe kicked his little legs, and when Sophia tickled his belly he began to crow with pleasure.

'How are the nights?' I asked.

'Luca wakes up at every little sound.'

'Does he cry a lot?'

'Oh, you know, when he's hungry.'

She reflected a moment.

'Luca says Giuseppe kicks him all night long.'

'Is he that lively?'

'He's a restless little fellow, and he usually sleeps between the two of us. I don't want him to fall out of bed.'

She looked at the whirling catkins. It was like the snow of yesteryear, the snow in which we saw her for the first time, her head tilted back and her mouth wide open. Except everything was different.

'You can catch these with your tongue, too,' Sophia said, 'but they don't taste of anything and they're really dusty.'

We walked to the ice-cream parlour together without saying very much. Occasionally we heard some noise from the pram and would both look at Giuseppe, the way young parents do. His dark eyes kept darting happily about.

Two days before the World Poetry Festival, I found Sophia sitting outside Venezia. It was a chilly morning, but the sun was out. She wore a poppy-red dress.

'Will you have an espresso with me?'

'I really ought to work.'

'One espresso.'

I gave in and sat down opposite her.

'Have you got a lot more to do?' she asked.

'The first poets are arriving today.'

I noticed goosebumps on her arms. Like her mother in the mountains, she simply ignored the cold.

'Are you going to Schiphol?'

'Yes, this afternoon and then back again in the evening.'

Beppi came out and reached for his grandchild. 'You'll only get coffee in exchange for this sweet little fellow,' he said to us.

'Gently,' Sophia said. 'He's just been fed.'

Giuseppe crowed with delight in the arms of his namesake.

'Shall we pinch each other's noses again?' my father asked and proudly carried him inside. He was more fun as a granddad than as an ice-cream maker.

For a while we watched the people go by. Shop assistants on their way to work, their heels tapping out a regular rhythm.

'My breasts are driving me insane,' Sophia said. 'They've been rock-hard for a couple of days now. They feel like they're about to explode.'

I couldn't not look, and I wondered if this might be one of those images I would keep seeing with my eyes closed, that would stay with me forever. Her breasts full of milk in a red dress. I hoped the image would fall through the filter, but I feared the worst.

My father returned with two cups of espresso. Giuseppe was now in my mother's arms. She was looking at the colours of the ice-cream with him — the pale green of the pistachio, the yellow of the mango-lemon, the amazing shade of the pomegranate-beetroot. A little later

Luca was standing beside them. He planted a kiss on the small head and then waved at us.

Sophia waved back. 'Will you join us?' she shouted.

'Just a minute,' Luca said when he came out with Giuseppe and sat down. 'I've got so much more to do.'

Giuseppe sat on his lap, clumsily sucking a finger. Drool dribbled out of his mouth.

'It's going to be hot,' Luca said. 'I'm curious to see if you'll get as many people as the ice-cream parlour.'

He was referring to the festival. We attracted an average of five hundred visitors a day, but far fewer on tropical days. The summer heat was the festival's Achilles heel. The ice-cream parlour, on the other hand, would have dozens of people queuing at any one time, a long line snaking down the street. They had never counted their customers. They didn't get the chance.

Luca smiled. He had won this competition. Perhaps he had won everything. At the age of eighteen I had made a choice, not an ill-considered one, but I could never have foreseen that the implications would be so big, and would only get bigger.

Giuseppe fidgeted. Unable to find his finger, he began to cry. Luca tried to console him by stroking his head, but to little effect.

I saw the anguish in my brother's eyes, a young, inexperienced father with a baby in his arms, and at that precise moment I lifted Giuseppe off his lap and held him to my chest.

Luca looked mightily pissed off.

As I rocked Giuseppe and gently patted him on his bottom, the crying briefly let up and he calmed down in my arms. But then he began jerking his head, and he was back to screaming at the top of his lungs.

Sophia took Giuseppe from me. 'I reckon he's still hungry,' she said and slipped her dress strap off her left shoulder. She bared her white breast and pressed Giuseppe against it. He sucked and drank and became intoxicated.

His fathers got up and went to work.

*

That evening I went to Schiphol for the second time that day to pick up a poet. This one had come all the way from Zimbabwe and had been recommended to us by the programmer of an African festival. He wrote that the poet lived in a small village, where he was a pastor as well as a dynamite specialist in the mines. In the evening, by the fire, he would read his self-penned poems. The poetry was unpretentious, his life sober. One of the poems we were sent told the story of a man who crouched down at a junction at the busiest time of day. He waited for a car to lose a hubcap, and then another one, and another, until at long last he had five. Five plates to eat from.

The poet carried nothing but a small hold-all, and never stopped looking around as we walked through the arrivals hall. In the car I tried to have a conversation with him. In pretty rudimentary English he told me about his journey, which had started two days earlier in a small village in southern Zimbabwe. He had never been outside his country before.

It wasn't the first time the festival had welcomed poets from remote corners. We'd had a poet who lived in a mud hut in the Sahel and another from a rural part of Chile, where he lived among an enormous flock of sheep. Likewise, the festival had hosted poets who opted to live in self-imposed solitude and wrote their poetry in the middle of nature, surrounded by the elements — like the Chinese poet Hanshan, who lived on a mountaintop and wrote his poems on rock faces, stones, and trees.

Sometimes it felt as if we plucked such poets from their natural habitat. In Rotterdam, they had to get used to the light in the evening and the wind that whipped past the tall buildings.

I had to explain the concept of food and drink vouchers to the pastor and dynamite specialist from Zimbabwe. In his village, people might have to work all day long to secure enough water. Once he understood what the vouchers were for, he walked to the bar and studied the bottles. He had never had alcohol, but had heard a lot about it.

It's like your first taste of ice-cream, albeit less innocent. The poet began to drink all of his vouchers, and by the time the doors opened he was pretty sloshed. Once the programme was underway, he fell asleep and snored through the recitation of a Georgian poet. The stage manager then had to help him onto the stage.

We ask all poets to read one poem during the first evening. Some visitors reckon this is nowhere near enough, and guests who only attend the opening night sometimes think we fly a poet over from the other side of the world for a single poem. But for the tanked-up dynamite specialist, it was virtually impossible to string more than two words together in front of the microphone.

When he discovered whisky on day three of the festival and became a bad drunk, I took him back to his hotel and placed him under house arrest.

You had to be strict sometimes, but above all fair. In the many years I have been working for the festival, I must have met some five hundred poets from all over the globe. Every year there will be a couple of difficult characters. Poets who demand a better hotel room than anyone else, who will only dine with the director, who refuse to shake hands with the women on the production team — you name it.

In Struga, the guest of honour gets to dine with the festival director at a separate table at the Hotel Drim restaurant every evening. Years after the event, in the Green Room of the Akademie der Künste in Berlin, I heard the story of two poets who discovered they had been at the same festival in Dubai but hadn't met. One of them had slept in the hotel penthouse and had pocketed a fee of ten thousand dollars, while the other had slept in a windowless room and had read in tiny spaces with scarcely any listeners.

At the World Poetry Festival, we paid each poet the same fee and nobody received preferential treatment. It's a tradition Richard Heiman had started, Victor Larssen had adopted, and I would continue.

After the poet from Zimbabwe had slept off his hangover, I picked him up from his hotel. He embraced me in the doorway of his room and refused the strip of vouchers waiting for him in the Green Room. That night he performed in an event with the Korean poet Ko Un. It was an exceptional evening: it was warm outside, the footpath cafés were packed, and people were queuing in front of the ice-cream parlour. Everybody was placing orders, chilling and chatting. Inside, in the cool darkness of the theatre's small auditorium, others were listening to poetry. Only half the seats were taken, most by a big group of regulars — aficionados — but also by some who had bought tickets at the last minute, curious to hear what followed the lines displayed on billboards all over town.

The poet stood at the lectern and read his poems, enunciating each word as carefully as he had once written them. Ko Un whispered his verses, as though his poetry was made of breath. At times there was applause, but some poems were followed by silence, the same silence as in the first few seconds after the final chord of a symphony, the poet impassive. It was unforgettable. A monument more lasting than bronze, as Horace described his poetry.

It was the fourth day of the festival, giving way to the fifth sometime in the night. A bunch of us were eating salt and pepper squid at the Chinese restaurant on Witte de Withstraat. It was already becoming light outside. A Ukrainian poet had stared at his chopsticks before deciding to eat with his hands. Sitting next to me was a translator whose pink nail varnish had chipped. She told me that her husband had run off with a poet she had introduced him to.

Festival days fly by. It's hard to keep track. The team and I stationed ourselves across the various rooms and auditoriums, but occasionally you had no choice but to skip part of the programme because you were talking to a poet or the programmer of another festival. The recommendations kept coming — must-read collections, promising new names. Nights with only three, four hours of sleep. The sky pale blue as you cycled home.

By the time the festival was over, the stage props stored away, the big banner above the entrance taken down, and the poets back on the plane, Giuseppe was ten days older.

I first saw him again at the ice-cream parlour. He was sleeping in the pram, which was parked beside the till. Sophia was behind the counter, wearing an apron and holding a *spatola*.

For a moment I was worried that Giuseppe had grown and might be sporting a thick head of hair, but he was just as tiny and bald as the last time I saw him.

'Is he still asleep?' I heard Sophia ask.

He was still asleep, his mouth open and his left hand splayed like a starfish on his chest. I tried to spot the differences. Were his fingers fatter? Had the down around his eyebrows disappeared? Was that a pimple on his cheek? I had missed ten days of his life, a third of his existence.

'What are you looking at?' Sophia asked. She had joined me.

'Everything. His nose, his ears, his eyelashes, the lines on his knuckles.'

'He's got beautiful long lashes.'

I looked, while at the same time searching for images in my memory.

'Has he grown?'

'Of course.'

Giuseppe moved his hands, shuddered, and then he opened his eyes. For a split second his dark irises were visible before they receded again. Maybe he had heard our voices.

'Hold him in your arms and you'll feel it,' Sophia whispered after a while.

If it had been up to me I'd have lifted Giuseppe right there and then, keen to feel what I couldn't see, but I was worried I'd wake him.

I leaned over to inhale his scent, the scent that hadn't changed, which remained as sweet as honey. What was it like to wake up beside him? To look at him, to nuzzle him while he was still asleep? I doubt Luca had the time in the morning. He got up at half-past five, sometimes even earlier.

'When did you get back to work?' I asked Sophia.

'Last Wednesday, when it was really hot.'

'What was it like?'

'He slept for nearly three hours.'

'What do you do when he wakes up?'

'I pick him up for a bit and tell him Mamma has to work.'

'And that works?'

'It's got to work.'

'Doesn't he cry?'

'It's what your mother did with the two of you.' She was still whispering, but the tenderness was gone. 'These are the busiest days of the year. I can't be the only one who's idle.'

I had momentarily forgotten that she was part of the ice-cream parlour, that she belonged to the other camp. It was the sun-kissed, tanned skin, the blonde hair that was back to its original lustre, which had fooled me. My mistake. I was the outsider, and perhaps Giuseppe too, for now, for the next couple of years. We had a summer and were free to go out. In the eyes of my family I had worked hard for ten days and now I was off again. They had never been to the World Poetry Festival, hadn't heard a single poet in all those years. It was impossible — the festival was held in June. The whole city was out and about.

'You can take him for a walk if you like,' Sophia suggested.

'I have to get back to the office,' I replied. 'I'm on my lunch break.'

It was the truth. My desk was littered with stacks of paper. Letters that needed answering, invitations to festivals in Brittany, Turkey, and Tasmania.

Sophia looked at me. She didn't smile.

'I'll have time at the weekend,' I said. 'I'm happy to take him for a walk then.'

It sounded terrible. I had fathered a child and could only take him for a walk at the weekend. But that was just the surface, the facts stripped of their context, of their complex and unbreakable connections.

Sophia returned to the ice-cream counter. I couldn't tell whether she was angry or simply needed to get back to work, but she didn't say a word. Yet when I emerged from the World Poetry offices in the evening, she called out my name, urging me to come over. Giuseppe was awake.

She lifted him out of the pram and handed him to me. 'So?' she asked. 'Can you feel that he's heavier, that he's grown?'

Giuseppe looked at me in surprise, the tip of his tongue sticking out of his mouth, and then he laughed, very briefly, without a sound, his laughing mouth oval and pinkish-red. Did he recognise me? Did he see Luca's face in mine?

'During the first month they gain a hundred and fifty grams in weight every week,' Sophia said. 'That's what the health nurse told us, anyway.'

It meant that Giuseppe had to be about two hundred grams heavier than the last time I held him in my arms. It was nothing, four scoops of ice-cream. I tried to feel it, but he was so light as to practically float in my arms.

'She didn't say he was too small?'

Sophia shook her head. 'Luca was a small baby, too,' she said. 'According to your mother, he weighed only five pounds at birth.'

What about me? How much did I weigh? I nearly said out loud. It made sense that my mother compared Giuseppe and Luca, but I didn't understand why Sophia did the same.

I held Giuseppe tight, his soft cheek against my nose, and closed my eyes. We were in the middle of the ice-cream parlour, surrounded by tables and customers. Beppi and my mother were looking at me, I was sure of it, as was Luca probably, from the kitchen. What was he thinking? Who did he see? His child with his uncle? His brother with his son?

I felt a hand on my shoulder — not Giuseppe's starfish, not Sophia's slender hand, but the ice-cream maker's claw of my father. He rubbed his thumb over the fabric of my shirt. Although he said nothing, I could hear him think. *Do you see now, Giovanni, that you made the wrong choice?* All this could have been mine: the ice-cream parlour, Sophia, a son as pure as an angel. *Do you see now?* His thumb dug deep into my flesh, into my muscles.

I looked at little Giuseppe and he looked at me. He laughed again, his lips trembling, as though his mouth wasn't big enough for his smile.

The distance would come; in fact, it was already here. All I needed to do was hand him back to his mother, turn around, and walk out underneath the red-and-white awning, to Eendrachtsplein, and from there to Veerhaven, to the restaurant where I had a meeting at a solid wooden table with linen napkins.

Sophia took him from me, but I couldn't pull myself away just yet. I had to have one more look, just one, at his baby legs, all soft and plump. No scratches, no scars. Unblemished.

Two weeks after the World Poetry Festival, I flew to Argentina. Victor Larssen had been invited to a small festival in Buenos Aires, but three days prior to his departure he had fallen ill. He was running a fever and his skin was covered in red spots. Chicken pox, it turned out. He had never had it as a child. Larssen was admitted to hospital, where he was to stay for the rest of the summer. I packed my suitcase and studied the programme on the plane. There would be poets from practically every Latin American country, including some big names such as Lêdo Ivo, but most of them were unknown, beyond their own borders, anyway.

I was picked up from the airport by a taciturn volunteer and driven to my hotel. Holiday Inn, Room 217. Grey curtains, grey towels, grey kettle. No art on the walls, but the note on top of the television welcomed me in four languages: Spanish, Portuguese, English, and French. I lay down on the bed and stared at a yellow stain on the ceiling for thirty minutes.

The festival's opening night consisted of a dinner for the poets and other guests in an old theatre. A large table had been set across the length of the stage. I was seated between the festival director and a close associate of the mayor, who had cancelled at the last minute. The evening featured no poetry, only food and drink. There would be plenty of time for poetry, which was to be read by the eighteen invited poets at locations across the city. The festival lasted six days.

After dinner I spoke to a few young poets from Buenos Aires. The men were all dressed in short-sleeved shirts while the women wore cotton dresses. Their faces were fresh with youth. They drank white wine and lit their cigarettes with matches they then casually tossed on the floor. This was their time. They performed a lot, published in magazines, and had tumultuous love lives. Poetry wasn't something that was taken lightly, as it was in Europe. It fulfilled an important role in the national culture. Its power was undiminished. People talked about Borges as though he were still alive. Macedonio Fernández was worshipped. Their lines ran through these young poets' veins, the rhythms were their heartbeat. *The taste of a fruit, the taste of water / That face given back to us by a dream, / The first jasmine of November, / The endless yearning of the compass.*

Around midnight, the group moved on to a nearby cocktail bar. There were two tall tables on the footpath outside, no bar stools. Others joined us — friends, nighthawks. There were lodgings above the bar, but the lights were on and the windows were open. The entire city appeared to be awake.

Opposite me, with one arm on the standing table, a young woman was smoking a cigarette. She was willowy like a model and started telling me about a party she'd been to as if we were old friends. But it took a while before she gave me her name. Elvira. She was a photographer with Italian ancestors.

'Whereabouts in Italy?'

'The North,' she said. 'Not far from Venice.'

That's all she knew; she had never been to Italy, never been to Europe.

I told her I was from the Province of Belluno, north of Venice, and that the first wave of Italian immigrants had hailed from this region. 'They went to North and South America in the hope of a better future,' I said. 'But some were plain old adventurers who left everything behind, including their wife and children in some cases.'

Elvira was sure her forefather had been an adventurer. 'Perhaps we're related,' she said with a smile.

'My great-grandfather went to America, but he didn't stick around.'

'A half-baked adventurer.'

'That's one way of putting it. He came back with a Native American headdress.'

'With what?'

'A feather headdress. He wore it on his head, pretending to be a Native American.'

No reaction from Elvira. She must have thought I was pulling her leg.

'Nobody believes the story,' I elaborated, 'but he is thought to have lived with the Blackfoot Indians and to have adopted their customs. Back home, we still have the white feather headdress.'

'It sounds like a myth.'

'I know.'

'What more do you know about him?'

'Not much. He never really settled.'

She lit another cigarette and offered me one too. I shook my head.

'Do you know the poets here?' I asked.

'Practically all of them. I've even photographed a few.'

'Have you read them, too?'

She laughed. 'They read to me.'

There was a small dent in her forehead, just below the hairline. Other than that, her face was flawless. She had lovely eyebrows, delicate, the hairs like little stalks.

'He wrote a poem for me.' She pointed to one of the poets I had spoken to after dinner. 'And so did he. Several, in fact.'

'Are you a muse?'

She blew out her cigarette smoke, close to my face. I needed no intoxicants; it was already happening without their influence.

I thought of Apollonie Sabatier, muse to Charles Baudelaire, but also to Théophile Gautier and Gustave Flaubert. All three had sent her erotic letters, but only Baudelaire's were intense and tortured, romanticism of the highest order. He dedicated a total of seven poems to her, Gautier four, while Flaubert based a character in a novel on her. Baudelaire was the only one who spent the night with her, a single night. Afterwards he wrote to her, 'You have a fine soul, but ultimately it's the soul of a woman.'

Elvira laughed. 'I'd hate to be a muse,' she said.

Her father was a painter. His work could be found in galleries

[223]

around town, as well as in the grand buildings in Recoleta. But at home the taps were leaky and the floor was always dirty — from footprints, daubs of paint, hardened brushes. Her mother was a simple woman who did everything for her husband and even posed nude for him on the cold tiled floor. She had no ambitions for herself. He had been her first love. She was sixteen when she met him in a café; he wore a grimy shirt and was twenty years her senior. He had cheated on her countless times and yet she couldn't leave him. It would be akin to treason. Elvira wanted to live her own life, independent, autonomous. And that's how she weaved her way through the lives of the young men who worshipped her, not just the poets. She was no muse; she was hard to forget, though.

'How old are you?'

She was twenty-two, her body like nectar.

She didn't ask me about my age, just as she hadn't asked me about my job. Perhaps she had no need to, as some women know everything just by looking at you.

In the bar across the street, someone turned up the music. A dark-skinned woman started dancing in the road, swaying her hips seductively. We both watched her. It seemed we had nothing left to talk about until Elvira suddenly said, 'You've got a wife.'

'What makes you think so?'

'Well, do you?'

'No, I don't.'

'I don't believe you. Your wedding ring is in the hotel, on the bedside cabinet.'

'I'm unmarried and unattached.'

She kept her eyes on me as she inhaled, and blew out the smoke seconds later.

'I have a son,' I said. 'He's two months old.'

It was the first time I had told anyone. It felt like a confession. It felt good.

At first Elvira said nothing. Perhaps she was waiting for me to elaborate.

'What's his name?' she finally asked.

'Giuseppe.'

'Do you miss him?'

'Yes.' I could say it, I could admit it, in the dark, in Buenos Aires, to a young woman I'd never see again, someone I'd know for one night only.

By now more women had started dancing, including some who had been in the cocktail bar. They had crossed the street with their glasses in hand and were now moving their bodies to the energetic music. Bar Miami, the joint was called. It sounded better than Ice-Cream Parlour Venezia. If my great-grandfather had gone to Argentina we might have owned a bar where people danced outside. But he had gone to North America and had returned home after a few years.

I was a half-baked adventurer, too.

Back in Rotterdam, I gave Giuseppe a stuffed toy I had bought at Buenos Aires airport. It was a grey dolphin, as soft as a peach. He clutched it gleefully, squeezing it in his little hands. The dolphin became his constant companion. He took it everywhere, sucked its beak, and often fell asleep snuggled up against it.

I would bring Giuseppe something from every country I visited. A marble elephant from India, a matryoshka doll from Russia, a tin car from Senegal. Luca said I was spoiling him, that I didn't have to give him a present after every trip. Later, when Giuseppe was a bit older, I started bringing back books of poetry from all corners of the world. Luca didn't like it one bit, and likewise my father always grumbled when I entered the ice-cream parlour with a slim, rectangular package. 'That's no present for a boy his age,' he would exclaim. 'He's going to be an ice-cream maker, not a poet!' But Giuseppe was curious and began to read them.

He had grown. I saw it the instant I stood before him with the dolphin in my hands. It was incredible, as if all the imperceptible little bits he had grown now added up to a tangible whole.

'You've grown bigger,' I said to him. 'You've gone and grown behind my back, but you can't hide it from me.'

He flailed his arms about and laughed.

'He's happy to see you,' Sophia said.

'I'm happy to see him, too.'

When he fell asleep shortly afterwards, I studied his face and ran my fingers over his skin. I discovered a scratch close to his knee. His very first scratch, little more than a dotted line. A few days later, it was gone.

His hair grew thicker and lighter in colour, the creases in the skin of his arms and legs deeper. He became more alert by the day, but he could also stare at an object for minutes at a time. The sleeves of his onesies didn't have to be rolled up anymore. And then the last day of the season arrived. Shortly after midnight, my mother stuck the note to the door. 'Back in March!'

The following morning the ice-cream parlour would be dismantled. The freezers would be emptied, the refrigerators cleaned, the cupboards cleared out. The ice-cream machines would be taken apart and given the once-over by my father. The display would receive a good scrubbing. Everything had to be switched off: gas, water, and light. Then the awning would be folded up and the key stuck in the lock. And once it had been turned three times, they would drive to Italy, via Germany and Austria, across the Brenner Pass, via Dobbiaco and Cortina d'Ampezzo, to the Cadore Valley. Like the other ice-cream makers, my father would sound his horn on the main street, and people would stick their head out of the window and wave at the cars entering the village.

It would be Giuseppe's first winter, his first time in Venas di Cadore.

In Venezia's Kitchen

The things that glitter like gold on the filter of memory: his blond hair, his teeth, his first steps. I clearly remember coming back from the International Istanbul Poetry Festival and hearing Giuseppe say his first word: 'Mamma.' Prior to that he had linked objects to certain sounds, but they weren't proper words yet. Sophia was incredibly proud and had Giuseppe repeat his first word over and over again.

I tried to teach him the Italian word for uncle. *Zio*. But he had trouble with the letter z, and kept saying 'io', which means 'I' in Italian. Whenever I entered the ice-cream parlour and Giuseppe saw me, he would exclaim in delight 'Io!' It always made Sophia laugh. She would jab her index finger at her son's chest and say 'Io', and then point to me: 'Zio.' But it was too complicated.

Luca has no recollection of Giuseppe's first words. They came during the summer Giuseppe was one year old. He could walk, but not all that well yet. He would bump into chairs or fall over on the paving stones, having tripped over his own feet. We all trotted after him so we could pick him up. Customers, too, often rose to their feet to keep the waddling baby safe.

'He's trying to escape,' said one of our regulars on the terrace. 'Look, there he goes again.'

I laughed when I heard that and said, 'He's already tired of the ice-cream parlour.'

'No, no,' my father said. 'He's practising waiting tables. Next year he'll be able to do it with a tray in his hands.'

Luca doesn't remember that, either. 'I was in the kitchen, churning ice-cream,' he'll say when you ask him about it. In fact, that's his answer to most questions about Giuseppe. Only after several consecutive days of rain and declining ice-cream consumption did he have time for his son. But an ice-cream maker is never happy on rainy days.

'Daddy' was Giuseppe's sixth or seventh word.

'You do remember the first ice-cream he ate, don't you?'

'I was the one who gave it to him,' my brother says to me. 'He cried; he thought it was too cold.'

I hadn't been there, but had heard the story from my mother afterwards. Luca had emerged from the kitchen with a tub of freshly made vanilla ice-cream. Giuseppe was in the stroller and clamouring for attention, but Sophia was at work. He was ten months old and at times he got by on only an hour of sleep. My brother fetched a spoon and held it out to him. 'This is the best vanilla ice-cream in the world, and it so happens that it was made by your father.'

Giuseppe opened his mouth, revealing two small teeth, both at the bottom. My brother inserted the spoon and his son's lips wrapped themselves around it. Cold numbs the tastebuds, it dampens everything. It takes a second, perhaps, and then you taste the sugar, a wave that builds and builds. But it took too long for Giuseppe. His eyes had closed, like those of all other family members about to get their first taste of ice-cream, but they simultaneously filled with tears. He squealed, as if someone had hurt him. His own father. The tongue-numbing vanilla came pouring out again.

'I won't eat it, either,' said Beppi, who had walked in with a tray. 'But the people are the worst. The people buying it. They're impatient, loud, and incredibly lazy. They sit down, scratch their fat bellies, fart, and expect ice-cream on the table within seconds.'

'Beppi,' my mother yelled. 'Don't force your poisonous ideas onto your grandchild.'

'Anita, will you please leave your husband alone?' My father leaned over the stroller. 'Your granny is an extremely difficult woman,' he said. 'Do you remember her having a go when I bought you that small crosshead screwdriver?'

Giuseppe didn't hear his grandfather. He was still bawling. He wouldn't have a second bite until the following season, when it melted on his tongue and he relished the flavour on his tastebuds, the sweetness that washed over him. 'Another bite,' he shouted. 'More!' All words he had learned to say by then.

'Such a beautiful tool,' Beppi muttered. 'And what does your granny do? She takes it away.'

One quiet morning, he had gone for a walk with his grandson and had taken the stroller into Spijkermand, the ironmonger. Like his grandfather, Giuseppe had been all eyes. They had spent longest staring at a pneumatic drill.

'That one,' little Giuseppe had said, 'that, that.'

'That one,' big Giuseppe had echoed, 'that one's nice, isn't it?'

But in the end he had bought him a stubby screwdriver, the kind for hard-to-reach areas. My mother told him to return the thing at once. 'Do you have any idea how dangerous that is to a baby?' she had said. 'It's not a rattle.'

'That's right,' my father responded. 'It's a stubby crosshead screwdriver.'

'What's Giuseppe supposed to do with it?'

'He liked it.'

'He likes everything! Are you planning on buying him a racing bike too?'

'No, of course not.'

'I want you to return that screwdriver right now.'

'No.'

'Oh, yes.'

'No.'

'In that case, *I'll* return it.'

'All right, all right, I get it. We're not supposed to enjoy life. Not when we're young, and not when we're old, either.'

My father took Giuseppe back to Spijkermand and returned the stubby screwdriver, but then on a whim bought the pneumatic drill instead. 'That one,' he said to the salesman. 'That one,' his grandson echoed.

With the pneumatic drill in the stroller, Beppi headed back to the ice-cream parlour. Giuseppe sat on his shoulders with a big smile on his face, oblivious to the dark clouds gathering above Venezia.

My mother wanted to hurl her *spatola* at Beppi, but she was afraid she might hit her grandchild.

Sophia was familiar with this kind of situation, absurd as it was. She knew she had to intervene. 'There's a shop with wooden toys on Nieuwe Binnenweg,' she said, 'and they've got beautiful tools. Why don't we go and have a look this afternoon?'

She had spoken calmly, quietly, without gesticulating, trying to sound as neutral as possible.

Beppi looked at the pneumatic drill in the stroller, perhaps realising briefly how ridiculous a purchase it was. Briefly, but long enough. That afternoon Giuseppe was given a large rectangular box containing a wooden saw and a wooden drill. His grandfather showed him how to use the tools.

Sophia kept the peace, engineered reconciliation, and kept the family together.

'Are you sure it was a pneumatic drill?' my brother asks.

We are in Venezia's kitchen. One ice-cream machine is churning. It's eleven o'clock in the evening. Sophia is in bed, Beppi and my mother are in Italy. Sara is serving ice-cream. A native of Vodo di Cadore, she has been working at the parlour for a couple of years now. Sara joined when my mother no longer wanted to leave Beppi alone in Venas, perhaps because she was getting on herself. Sara is in her early twenties, plain but extremely reliable. She stays all season and sleeps in the attic. Luca and Sophia sleep on the floor below, in my parents' old room.

'Mamma told me the story,' I say.

'Sometimes I get the impression that you make stories up. Or you change or swap things round to fill gaps.'

'It was the kind of drill you use to break through walls. A gigantic contraption, quite unsuitable for a ten-month-old child. That's what she told me.'

'I'm not talking about the drill,' my brother says.

We're silent. The humming sound of the Cattabriga's motor fills the kitchen as the scraper blade rotates almost noiselessly through the fluid mass. The ice-cream is nowhere near done.

Sometimes we sit outside, but that means Luca has to get up when there's someone in front of the counter. Sara is off two nights a week, which is when Luca does the serving. But he gets to sit down most of that time. It's not that warm anymore. October, the last month of the season. There are hardly any customers after ten.

We talk and we don't talk, we look at each other and we look away. Giuseppe has been gone for nearly three months. He hasn't phoned again, but we did receive a postcard with a picture of a Native American wearing a beautiful, multi-coloured headdress. The postmark shows it was posted a week earlier, in Mérida. The address was not in Giuseppe's hand; the handwriting was more rounded.

'It was written by a girl,' I tell my brother. 'He's in love.'

Luca doesn't believe me. He believes the postcard is from a customer. It is not uncommon for the ice-cream parlour to receive postcards from exotic countries.

'But there's no text on it,' I say.

'There is on the front,' my brother reacts. 'Greetings from Mexico!'

Sometimes we are pleased to see a customer, so Luca has to go inside to get a cup or a cone, or to make a milkshake for a lonely man.

There are no such disruptions in the kitchen, where Luca only has the machines to hide behind. He still sends me away when the ice-cream is ready. Since he wants to be alone for that, I go home, and we meet again the following evening.

We talk and we tell each other everything we know, trying to weave

[231]

together two halves: what I remember and what Luca remembers.

'Sometimes I get the idea that you suppress things,' I say. 'That you say you don't remember something just so you don't have to talk about it.'

'What am I supposed to remember? Look around you. Look at the tiles, the cabinets, the ice-cream machines, the worktop.' He's talking louder and louder. He's angry. Like Beppi, he feels betrayed. Everybody has turned against him. Even his own brother. 'Look at the strip lights, the metal containers. That's what I saw, day in, day out. That's what I remember.'

How many summers has my brother skipped now? How many has he sacrificed?

'And if I wasn't here, I was outside or behind the espresso machine or serving ice-cream.'

The first couple of years after my father retired, Luca was forced to work for two. He would make ice-cream in the mornings and evenings and then wait tables the rest of the time. My mother would be behind the counter with Sophia. She managed to keep this up for five years, before deciding to stay in the mountains with Beppi. She had worked until she was nearly seventy. Her hair had turned the colour of fig-and-almond ice-cream. The following season Sara came along, but they were still one person short. Until Giuseppe turned sixteen, that is, and was no longer of school age.

'You think I know more about him than you, but I reckon it's the other way around.'

I remember Giuseppe's first day in the ice-cream parlour. It was the middle of June, so the schools in Italy had closed. He had travelled alone by train, a rucksack over his shoulders, headphones over his ears. A typical teenager. His clothes smelled of the stuffy compartment he had travelled in from Milan. Over a thousand kilometres. Later that same evening, he was put to work.

I could tell from his face, from the sad frown between his eyebrows, that he didn't fancy it one bit. His friends in Italy were not working, free to enjoy the balmy evening. The sky was as blue and empty as the long days ahead of them. But he had to walk up and down the terrace and take orders. This was the first summer that was taken from him.

He had helped out in the ice-cream parlour before. As a little boy, he had made ice-cream with my brother. Separating eggs, pureeing fruits, grinding nuts. Giuseppe had come up with a new flavour. Apricot, peach, mango, plum, and a touch of orange — his very own ice-cream. He and Luca scooped it out of the Cattabriga, their thumbs around the handle of the *spatolone*, which was nearly twice as big as Giuseppe himself. Later he had cleared tables, the tray in both hands like the wheel of a lorry. And when he was finally tall enough to see over the counter, he had served ice-cream, too. Alongside his mother, occasionally snacking on the sprinkles.

But when he'd had enough or he wanted to play, he was always allowed to go. Usually he would run off to the square on Schiedamse Vest, where he played football with other boys from the neighbourhood. He was incredibly quick, and yelled out their names when he wanted someone to pass him the ball. Sometimes he would come back to the ice-cream parlour with ten little boys, their cheeks flushed, their hair wet with sweat. They were all given a cone, and they licked their ice-cream with the sun high above them. Summers were still summers back then.

I felt for Giuseppe when he had to work in the ice-cream parlour and couldn't get away anymore. He looked uncomfortable, tortured, but Luca seemed oblivious. He suppressed it and continues to suppress it.

Mid-week I suddenly spotted Giuseppe in the theatre's large auditorium. I thought I must be mistaken, that it was a young man who was the spitting image of him — the same innocent face, the same long, dark hair. But it was him all right. He was the first member of the family to come to the World Poetry Festival. I tried to establish eye contact, but he didn't see me. His eyes were on the stage, where the South African poet Gert Vlok Nel was reading. A big bloke with strong arms, but with poetry that was wistful and personal, like the songs he sang in cafés while strumming his guitar. A sailor with a velvet voice. He looked at the audience as if looking at a woman he hadn't seen in years.

After the performance, I lost sight of Giuseppe. I couldn't see him anywhere in the foyer or at the bar. I wanted to introduce him to Gert Vlok Nel, the poet who smelled of his poetry, of whirlwinds and gum trees, of a canoe made of zinc. The three of us could have a beer or something, I thought.

Giuseppe had stalked off after an argument with his father. I got the story not from Giuseppe but from Luca. 'He didn't want to work,' my brother said, 'because he'd worked all day. He reckoned he deserved an evening off.'

Luca couldn't get his head round it. His father had spent fifty-seven years in the ice-cream parlour, while he had racked up some thirty years, and now Giuseppe complained after a mere four days. 'You work eight months and then you get four months off,' he told his son. 'That's how it works, that's the life of an ice-cream maker.'

'I'm not an ice-cream maker.'

'Yes, you are. We're all ice-cream makers.'

'Uncle Giovanni isn't.'

My brother exploded. 'Uncle Giovanni is a traitor!' he yelled.

'No, he's not.'

'Yes, he is. He abandoned us.'

'He just does as he pleases.'

'We can't all do as we please. Some of us have to work!'

They were in the kitchen. The door was closed, but everybody could hear them: Sophia and Sara, and the customers sitting inside and spooning up their ice-cream coupes with fruit and whipped cream.

'Uncle Giovanni works for the World Poetry Festival.'

'That's not work. Not real work, anyway. Do you know who pays for that festival? Not the people who visit it, but the people who have real jobs, who pay tax, because that's what subsidises the festival, including your uncle's salary. I work for him.'

'You're just jealous.'

'No, I'm not.'

'Yes, you are.'

'You're sixteen and you don't know everything there is to know,' Luca said. 'And now shut up and get to work.' The father had spoken his final word to his son.

Giuseppe had gone to work, with that deep frown in his forehead, but at eight o'clock he had taken off his apron and without another word he had walked out, under the red-and-white striped awning.

'Sophia called out his name, but he didn't turn round.'

'I saw him,' I said. 'He was at the festival. I spotted him in the audience.'

'What?'

'He was listening to a poet.'

It still bothers him. It keeps coming up; we keep talking about that evening. 'He did it to taunt me,' Luca claims.

'He did it because he was curious.'

'No. He did it to hurt me. He knew how much I'd mind, otherwise he'd have gone to the cinema, or the park.'

We can't agree. He hadn't seen the way Giuseppe listened to the South African poet. Riveted, moved. Not driven by vengeance.

'Was he already drinking beer by then?'

'Why do you ask?'

'Because I want to know.'

Luca doesn't know how Giuseppe looked at Gert Vlok Nel. I don't know whether he was already drinking alcohol. We fill in the gaps of the story.

'I reckon he was. He's been sixteen for some time. In the winter I'd taken him to Bar Posta and we were both the worse for wear as we walked home. Yes, now I remember. Giuseppe was drunk on two beers, me on the pleasure of seeing him again, of sitting in a bar with him. It was the first time he'd come along.'

We listen carefully when the other is telling a story only he knows, the way Luca had listened to me in the kitchen a couple of days earlier when I told him about the occasions when I had seen Giuseppe play football on the square on Schiedamse Vest. 'He was the best,' I said proudly. 'All the boys wanted to be on his team.'

'Did you see him score a goal?'

'He cheered and the other boys ran up to him and jumped all over him. They hugged like professional players.'

'What were you doing there?'

He sounded pissed off, which was not unusual for him in the middle of a conversation, but he must have realised it because he immediately followed up with another question. 'Had you made your way to that square especially for him?'

I nodded. I had just come back from Sweden, where I had attended the Gotland Island Poetry Festival with a bunch of Dutch poets. Tomas Tranströmer had listened to them in his wheelchair. I had headed straight to the ice-cream parlour with my suitcase, but Giuseppe wasn't there. He was playing football on some square. Sophia pointed in the direction of Westblaak. 'Somewhere over there,' she said. I remembered the place. Luca and I used to play football there when we were young. Since then white lines had been painted on the square: sidelines, goal lines, a centre circle. The goals were gigantic.

'He was completely absorbed in the game and barely glanced at me. But when he scored, he ran up to me and gave me a high-five. "Did you see that, Uncle?" he yelled. "With my heel! Did you see?" And then he ran back onto the square and they all jumped on top of him. He spent two-and-a-half months of the year in the Netherlands and yet he was one of them.'

'I've never seen them play football,' Luca said. 'I've seen them sit on the terrace, though. Giuseppe would run into the kitchen and tell me, while catching his breath, that all of his mates were outside, that he wanted to treat them to ice-cream and that Mamma had said to ask me. To be honest, I didn't approve, but I knew he'd be overjoyed if I said yes. That smile — I did everything to see it.'

It was the beaming boy's smile I had seen in Venas di Cadore. Giuseppe was six years old when I went to visit him at his grandma's, where he lived. During his first five years, he had come along to the Netherlands every season, like Luca and myself, but as soon as he had to go to school he stayed behind in Italy. Sophia struggled to come to terms with it. She never stopped missing her son. Luca didn't let on. He prepared ice-cream, got up early, and went to bed in the middle of the night. Besides, his own parents hadn't been able to take him along. That's how it works, that's the life of an ice-cream maker.

Sophia didn't have the heart to send Giuseppe to the boarding school in Vellai di Feltre, the one where the nuns had beaten us and Luca had crawled into my bed at night. Her mother was prepared to take Giuseppe under her wing, take him to school, cook for him, and wash his clothes.

It was spring when I went to see him for the first time. April. The sky was clear, the mountaintops covered with dazzling snow. I had hired a car at Venice airport, a metallic automatic SUV. Giuseppe ran outside when I got out. Sophia's mother stood in the doorway, joined a moment later by her husband. And then, without warning, he jumped into my arms, which were shocked at the weight, as were my back muscles.

'Zio! Zio!' he exclaimed.

I lifted Giuseppe and held him up like a trophy. *You're mine*, I thought. *You're mine*. And in the days to come he would indeed be mine, as Sophia and Luca were away, working.

Giuseppe laughed. He was late to lose his milk teeth. They were a virginal white.

His smile seems to beam right across the years. Together with the paintwork of the car in the background and the sun illuminating the snow in the distance, it creates an echo of light.

'Zio!'

These are luminous memories. We live on top of gold, but we just can't reach it.

'Of course I missed him,' my brother tells me one evening in the kitchen. 'It's not as if an ice-cream maker has a heart of ice. Like everyone else, he's got arms that want to hug, that want to throw a little boy high up in the air and catch him again a second later. You're busy, sure, and you're always on the go, but your thoughts never let up. Even as the ice-cream is churning, as the cylinder needs emptying, as the machine needs refilling.'

He falls silent and stares at the worktop, which is full of pineapples. They need to be peeled and pureed. After that, the puree has to be boiled in syrup before being pressed through a sieve and allowed to cool. I have no idea what my brother is going to add to the sorbet base. Perhaps just a splash of lemon juice, or some beaten egg whites for a creamier texture, for ice-cream that feels like a cloud in your mouth. But perhaps he's going to add something entirely different. I see some ginger and a bunch of fresh mint. It's alchemy.

'Underneath this strip lighting I also thought back to the time when we were separated from Mamma and Beppi,' Luca says. 'The nuns who read our letters and got angry when you wrote that you missed your parents.'

'They made us rewrite the letters.'

'We were expected to write what we had learned, that we emptied our plates like good boys and prayed every day. The days in the ice-cream parlour are long, but the days at boarding school were interminable.'

The days the grass turned green and the dandelions shot up. The days when the sun brought warmth and banished the whiteness of winter from our skin.

The days I spent with Giuseppe while he stayed at his grandmother's. Everybody was in Rotterdam: Beppi, my mother, Sophia, Luca. I walked through the village with Giuseppe, holding his hand. We went to the baker's and the butcher's, we bought a newspaper or a magazine for Sophia's mother. There were very few people about, so there were no queues anywhere. In the evening it was dead quiet in the village. The pizzeria only opened at the weekend; in Bar Posta, old, worn-out men stared into the middle distance, their wives asleep in the lonely conjugal bed. Empty clotheslines, closed shutters, here and there some fresh, new geraniums on a balcony. Spring in Venas di Cadore.

I picked Giuseppe up from school and went to the forest with him. We went looking for pinecones and built huts, did battle with branches that doubled up as lethal swords. We rolled around the fields when the farmers weren't looking.

Days of bliss and days of a thousand questions. *May I sit in the front? May I drive? Can you make me a bow and arrow? Can you ask Gran to make pancakes tonight? Will you catch me if I jump off this branch? Will you play football with me? Twirl me around, please! And again!* Round and round and round. Churn, churn, churn. And then we would lie together in the grass, giddy, watching the sky spin.

Then, when everything had spun to a halt, there were the other questions.

'How much longer are you staying in Venas?'

'Four more days. I'm going back to Rotterdam after the weekend.'

'And then?'

'Then I'm going to Santiago.'

'Where's that?'

'In Chile.'

'Can I come with you?'

'No, you can't.'

'Why not?'

'You have to go to school.'

'I don't want to go to school; I want to come with you.'

Giuseppe clambered on top of me, his face a mere few centimetres above mine.

I looked at his wispy eyebrows and his dark eyes, at his smooth skin and at the lock of blond hair that touched my face. I was still in love.

'Why can't I come with you?'

'You can do plenty of travelling when you're grown up,' the uncle said to his nephew.

Giuseppe groaned. That wasn't the answer he wanted to hear.

'When am I going to Rotterdam?' he asked.

'In June, at the start of summer.'

He didn't say anything, but a frown appeared in his delicate forehead.

'Who do you miss the most?' I asked.

'Mamma.'

'What about Papa?'

'Him, too.'

'What about me?'

'You're here now.'

'But when I'm gone, when you're staying with Grandma and Granddad?'

He gave this some thought. 'I miss you in winter,' he said, 'when I'm in my own house.'

The house where I was staying, which was otherwise empty, where everything — the chairs under the kitchen table, the plates in the cupboards, the tools in the basement — awaited the return of its residents. I hadn't lived there for years. My place had been taken. Giuseppe now slept in my bedroom.

On one occasion I took him to his house, because he kept asking me to. He wanted to pick up a toy car he had forgotten to take to Sophia's parents' house.

'You're sleeping in my bed,' he said when we were in his room.

'You're sleeping in *my* bed,' I countered, but Giuseppe didn't seem to hear. He was looking for the car among all his other toys. He failed to notice that I hadn't changed the bed linen and that I was sleeping under his sheets. Nor was he aware of the silence in the house, the stillness of the objects and the furniture waiting for his parents' and grandparents' return. He happily drove his red racing car up and down the landing.

'Zio, look! If you pull it back, it shoots forwards.'

The racing car zipped to the far side of the landing, where it crashed against the wall, but Giuseppe didn't run after it. He turned round and went back into his room.

'I want to get changed,' he said.

'Why would you want to get changed?'

'These clothes aren't comfy.'

He opened the wardrobe and pulled out a pair of trousers, a pullover, and a t-shirt. At first I didn't really get what he was doing, but once he had changed, I realised what this was all about. He had taken off all the clothes Sophia's mother had dressed him in. They were smart clothes, trousers with a sharp crease and a crisp white shirt. His Sunday best, clothes for church.

I had noticed on my first day that Giuseppe was looking very dapper, but I thought Sophia's mother had rigged him out like that especially for me, just as we used to have to wear tight trousers and itchy jumpers when we had visitors. But she dressed her grandchild in his Sunday best seven days a week, just as she was never seen without shiny high-heeled shoes.

'At least I can get these trousers dirty,' Giuseppe said.

'But not the others?'

'Gran doesn't like anything to get dirty.'

'I think she loves you very much.'

'She gives my hair a side parting every morning.'

We want to pass so much on to the next generation. Ice-cream, poetry, tools. A way of life. Nothing must get lost, or it would feel like a betrayal of your own nature.

When I returned Giuseppe to his grandmother, she looked at him like one would at a mongrel. Then again, she didn't look much more kindly on her husband, who was now at home all day. There were hardly any glasses factories left in the region. The Chinese had triumphed. Sophia's father's factory had closed down, too; he had been given the choice between relocation or early retirement, and he had opted for the latter. Now they had entered a tricky phase of marriage: the phase where you're at each other's throats. Sophia's mother still looked good, but she was no longer as fancy-free as a few years back. She could be extremely frosty, and her face had hardened. And she often had a glass of wine in her hand. Perhaps it was Giuseppe who stopped her from returning to Modena, or perhaps she simply lacked the courage to start all over again.

The four of us ate dinner together. Polenta with gorgonzola. Sophia's father smiled at his grandson every now and then, but Giuseppe didn't pay much attention. He was hungry and he was fonder of his other granddad. In winter the two of them would retreat into the basement, where they let the machines whizz and whir. My mother detested it, but there was nothing she could do about it.

After the table had been cleared and Giuseppe was asleep, Sophia's mother said to me, 'He's got your eyes.'

We were having a glass of wine. Her husband was sitting on the couch, watching television. I could keep his wife company, as far as he was concerned.

'He resembles you more than Luca,' she said. She took a big gulp, her face hard as stone.

She knew two things, or three, rather. Firstly, that it had taken a long time for Sophia to get pregnant, and secondly, that I had always had a soft spot for her daughter. Those years ago when Luca and I had buzzed around Sophia like flies, turning up on her doorstep practically every day, often it was her mother who answered the door and at some point told her to choose.

And thirdly, she knew I was naughty.

'It's the sun,' I replied. 'Giuseppe and I spend a lot of time outdoors. Luca is always inside. He never sees the sun.'

Giuseppe had chased the sun. The glorious sun over Central America. He hadn't lasted three summers in the ice-cream parlour. The second summer, when he was expected to help in the kitchen too, had been the worst. Luca wanted him to learn to make all the different flavours, but Giuseppe had no interest in making ice-cream at all.

'It's bad enough having to work here,' he had said to Luca. 'Now you're locking me in the kitchen, too.'

'An ice-cream maker has to learn to make ice-cream.'

'I don't want to make ice-cream.'

'I had to learn it once.'

'I don't see why I should do what you had to do.'

'Because it's a tradition,' my brother replied. 'Because your grandfather and great-grandfather learned it, too. Because this ice-cream parlour is owned by our family and passed down from father to son.'

My brother had never told him that he wasn't his father. Dozens of times the truth had been on the tip of his tongue and he had been on the verge of spitting it out, but he always managed to check himself. He had wanted to throw Giuseppe out, had wanted to disown him, had wanted to whack him over the head with the *spatolone*, just as Beppi had been close to despair when I started reading poetry.

Sometimes Giuseppe turned to his mother for comfort, but she served ice-cream seven days a week; spring and summer offered little time for comfort. Once he rang the doorbell of the World Poetry offices. I let him in and we sat down at the large table in the library. He said nothing, not a word, just kept staring at the tabletop.

I saw myself when I looked at him, and perhaps my brother saw me — the traitor, the enemy — when he looked at Giuseppe.

'Only poets stand to gain from melancholy,' I said, as Heiman had once said to me. 'We ordinary mortals have a duty to be happy.'

He looked at me, but didn't react. I saw that he had tears in his eyes and his lips were trembling. Numerous lines of poetry popped into my head, hundreds of words that might have brought solace, but I did what Heiman had never done. I put my arms around Giuseppe and held him close. I hugged him.

'You never told him?' my brother asks me now.

'Never.'

'And no one else, either?'

'Nobody.' Except that young woman in Buenos Aires, but she didn't count. She had been engulfed by the past, swallowed up by time.

I had never struggled with it. It had never been on the tip of my tongue. I had fathered Giuseppe, but he was Luca's and Sophia's son. I was his uncle, an uncle who loved him and who visited him in spring, an uncle who brought him gifts from around the world. An uncle who missed him sorely at times.

'The winters were the hardest,' I say.

'The winters were the best,' Luca says.

The winters that are summers for ice-cream makers. Despite the short, dark days, despite the cold and the smoke from the chimneys, winter was the main, the sumptuous season in the Cadore valley. Up in the mountains, a weight would fall off your shoulders.

'I would watch the snowflakes with him,' my brother tells me. 'We tried to catch them with our tongues, competing as to who would be the first to catch two at once. Giuseppe always won, because he has the same long tongue as his mother.'

I can picture them walking through the falling snow: my brother and his son, clutching each other's hands, links of a chain that can't be broken.

'When he was a bit older, I went up to the attic to retrieve the sledge that Beppi made for us. The three of us — Sophia came along too — went downhill, but we fell off at the first bend. Initially Giuseppe cried, but when he saw his Mamma and Papa laughing, he also roared with laughter. "There's snow in my collar!" I exclaimed. "There's snow in my bra!" Sophia shouted. "There's snow in my underpants!" Giuseppe yelled.'

I remember a winter when I woke up with Jim Morrison in three different hotel rooms.

'He could stay out all day and have snowball fights with his friends. When you summoned him back in for dinner, you'd have to watch out for stray snowballs. This one time we all lay in wait for him outside — Beppi, Mamma, Sophia, and I — and bombarded him until he begged for mercy. Of course he was angry and upset, but when Mamma told him she'd prepared *ossobuco* everything was forgiven, and a little later the five of us were sitting in the warm kitchen with a steaming plate in front of us.'

Some evenings, my brother is quiet, happy to listen to me or to the humming of the Cattabriga's motor, but this evening the memories surface quite naturally, one after the other, reminiscent of the way Fernando Pessoa walked to his desk on 8 March 1914, picked up a sheet of paper, and wrote more than thirty poems in a row.

It's impossible to tell everything, the whole story. We don't actually know it. We weren't present at everything. We tell each other what we know. We try to solve a riddle.

On one of the evenings we were sitting outside, Luca suddenly said, 'Sometimes I think you told him, "Go to Mexico. There's no need to come back. Live your own life. Go ahead."'

'Are you blaming me?'

He looked around, perhaps hoping for a customer, but no such luck.

'Yes, sometimes I blame you,' my brother replied, 'but often enough I blame myself. I just can't forget that time I nearly laid into Giuseppe in the kitchen. We were having the umpteenth argument about his hair. He always wore it down, although I'd asked him a hundred times to wear it in a ponytail or to go to the hairdresser's. It's incredibly dangerous when you're standing over a churning Cattabriga. You've heard the story of the ice-cream maker who was strangled by his own ice-cream machine, right? His tie got caught. I was terrified that Giuseppe's hair might get snarled up. Besides, it was unhygienic, too. His hair ended up in the ice-cream. We'd already had a complaint from someone about a hair in a scoop of banana ice-cream. It was Giuseppe's, I was certain of it. It was long and dark, practically black. I saw it with my own eyes.

'Sophia always said I shouldn't be too hard on him, to give him a bit more space, but she wasn't there in the kitchen with him. She thought he just needed time and that everything would be fine. The problem is that there is no time in an ice-cream parlour. Yeah, sure, there's time in winter, but not in summer, in a kitchen measuring two-by-three, with churning ice-cream machines and crates of fruit stacked up to the ceiling. So what I did was I booked him an appointment with the hairdresser's. With Lagerman, around the corner. His customers all walked out with handsome crewcuts that wouldn't look out of place in the navy.

'Remember we always wanted to go there when we were little, but Mamma thought they were too expensive? When I told Giuseppe they were expecting him, he refused to go. Wild horses couldn't drag him there. So then I told him I'd do it myself. I'd had enough. His hair was getting longer and longer and it was always in his eyes. I tried to find a pair of scissors, but we don't have any scissors in the kitchen. You don't need scissors to make ice-cream. But I carried on looking, because I just couldn't believe it, and do you know what he said then? He asked me why I hadn't made another son. A son who did want to be an ice-cream maker. With short hair. That really hurt and I became absolutely livid. I caught sight of the knife for halving melons. I grabbed hold of it and squeezed the handle. I'm going to cut off his hair, I thought to myself. And then I charged at him, but before I had a chance to raise the knife he'd already left the kitchen.'

'When did this happen?'

'A week before he told me he'd bought a ticket to Mexico.'

Then, finally, someone turned up to buy an ice-cream.

To be honest, I often blamed myself. Perhaps I had told Giuseppe too much about my job. Perhaps I had tempted him with a life that wasn't meant for him. I knew he was expected to work in the ice-cream parlour and that one day it would be his. There was no other son, no brother who could shoulder his fate instead.

I had told him about Medellín, about Struga, about Tel Aviv. About the poetry festival in Mongolia, which took place in the capital as well as in villages and in round felt and wool tents out in the Gobi Desert. About the camel rennet vodka I had drunk, and the poets who had sung with trembling voices. *Evening descends on the yurt / Nocturnal black / Condenses the shadows / Darker than all the nights / Of one long winter.*

About my meeting in Chicago, in one of the skyscrapers on the Magnificent Mile where The Poetry Foundation, the organisation that manages Ruth Lilly's bequest, had its headquarters.

'Who's Ruth Lilly?'

'A lady who submitted poems to *Poetry*, a small literary journal, her whole life, but never saw any of them published. She did, however, always receive a note from one of the editors, Joseph Parisi, who wrote everybody personal rejection letters. At the age of eighty-seven, Ruth Lilly donated two hundred million dollars to *Poetry*.'

'And what were you doing in Chicago?'

'I was pitching to the board of The Poetry Foundation, some twenty officials from Chicago's cultural elite who watch over those two hundred million dollars. The chairman wasn't in attendance. He was on a plane to New York and dialled in via a box — a small square speaker on the table in the middle of the room, like you see in films. They thought the plan was interesting, but didn't have the budget for it.'

About the festival in Huangshan, which was organised by four friends who used to spend seven days a week drinking wine and writing poetry. When it dawned on them that such a lifestyle was too romantic and didn't bring in any money, they switched to drinking and writing poems three days a week. In the remaining time they each founded a business — a taxi company, a hotel, a restaurant, and an opera house — and used the money they earned doing this to organise their own festival with poets from around the world. Thanks to their financial independence, the Chinese government had nothing whatsoever to do with the festival. In fact, they probably didn't even know about it. The plane tickets, the booklets of translations, the excursions to ancient cities, and even the lengthy foot massages were paid for by the organisation itself. There was no mention of the festival on the internet. There was no audience. The poets recited their work in celebrated gardens, standing in front of a lone pine tree. Or dangling from a cliff in the Yellow Mountains. The four friends would listen with blissful smiles on their faces.

'What kind of hotel did you stay in?'

'The Xin An Country Hotel.' On the desk stood a box of tissues smelling of roses; a large painted porcelain vase served as a chair. The window overlooked a classic garden with carefully tended trees and a small bridge across a pond. Every morning at eight-thirty, a woman raked the grass with a broom made of reeds.

About the recital in Barrancabermeja, a couple of days after the festival in Medellín. I was in an armoured vehicle with four poets, and the driver had an automatic rifle on his lap. Behind us was a second car with two more men with automatic weapons. We were on our way to the country's biggest oil refinery. It was five in the morning and all the day labourers had gathered in a field. Six hundred men, twelve hundred black hands. The sun rose above the land while the poets read from sheets of paper they had pulled out of their pockets seconds earlier.

Giuseppe's eyes were ablaze, as though he were one of the labourers, and the light washed over him while the poets' words poured into his ears and churned up his mind.

Oscar Wilde had once read to the miners of Leadville, Colorado. He had decided against poetry or his sole novel, *The Picture of Dorian Gray*. Dressed in a velvet suit, he had read from the autobiography of Benvenuto Cellini, a sixteenth-century Italian artist who had affronted popes and sovereigns, had frequented whores and entertained mistresses and was said to have committed several murders. The miners loved his recital and clamoured for Wilde to return the following year. With Cellini.

Giuseppe, too, wanted more.

We haven't talked much in recent years, Luca and I. He would occasionally sit down with me when I popped into the ice-cream parlour, or invite me into the kitchen. I would ask how Giuseppe was, how he was doing in school, and whether he had a girlfriend. Luca would answer me while he carried on working or quickly downed an espresso. Sometimes he would volunteer that he had spoken to Giuseppe on the phone and that he sent his regards. We avoided the other issues, a proper conversation. It wasn't as bad as the twelve years he barely spoke a word to me, but not an awful lot was said. We didn't want to hear the other's stories. It was envy. The winters Giuseppe spent in Venas, the spring when I walked through the fields with him, while Luca was hunched over an ice-cream machine in Rotterdam.

Now the untold stories bring us together and we hang on every word. Almost every word. There are still some things my brother doesn't want to hear.

It goes without saying that I introduced Giuseppe to Shelley's poem, the poem that had turned my world on its head when I was fifteen. *'Narrow / The heart that loves, the brain that contemplates, / The life that wears, the spirit that creates / One object, and one form, and builds thereby / A sepulchre for its eternity.'* Giuseppe, likewise fifteen, his hair still short, gave me a glassy stare. Perhaps I'd had the same look in my eyes when I heard the poem for the first time. Eventually he managed to formulate a response. A single word. 'Nice.' But Luca won't want to know.

'Please don't bother me with lines of poetry,' he will say. Or, 'Can you leave the poetry out of this, please?'

So I don't mention the poets Giuseppe liked to read, the lines he knew off by heart. Nor do I tell him about the time Jules Deelder sat outside and Giuseppe asked the poet to autograph one of his collections. *'To Giuseppe,'* he dedicated the book. *'The coffee is black and the ice-cream flavours a bit whack.'*

Frans Vogel walked past the ice-cream parlour every now and then, but he never sat down. Perhaps my father had chased him away once. He looked like a vagabond. You'd recognise him by the plastic bag he always carried with him. It was full of books of poetry he was trying to flog to bookshops around town.

I had told Giuseppe about the first time the World Poetry Festival had welcomed poets from China. This was back in the Seventies. Before then it had been unthinkable for writers to be allowed to travel outside the strict Communist country. There were no translations, but the audience, aware that this was a special occasion, listened respectfully to the three poets from the People's Republic. Until, that is, Frans Vogel got up and yelled at one of the muttering Chinese men on the stage, 'Louder! I can't hear you!'

Giuseppe had asked for Vogel's most recent volume and had been particularly impressed with its motto by Breyten Breytenbach: 'The function of the poem is to fuck the words good and hard.'

I don't say a word about Boris Ryzhy. After I gave him *Wolken boven E*, Giuseppe wanted to know everything there was to know about the poet, a young Russian who wanted to sing like a drunken whore.

His poetry was saturated with melancholy and despair. He was both a poet and a street fighter. Giuseppe was hooked by the direct and plain language, the drunkards and junkies that peopled his poems. Ryzhy had a huge scar across his face. He claimed he had sustained it in a fight, but in actual fact he'd had a nasty fall as a child.

His appearance at the World Poetry Festival had been a disgrace. Drunk for most of the time, his behaviour was completely out of order. And given his atrocious English, it was practically impossible to communicate with him. The audience was disappointed. Ryzhy staggered up to the lectern and read his poems in the wrong order, so they didn't correspond with the projected Dutch and English translations.

Less than a year later he hung himself in his parents' house in desolate Yekaterinburg. 'I loved you all, I kid you not! Your Boris,' he had jotted down on a piece of paper found on his desk. Twenty-six he was, the same age as Lermontov, who had been shot in a duel he didn't think was serious.

I won't read my brother the poignant poem Boris Ryzhy had read during the closing night of the festival. Written for his son, it starts with the lines,

> *When I return from Holland I'll give you Lego*
> *and we'll build a beautiful castle, you and me.*
> *You can make them come back, the years and the people,*
> *and love too — mark my words, you'll see.*

Every time I read the poem, my eyes linger over the line *We'll live and loiter until the snow falls*, and then I think of the sun Giuseppe is chasing. The sun so rarely seen by the ice-cream maker.

Instead I tell Luca about the Tre Cime di Lavaredo, the three colossal rock formations that are visible for a second and a half as you drive up the road between Cortina and Dobbiaco.

'Did you take him to the Tre Cime?'

I nod. The two of us had walked up there on a clear day, a rucksack slung over my shoulders, a drink bottle hanging from his belt.

'When was this?' Luca wants to know.

I need to think about it, calculate back. 'He was seven,' I reply.

My brother is silent. He is calculating back too, to the spring when Giuseppe was seven, to the ice-cream parlour where both Beppi and our mother were still working at the time, to the flavours he made that season.

'What did he make of it?' he asks. It was hard for him not to be envious, but to keep asking, to find out more.

I remember Giuseppe walking faster and faster as we approached the Tre Cime. There are different walking trails leading up to the peaks, one of which starts from a large car park some fifteen minutes away, but we had risen early and had walked all morning. In his right hand Giuseppe held a stick he had found. His left hand was in mine. We had removed our pullovers. It was a warm day in May, with hardly any snow on the peaks around us.

The Tre Cime don't suddenly appear out of nowhere — you can see them from a distance — but with each step they grow bigger and more spectacular. Giuseppe, who had been talking nineteen to the dozen about his plans for the summer, didn't breathe another word as we walked along the narrow path among the rock fragments. He appeared to be hypnotised by the mountain in front of us. The mountain his father and grandfather had never seen. Not from up close, anyway.

Then we came to a halt and looked up, at the gigantic peaks and the sharp contours of the rocks, a trident that had risen from a tropical primal sea two hundred and seventy million years ago. Fossilised coral reef. He couldn't take his eyes off it. It was terrific to stand there with Giuseppe. To look, to be silent, to hear him breathe. To hold his hand and squeeze it with all my love.

'Zio!' he suddenly exclaimed. 'Look! There are people.'

I looked towards the spot he indicated, halfway up the overhanging north cliff of the Grande Cime. It took me a while but then I saw two tiny dots. Mountain climbers.

'Would you do that?' Giuseppe asked.

'No.'

'I would.'

The next moment he pulled at my hand, intending to walk up the rocky slope to the base of the rock tower.

'He wanted to climb the Grande Cime,' I say to my brother.

At first Luca doesn't react, but then he smiles, as though picturing his precocious son, tugging at his uncle's hand.

We both picture him tugging and trying to break free, keeping at it until the link is severed.

Now it's autumn and the nights are closing in. The ice-cream parlour will be open for just a few more days. People are wearing coats again, and the leaves on the trees are yellow. There's still the occasional queue, but only at the weekend. It's not a bad autumn at all; it doesn't rain much.

'We're talking about him as if he's dead,' my brother says.

'He isn't.'

'How do you know?'

I don't respond.

'I asked you a question,' Luca says.

At first I want to remain silent, just like he never used to answer when I asked him something, but Luca perseveres. He keeps repeating the question. His words ricochet off the kitchen tiles, the same white tiles that amplified the frequent fights between Giuseppe and my brother.

'Because I'm his father.'

All goes quiet. Even the ice-cream machines appear to fall silent for a moment. Then slowly the sound returns: the blade starts scraping, the ice-cream starts whispering again. And Luca opens his mouth. I expect him to explode, but he isn't angry. 'I was afraid you'd say that,' he says, 'and I hope you're right.' He looks at me with tears in his eyes. 'I can't live without him, and nor can Sophia.'

Maybe I can. I was used to always being away from Giuseppe. From the beginning, from the day he was born. He was always a small, distant dot, but I could see him when I focused long and hard enough. The way I can see my brother in the ice-cream parlour when I have my mother on the line. It happens automatically. My memory makes it happen.

Luca would say I was making things up or getting my stories all mixed up to fill the gaps. A huge gap.

And yet I see Giuseppe before me, walking down the street in Mexico, in Michoacán or Colima, or along the white beach of Chacahua, where pelicans plunge into the waves and resurface with fish in their beaks. A tiny dot, growing ever more distant. The ice-cream maker in search of perpetual summer.

Could it be that I know more because I'm his real father? Or do we both not know him all that well, because we only know part of him?

'Sometimes I think I'd lost him before he even set off,' Luca says.

I could say the same; he'd always been lost to me.

There are moments when I think Giuseppe knew, that he could see it, just like Sophia's mother saw it.

Luca and I are in our late forties. We are men with wrinkles, thinning hair and crowns on our teeth, but we look less alike now than we did twenty years ago. My brother is heavier and stockier, due to muscle I don't have. His shoulders are firm and broad. I'm slight, skinny even, compared to Luca. Time has magnified the differences between us. It's no longer just the colour of our skin. My brother's gait is different; his back is hunched.

On West-Kruiskade, not far from the ice-cream parlour, is a Halal butcher. Benali. The old Moroccan butcher himself no longer works there since his sons took over the business, young men who have always worked in their father's shop. His oldest son, however, is a writer. He has published a couple of novels, including a bestseller, and now lives in Amsterdam. A life of ambition and adventure, of book launches and frisson with young women working at publishing companies, of getting up late. Every now and then the writer takes the train to

Rotterdam, and occasionally I see him sitting outside Venezia with one of his brothers. The butcher is pale, like the strip lighting over his head, balding and with a body that betrays his enormous strength as much as the gruelling nature of his work. His brother, who wears a hip Italian cap, is darker and as fit as a marathon runner. One is exhausted, laid low, the other bursting with energy and plans. An ox and a stallion.

Giuseppe once waited on the brothers outside. They had ordered ice-cream. He noticed the parallel immediately.

'You see those two?' he said to his mother while she scooped their ice-cream. 'It's as if Papa and Uncle Giovanni are sitting there, except younger and Moroccan.'

Sophia laughed, but Giuseppe persisted. 'I reckon the one with the cap is flirting with you,' he said. 'See how he looks at you?'

'He's a handsome man.'

'What about his brother?'

She didn't react, at least not directly. She thought about her answer and then said, 'The other man strikes me as shy.'

'Who do you think I look like?'

'You don't look like them at all.'

'That's not what I meant.'

Sophia stopped scooping. 'Then what *do* you mean?'

'I mean, do you think I look more like Uncle Giovanni or Dad?'

She had to squeeze her *spatola* tight so it wouldn't fall from her hand. 'You look like me,' she said, forcing a smile.

'Everybody thinks I look more like my uncle.'

Giuseppe looked at his mother, but her eyes were cast downward, at the ice-cream in the display.

'Wouldn't you say so?' he asked.

Now Sophia met his gaze. 'If you work from morning till night,' she said, 'if you slave away all summer, if you spend years in the kitchen, you'll eventually come to resemble your father.' She carried on scooping ice-cream for the butcher and the writer. 'Don't you worry about that.'

*

Sophia, the fairytale princess of my childhood. The girl who had emerged from a flurry of snow and who had enchanted me. The woman who had married my brother and who had made a child with me. The woman who had brought reconciliation and had kept the family together. She is lying in bed now, refusing to come out.

It started mid-August, a week after Giuseppe left. At first Sophia started getting out of bed later and later — at eleven, at eleven-thirty, long after midday. Then she stopped getting up altogether. My brother reckons the pattern's the same as when she couldn't get pregnant. History repeats itself. But this time there was nobody to take over from her. Luca was already working for two, because Giuseppe was away; Sara had replaced my mother. My brother was obliged to hire a student for the rest of the summer, and for the evenings in autumn. Now and again I see the kid behind the ice-cream or waiting tables, looking like a stray who has been taken in by a strange family, a family that's not a family anymore.

My father is in the basement in Venas, polishing a new heart, while my mother is studying the weather forecast in the kitchen. Giuseppe is somewhere in Central America. Luca empties one of the ice-cream machines in Rotterdam. I'm off to Estonia tomorrow.

The woman who had kept the entire family together is lying in the dark, behind permanently closed doors. It's warm and airless inside the bedroom. Sophia has buried her head under the covers. Her long hair appears to have been robbed of its lustre once and for all. My brother has told me that nothing can pull her from this drowsy underworld. The room smells stale. When Luca draws the curtains and opens a window, Sophia starts yelling from under the sheets, but it sounds as if she is yelling from a deep sleep. Her cries are barely audible and she doesn't stop until he has left the room. She doesn't answer any of his questions. She won't let him touch her. He's unable to comfort her.

I walk under the red-and-white striped awning and into the ice-cream parlour, past the display and the till, through the door leading to the stairs. Nobody asks me what I'm up to. Sara is behind the counter, staring out of the window. Luca is in the kitchen. I have his permission to go upstairs. 'You've worked miracles before,' he said. Then he went back to work.

Back when I first climbed the stairs to see Sophia, I skipped every other step, and when I visited her to see my newborn son I soared up the stairs. This time I don't have to go up to the attic, and yet the ascent takes me longer. I grip the banister and hear the steps creak under my shoes. Why am I doing this? What debt do I still owe? Why not turn on my heels, walk under the awning, and make myself scarce?

A line by Boris Ryzhy waltzes around my head. *You can make them come back, the years and the people.* But I doubt if the miracle will repeat itself. Sophia won't answer the door in a dress with peonies, she won't have flushed cheeks; there'll be no golden braid. This time round she'll lie in bed with chapped lips and dark circles under her eyes. Withdrawn, worn out by grief. She's waiting for Giuseppe. Only his return can pull her out of this woe.

I walk through the dining room to Luca and Sophia's bedroom. The table is still littered with plates and glasses from dinner. Flies are gorging on the food scraps. The kitchen counter is crammed, and encrusted pans fill the sink. It looks forlorn, condemned. My brother can't manage without Sophia, and the ice-cream parlour can't manage without Giuseppe. Maybe he'll hold out for a couple of seasons, with the help of extra staff, but in the end you need a son, a successor.

Giuseppe had brought the ice-cream machines to a halt on the day he was born; now they may grind to a halt for good.

I place my hand on the door handle, but don't enter just yet. There's no sound behind the door. No rustling of sheets, no coughing, no snoring. Sophia doesn't stir. I have no idea if she'll listen to me, if my words can rouse her from her torpor. What do we know about the workings of a heart? How can you make it forget the pain, how can you give it hope again?

Then I press down the handle and open the door. The hinges creak, the heat hits me in the face. It's dark and dead quiet. My head is spinning when I enter the room. Everything is churning.

A Beginning, an End

After two bitterly cold winters and a summer filled with cicada song, Giuseppe returned. Azure skies, days of St John's wort, clover, and water milfoil. Time had advanced mightily yet leisurely in the Cadore Valley, had unfurled the seasons and pulled them back in again. Trees had been cut, cows had calved, boys had grown into men. Maria Grazia felt their eyes on her body, but she walked on quickly when anyone accosted her in the street. She hid in her room or went to the forest, visiting places she had been to with Giuseppe. She found them all: the place where the light fell in spokes between the tree trunks and where they searched for pinecones, the meadow where they picked dandelions, the patch of grass in which they lay like a life-sized clock. Only the Antelao was too daunting.

A year had passed since Giuseppe's disappearance. Everyone had been perplexed. His mother had sat waiting for him in his room for days, the window he had climbed out of left open as if in expectation of an imminent return. He had set off in the half-light of the early morning without leaving a note, without a word to his brothers and sisters. Maria Grazia could have solved the mystery, but she was afraid to tell Giuseppe's mother what had happened the night before his departure — the night in which she had confessed her love to him and had begged him for a child. She kept it inside, a secret. At times she was consumed by guilt, but some days she couldn't believe Giuseppe had left because of her. What had she done wrong? She had shown her body to him, her white breasts and amber-coloured nipples.

Nobody knew where Giuseppe might be. The first couple of days, all the men in the village went out searching: the metalsmith, the locksmith, Enrico Zangrando, his father. The man who had always whistled while out and about now walked quietly through the countryside. They went on long hikes in the mountains and stood on the glacier of the Antelao. They thought he might have fallen while harvesting snow.

In autumn, two months later, when the woodcutter stood at the corner of the Volksgarten with his stove, and the aroma of roasted chestnuts filled the streets of Vienna, people were still looking out for him. For a split second Bruno thought he spotted him across the street, but even as he called out Giuseppe's name he knew it was someone else, a young man with the same strong shoulders and dark hair, but a different face. Delicate and carefree.

As time went by, Maria Grazia kept her faith in Giuseppe's return. She was convinced he was thinking of her, wherever he might be. She waited for him. All summer long. The farmers gathered in the hay once more; fruit was cooked and preserved in jars. Hailstones the size of walnuts fell from the sky as thunderstorms swept across the villages.

'How long do you intend to wait for him?' her mother asked.

Maria Grazia didn't respond. She looked out at the dark clouds.

'Do you want to be left on the shelf?'

Again, no response, just a deepening furrow in the girl's forehead. Two days ago, the mother had seen her daughter emerge from the forest, holding the hem of her dress and looking at the pinecones she had gathered in there.

'Maria Grazia,' her mother said. 'I asked you a question. Do you want to be left on the shelf?'

'No.'

'Then maybe you ought to look around you once in a while and not always down at the ground.' She looked at her daughter, who was more beautiful than her other daughters, the most beautiful girl in the village. It was unbearable. The sadness around her mouth, the film covering her eyes. 'He won't be back,' she said. 'Forget about him. Start looking for someone else — a man who doesn't just walk off, who gets up in the morning and goes to work. You hear me? He won't be back!'

She paid no attention. Maria Grazia heard her mother talking, but the words didn't register. She knew that one day he would knock on their door, as he had done when she was younger. She could picture him walking through the village — dirty clothes, threadbare shoes, finally returned from a long journey. She had dreams, lucid-like visions.

Yet her heart wasn't narrow, as in Shelley's poem, the heart that loves one object. Maria Grazia's heart was strong and steadfast.

The summer passed and she continued to wait for him. The autumn that followed was mild but wet. The clouds were trapped between the mountains. It rained for five consecutive days. The streets were flushed clean, and the water of the Piave turned a rusty brown. Then the second winter arrived, even colder than the first. The temperature dropped to twenty degrees below zero, and the wind was as sharp as a scythe. Those who had no business outside stayed in, in front of the burning stove. It was for this the trees had been cut down, the trunks cleaved. It was for this a vast stockpile of wood had been prepared in the middle of summer. The snow didn't start falling until January. Most people had anticipated it. It was in the air, you could smell it. Within an hour the fields were white, and by evening the roofs were covered in a thick blanket of snow.

The following morning, children emerged from their houses and ran through the snow with flushed cheeks. The sun brought light and warmth; the sky was cornflower blue. People shovelled the snow off their doorsteps, and streets were cleared with the help of oxen, which blew little clouds through their wet nostrils. Only Maria Grazia stayed inside, in her room with the blankets pulled over her head so as not to hear the cheerful noises outside.

The girl who had turned to the sun like a sunflower and who had traced circles on her arms with dandelion milk, the girl who had become a woman in the course of a single summer and had taken boys' breath away by looking them straight in the eye and parting her lips a little — she was in bed and wouldn't come out.

A crying shame, the men of the village thought. But none of them were capable of rousing Maria Grazia from her lethargy.

January turned to February turned to March. Everything melted, dwindled, trickled, and evaporated, except the snow on the glaciers, the necklace around the peak of the Antelao. When Giuseppe saw it sparkling from a distance, he knew he was nearly home. His clothes were indeed dirty, his soles threadbare. He had been gone for almost two years. His nose and forehead were tanned by the sun.

The first person to spot Giuseppe in the Cadore Valley had been so stunned and delighted he barely took in the traveller's words. According to the bricklayer Pietro Zaetta, Giuseppe was supposed to have said, 'Greetings, paleface.' But he wasn't entirely sure.

The news reached the village before Giuseppe himself, spreading through the streets and houses like wildfire. His father, his mother, his brothers and sisters all came out and made their way to the main road. There he was, in the distance, a black dot getting bigger and bigger. They couldn't wait to take him into their arms.

Maria Grazia threw off the blankets and stepped out of bed. She had heard the shouting, the screams of disbelief and joy. Children were yelling his name. Her legs had to get used to the weight they had to carry, her eyes to the light outside. She felt as though she was still dreaming when she laid eyes on him. He had turned into a giant, bigger and stronger than when he left. She didn't know it then, but he had built a skyscraper, constructed a railway line, since he had left their valley.

Giuseppe was pulled inside by his mother, but later that same evening he knocked on his neighbour's door. She looked into his eyes, dark-blue eyes that had seen the Atlantic Ocean and the vast emptiness of the Great Plains. Giuseppe didn't look away. He was no longer afraid. He didn't take his eyes off her and saw how beautiful she was, despite her dry skin and dull hair. She had a beauty that outshines all else.

In his cardboard suitcase, he had carried back with him a Native American headdress and a pair of jeans with pockets filled with red sand from the prairies of South Dakota. He had put down railway sleepers under the burning sun, hunted buffalo in Wyoming, and gawped at a woman in a silk dress whose perfume had intoxicated him in New York, but he had come back. The threads hadn't snapped; the gossamer remained intact. It had brought him back to her.

And now it was spring. The highest peaks were covered in snow, the fields were turning green, and down by the river the air was thick with the smell of cut logs. Giuseppe climbed the Antelao with Maria Grazia and stole snow from the king. They experienced everything afresh. He saw the tiny beads on her nose; she saw the wet patches on his clothes. They had to squeeze their eyes shut in the blinding light, and the sweat on his bare arms evaporated. The snow melted in the straw basket.

Down in the valley, in the basement, he set the wheel of the ice-cream machine in motion, the wheel that had been still for so long. They made sorbet out of apricot jam and ate it together, spoon after spoon, but on the days that followed Giuseppe sold various flavours of ice-cream by the side of the main road, gradually attracting more and more people. His thumb became calloused, while her skin turned the colour of honey, and her long hair shone in the sun.

No longer afraid, he now spoke the language of love. They had a baby: my father's father, my grandfather. And so the ice-cream machine kept churning.

List of Cited Poems

p. 5: 'Today' by Nurit Zarchi, translation by Lisa Katz, in *Prairie Schooner*, vol. 79, no. 1, Spring 2005, p. 62.

p. 7: 'What It Is' by Erich Fried, based on the translation by Anna Kallio (some punctuation has been added), *The Adirondack Review*, vol. IV, no. 1, Summer 2003, available at http://www. theadirondackreview.com/transfried.html.

p. 41: *Epipsychidion: verses addressed to the noble and unfortunate Lady, Emilia V—, now imprisoned in the convent of* — by Percy Bysshe Shelley, Charles and James Ollier, London, 1821, available at http://www.poetryfoundation.org/poems-and-poets/poems/ detail/45119.

p. 42: *Adonaïs: an elegy on the death of John Keats, author of* Endymion, Hyperion, *etc.* by Percy Bysshe Shelley, Charles and James Ollier, London, 1821, available at http://www.poetryfoundation.org/ poems-and-poets/poems/detail/45112.

p. 52: 'First Day of Spring' by J.C. Bloem, translation by Laura Vroomen.

p. 72: 'Ode to the Ice Cheese' by Yang Wanli, c. 1100, quoted at http://www.silkroadgourmet.com/the-origins-of-ice-cream.

p. 84: 'The World Turned Upside Down' by Maura Dooley, in *Life Under Water*, Bloodaxe Books, Hexham, 2008.

p. 94: 'A Martian Sends a Postcard Home' by Craig Raine, in *A Martian Sends a Postcard Home*, Oxford University Press, Oxford, 1979, p. 1.

p. 97: 'But the Sky is Always Bluer' by Rino Gaetano, translation based on that submitted by Riccardo (some lines have been altered), 2007, available at http://lyricstranslate.com/en/ma-il-cielo-e039-sempre-piu039-blu-sky-always-more-blue.html.

p. 105: T.S. Eliot, as quoted in 'An Encounter with T.S. Eliot', 2007, available at https://donmehwest.wordpress.com/my-encounter-with-ts-eliot.

p. 117–18: 'Just Living' by Patrick Lane, in *Selected Poems: 1977–1997*, Harbour Publishing, Pender Harbour, 1997.

p. 130: 'I Would' by Antjie Krog, translation by Tony Ullyatt, 2012, available at http://versindaba.co.za/2012/01/12/antjie-krog-vert.

p. 140: 'Touch' by Manglesh Dabral, translation based on that by Sudeep Sen (some lines have been altered), 2008, available at http://www.poetryinternationalweb.net/pi/site/poem/item/12586/auto/0/TOUCH. Poem appears in *Mujhe Dikha Ek Manushya* (*I Saw a Human Being*), Radhakrishna Prakashan, New Delhi, 2008.

p. 143: 'Thinking of something, carelessly' by Marina Tsvetaeva, translation by A.S. Kline, 2010, available at http://www.poetryintranslation.com/PITBR/Russian/Tsvetaeva.htm#_Toc254018915.

p. 196: 'I was stolen by the gypsies ...' by Charles Simic, in *New and Selected Poems: 1962–2012*, Houghton Mifflin Harcourt, New York and Boston, 2003.

p. 200: First quote taken from 'The Unfaithful Wife' by Federico García Lorca, translation by Lynn Margulis and Richard Guerrero, in *The Massachusetts Review*, vol. 44, issue 3, Autumn 2000, p. 338; second quote taken from 'The Unfaithful Housewife', translation by Conor O'Callaghan, in *Poetry*, June 2011, available at http://www.poetryfoundation.org/poetrymagazine/poem/242108.

p. 209: 'Cradle' by Ida Gerhardt, translation by Laura Vroomen.

Poem appears in Gerhardt, *Collected Poems*, Athenaeum–Polak & Van Gennep, Amsterdam, 1980.

p. 222: 'Shinto' by Jorge Luis Borges, translation by Hoyt Rogers, in *Selected Poems* (edited by Alexander Coleman), Viking, New York, 1999, p. 457.

p. 246: 'Solitude' by Galsan Tschinag, translation (from the Dutch) by Laura Vroomen.

p. 250: 'When I return from Holland I'll give you Lego ...' by Boris Ryzhy, translation (from the Dutch) by Laura Vroomen.

Acknowledgements

I'm greatly indebted to the Olivo family of ice-cream parlour Venezia in Rotterdam. They spoke to me at length about their family history, invariably over an ice-cream, milkshake, or espresso. Likewise, they welcomed me in Venas di Cadore, where I was introduced to members of their extended family and other ice-cream makers who provided me with invaluable information.

I'm extremely grateful to Bas Kwakman, director of the Poetry International Festival in Rotterdam. Over the course of several conversations he told me extensively about his work and travels. He also showed me his collection of drawings of hotel rooms. I really appreciate his openness.

I would like to thank Dorine de Vos for the wonderful and peaceful spot ('the servant's room') where I was able to write this book, not to mention the many espressos she made me.

The following sources have been of greater or lesser importance:

Bovenkerk, Frank et al., *Italiaans ijs. De opmerkelijke historie van de Italiaanse ijsbereiders in Nederland (Italian Ice-cream: the remarkable history of Italian ice-cream makers in the Netherlands)*, Boom, Meppel/ Amsterdam, 1983.

David, Elizabeth, *Harvest of the Cold Months: the social history of ice and ices*, Michael Joseph, London, 1994.

Oltheten, Harry, *Elio Talamini. Entrepeneur en visionair* (*Elio Talamini: entrepreneur and visionary*), Fortis Age, Deventer, 2005.

Reinders, Pim, *Een Coupe Speciaal. De wereldgeschiedenis van het consumptie-ijs* (*The Scoop: a world history of gelato*), L.J. Veen, Amsterdam/Antwerpen, 1999.